THE BRIDGE OF ECHOES

THE BRIDGE OF ECHOES

BROOKWOOD MYSTERIES
BOOK 2

JORDAN JACE

EPub ISBN: 978-1-967657-47-6

Print ISBN: 978-1-967657-48-3

To Alice—my partner in love, words, and wonder.

Thank you for believing in every story, and for sharing this beautiful journey of writing together.

CONTENTS

FOREWORD

Some bridges carry more than footsteps—they hold secrets, vows, and echoes that refuse to die.

In The Bridge of Echoes, the highly anticipated second installment of the Brookwood Mysteries, bestselling intrigue and romance collide once more as Marley Taylor and Damien Hawthorne step deeper into the shadows of Brookwood's haunted past.

When an unusual fog clings to the town's covered bridge, Marley begins hearing voices in the mist. A child whispers warnings, a woman's voice pleads for someone who never came, and dreams pull Marley into visions of a nineteenth-century bride who vanished without a trace. Each haunting leaves her more determined to uncover Annie Wren's forgotten story.

But Brookwood has long memories—and its people prefer silence. Whispers turn into gossip. A child sketches "the lady on the bridge at night." A café owner deflects questions about a bride who never reached the altar. And when Marley discovers an unfinished poem pressed into an old letterpress plate, initials etched faintly at its edge, she begins connecting Annabelle to Callum Marwick, heir to one of Brookwood's founding families.

Damien, ever the rational protector, fights to dismiss the evidence even as it chips away at his disbelief. His own family's tragedies—and the sleepwalking of his young daughter —stir doubts he can no longer ignore. As Marley records every dream, vision, and trace of ink in her journal, Damien is torn between his fear of repeating history and the undeniable pull he feels toward Marley herself.

From candlelit trances and eerie jazz melodies that echo through rehearsal halls, to séance reenactments that spiral out of control, to a ledger that reveals Annabelle's very name scratched out of Brookwood's burial records, each clue pushes them closer to a revelation the town has buried for more than a century. What begins as Marley's search for a silenced woman turns into a reckoning with the town's identity, its hidden healer lineage, and the power of ancestral vows unfulfilled.

As Marley and Damien gather the ring, ribbon, music box, and letters that belonged to Annabelle and Callum, the bridge itself begins to respond—mist parting, voices rising, and one final apparition that forces Brookwood to confront its own truth. And when the chapel bell rings for the first time in over a hundred years, Marley knows she has brought Annabelle home. But some doors, once opened, cannot be closed.

The Bridge of Echoes is a sweeping tale of mystery, romance, and generational healing—a story of how love lost can echo through centuries, and how courage in the present can quiet the past. Readers who devoured The Bookshop Secret will find themselves pulled even deeper into the mist, where every revelation comes at a cost, every silence hides a wound, and every choice Marley and Damien make will shape not only their fragile bond, but the fate of Brookwood itself.

And as the mist finally clears, a new light emerges. A lighthouse, long dark, flickers awake for the first time in seventy years—signaling that Brookwood's story is far from over.

Prepare to be haunted, enthralled, and moved in equal measure. The Bridge of Echoes is not just a mystery to be solved—it's an invitation to step onto the bridge, listen closely, and decide what you believe before the echoes fade.

The Brookwood Mysteries is a continuing saga blending gothic suspense, slow-burn romance, and community legacy storytelling. Each book resolves one haunting while weaving threads toward the next, inviting readers to not only unravel the mystery but to belong to the town itself.

PROLOGUE

The fog returned as if summoned by memory rather than weather, folding itself over Brookwood's streets in hushed layers. By late afternoon the bay had dissolved into mist, and the covered bridge—its ribs and rafters rising like a skeleton out of history—stood half-swallowed in gray. To Marley Taylor, standing at the bookshop window, the sight felt less like the day's inevitable weather and more like the threshold to another story waiting for its telling.

She had grown familiar with Brookwood's rhythms over the past months, but the bridge carried something different —an unsettled pulse, an echo that seemed to live in the timbers themselves. The town treated it as a landmark, picturesque in postcards and pleasant in daylight, but Marley had begun to notice how conversation shifted whenever its name surfaced. Brookwood lived with the bridge the way one lives with an old scar: admired from afar, never touched without remembering the pain it once carried.

That evening, she lingered in the shop longer than usual, stacking the last of the returned volumes and brushing dust from the counter where light had pooled like honey. On the shelves, the small first run of *The Book of Brookwood* had already thinned; neighbors had carried copies home, some with curiosity, others with reverence. The book had given voice to records long muffled, and while not everyone welcomed it, Marley had felt a subtle shift in the town's atmosphere—less silence, more listening.

Still, with listening came weight.

The ledger, Clara's legacy, waited in the back room with its measured lines and secretive symbols. The music box lay patient, a keeper of tunes that shifted depending on who opened it. And now, a new artifact rested on her desk wrapped in oilcloth: the iron triangle delivered by a boy with flushed cheeks and words rehearsed by his grandmother—*for the book lady who hears things.* Marley had not yet struck it. Its spiral etching seemed to breathe when the lamplight touched it, and she hesitated to release whatever sound it guarded.

When Damien Hawthorne arrived, shaking mist from his coat, he carried with him another fragment: a broadside proof dated 1891 from *The Brookwood Echo.* Its headline declared a petition about a grove, but the columns beneath were blank—as though the story had been silenced in the very act of being born. He had placed it in her hands with that familiar mixture of caution and trust, the weight of shared discovery passing easily between them.

Now, hours later, Marley replayed the scene in her mind. She traced the raised ink of the broadside with her fingertips, remembering how Damien's eyes had lingered on her face when she read aloud the title. The *Echo.* The word itself seemed chosen to resonate beyond time. A newspaper built on repetition, on voices carried back across years, on truths too large to vanish quietly.

She pressed her hand against the shop's window, feeling the cool glass beneath her palm. Outside, the fog pressed close, almost affectionate. The lighthouse beam carved a pale stripe across the mist, sweeping rhythmically, a heartbeat no storm had yet extinguished. And from somewhere deep in the fog, she thought she heard it again: not quite a sound, more the absence of silence. An echo without origin, waiting.

Marley turned back to the counter where the triangle lay hidden under its cloth. She hesitated, then drew the object free. Its weight surprised her; heavy for its size, dense with use and memory. She lifted the striker, poised to test its voice. But just as her wrist tilted, the bell over the door gave its faithful ring, and Damien's voice cut through the quiet.

"I thought you'd still be here."

She smiled faintly. "Where else would I be?"

He set a second broadside proof on the counter, this one folded as carefully as if he'd feared it might dissolve. "Fenwick found more. All the same date. All the same blank silence."

Marley smoothed it open, tracing the void where words should have been. "It feels deliberate. Not a mistake."

"Not a mistake," Damien agreed. His voice carried that academic precision he couldn't quite shed, but beneath it lay something more personal—fear, perhaps, or longing. "Someone wanted the Grove forgotten."

They spoke the word together—*Grove*—and for an instant the lamps flickered, as though the shop itself had listened too closely.

Neither of them said what they both knew: the ledger's whispers, the triangle's inscription, the broadside's headline—they were all leading in the same direction. Toward a place the town no longer admitted it possessed. Toward something Brookwood had buried with intention.

Marley wrapped the triangle again and slipped it into her satchel. She added the broadside proof and her notebook, where pages of half-legible dreams recorded themselves in her uneven script. "If the bridge is where echoes live," she said softly, "then maybe that's where we should begin."

Damien nodded, his hesitation tempered by the way her words steadied his own thoughts. "Close early?"

She turned the sign on the door to *Back at Dusk*. Together, they stepped into the fog.

The town had surrendered to silence, lanterns glowing in their glass cages, windows lit like small hearths along Main Street. At the mouth of the lane, they paused before the weathered placard with its ghost-letters—E, O, the remnants of *ECHO*. Marley brushed the wood with her fingertips. "It was always telling us its name. We just forgot how to read it."

When they reached the bridge, its timbers groaned as though welcoming their weight. The river's patient rhythm rose through the boards, a language older than the town. In the satchel, the triangle pressed heavier against her hip. She loosened the strap and let the bag rest on the railing.

"Not yet," she whispered, answering Damien's unspoken question about striking it. She turned her face toward the water, listening. The mist thickened, and for a breath it shaped itself into what might have been a figure at the far end of the bridge—narrow, uncertain, waiting. Marley did not call out. She only listened, because listening was what the town most needed and what it least knew how to do.

When they finally returned to the shop, she unwrapped the triangle and gave it one clean strike. The sound traveled no farther than the room, yet it seemed to linger, nestling into shelves and rafters as though the wood had been waiting to hold it. The quiet afterward felt altered, tender.

Damien's expression softened. "Tomorrow," he said, "we go to the mill. We ask what it remembers."

Marley touched the ledger, the broadside, the triangle—threads weaving themselves into a pattern she could almost recognize. She did not say aloud what she felt settling deep within her: that tomorrow the echoes would not only answer, but begin to call her by name.

THE MILL LOOMED over the river like a relic that refused to surrender its bones. Its broad windows reflected the fog in milky panels, and its timbers—blackened with age, water, and time—creaked whenever the wind slid through them. For most of Brookwood, the building was little more than a place to buy nails, twine, and the occasional plank of seasoned wood. To Marley, standing at its threshold with Damien's key in her hand, it felt like a library that had gone to sleep long ago and needed careful waking.

Damien glanced at her as he fitted the key to the side door marked *Society Records – Authorized Only.* "Fenwick gave this up too easily," he said. His voice was quiet, though the street behind them was empty. "Either he's finally tired of guarding ghosts—or he wants us to see something."

Marley lifted her satchel higher on her shoulder. Inside, the triangle wrapped in cloth seemed to press its presence against her ribs, as though aware of where they were going. "Either way," she said, "we can't ignore it."

The lock yielded reluctantly, and the door swung open on a room steeped in dust and neglect. The smell of paper, ink, and mildew greeted them—a heavy perfume of forgotten years. Tall cabinets leaned under their own weight, folders and ledgers stacked like uneven bricks. Lamps burned low along the central table, their light more suggestion than clarity.

Marley stepped inside and felt an almost physical hush settle over her shoulders. It was not silence exactly, but the attentiveness of a place that had been waiting. She set her hand on the nearest cabinet, and for a moment she thought she felt the faint hum of metal beneath her palm—as though memory itself had a pulse.

Damien unrolled the broadside proof and set it on the table, its blank columns yawning. "If this story was silenced," he said, "its shadow will still be here. The Society kept everything—even the things they wanted forgotten."

They split the room between them. Damien began with the ledgers, pulling drawers carefully, his fingers moving with the scholar's caution he never seemed to lose. Marley gravitated toward the boxes labeled in uncertain scrawl: *Festival Posters—1910s, Church Circulars, Miscellaneous Ephemera.* She lifted lids, brushed dust from paper edges, and found herself reading headlines that had not been touched in decades: *Harvest Dance Raises Funds for Harbor Repairs, Youth Choir Performs at Chapel Dedication.* They were ordinary stories, lives caught mid-sentence, but in their ordinariness she felt the outline of what was missing.

At the bottom of a box labeled *Festival Posters—1910s,* her fingers touched wax paper instead of folded newsprint. She drew it out carefully. Beneath the wrapping was a wooden frame no larger than a book, and inside the frame gleamed the faint gray of unfinished metal. Her breath caught.

"Damien," she said, her voice thinner than she intended.

He crossed the room in two quick strides. Together, they bent over the frame, and the lamplight revealed its surface:

an incomplete printing plate. The letters had been etched but not finished, their lines shallow in some places, broken in others. Enough remained, however, to read the headline: *Petition Regarding the Grove.*

Marley's fingers trembled as she traced the incomplete words. The plate felt colder than the air, as though it had never warmed to human touch. "They began to set it," she whispered. "They meant to print it."

Damien's jaw tightened. His eyes scanned the broken letters with something close to fury. "But never did."

The silence that followed was heavier than before. Marley felt as though the room itself leaned closer, waiting for her to acknowledge what she held. She looked at Damien, and he met her gaze, the lamplight reflecting in the gray at his temples.

"Someone stopped this deliberately," he said. "The blank proofs, the unfinished plate. Someone wanted the Grove erased."

Marley set the frame gently on the table beside the proof. The two artifacts mirrored one another: one with its columns empty, the other with its letters arrested mid-formation. Together, they were louder than any complete article could have been.

Her hand went to her satchel, where the ledger waited. She remembered the warning written in its cramped, insistent hand: *When the bell forgets to ring, remember the Grove.* The phrase echoed now with sharper resonance. This was not metaphor. It was direction.

Damien bent lower, examining the plate's edge. "Here," he murmured. "Do you see it?"

Almost invisible, etched small as a craftsman's mark, was a spiral of seven stones. Marley felt the breath leave her lungs. It was the same symbol carved under Clara's desk, the same spiral she had traced like a worry stone.

Her throat tightened. "The Circle."

Damien nodded grimly. "They were going to print it. They were going to make it public. And then—"

"Someone silenced them," Marley finished.

Her thumb rested lightly on the spiral, careful not to mar the delicate etching. The metal seemed to hum faintly under her skin. She remembered Clara's words, written in a margin: *The circle holds both knowing and not-knowing with the same hand.*

The plate pulsed with that very paradox. It was both revelation and silence, an artifact of truth almost told.

Marley wrapped it again in its wax paper, her hands steady now. She slipped it into the satchel beside the triangle. The weight shifted, heavier than it should have been. She thought of ballast, of anchors, of objects that knew their own importance.

Damien leaned against the table, watching her. His face was a study in conflict—determination edged with worry. "You realize what this means."

"It means," she said, her voice firmer than she felt, "that Brookwood's story was interrupted, not erased. It means someone tried to carry truth across the bridge, and someone else made sure it fell."

His expression softened, though the concern in his eyes remained. "It also means there are people—past or present —who wanted this hidden. And they may not be done wanting it hidden."

Marley shouldered the satchel, the strap biting a little into her collarbone. She thought of the mist at the bridge forming into something almost human, the whisper of a child's voice months earlier calling her name. She thought of how silence itself seemed to wait for her. "Then we'll give it a spine," she said.

Damien tilted his head, half a smile breaking through. "A spine strong enough to carry echoes."

The clock in the corner ticked, an ordinary sound that felt impossibly fragile in the heavy room. Marley touched the plate through the satchel's canvas, steadying herself. "We follow it," she said. "To the Grove."

They locked the archives carefully behind them. Outside, the fog still pressed low across the harbor, but now threads of late sunlight angled through, setting the water to a dull gleam. As they descended the steps, Marley thought she heard it again: the faint arrhythmic ticking of type being set, though no hands moved across ink or paper.

She closed her eyes, and the sound faded. But the certainty it left did not.

The story had begun to echo. And echoes, she knew, always find their way home.

By dusk, Brookwood seemed suspended in a half-light, the fog lifting just enough to reveal the harbor lamps and blur the line between water and air. The lighthouse beam swept its familiar arc, untroubled, but to Marley the rhythm felt less like a safeguard tonight and more like a summons.

She stood at the bookshop door with the satchel heavy against her hip. Inside it lay the unfinished printing plate, still wrapped in wax paper, the ledger with its warnings, and the iron triangle folded in cloth. Damien had stayed behind, conceding that she needed to go first, though his worry had lingered in the way he adjusted her strap, in the way his hand hesitated before letting go of her arm.

"You can call me," he had said. "For any reason or for none."

She carried his words like another object in the bag—weightless, but present.

The lane sloped toward the bridge, and Marley followed it as one follows an intuition: not quickly, not carelessly, but with the quiet surety that hesitation would not protect her. At the mouth of the lane, she paused again before the weathered placard with its ghost-letters. Her fingertips brushed the wood. *ECHO.* The fragment seemed almost to pulse under her skin, as though the word itself remembered being whole.

She crossed onto the bridge. The boards yielded underfoot with the honesty of old timber. The river spoke beneath her, its arithmetic slow and tireless, carving sound into syllables that only the patient could translate. She went to the center span, set the satchel on the beam, and lit the lantern. Its glow pressed back a small circle of mist, enough to see the curve of rafters overhead and the pale path of the water below.

One by one, she unwrapped the contents: the iron triangle with its striker, the unfinished plate with its headline half-etched, her notebook with its blank page waiting. The triangle lay on the wood like a small heart, dense and cool. She held the striker loosely, unwilling to release its sound too soon.

"Why here?" she whispered, not to the river, not to the air, but to the bridge itself—the way she had learned to speak at Clara's desk.

The bridge answered in the only way bridges know: by holding.

Marley opened her notebook and copied the plate's title across a fresh page: *Petition Regarding the Grove.* Beneath it she wrote the phrase from the ledger again: *When the bell forgets to ring, remember the Grove.* The words looked different here, under the lantern's light, as if the ink had been waiting for this setting to reveal its weight.

She closed her eyes for a moment, listening. The ordinary sounds of the town faded until there was only the river's slow pulse. Then, beneath it, she heard something more: the faint hush of mist shaping itself, a braid of air twisting into form at the northern mouth of the bridge.

Her breath caught. The mist narrowed, lengthened, gathered at the waist until it resembled the suggestion of a figure standing still, watching. Marley did not move.

"Marley," a voice said.

It was not Clara's. It was not the deep cadence of the Circle women in her dreams. It was a girl's voice, no louder than the scrape of a leaf along the planks, but clear. A voice that came not from outside her, but through the echo the bridge held.

Her fingers tightened around the striker. "I hear you."

The mist did not advance. It re-gathered itself, the way a careful thought does when someone has promised to listen.

"Say it back," the voice said.

Marley's throat tightened. She understood instinctively —this was not a command to repeat words she did not know. It was an instruction to answer, to prove she was listening. She lifted the striker and gave the triangle one clean strike.

The sound leapt across the span, ringing against rafters, ribs, and pilings. It traveled into the water and came back altered—not a repetition but a recognition, like a name spoken by someone who loved her. The wood seemed to hold it, reluctant to let it go.

For an instant, Marley thought she saw light in the fog—

three short flashes, two long, like the lighthouse's old pattern long since retired. She answered with two slower taps. The sequence nested itself into the night, hers and the town's history layered together.

The mist at the far end of the bridge quivered. The girl's voice came again, closer this time: "Bring the bell. To the Grove."

Marley lowered the striker, her pulse quickening. "Which grove?" she asked, though she suspected the answer.

"The one they almost printed," the voice said, threaded with a humor that startled her—the humor of a child who knows adults are slower to see what is plain. "The one that remembers what the town forgot."

Her mind filled with images: the east bank beyond the mill, the pale birches, the shallow dip where water gathered after storms, the stand of stones Clara's map had left blank. A place overlooked, but not empty.

"What do I do when I get there?" she whispered.

"Listen. Say it back. Bring the bell."

The words sank into her chest with the weight of a vow.

A heron lifted upstream, its wings breaking dusk into syllables. The mist shifted as if in answer, loosening. Marley's hand trembled, not with fear but with the ache of recognition.

"Wait," she said quickly. "Your name?"

For a heartbeat, the mist held. Then it loosened entirely, drifting into air. But as it went, a single syllable skimmed the span and lingered on the railing like salt drying after a tide: "Lena."

Marley repeated it softly. "Lena."

The name settled into the bridge, into the water, into her notebook when she wrote it down beneath the ledger's line.

The lantern's flame did not quiver, yet she felt the atmosphere change, as if the bridge itself had accepted her answer.

She gathered the triangle, the plate, the notebook. The satchel felt heavy again, not as burden but as ballast. Staying a while longer, she let the silence deepen into steadiness. Then, when the air chilled her hands, she returned along the planks, each step ringing a little more sharply than it should have, as though the bridge had memorized her presence.

Main Street glowed faintly as she re-entered the town. Through the café window she saw the last of the sitters, hands cupped around warm mugs. A fisherman's laugh drifted from the docks. The lighthouse beam swept its clean arc. Ordinary life folded itself around her, yet nothing felt ordinary.

At the bookshop door, Damien opened it before she could fit the key. His face was lined with the concern he had carried all day, but his eyes held steady. "Well?"

Marley stepped inside, and the bell over the lintel rang its faithful note. She set the satchel on the counter, unwrapped the triangle, and said, "The bridge spoke."

He waited.

"A name," she said. "Lena. And an instruction."

"What instruction?"

"To bring the bell to the Grove."

Damien exhaled slowly, as if making room for the words. He nodded once, a gesture that felt less like agreement and more like signing his name to a shared oath. "Then tomorrow we ask the mill what else it remembers. And tomorrow night, we go east."

Marley touched the cover of *The Book of Brookwood* still waiting on the counter. She thought of its promise—*to keep the circle whole*—and felt how it aligned with Lena's voice. This was how beginnings arrived in towns like theirs: not with trumpets, but with a small bell carried in a satchel, waiting to be struck where memory had been denied.

Damien poured two cups of tea, and they drank in silence. Through the front window, the fog eased back half a step, as if giving them room. In the satchel, the triangle waited. The unfinished plate whispered its headline. And the bridge, once silent, now carried a name.

Lena.

The echoes had spoken. And Marley knew the Grove was waiting.

1

THE WINTER MIST

The fog arrived with winter's discipline, thick and determined, as though it had a duty to shroud the town and would not be dissuaded. Brookwood often wore mist like a shawl, the bay sending it inland in the evenings, but tonight it clung with unusual weight. Main Street blurred into suggestion; lamps glowed like captive moons; and the covered bridge stood half-lost in a pale curtain, ribs and beams fading into absence.

Marley Taylor paused at the end of the lane, her breath visible in the raw chill. She had walked this way many evenings since autumn, drawn not by errand but by instinct. The bridge had become, for her, less a crossing and more a question. Every time she approached it, the sense grew stronger: that it was not simply an artifact of nineteenth-century engineering but a listening place, a span built to carry not only footsteps but echoes.

Tonight, the fog gathered around its entrances like sentries. The boards creaked under her shoes, damp with condensation. The lantern she carried threw a pale circle ahead, but the mist swallowed it quickly, so that beyond a few feet there was nothing but gray. The bridge felt longer than usual, stretched by weather and by waiting.

At the midpoint, Marley stopped. The river beneath moved with slow insistence, its sound muffled by the fog but steady, a kind of arithmetic she could almost count if she closed her eyes. She let the silence deepen. Then she heard it: faint, arrhythmic, a whisper barely distinguishable from the sigh of the water.

"Mar—"

Her name, or close enough that her breath caught. She turned sharply, lantern lifting, but the mist offered no shape. The word had been no louder than a thought spoken half in sleep, and yet it had lodged in her as firmly as if a hand had pressed it into her chest.

She steadied herself against the railing, fingertips brushing cold wood. "Who's there?" she asked, though her voice was thin.

No answer. Only the ordinary insistence of the river.

She stayed longer than she meant to, listening. The sound did not repeat. But the impression lingered—an echo without source, a syllable released into the fog with nowhere to land. At last she turned back, her steps quickening over the planks. When she reached the far end, she glanced behind her once more. The bridge stood veiled, ribs lost in mist, as if it had absorbed the voice and meant to keep it.

By the time she returned to the bookshop, the lamps in the windows looked warmer than usual, like a hearth after exposure to wind. She let herself in, the bell over the lintel writing its small familiar word in the air. The scent of paper and wood oil steadied her. She set the lantern down and rubbed warmth back into her hands.

Damien Hawthorne sat at the counter, spectacles sliding

down his nose as he examined a stack of broadsides Fenwick had delivered. His dark hair was still damp from the weather, and his jacket draped carelessly over the back of a chair. He looked up at her entrance, his expression a mix of relief and quiet reproach.

"You went to the bridge again," he said, more statement than question.

Marley hesitated before answering. "I needed to."

His mouth tightened, the line between worry and irritation clear. "You know how the fog plays tricks. Sound bends. Carriages on the other side of town can sound like they're whispering beside your ear. It's atmospheric illusion, nothing more."

She slid onto the stool opposite him. "I heard my name."

"Echoes," Damien said. His tone was careful, too careful—the voice of a man determined to keep concern within the boundaries of reason. "Your voice can bounce back from the beams without you realizing. You think you're hearing someone else when you're really hearing yourself."

Marley studied him. The lamplight drew out the gray at his temples, softened the angles of his jaw. He was speaking like a tutor, measured, patient, dismissing gently without dismissing her. But beneath it she saw the flicker in his eyes —the part of him that knew her well enough to recognize when she would not be argued down.

"Maybe," she allowed. Then, after a pause: "But it didn't feel like me. It felt...other."

Damien removed his glasses, folded them carefully, and set them on the broadsides. "Marley, you've been living in Clara's legacy for months now. The ledger, the Circle, the objects that still hum when you touch them—it's natural your mind would start hearing things in patterns. You've immersed yourself in echoes so long you're bound to imagine them."

"Imagine them?" she echoed softly, tasting the word.

He sighed, rubbing his temples. "I'm not saying you're wrong. Only that you're human. And humans see faces in clouds, hear names in wind, because we're built to find meaning even when there isn't any."

Marley reached for the notebook that lay half-hidden under the counter. She had started carrying it since autumn, its pages already cluttered with sketches, half-legible quotes, and fragments of dreams that would otherwise dissolve by breakfast. Tonight, she opened it to a fresh page and wrote in deliberate strokes: *Winter Mist. Heard my name on the bridge. Female voice? Faint. One syllable—Mar—*

She set the pencil down. "If it's only illusion, then it won't matter if I write it down. But if it isn't—if it's part of the pattern—then I need a record."

Damien watched her, his expression caught between skepticism and reluctant respect. "A dream journal?"

"Not just dreams," she said. "Anything. Words in the fog. Names that don't belong to me. Fragments that seem like nothing until you see them together. Clara always said the Circle kept ledgers not to prove they were right, but to remember what had happened. Even the small things."

He leaned back in his chair, exhaling. "And what will you do when the notebook fills? Publish another book the board refuses to endorse?"

Her smile was brief, dry. "Maybe. Or maybe I'll understand the bridge."

The bell over the door rang before Damien could answer. A gust of cold air followed, and Sophie darted in, cheeks flushed, hair damp with fog. She carried a folded sheet of paper like a prize.

"Look!" she said, spreading it on the counter. A sketch, rough but eager, showed the bridge beneath its rafters. And at the midpoint, drawn in lines darker than the rest, was the figure of a woman standing alone.

Damien stiffened. "Where did you see this?"

Sophie shrugged, suddenly shy. "I didn't see it. I just drew it. Nana says sometimes your hand knows before your head does." She glanced between them, sensing their tension. "Is it wrong?"

Marley touched the edge of the drawing gently. The figure's face was nothing more than a shadow, but the posture—waiting, patient, half-formed—sent a tremor through her.

"No," Marley said softly. "It isn't wrong."

Damien folded the sketch carefully, as though by doing so he could also fold the question it raised. "It's late," he said. "Go warm up by the stove."

Sophie skipped toward the back, humming. The drawing lay folded in his hand, and his eyes met Marley's.

"Atmospheric illusion," he said again, but this time his voice lacked conviction.

Marley closed her notebook, slid it into her satchel, and answered without words. She only lifted her gaze toward the window where the fog pressed close, thick as breath, as if listening.

THE FOG DID NOT RETREAT OVERNIGHT. By morning it lingered low across the harbor, veiling the fishing boats until their masts looked like thin black reeds pushing through a white field. Marley stood at the window of her small apartment above the shop, notebook open against the sill, and listened to the town breathe under the mist. Even at this early hour, Brookwood's rhythms sounded muffled: the clatter of pans from the bakery, the faint thump of oars in their locks, the cry of a gull somewhere higher than the fog allowed the eye to follow.

She dipped her pencil and began to write:

January 8. Fog unusually heavy. Bridge half-lost. Heard voice—one syllable—Mar. Distinct. Not echo, not my own voice. Female, young. Sophie's drawing: woman on bridge. Pattern?

The act steadied her. Clara's journals had taught her this: impressions grew slippery when left unpinned. Dreams dissolved by noon. Sounds eroded by logic. But on paper, they held their ground. The ledger had not lied, and Marley did not intend to let her own record scatter into half-memory.

When she came down to the shop an hour later, Damien was already at the counter, a stack of documents spread before him. He had the look of someone who had not slept enough but would never admit it. His spectacles perched low again, and the corners of his mouth tightened when he saw her notebook in hand.

"You started it," he said.

She set the notebook beside the register. "I did. I don't want to lose what I heard."

Damien tapped one of the documents with his finger. "You heard it in fog, Marley. A natural amplifier. Sound refracts differently when the air is saturated. What you think is a voice is likely a fisherman calling upriver or the echo of your own footsteps."

Marley studied him quietly. He wore skepticism like armor, but she knew the man beneath—the one who had touched the unfinished plate with reverence, who had seen symbols etched by the Circle and not turned away. "You believe in echoes," she said softly. "You just want them to behave."

His jaw flexed, the only sign that her words had struck deeper than he wished. He lifted another sheet from the stack, showing her a record of town meetings from the 1880s, columns of ink faded to brown. "Look at this. Notes from a December gathering. The clerk mentions *'fog thicker than usual, bell could not be heard across the river.'* That's what you heard: weather, not whisper."

She traced the edge of the page but did not argue. "Then let's say you're right. What harm is there in me keeping a record? At worst, it proves you right later. At best—"

"At best it convinces you that your imagination has merit."

"At best," Marley said evenly, "it helps us hear what the town itself is trying to remember."

The firmness in her voice quieted him. He leaned back in his chair, rubbing his temples. "You sound like Clara."

"I'll take that as praise."

For a long moment, neither spoke. The fog pressed against the window like a curious child, thick enough to make the lamps on Main Street glow even in morning.

Finally Damien sighed. "Write, then. Keep your journal. But don't let it pull you under." His eyes met hers, shadowed with a worry he rarely confessed. "You remember what happened with Jackie."

Marley did. His late wife, lost too young. He had never told her every detail, but enough had surfaced—Jackie's dreams, her strange certainty that voices spoke through the bridge, her decline into exhaustion and silence. To Damien, the bridge was not only history. It was danger.

She reached across the counter and rested her hand briefly on his. "I'm not Jackie. And this isn't the same."

He didn't answer immediately. When he did, his voice was roughened at the edges. "Just promise me you'll keep one foot in the present. Keep your records, yes—but keep your life too. Teach Sophie. Bake with Mrs. Bennett. Argue with me about coffee. Don't disappear into fog."

"I promise," Marley said, though she knew the line between presence and disappearance was thinner than either of them admitted.

That evening, as the shop closed and the lamps burned low, she found herself drawn again to the bridge. The fog clung even thicker than the night before, as if layering itself in response to her persistence. The town's outlines softened into suggestion. She carried her notebook beneath her coat, its weight light but insistent.

At the midpoint of the span, she stopped and waited. The boards creaked softly under her shoes. The river murmured its patient syllables. For a long while, nothing. Then—

"Write."

The whisper brushed her ear like breath. She spun, lantern raised, but the mist showed only itself. The word had been clear, a command rather than a suggestion.

Her pulse beat high in her throat. She pulled the notebook free, opened to a fresh page, and wrote the single word in her own hand: *Write.*

The air grew stiller, as if satisfied. The fog thickened briefly at the far end of the bridge, a braid of whiteness gathering before loosening again into air.

Marley shut the notebook and clutched it to her chest. The page already felt less like her handwriting and more like a record taken down for someone else.

When she returned, Damien was waiting at the shop

door, coat on, arms folded. His expression carried both relief and disapproval. "You went alone again."

"I had to."

"What did you hear?"

She hesitated, then opened the notebook and showed him the single word. *Write.*

Damien's mouth tightened, but he did not mock. Instead, he looked at the word for a long time, then closed the book gently and handed it back. "Atmospheric illusion," he said, but the phrase lacked strength now, spoken more out of habit than belief.

Marley tucked the notebook away. "Illusion or not, I'll keep writing. If the mist wants a record, I'll give it one."

Damien turned the key in the shop door and held it open for her. "Just remember—echoes don't always belong to the living."

Marley stepped past him, the notebook warm against her ribs. "Neither do stories."

The bell over the lintel rang as the door shut, a sound so small it should have been ordinary. But to Marley, it carried the weight of an echo, a voice keeping time.

Marley woke before dawn with her pulse thrumming as if she had run in her sleep. The fog pressed against her windows, pale and insistent, and though the room was quiet, she carried the memory of words spoken in the night. They had not come in the shape of dreams exactly, but in the half-space where sleep thins into awareness.

She reached for her notebook before the sensation dissolved. Her pencil scratched across the page with hurried strokes:

January 9. Dream? Waking vision? Heard voice—female, clear. Not just "Mar." This time: "Wait." Felt like warning. Or invitation.

She underlined the last word twice, then closed the notebook firmly as if to keep the voice contained within its covers. The act steadied her, but only partly. For the first time, she wondered if writing was not simply record but ritual—that the fog itself required her acknowledgment, that failing to set down the words might risk losing them forever, or worse, letting them seep into her unnoticed.

By the time she came downstairs to open the shop, the street was already stirring. The bakery's door swung open to let out the smell of yeast and cinnamon, but the fog still clung low, thickening around the bridge like a veil not yet lifted. Marley kept glancing toward it as though it were watching her back.

Damien arrived mid-morning, his coat damp, his hands carrying a folder of student essays. He dropped them on the counter and reached for the kettle without speaking, as though the ordinariness of tea could anchor the room against whatever storm might be gathering. Marley waited until he poured two cups before setting her notebook beside him, open to the most recent entry.

He scanned it quickly, his brow furrowing. "You're writing even the dreams now."

"They don't feel like dreams."

"They are," he insisted, but without conviction. His fingers tightened around the cup. "Marley, this is what I'm afraid of—once you begin believing every shadow and syllable carries meaning, you stop sleeping, stop eating. You let it consume you. That's what happened to Jackie."

Her heart twisted at the name, but she did not flinch.

"I'm not Jackie. I'm not walking into this blind. I know the risk of obsession, Damien, but I also know the risk of ignoring what keeps calling." She tapped the page. "You read Clara's journals. You've seen the ledger. This isn't only in my head."

He pressed a hand across his eyes, pinching the bridge of his nose. For a long moment he said nothing. When he lowered his hand, the stern line of reason remained on his mouth, but his eyes betrayed fatigue, doubt, and something nearer to fear.

"What if you're right?" he asked quietly. "What if there are voices in the fog? What if the bridge is holding something it shouldn't? What then?"

Marley exhaled slowly. "Then we keep listening until we understand. And if listening means writing, then I'll keep writing."

Damien shook his head but did not argue further. The silence between them was not agreement, but it was not dismissal either. It was the silence of two people standing at opposite ends of a question they both feared to finish.

That night the fog thickened again. Marley went to the bridge with notebook and lantern, her breath visible in the frozen air. At the midpoint she stopped, leaning against the railing, the river's sound muffled but steady below. She waited, pencil poised.

The voice came sooner this time.

"Not alone."

Clear, insistent, carrying more weight than the faint syllable she had heard nights before. Marley's hand trembled as she wrote it down. The letters seemed darker than her pencil could account for, as though the fog itself had pressed into the page.

Her throat tightened. "Who?" she asked aloud, though the air swallowed her words.

The mist shifted at the far entrance of the bridge. She thought she saw the faint braid of a figure again, but it loosened before she could fix her gaze. The only answer was a repetition, softer but still distinct: "Not alone."

She backed toward the lane, notebook clutched against her chest, the words pulsing on the page as though they were still being spoken.

When she returned, Damien was waiting by the shop fire, arms folded, the posture of a man who had already been pacing. His eyes went first to her hands, to the notebook, then to her face.

"You heard it again."

"Yes." She opened the notebook, showed him the words.

He looked at the page, then at her, his rational façade struggling to hold. "Marley, this is—" He stopped, jaw tightening. "This is the same phrase Jackie wrote. Once. Just once, weeks before—" His voice broke off. He pressed his lips into a hard line.

Marley felt a chill deeper than the fog had given her. "What phrase?"

He closed his eyes briefly, as though conceding something long held. "She wrote *Not alone.* Just that. I found it in her journal after. I convinced myself it was nothing—a fragment, a thought, not worth carrying. But now—"

He didn't finish. His hand hovered above the notebook, not touching it, as if to do so would be to acknowledge too much.

Marley closed the book gently. "Then maybe it's not warning. Maybe it's promise."

Damien's laugh was rough, humorless. "Or curse."

They sat in silence, firelight shifting across the spines of books, across the spiral carved into the desk that seemed to hum beneath Marley's palm.

The fog pressed against the windows, thick and patient.

And Marley knew, with the certainty of someone standing at the threshold of a story, that the voices had only begun to speak.

2

THE VOICE IN THE WATER

The fog had not yet lifted when Marley left the shop the next morning, her satchel slung over her shoulder, notebook tucked inside. The town was muted, as though wrapped in cotton. Even the gulls seemed reluctant to cry, their silhouettes barely discernible above the harbor. She had not meant to go back to the river so soon, but her feet carried her toward it with an insistence that felt less like choice and more like obedience.

The covered bridge loomed first, ribs fading into mist, but today Marley did not cross it. She turned down the narrow path that wound toward the bank, her boots soft against the damp earth. The air smelled of brine and cedar, a winter dampness that clung to her skin. She paused at the water's edge and listened.

The river ran steady, hushed beneath the fog. Then, faint as a thread pulled through fabric, a child's voice surfaced.

"Marley."

Her name, spoken with urgency. She turned sharply, but

the bank lay empty. She took a cautious step forward, heart tightening.

Again the voice: "Marley… Annabelle waits…"

The last word dissolved in the mist, but the syllables carried. Marley's breath caught, cold searing her throat. She knelt and opened her notebook, hands unsteady, and wrote quickly before the words slipped:

January 10. Heard child's voice at riverbank. Clear. Female. Said: "Marley… Annabelle waits in the water."

Her pencil pressed harder than she intended, the letters dark grooves in the page. She repeated the phrase silently: *Annabelle waits in the water.* The name clung to her as though spoken for her alone.

The fog shifted at the edge of her vision, a braid of whiteness curling low to the ground. She thought of Lena, the girl at the bridge, her voice threaded with humor and instruction. This was different. Younger, more fragile. A tone that sounded not instructive, but desperate.

She closed the notebook firmly, heart drumming. The name Annabelle echoed in her chest, familiar yet strange, as if she had always known it without knowing she did.

Behind her, footsteps approached, crunching damp leaves. She spun, relief flooding her when she saw Damien emerging from the fog. His coat collar was pulled high, and his hands were thrust deep into his pockets.

"You came," she said, breath unsteady.

He nodded once. "I saw your shop was closed. I knew where you'd be." His eyes scanned her face. "What did you hear?"

Marley handed him the notebook, the page still fresh with pencil strokes. He read it, his brow furrowing.

"Annabelle waits in the water," he murmured. His tone

was not skeptical—just quiet, as though the words themselves carried a weight he could not dismiss outright.

Before she could answer, Damien crouched, brushing back the grass near the bank. Marley followed his gaze and felt her stomach lurch.

Footprints. Small, bare, pressed deep in the damp earth.

They led down the slope toward the water, each one distinct until the last pair disappeared at the edge where river met land.

Damien touched the ground with careful fingers, as though verifying they were not tricks of shadow. His face paled. "These are fresh," he said. "No more than an hour old."

Marley's throat tightened. "Children don't walk barefoot in winter."

He rose slowly, scanning the river's surface. Nothing but mist and rippling current. His rational armor cracked then, just for a moment, and she saw fear slip through.

"Whoever made these," he said carefully, "didn't come back."

Marley clutched the notebook to her chest, the phrase *Annabelle waits in the water* burning against her skin as though it had been spoken onto the page rather than written by her hand. She glanced again at the footprints dissolving into the river, and for the first time since she had begun hearing voices in the fog, she shivered with more than cold.

Because this was not only sound. This was evidence.

And evidence, unlike echoes, demanded an answer.

THE FOOTPRINTS WOULD NOT RELEASE her gaze. They clung to the riverbank with the insistence of testimony, each indentation holding a shape of toes and arch, pressed deep enough that the water could not yet erase them. Marley crouched, her breath fogging the cold air, and pressed her hand into the soil beside one of the impressions. The earth was damp, pliant, cold. Her handprint looked shallow by comparison, as if whatever had walked there carried more weight than a body should.

Damien stood just behind her, his posture taut, arms folded across his chest. "We need to think rationally," he said, though the words sounded thin against the mist. "Someone could have come early to fish, taken off their boots, maybe slipped—"

"Children's feet," Marley interrupted, her voice steady. "Look at the size."

He hesitated, then crouched beside her. His brow furrowed, the muscles of his jaw tightening as he measured the length of the print with his hand. Small. Bare. No more than nine years old. His silence confirmed what she already knew.

"They go one way," Marley said, gesturing along the trail. "Down to the water. Nowhere else."

Damien straightened, scanning the fog. "The current's strong this time of year. If someone—" He stopped himself, his rational explanation catching in his throat.

Marley turned her face toward the river, the mist curling off its surface like breath. "It wasn't only footprints. I heard her. A child's voice. She said my name. And then..." She opened the notebook again, showing him the line etched in dark pencil: *Annabelle waits in the water.*

Damien read it, lips tightening. "You could have imagined it. You've been listening for voices—your mind fills the silence with patterns."

Marley's eyes lifted to his, steady. "Then how do you

explain these?" She pointed again to the prints, her hand trembling not from cold but from the certainty pressing in on her.

He said nothing. His silence was louder than any rebuttal.

The river moved slowly, the faint ripple of its current breaking against the pilings of the bridge upstream. Marley felt the pull of its sound, the way it seemed to carry more than water—memory, perhaps, or names whispered into its depths. *Annabelle waits in the water.* The phrase gnawed at her, not as metaphor but as message.

She flipped to a new page in the notebook and wrote the words again, deliberately, letting each letter carve deeper: *Annabelle waits in the water.* She underlined Annabelle's name three times, then circled it.

When she looked up, Damien's expression was unreadable. His rational façade was still in place, but she saw the strain around his eyes, the way his hands tightened into fists at his sides.

"You've heard that name before," she said quietly.

His eyes flicked to hers, startled, then away. "It's a common enough name."

"Not to you," she pressed. "Not here. You recognized it."

He turned away, gazing upriver where the fog thickened around the bridge. His voice, when it came, was low. "There was an old story. One of the founding families. A girl who went missing near the bridge in the 1880s. But there's nothing in the records—only fragments. A census, a mention in church notes, then gone. Annabelle Warren. The Society never speaks of her."

"Annabelle Warren," Marley repeated, the name tasting like recognition though she had never heard it. She wrote it beneath the phrase in her notebook: *Annabelle waits in the water – Annabelle Warren (1880s?)*

Damien's mouth hardened. "Don't romanticize it. People vanish. Records fail. History is full of ghosts that belong to ink and not to us."

"And yet here are footprints," Marley said.

He exhaled sharply, a sound caught between frustration and concession. "I can't explain that."

The admission hung between them, fragile and heavy. Marley closed her notebook with deliberate care, as though sealing the words inside gave her some control over their weight. But in her chest, the phrase pulsed louder than before. *Annabelle waits in the water.*

She thought of Lena, the girl's voice at the bridge, instructing her to bring the bell to the Grove. Now another name had entered, stitched to water and fog. Annabelle. A second thread weaving itself into the pattern.

Damien reached for her arm, his touch steady but firm. "Promise me something. If you hear her again—if you hear anything—don't go chasing it into the river. Don't follow where it leads. Write it, record it, but don't step into the water."

His eyes held hers with an intensity that startled her. Beneath his rational words lived fear, sharp and unspoken, as if he carried memory heavier than logic could erase.

"I promise," Marley said, though the words felt thin even as she spoke them. Because already, some part of her knew: the river was not finished speaking, and promises made in daylight seldom held against fog.

The water shifted against the bank, a ripple with no source. Marley shivered and closed the notebook tighter.

Damien bent one last time to study the footprints. When he straightened, his shoulders bore the weight of unease.

"We'll tell Fenwick," he said finally, though his tone made it sound like obligation more than intention. "Maybe the records will have more. Maybe Annabelle Warren was more than story."

Marley looked at the river, at the mist thickening over its surface. "She is more than story." Her voice was certain, quiet but unyielding. "She's waiting."

THAT NIGHT the fog returned heavier than before, thick enough that lanterns along Main Street glowed like blurred embers. The bridge was all but invisible, its ribs swallowed by whiteness. Marley sat at the desk in the back of the shop, the notebook open, the words *Annabelle waits in the water* underlined so many times the pencil had nearly torn the page. She traced the phrase with her finger until the graphite smudged against her skin.

The name clung to her mind as though it had always belonged there. Annabelle. It felt less like discovery and more like remembering something she should never have forgotten. She thought of the footprints pressed deep into earth, vanishing at the river's edge. She thought of the child's voice, urgent, pleading. And she thought of Lena, the bridge-girl, who had spoken of the Grove. Two names now. Two voices. A pattern taking shape.

The spiral carved into the underside of Clara's desk pressed cool against her palm, as though reminding her she was not the first to sit with riddles that blurred the line between past and present. Clara had written: *The circle holds both knowing and not-knowing with the same hand.* Marley closed her eyes and breathed. Then she wrote across the next page in deliberate strokes:

Not imagination. Not illusion. A message. Annabelle waits. The river holds what the town buried.

The sound of the bell above the shop door startled her. She looked up to see Damien stepping inside, his hair damp, his expression drawn. He carried his coat over one arm, and the weariness in his posture told her he had walked the long way from the mill instead of cutting through town.

"You're still at it," he said, voice low.

She gestured toward the notebook. "It won't leave me."

His eyes flicked to the words visible on the page, then away. "You're letting it in too much."

Marley closed the notebook with care. "And you're trying too hard to keep it out."

The words landed between them with more force than she expected. Damien lowered himself into the chair opposite her, rubbing his temples. For a long moment he said nothing, only stared at the lantern flame shifting on the desk. When he finally spoke, his voice was stripped of the usual armor.

"I can't deny the footprints," he said. "I can't explain them either. But Marley—" He broke off, searching for the right shape of words. "When Jackie began hearing things, it started just like this. A name. A plea. She wrote them down, night after night, until the journal was all she carried. She stopped sleeping. Stopped living. And then she was gone."

Marley's throat tightened. "Gone?"

"Not in body," he said bitterly. "But in herself. She was hollowed out by listening to voices no one else could hear. And when she died, I couldn't help but think the bridge had been claiming her long before the illness finished the work."

His voice cracked on the last word, and silence spread between them.

Marley reached across the desk and rested her hand lightly on his. "I'm not Jackie," she said softly. "But I will not pretend I don't hear. If voices are calling from the river, if Annabelle is waiting, then someone has to listen. Someone has to write."

Damien closed his eyes briefly, as if conceding to something he wished he could still deny. His fingers curled around hers for one brief, unguarded moment before withdrawing.

The silence pressed heavier, broken only by the soft hiss of the lantern. Then—

A sound.

Faint, distant, but distinct. Marley's head lifted sharply. It was not the bell, nor the creak of timber. It was a voice, threading through the fog beyond the window, carried thin but undeniable.

"Marley..."

Both of them froze.

The voice came again, closer this time, urgent: "Marley... Annabelle waits..."

Damien rose so fast his chair scraped the floor. He crossed to the window, peering into the fog. The glass showed nothing but pale shifting whiteness. His shoulders stiffened. "Tell me you heard that," he said, not turning.

Marley had already opened her notebook, pencil trembling in her hand. "I heard it." She wrote quickly: *Heard again, from outside shop. Clear. Annabelle waits...*

Damien's hand pressed against the glass as if bracing himself against something pressing in from outside. "It wasn't just you this time," he said, his voice strained. "I heard it too."

The words cracked something in the air. For the first

time, his skepticism faltered not in silence but in confession. He turned, his face pale, eyes shadowed.

"This isn't possible," he whispered. "And yet—"

Marley closed the notebook firmly, her pulse quickening. "Then we agree. It's real."

He looked at her for a long moment, his rational façade dissolving under the weight of what he could no longer deny. Finally he nodded once, as though signing a contract he could not escape.

"Tomorrow," he said. "We go back to the river."

Marley pressed her palm against the notebook, the words inside thrumming like a heartbeat. She knew already what the voices would say. They would call her name. They would ask her to listen. They would press Annabelle's presence deeper until it rooted itself in every breath she took.

The fog thickened outside the window, pressing against the glass, as if listening too.

And in the silence that followed, both Marley and Damien understood: the water did not only reflect. It remembered.

3

COFFEE GROUNDS AND CLARITY

The café was one of the few places in Brookwood where fog felt like a companion instead of an intrusion. Its windows, always steamed from the kettles and ovens, blurred the view of the harbor into watercolor. The scent of cinnamon, clove, and dark roast coffee wrapped every visitor in the kind of warmth that made them linger longer than they planned.

Marley pushed the door open, the bell giving a cheerful jingle that felt almost irreverent after the gravity of the riverbank. She carried her notebook tucked beneath her arm, its pages already heavy with the words she could not shake. *Annabelle waits in the water.* She had written the phrase so many times the letters seemed to etch themselves onto the paper of their own accord.

Evelyn, the café's owner, glanced up from behind the counter. She was a broad-shouldered woman with a mane of silver hair she refused to tie back, her laugh the kind that filled the whole shop when she let it out. Today she wore a cranberry-colored apron, flour dusting her hands.

"Well, if it isn't my night-walker," Evelyn said with mock

sternness. "You've been haunting the bridge more than the ghosts themselves."

Marley smiled faintly, unzipping her coat. "News travels fast in this town."

"In a town this size," Evelyn said, "news doesn't travel—it spreads like steam." She poured a cup from the fresh pot and slid it across the counter. "On the house. You look like you need grounding."

Marley accepted, wrapping her hands around the cup. The warmth sank into her palms. "Grounding sounds good."

Evelyn leaned against the counter, eyes glinting. "Speaking of grounds—want to know your fortune?"

Marley blinked. "My fortune?"

"Coffee grounds. Old trick my grandmother used to do for fun. Nothing serious. Just patterns in the bottom of the cup. You'd be surprised how many truths hide in a good dark roast."

Marley hesitated, then took a sip, curious. "All right. Show me."

"Drink it down first," Evelyn instructed. "Leave a little at the bottom, swirl it, then tip it over onto the saucer."

Marley obeyed, feeling slightly foolish but intrigued. She drained the cup, leaving a dark residue, and handed it over. Evelyn swirled the liquid with the practiced hand of someone who had done this too many times to dismiss entirely, then tipped the cup upside down. The coffee slid slowly down the porcelain, leaving behind shapes like ink blotches, curling into patterns.

Evelyn lifted the cup, peered inside, then chuckled. "Well, would you look at that. A fish. That's luck in some cultures. Prosperity in others."

Marley leaned closer. "I see it."

Evelyn tilted the cup again. Her laughter softened. The color drained slightly from her face. "And that..." She hesitated. "That looks like a bridge."

Marley's heart quickened. She stared into the cup. Against the pale porcelain, the grounds had formed an arch with darker vertical lines like planks. She could see it plainly—the covered bridge, Brookwood's own, standing in miniature at the bottom of her cup.

Her hand tightened on her notebook. "What does it mean?"

Evelyn set the cup down more quickly than necessary, wiping her hands on her apron as if to erase the image. "It means nothing. Shapes are shapes. People see what they want to see."

"You saw it too," Marley pressed.

Evelyn busied herself with the kettle, avoiding Marley's gaze. "Superstition. That's all. My grandmother used to scare us with stories, that's how small towns work. You pass on the myths, and they grow taller every generation."

Marley lowered her voice. "The bridge bride. That's what people whisper, isn't it?"

Evelyn froze for a fraction of a second before recovering, slamming the kettle back onto the counter harder than needed. "Old nonsense. Don't fill your head with it. Folks like you—newcomers, dreamers—you'll start believing and before you know it, the town will blame you when the fog comes thicker."

The words stung, but Marley didn't back down. "It's already too late. I hear her. Annabelle. The water isn't quiet anymore."

Evelyn's eyes snapped to hers, sharp with something between fear and anger. "Stop," she said firmly. "Don't speak her name. Not here. Not in daylight. Some stories don't need breath to stay alive."

The café door swung open, the bell ringing bright. Damien stepped in, shaking fog from his coat. His timing felt less like coincidence than inevitability. He saw Marley, then Evelyn's rigid stance, then the coffee cup still sitting between them. His eyes narrowed.

"What's this?"

"Nothing," Evelyn said quickly, turning away.

Marley closed the notebook, sliding it back into her satchel. "Evelyn was showing me how to read coffee grounds."

Damien's gaze sharpened. "And you saw the bridge, didn't you?"

Evelyn muttered under her breath and disappeared into the kitchen, leaving them alone in the hush of steam and clinking cups.

Damien crossed to Marley's table, lowering his voice. "Don't let it consume you. Coffee cups, footprints, voices in fog—they'll eat your mind if you give them too much power."

Marley looked down at her hands, the faint smudge of graphite still dark on her fingertips. "What if they're not illusions, Damien? What if it's all connected?"

His jaw tightened. "Then the danger is even greater. Because once the stories get hold of you, they don't let go."

The warmth of the café pressed around them, but Marley shivered. The coffee cup still sat on the counter, grounds forming the bridge's silhouette, as if daring her to look again.

. . .

THE CAFÉ SETTLED into a quieter rhythm after Evelyn slipped into the kitchen, her retreat leaving the air thick with unspoken weight. A few regulars lingered by the window, their conversations muted under the fog-pressed glass. The hum of the espresso machine filled the silence Evelyn had left behind, but Marley felt the absence more than the sound—the sudden hollow where explanation should have been.

She turned her cup slightly, peering into the grounds once more. The shape had not changed. The bridge stared back at her in miniature, its ribs stark, its arch unmistakable. It felt like confirmation, like the echo of what she had already been hearing in the mist and water.

Damien leaned against the counter, arms crossed. His voice was low, clipped. "You see? This is what I warned you about. People here feed the fog with stories. You're not the first to sit at this counter and hear whispers of brides and ghosts. And if you let it, you'll start believing every smudge of coffee is a prophecy."

Marley lifted her gaze to him, steady. "It isn't only stories. I've heard her. Annabelle. And now even Evelyn reacts when the bridge comes up. That isn't coincidence."

Damien's jaw tightened. "Evelyn is practical. She runs this café with her hands, not her head in clouds. If she won't talk about it, it's because she knows nothing good comes from stirring the past."

"Or because she knows too much," Marley countered.

The words hung between them, heavier than either expected. Damien broke eye contact first, staring toward the fogged window as though the blur of harbor lamps might anchor him.

The kitchen door swung open, and Evelyn reappeared with a tray of scones. She moved quickly, as if busyness could shield her from conversation. But Marley stood and intercepted her.

"Evelyn," she said softly, not loud enough for the customers by the window to hear. "You knew her name. Annabelle. Didn't you?"

Evelyn's hands froze on the tray. The clatter of a spoon hitting porcelain from another table filled the silence that followed. Finally Evelyn exhaled, long and slow. "I knew the whispers. My grandmother used to hush us if we said it aloud. 'Don't call her,' she'd say. 'She's still waiting, and she'll think you're the one she's meant for.'"

"Waiting for what?" Marley pressed.

Evelyn's eyes darkened. "For the man who never came. For the vow that broke. For a crossing never made." She set the tray down with deliberate force, as if ending the conversation. "But it's just a story. A warning for young women not to wait too long for love, or not to trust men who promise more than they can give. Folklore. Nothing more."

Marley studied her face, searching for cracks in the practiced dismissal. There was fear there, yes—but also a knowledge Evelyn could not hide entirely.

"The bridge bride," Marley said softly.

Evelyn's lips pressed into a thin line. "That's what they called her. A girl who stood waiting on the bridge until the mist took her. Or the water did. Or her own despair. Depends who tells it. My grandmother swore she heard footsteps on the boards at night long after the girl was gone. Swore she heard humming in the fog. But grandmothers say many things."

Marley opened her notebook, jotting quickly: *Bridge bride. Waiting. Vow broken. Footsteps. Humming.* She underlined the words until the paper dented. "That's not nothing," she whispered.

Evelyn's eyes flicked to Damien, sharp with unspoken reproach. "You see what you've started? She'll go chasing it, just like—" Evelyn stopped herself, biting the rest of the sentence.

"Just like who?" Marley asked.

But Evelyn shook her head, retreating toward the kitchen again. "Some stories should stay buried."

The door swung shut behind her, leaving Marley staring at the wood as though it might yield answers.

Damien stepped closer, his voice taut. "You see what happens? Every time you press, they'll give you pieces—just enough to keep you coming back. It's a cycle. The town has lived with it for generations, and they've learned the safest way is to leave it alone."

Marley closed her notebook with care, the pencil still clutched in her hand. "But leaving it alone didn't stop the voices. Didn't stop the footprints at the river. Didn't stop Evelyn from flinching when she saw the bridge in the cup. Silence doesn't protect us, Damien. It only protects the secret."

His expression shifted, a flicker of something like fear beneath the frustration. He leaned closer, lowering his voice so the other patrons couldn't hear. "You think you're listening to the past. But what if the past is listening back? What if it doesn't care who it answers, so long as someone keeps asking?"

The thought sank between them like a stone into deep water.

Marley's hand moved unconsciously to the notebook again. "Then maybe it's meant to be me."

Damien's eyes locked on hers, shadowed with both admiration and dread. "That's exactly what Jackie said."

The café's warmth suddenly felt fragile, a thin shield

against the fog pressing harder against the windows. The bridge bride's story had been named, however reluctantly. And with the name came weight, the kind of weight that did not easily loosen.

Marley sat back down, notebook open, pen ready. She had no intention of letting silence win.

Perfect.

THE FOG outside the café pressed so thick against the windows that the lamps glowed like muted halos. A pair of fishermen finished their meal at the far table, their murmurs low, while Evelyn busied herself in the kitchen, the clatter of pans a deliberate barrier.

Marley sat with her notebook open, pen poised, the steam from her untouched coffee curling upward in a slow ribbon. Damien stood opposite, his arms folded, his posture radiating impatience that could no longer disguise the strain beneath it.

"You need to stop," he said finally, his voice sharper than before.

Marley didn't look up. She finished writing Evelyn's exact words—*She's still waiting, and she'll think you're the one she's meant for*—before lifting her eyes. "Stop what? Writing down what I hear? What I see?"

"Chasing shadows," he snapped. His hand tightened around the back of the chair until his knuckles whitened. "Evelyn gave you a story, that's all. Folklore. A tale to keep girls from wasting their lives waiting for men who don't return. It's caution dressed as myth. Nothing more."

Marley studied him, calm in her defiance. "Then why did she flinch when she saw the bridge in the coffee cup? Why did she shut down the moment I asked about

Annabelle? People don't react that way to harmless stories."

Damien exhaled, the sound rough. "Because she knows how stories feed on belief. The more you talk about them, the more they grow. Evelyn doesn't want to give the fog another voice."

Marley leaned forward, her hand flattening on the notebook. "Or she doesn't want to admit the fog already has one."

Silence stretched. The fishermen paid their bill and left, the bell over the door jingling brightly before the heavy door shut again. Now it was just the two of them, the café and its steam and its ghosts.

Damien lowered himself into the chair opposite her, his voice dropping to a quieter register. "Marley, I need you to hear me. This is the same path Jackie took. She started with whispers, then names, then visions she swore were real. And by the end, she couldn't separate her own mind from the echoes. She believed the bridge was speaking to her. And it broke her."

Marley's chest tightened, but she held his gaze. "Maybe it wasn't madness. Maybe she was right. Maybe she was hearing what the rest of you were too afraid to admit."

His hand slammed flat against the table, hard enough to rattle the cup. A few heads turned from the other side of the café, but quickly looked away. Damien lowered his voice again, fierce but contained. "Don't you dare romanticize it. I watched her unravel, Marley. Day after day. I buried the woman I loved because she believed too much. Don't tell me it was wisdom in disguise."

Marley didn't flinch at the outburst. She let the silence settle again, then spoke softly. "I'm not Jackie. And I won't let the bridge break me. But I won't ignore it either. If

Annabelle is still waiting, if her story is unfinished, then it matters. You can choose to look away. I can't."

Her words hung between them, sharper than she intended, but true.

Damien's expression shifted, anger fading into something closer to anguish. He rubbed the bridge of his nose, eyes closing briefly. When he opened them again, the vulnerability in his gaze startled her. "Do you even hear yourself? You're already speaking like she did. About unfinished stories and voices that matter. You think you're stronger, but obsession has a way of convincing you you're invincible—until you're not."

Marley tapped the notebook with her pen. "This isn't obsession. It's discipline. Record, observe, verify. I don't run into the fog blindly—I write. That's how I stay grounded. That's how I stay present."

He leaned forward, voice urgent. "And what happens when the notebook fills with words you didn't write? What happens when you wake and find the pages filled in your sleep?"

She froze. His words struck too close. She thought of the ink-stained hand from nights ago, the page she did not remember tearing from Clara's journal. A chill rippled through her, but she did not let him see it.

"If that happens," she said quietly, "then it means the story wants to be told. And I'll keep writing until it's finished."

Damien sat back, defeated, running a hand through his hair. "God help you, Marley. Because nothing I say will change your mind, will it?"

She closed the notebook with a firm snap. "No. Because the fog has already spoken. And the water too. Pretending otherwise won't silence it."

For a long time neither moved. Evelyn returned briefly, refilling cups without meeting their eyes, then retreated again. The café seemed to lean into its own silence, the only sound the faint hiss of steam from the kettle.

Finally Damien stood, sliding his chair back. His voice was softer now, weary. "Then if you're determined, at least let me stand beside you. I'd rather fight the fog at your side than lose you to it alone."

Marley felt her throat tighten. She nodded once, words failing her.

He picked up his coat, pausing at the door. "But remember this—stories don't just consume those who chase them. They consume those who love the ones who do."

The door shut behind him, leaving Marley with her notebook, her cooling coffee, and the bridge still etched in grounds at the bottom of her cup.

She opened the notebook one last time and wrote, hand steady:

Bridge bride. Annabelle waits. Voices persistent. Damien afraid. Must keep listening.

She underlined the last phrase twice. Then she closed the book, slid it into her satchel, and rose.

Outside, the fog thickened, swallowing Damien's retreating figure. Marley stepped into it, her breath visible, the word *Annabelle* whispering through her chest like a heartbeat.

And for the first time, she no longer feared the waiting. She feared what would happen if no one answered.

4

TOWN GOSSIP

It began the way most things began in Brookwood: with whispers. The kind that slipped between hands over market stalls, threaded into idle chatter at the docks, and carried with steam from teacups in the café. Marley had lived in town long enough to recognize the shift in tone—how a name spoken casually could tilt into suspicion when repeated too often in the wrong places.

Now it was her name.

She felt it first in the bakery when the woman behind her at the counter lowered her voice but not enough to keep Marley from hearing. "That's her. The one who walks the bridge at night. The fog's thicker since she came."

The words pricked her skin, though she kept her posture straight, collected her loaf of bread, and offered the baker her thanks with steady politeness. When she stepped outside, the fog had already thinned in the late morning sun, but the sense of being watched clung heavier than any mist.

Later, at the grocer's, she noticed a similar look. Not

hostile, not yet, but wary. As though her presence carried with it something unstable, something contagious.

By afternoon, she escaped into the café, seeking warmth and the steadiness Evelyn provided when she wasn't bristling against questions. The place was crowded, the tables filled with fishermen, schoolteachers, and shopkeepers avoiding the damp. The hum of conversation should have comforted her, but she heard it again: her name, low, threaded into the murmur. She caught fragments —*bridge... not safe... stirring things best left quiet.*

Marley set her satchel on the counter, pulled out her notebook, and forced herself to write it down instead of reacting. *January 12. Whispers growing. Locals wary of me. Afraid of bridge. Afraid I'll wake something.*

The act steadied her, though her hand trembled as she capped her pen.

Damien arrived not long after, his expression tired from lectures at the college, his shoulders hunched against weather and weight. He spotted her at the counter and slid onto the stool beside her, ordering tea instead of coffee as if to mark his resistance against Evelyn's fortune-telling games.

"You've heard it too," Marley said softly, not looking at him.

"Heard what?"

"The gossip. The whispers." She turned her notebook so he could see the line she'd written. "They think I'm stirring things. That the fog, the voices—it's my fault."

Damien sighed, rubbing the back of his neck. "People will always find someone to blame when they're afraid. You give them a story they don't understand, and they'll place the weight on the closest shoulders. Don't feed it."

Marley closed the notebook gently. "What if they're right? What if I am stirring something?"

His jaw tightened, but he met her eyes. "Then stop."

She studied him, the firmness in his tone, the refusal to bend. "You still don't believe any of it's real, do you? Not the voice, not Annabelle, not the footprints at the water."

Damien hesitated, and in that pause Marley saw the crack in his certainty. But then he shook his head, resolute. "I believe you believe it. That's enough to worry me. But no—I don't believe voices linger in fog, or brides wait on bridges. I believe in history, in trauma passed down like broken inheritance, in superstition woven so tightly into memory it feels like truth."

Marley wanted to argue, but Evelyn approached with a pot of tea, filling Damien's cup before topping off Marley's. She lingered just long enough to glance at Marley's notebook, lips pressing thin before she retreated again. Another deflection. Another silence where explanation should have been.

The café door opened, bell bright, and a family stepped in—two parents shaking damp from their coats, a boy no older than six skipping ahead to the counter with paper and crayons clutched in his hand. Evelyn greeted them warmly, ushering them toward a corner table. The boy immediately began to draw, his tongue poking out in concentration.

Marley let the distraction pull her eyes away from Damien's sternness. She watched the child scribble dark lines across the page, then curves, then shapes that took form faster than expected. He colored with determination, as though sketching something he had already seen clearly in his mind.

When Evelyn brought over their order, the boy held up his drawing proudly. Evelyn froze for the briefest second before recovering, patting his shoulder and laughing too loudly. The parents smiled indulgently, not noticing.

Marley caught the image as Evelyn carried the tray past. It was the bridge. The covered arch, drawn in rough but certain lines, the planks marked like ribs. And at the center of the bridge, darker than the rest, a figure. A woman.

The boy announced for anyone listening, "That's the lady who stands on the bridge at night."

The café went still for a breath too long, the way places do when words land heavier than expected.

Marley's pulse quickened. She opened her notebook without thinking and wrote the child's words down exactly. *The lady who stands on the bridge at night.*

Damien's hand covered hers suddenly, firm. She looked up, startled, to find his expression caught between fear and anger.

"Enough," he said quietly. "Don't make this into more than it is."

But Marley knew, with the certainty of ink pressed deep into paper, that it already was more. Much more.

BY THE FOLLOWING DAY, the whispers had grown into a low, persistent hum that seemed to follow Marley wherever she went. At the post office, the clerk handed her letters with a smile too bright, too forced, as if masking unease. Outside the general store, two men spoke in lowered voices, their conversation halting the moment she passed. Even in church that Sunday, she felt eyes linger a moment too long, heads bending together when she sat down.

It wasn't what people said aloud—it was what lived in the silences after her name was mentioned.

That afternoon, she walked through the square with

Damien at her side, the notebook pressed firmly against her ribs inside her satchel. The air was heavy with mist again, a veil clinging low and refusing to burn off despite the pale sun overhead. Children darted between benches, their laughter carrying easily through the damp air, but the adults stood in smaller clusters, their words muffled, wary.

Marley caught fragments—*bridge bride... not safe... shouldn't meddle.* She slowed her pace, straining to listen, but Damien's hand on her elbow urged her forward.

"Don't," he said.

"Don't what?"

"Don't listen to them. It will only make it worse."

She stopped in the middle of the square, forcing him to halt with her. "They think I'm summoning something. That I'm the reason the fog hasn't lifted. Don't you hear them?"

Damien's jaw worked, his expression taut. "I hear them. And they're afraid because you're giving the fog more power than it deserves. You walk at night, you talk about voices, you ask about the bridge bride—and people notice. They always notice."

Her hand went instinctively to her satchel, gripping the notebook through the canvas. "So you think it's my fault too? That by writing it down, by listening, I'm feeding the story?"

"Yes," he said flatly. "You are. History is fragile. Memory is fragile. Stories survive because people repeat them, and the more you repeat them, the more real they feel. That's how myths grow. You think you're uncovering truth, but you're breathing life into superstition."

Marley's voice sharpened. "What about the footprints? What about the voice you heard outside the shop? Was that superstition too?"

Damien's eyes flicked away. The hesitation was small,

but she caught it. "There are explanations—natural ones. The ground shifts near the bank, the river plays tricks with sound. We both know fog distorts perception."

"And yet you heard it."

His silence was louder than any argument.

Marley stepped closer, lowering her voice so only he could hear. "Maybe the gossip isn't just fear. Maybe it's part of the echo. Maybe the whole town has been repeating fragments for so long they've forgotten they're pieces of a real story. Every whisper is like the bridge itself—holding what was left unfinished."

Damien exhaled sharply, shaking his head. "You're turning hearsay into scripture. People gossip, Marley. That's all. It doesn't mean the fog is talking."

"But what if it does?" she pressed. "What if the gossip is how the past keeps itself alive? What if Annabelle's story survived not in records or ledgers, but in whispers that never stopped?"

His eyes hardened. "Do you even hear yourself? You're trying to sanctify rumor. That's dangerous. Gossip isn't truth. Gossip destroys people."

The edge in his voice stilled her. Around them, the hum of voices carried on, indifferent to the argument threading between them. For a moment she saw him not as skeptic but as a man marked by loss, his every word heavy with the shadow of Jackie's unraveling.

Marley softened her tone, but not her stance. "I'm not chasing shadows for the sake of drama. I'm listening for what's real. And maybe the town's gossip is closer to truth than the official histories you cling to."

Damien's face darkened, his rational mask straining. "And if listening costs you what it cost her? If you become nothing more than a vessel for their fears? Will you still call that truth?"

She held his gaze, steady, unflinching. "If I don't listen, no one will. And then Annabelle will keep waiting."

The words seemed to strike him harder than she intended. He turned sharply away, staring down the lane as if searching for something solid. The fog thickened at the far end of the square, the covered bridge only a pale suggestion through the mist. Its ribs rose faintly like the bones of an animal too stubborn to lie down.

Around them, the townsfolk continued their murmurs, weaving Marley's name into the tapestry of superstition. She felt it, a vibration in the air—an echo not confined to the bridge but stretching through Brookwood itself.

She opened her notebook again, ignoring Damien's look of dismay, and wrote:

January 13. Gossip intensifying. Whispers about me stirring things buried. Feels like echo. Not malice—memory. The bridge bride lives in rumor as much as in silence.

She closed the book, satisfied. "If they're repeating her story, then I'll record it. Even gossip can hold truth."

Damien's hands tightened into fists at his sides. "And even truth can destroy."

The words landed heavy, his fear laid bare at last. But Marley did not flinch. She only tucked the notebook back into her satchel, as the fog shifted and the bridge's outline loomed larger, listening.

THE CAFÉ WAS loud with mid-afternoon chatter, the air thick with the scent of fresh bread and coffee grounds. Marley and Damien had taken their usual seats near the window, though today the fog outside pressed so tightly against the glass it was like looking into a blank wall. Inside, warmth hummed, but Marley still felt the weight of the town's murmurs clinging to her shoulders.

At the counter, a small boy sat with a stub of crayon clutched in his fist, tongue poking from the corner of his mouth in concentration. His parents talked quietly with Evelyn, leaving him to fill the sheet of paper before him. The sound of crayon scraping on wood punctuated the clink of cups and the hiss of the kettle.

Marley noticed him first. Something in the way his head tilted, the speed of his hand, reminded her of Sophie's earlier sketch—the figure on the bridge, dark and waiting. Her chest tightened. She tried to look away, but her gaze kept drifting back.

Finally, the boy lifted the paper proudly. "See?" His voice carried across the room, clear enough that the whole café heard. "That's the lady who stands on the bridge at night."

The café fell silent for a beat too long. Evelyn's laugh came a moment later, forced and brittle. "Oh, that's just imagination, sweetheart. You've been listening to too many old stories."

But Marley's heart thudded against her ribs. From her seat, she could see the drawing. The covered bridge was unmistakable: arched, lined with planks. And at its center, a figure shaded in dark strokes, taller than the boy had drawn the bridge itself. A woman, faceless but certain.

Damien stiffened beside her. His hands curled on the table, knuckles whitening. For once, he didn't rush to explain it away. He just stared at the crude drawing, his jaw clenched, his breath shallow.

Marley pulled her notebook from her satchel, opened to a fresh page, and wrote the boy's words exactly: *The lady who stands on the bridge at night.* She underlined it, then added: *Second child to draw her. Different family. Same description.*

Damien caught her hand before she could set the pencil down. His grip was firm, almost desperate. "Stop," he said hoarsely.

She looked at him, steady. "You saw it. You heard him."

"It's coincidence," Damien said, but his voice cracked. "Children repeat what they overhear. They draw shadows because we plant them there."

"Not this," Marley said quietly. "Not two different children, two different drawings. Not the same woman standing where I've heard her voice."

Evelyn whisked the boy's paper away with a too-bright smile, tucking it against the counter before his parents could study it. "Lovely work," she said, pressing a scone into his hand. "Why don't you eat this instead?"

The boy grinned, unconcerned. But Evelyn's glance toward Marley was sharp, a warning glimmering beneath her careful mask.

Marley felt the words rising in her throat, but Damien's hand pressed tighter, urging silence. His eyes pleaded with her—don't make this worse, don't give the room another reason to whisper.

But it was too late. Marley could feel the weight of every gaze in the café settling on her, the murmurs already forming in the air. Her name, her walks at night, her notebook always open. *She's feeding it,* they would say. *She's keeping the bridge alive.*

She shut her notebook firmly, sliding it into her satchel, though her decision did not change. She had recorded it. That was enough for now.

Damien released her hand, leaning back, running his fingers through his hair. "You're letting this consume you," he muttered, low enough only she could hear. "I won't watch it happen again."

Marley's chest tightened, but her voice was calm, resolute. "I'm not Jackie. I won't vanish into the fog. But I can't ignore what the children see, what the voices say. Annabelle's waiting. The bridge bride is waiting. If I don't write it down, no one will."

He turned to the window, to the wall of fog pressing so close it seemed to breathe. His shoulders slumped, the fight draining. "And what if writing it down makes her stronger?"

Marley laid her palm over her satchel, feeling the notebook's weight. "Then at least she won't be forgotten."

The silence between them deepened, taut as a rope pulled to breaking. Around them, the café slowly resumed its chatter, though quieter now, wary. Evelyn avoided their table. The boy munched his scone, unconcerned with the echo he had loosed into the room.

Marley opened her notebook one last time, added a final line beneath her notes: *The town already knows her name. I will not pretend otherwise.*

She shut it gently, her decision settled.

Damien's eyes flicked toward her, shadowed with fear, but also with reluctant recognition. He had heard the boy. He had seen the drawing. And though his lips still formed the shape of denial, the cracks in his certainty widened further.

Outside, the fog pressed heavier, and in its folds Marley almost thought she saw movement—something like the curve of a shoulder, the suggestion of a figure waiting mid-span. She blinked, and it was gone.

But the echo remained.

And she knew, as surely as she knew her own name, that the lady on the bridge was no longer content to be whispered about.

5

—————

THE LETTERPRESS DISCOVERY

The bell over the print shop door gave a tired jangle, and with it came the scent Marley had come to love: old oil, oxidized ink, paper that had learned to breathe slowly. Unlike the café's warmth or the bookshop's sap-and-sawdust sweetness, this air was metallic and mineral—iron rails and river stones. The shop had been Fenwick's once, in the years before the Historical Society absorbed his energy and patience; now his niece, Tessa, kept it humming with wedding invitations, town notices, and the occasional run of broadside posters.

"What are you after?" Tessa asked, pushing her hair beneath a red kerchief as she glanced up from the Vandercook. The roller made a low contented purr as it coasted to a stop. "Please don't say gold foil. I'm not that kind of magician."

"Just looking," Marley said, trying to sound casual and failing. "Historical plates, proofs—anything retired to the back room that shouldn't be forgotten."

Tessa's eyebrow flicked up. "The back room is where dust goes to retire."

"I get along with dust."

That, at least, won a smile. "Help yourself. Mind the stacks. They have their own politics."

Marley moved past the type cabinets—the familiar grid of the job case, small capitals sleeping beside ligatures—toward the dimmer space beyond the press. The back room was a narrow throat lined with shelves. Galley trays leaned like neglected shingles, each corrugated with a history of fingerprints. Quoins and furniture sat in cigar boxes, the small architecture behind every page.

Her fingers grazed labels in fading pencil: *Menus 1964*, *Fourth of July*, *Chapel Circulars*. She stopped at a tray with no label at all—just an X scratched into the wood and a rubber band turned brittle with age. Inside, wrapped in waxed paper gone translucent in places, lay a small plate, copper-faced on a lead body. Marley recognized the weight before she felt it in her palm; the old plates insisted on their own gravity.

She peeled back the wax paper. The metal shone dull, pitted in the corners, but the etched face held. A few words waited there, reversed and raised just enough to catch the light like tiny shoreline.

...waited beneath the sycamore tree...

Her breath caught. Even backwards, the line assembled itself in her mind with ease. She heard it in Evelyn's grandmother's hush, in the boy's unabashed announcement, in the voice from the riverbank—waiting. Marley tasted the word and felt it settle, familiar and new.

Tessa's voice floated from the doorway. "Find something reckless?"

Marley didn't look up. She ran her thumb along the plate's edge, and there it was—smaller than a craftsman's mark, almost an afterthought: two letters cut with a needle-fine hand.

C.M.

She felt the room shift around that pair of initials, the way it had shifted when the triangle rang in the shop, when the unfinished broadside proof lay blank as a withheld confession. C.M.—present at the edges, claiming nothing and everything.

"May I?" Tessa had come closer, cautious, as if approaching a sleepwalker.

Marley turned the plate to her. "Do you see it?"

Tessa squinted, then nodded, slow. "Someone set a poem?"

"Or began to." Marley ran her finger a second time above the reversed line. "It's unfinished."

"That happens," Tessa said, but the lightness in her voice thinned. "Wedding poems abandoned after broken engagements. Eulogies no one wants to read in the bright light of morning."

"Who would sign with initials?"

"Apprentices sometimes cut their pride where the boss won't see." Tessa shrugged. "And ghosts are particular about signatures."

"Ghosts?"

"I'm a printer," Tessa said. "The dead talk in lead all the time. Don't let Fenwick hear me say that."

The doorbell jangled again, then stilled. Damien stepped in with his coat open, river-cold on his collar. He took in the press, the ink, Marley's posture—the way she leaned toward the plate like a listener offering the better ear —and his expression sorted itself into worry first, then duty.

"Tessa," he said by way of greeting. "And what have you dug from the riverbed now?"

Marley held out the plate without preface. He took it carefully, as if held heat might bloom from the metal. He read the line in the mirrored relief, then inverted it in his head with a frown that wasn't skepticism so much as bracing.

"She waited beneath the sycamore tree..." he read softly. The unfinished ellipsis seemed to spread in the air.

Tessa leaned on the doorjamb, wiping her palms on the kerchief. "Sounds like something romantic until you put it in Brookwood's mouth."

"Sycamore," Damien repeated, turning toward Marley. "On the east bank, isn't it? Near the old path to the Grove."

Marley nodded. She saw the tree in her mind—its pale, shedding bark; the way its roots gripped the slope as if the earth itself might slide away if not held. She'd stood near it months ago to watch sunrise burn fog from the river. She had thought then it looked like a skeleton learning to love the light.

"Do you see the initials?" she asked.

He tilted the plate and found them. "C.M." He said it as a confirmation, not a question. "Marwick."

Tessa whistled softly. "As in the family with the good money and the bad luck?"

Damien's mouth thinned. "As in a founding family. Land titles. A ferry business that never outlived the bridge. And a daughter who vanished sometime in the winter of 1887—Celia." He handed the plate back to Marley, then adjusted his glasses as if the gesture might make the next sentence easier. "The census the next spring lists a son, Callum. The ledger from the chapel lists a vigil without naming for whom."

"Two C.M.'s," Marley murmured. Celia and Callum, daughter and son. The initials on the edge made room for both, and in that looseness something opened: a story not yet choosing its speaker.

Tessa had gone quieter. "If this came with the shop, it came from Fenwick's great uncle. He set eulogies, playbills, a scandal or two. We keep the plates because lead is heavy and guilt makes poor kindling."

"Do you remember where this tray came from?" Marley asked. "Any sense of who tucked it away?"

Tessa shook her head. "We lose the map when we stop asking and the labels give up. But I know where the sycamore is. We all know it. It's a landmark disguised as a tree."

Marley turned the plate over in her hands again, palms reading the nicks like Braille. "She waited beneath the sycamore tree." The upright version lined itself in her head. "It reads like a poem and a police report."

Damien did not smile. He glanced at the Vandercook, at the type drawers, at the walls where old broadsides hung crooked in their frames like neighbors left to age without vanity. "The town recorded what it could afford to remember," he said. "What it couldn't afford, it turned into rhyme."

Marley set the plate on a clean sheet of newsprint and took out her pencil. "May I make a rubbing?" she asked Tessa. "Just the line and the initials."

Tessa slid a graphite stick across the table. "Don't press too hard. The dead dislike being handled, but they love to be heard."

The paper received the relief in a grainy whisper—the reversed letters shading dark until the sentence read correctly, shallow and haunted: **She waited beneath the sycamore tree...** Then, in the lower margin, the tiny fidelity of **C.M.**

Holding the rubbing felt like holding breath. Marley folded it carefully and slid it into her notebook. The action steadied the agitation in her chest; to record was to anchor.

Damien watched her, his voice quieting without softening. "If 'C.M.' marks the plate and the Marwick name marks the town, then whatever happened near that tree wasn't only grief. Families that shape towns sponsor their stories. They don't sign them unless they mean to control the ending."

"Or ask for one," Marley said.

He looked at her then, meeting the suggestion he heard in her voice. "Don't leap."

"I'm not leaping," she said. "I am stepping." She tapped the line with one finger, just above the graphite. "It's not only that she waited. It's where. The sycamore. The east bank. The Grove."

Tessa cleared her throat, as if to cut a thread before it tangled. "Before you two turn this plate into a séance, tell me what you want done with it. I can inventory it, tag it, drop it at the Society. But if it leaves this room, it may never come back."

"Let it stay for now," Damien said quickly. "But may we borrow the rubbing?"

Tessa nodded. "Take the newsprint. Take the plate in your heads, not your hands."

Marley wrapped the plate again in its wax paper, returning it to the tray as if laying a warm body back into bed. She could not shake the sensation that the metal still held a faint warmth—someone else's hand, or hers, or some temperature common to memory and lead.

When they stepped into the front room again, the Vandercook gave its slow purr at Tessa's touch, and the rollers picked up ink with their patient appetite. Marley glanced at the racks where drying sheets hung like skin. She thought of how words reversed themselves first to be made legible later—how truth often required a mirrored labor to read correctly.

Outside, the afternoon had leaned toward a dim, indifferent light. The fog kept its station by the river. Marley pressed the rubbing to her chest under her coat like a talisman that could mind its own voice.

On the sidewalk, Damien buttoned his collar and, after a beat, said, "Celia Marwick left no gravestone." He did not look at her when he added, "But the records list a donation to the chapel that winter—a bell rope."

"The bell that hasn't rung since," Marley said. The thought landed with the weight of something that knew—an echo that had found its cavity. "She waited beneath the sycamore tree... and when the bell forgot to ring—"

Damien gave a short, unhappy sound. "Don't finish the sentence."

Marley didn't. She held the rubbing tighter and looked past him toward the faint silhouette of the east bank sycamore, its pale bark a ghost in daylight, its roots stained with the season's damp. The poem fragment hummed in her hands; the initials on the plate's edge felt like two fingertips pressed through time, asking for the rest of the line.

She would write it down when she reached the shop— every letter, every hesitation. She would note the burr in the copper where the graver had lifted, the faint scratch where a hand had steadied. She would add **C.M.** to the ledger of names that had begun to gather like lanterns at the bridge.

And that night, she would stand near the sycamore with her notebook under her coat and listen for the river to choose its voice.

· · ·

THE FOG LINGERED as Marley and Damien carried the rubbing back through town, the folded sheet of newsprint cradled between them like a fragile relic. Neither spoke until they had reached the bookshop. Inside, with the door locked against the late afternoon chill, Marley spread the rubbing across Clara's old desk, smoothing the paper with care.

The words stood stark in graphite, the reversed etching now legible:

She waited beneath the sycamore tree...

Below, the initials sat like a whisper carved into the margin: **C.M.**

Marley traced them with her fingertip. "Celia Marwick," she said softly, as though testing the sound.

Damien had taken off his coat, but his hands still lingered in his pockets. His face was taut, shadowed with memory. "Or Callum. Her brother. The family had both. But it was Celia who disappeared."

He leaned closer, adjusting his glasses. "The records say nothing outright—only gaps. A line of attendance crossed out in the school ledger. A note about illness in the church register. Then silence. And then—" He exhaled, the words reluctant. "The donation to the chapel. A bell rope, gifted by the Marwicks in the winter of '87. As if sound could atone for silence."

Marley scribbled quickly in her notebook: *Celia Marwick – vanished 1887. Sycamore tree. C.M. initials etched into plate. Bell rope donation.* She underlined Celia's name three times, pressing until the pencil tip nearly broke.

Damien's voice lowered, as though speaking to the floorboards themselves. "There was rumor she was last seen on the bridge. Some said she'd gone to meet someone. Others said she waited too long in the fog, and the river took her. But no official record—only what the town traded in whispers."

Marley's chest tightened. "And now the plate. The words. The initials. It's not just rumor. Someone began to print her story."

Damien gave a sharp shake of his head. "Or to dress gossip in ink. You know as well as I do that type is hungry for drama. One unfinished line doesn't prove truth."

"But it proves intention," Marley countered. "Someone thought her story mattered enough to set it into metal. And someone else stopped them before they finished."

She glanced at the rubbing again, at the ellipsis that trailed into absence. The incompleteness felt louder than any finished poem.

"She waited beneath the sycamore tree..." Marley whispered, completing nothing, because no ending felt safe.

Damien paced the length of the shop, the boards creaking under his step. "The sycamore is older than the bridge. Older than the chapel. It's been a meeting place as long as there's been a town here. If Celia was there—" He broke off, shaking his head again. "It doesn't matter. We can't assume."

Marley rose from the desk, notebook in hand. "Then we verify. We go to the tree. We see what waits."

His expression hardened. "And if the tree is only a tree? If the poem is nothing more than an apprentice's flourish?"

She met his gaze. "Then I'll have written it down. And nothing will be lost."

For a long moment he said nothing, his breath rough in the quiet. Then he dropped into the chair opposite her, elbows braced on his knees, head bowed. "You sound exactly like her," he murmured.

"Like who?"

His eyes lifted, pained. "Jackie. She spoke of waiting. Of things buried in the town's silence. She swore the bridge would finish her sentences if she only kept writing. And I told her—" His voice cracked. He closed his mouth, pressing his lips together hard.

Marley reached across the desk and laid her hand over his. "I'm not Jackie. But maybe she wasn't wrong either."

He didn't answer.

The fire in the stove snapped, sending sparks up the chimney. Outside, the fog pressed against the windows as though listening. Marley felt the rubbing hum beneath her palm, the graphite line still carrying the plate's intention.

She waited beneath the sycamore tree...

The unfinished sentence felt less like absence now and more like invitation.

Marley opened her notebook to a new page and wrote, slowly, deliberately: *If Celia waits, the river remembers. If the river remembers, the bridge repeats. If the bridge repeats, then I must record.*

She underlined the last words, anchoring them.

Damien watched her, his face unreadable. "You'll go to the tree," he said at last, resignation woven into his tone.

"Yes," Marley answered. "And I'll bring the notebook. And the bell rope, if I can find it."

He closed his eyes briefly, weary. "Then God help us both."

BY DUSK, Marley could no longer bear the weight of the unfinished line without seeking the place it named. The rubbing of the plate lay folded in her satchel, the graphite smudging faint shadows onto the paper like a bruise that refused to fade. She kept touching it as she and Damien walked the path eastward, the fog thickening again with the evening tide.

The sycamore revealed itself slowly, pale bark ghostly against the dimming light, its roots twisted into the bank as though clutching the earth to keep it from slipping into the river. Its crown had long since shed its leaves for the season, and the limbs rose like skeletal arms, wide and reaching. Beneath it, the ground was soft with damp and leaf rot, the air heavy with the scent of wet soil.

Marley stopped at its base and pulled the rubbing free. She unfolded it carefully, pressing it against the trunk as though returning words to their source.

"She waited beneath the sycamore tree..." she whispered.

Damien stood a few paces behind her, his coat collar up against the chill. His face was shadowed, but his eyes kept shifting between the tree and the river. "You see a poem," he said. "I see a caution written in metaphor. Waiting leads to nothing but silence."

Marley traced the graphite initials. "C.M. If it was Celia, then this tree wasn't just a metaphor. It was where she stood. And someone began to set it in type because they wanted her story to last."

"Or because they wanted to warn others not to follow her," Damien countered. But his voice lacked its usual certainty.

Marley knelt, brushing away damp leaves at the base of the trunk. The earth smelled raw, newly turned though no spade had touched it. Her fingertips caught against something hard. She pulled gently and revealed a small shard of metal, green with oxidation. A fragment of a buckle, perhaps, or clasp. She held it up, mud streaking her palm.

Damien stiffened. "Where did you—"

"Here," Marley said, pointing to the root hollow where it had lodged. "Buried shallow. The river would have carried it away if not for the tree."

He stepped forward reluctantly, taking the fragment from her hand. His thumb rubbed across its surface until the faintest suggestion of an engraving showed—worn, but not erased. A looped letter, maybe an *M*.

"Marwick," he said quietly. The name tasted bitter on his tongue. "It could be coincidence."

"But it could be her," Marley pressed. "Celia. Standing here, waiting. Just like the plate says."

Damien closed his fist around the fragment, his shoulders bowing under weight. "The Marwicks never spoke of her disappearance. Not in public. But there were rumors. That she loved someone her family forbade. That she left to meet him and never returned. That the river took her, or that she walked into it herself. I tried to bury those fragments because rumor destroys the living. But they keep surfacing."

Marley rose, brushing soil from her knees. "Fragments are echoes. And echoes demand to be heard."

The river lapped against the bank, slow and heavy. The fog seemed to shift closer, wrapping the tree in a pale cloak. Marley pressed the rubbing flat against the trunk once more, the words aligning with bark.

"She waited beneath the sycamore tree..." The unfinished line trembled in the air. Marley lifted her notebook and wrote quickly: *Sycamore tree east bank. Fragment of metal clasp (possibly Marwick). Fog heavy. Poem incomplete. Waiting feels present.*

Damien watched her, his face drawn. "Do you understand what you're doing? Every word you write, every fragment you gather—you're weaving her back into the town's fabric. You think you're uncovering truth, but you might be resurrecting a grief this place chose to bury."

Marley met his gaze, unwavering. "And what if it wasn't the town's choice? What if it was forced silence? What if the Marwicks made sure her story was never told? Doesn't she deserve to be remembered?"

His fist tightened around the clasp until his knuckles whitened. For a long moment he said nothing, only stared at the tree as though seeing two centuries layered into one. Then, slowly, he opened his hand and set the fragment into Marley's palm.

"Record it," he said hoarsely. "But remember—truth has teeth. Once you feed it, it won't stop biting."

Marley closed her fingers around the metal. The fragment was cold, but it pulsed in her hand as though warmed by memory. She slipped it into her satchel beside the rubbing, her notebook already waiting to hold the next line that surfaced.

The fog pressed closer. In the quiet, Marley thought she heard the faintest thread of a voice—high, young, trembling like breath caught in winter air.

Waiting...

She froze, eyes wide. Damien's head snapped toward the river, but the sound had already dissolved into mist.

"You heard it too," Marley whispered.

He didn't answer. His silence was its own confession.

Marley opened her notebook and wrote a single word, dark and insistent: *Waiting.*

Then she closed it with a steady hand, her resolve stronger than before. The initials on the plate were no longer faint etchings at the edge of metal. They were names, stories, lives pressed into silence, now stirring again.

And she knew—the sycamore, the bridge, the Grove— were no longer passive landmarks. They were listening.

6

BRIDGE DREAM #1

The bridge rose in moonlight, ribbed beams glinting like bones polished by the river. Fog clung along its rafters, pale ribbons trailing through the arches, and in the stillness Marley saw her: a woman standing at the midpoint, shrouded in skirts that brushed the planks like restless water.

The gown was from another century—fitted bodice, sleeves tapered, fabric heavy enough to belong to winters past. The pale light caught the sheen of satin worn to exhaustion. Her hair was dark, pulled low in a knot at the nape, strands loose from damp. She did not look spectral. She looked alive. Alive and waiting.

Marley's breath caught in the dream, though her body did not move. The woman's posture was taut, spine straight, chin lifted toward the dark at the far end of the bridge. Her lips parted and shaped a name—so soft Marley at first mistook it for river-song. Then the sound formed clearly.

"Callum."

The name echoed in the mist, syllables trembling along the beams as though the bridge itself breathed it back.

"Callum," she said again, louder, her voice threaded with desperation. "Callum, come back."

Marley's chest tightened. She wanted to move forward, to answer, but her feet would not lift. She could only watch as the woman turned, searching the emptiness with wide eyes that gleamed with something raw—fear, grief, longing all tangled into one.

The gown clung darker at the hem where fog curled upward, as though the mist itself had hands pulling her down. Still she called, again and again:

"Callum!"

The bridge planks began to moan under the strain of her voice, groaning like timbers drowning. Marley felt the vibration under her own soles though she had not taken a step.

Then the woman looked directly at her.

For a suspended moment, Marley felt herself pierced by that gaze—two centuries collapsing into a single instant. The woman's lips moved again, slower now, her tone no longer pleading but resigned, almost warning.

"You must write what I cannot."

The dream fractured.

Marley jerked awake in darkness, breath ragged. Her hand throbbed. She sat upright in bed, fumbling for the lantern at her side. When its flame caught, she froze.

Her right hand was smeared in black ink. The lines streaked across her palm and fingers were not random smudges but loops and curves, cursive strokes pressed hastily as if written in sleep. She lifted her palm to the light and saw letters, broken but undeniable:

C... M...

The same hand that had etched the plate.

Her notebook lay open on the nightstand. She grabbed

it with trembling fingers and turned the pages. On the blank sheet where she had left off, words now sprawled in elegant script not her own:

Callum.

The ink was fresh enough to smear when her fingertip brushed the curve of the "C."

Her throat tightened. She pressed her palm flat against the page as if to still it, as if the ink might keep writing if left alone.

The lantern flame flickered. The fog pressed harder against the window. Marley whispered aloud, her voice unsteady: "I heard her. I saw her."

Her hand trembled as she dipped her pencil and wrote beneath the ink: *Dream of woman in 19th-century dress, calling for Callum. Ink on my hand when I woke. Name written in cursive style. Matches plate initials: C.M.*

She shut the book firmly, as if containing what the night had forced into her. But the ink on her hand refused to fade, staining her skin like a vow she had never spoken.

She sat motionless for a long time, listening to the faint creak of the beams outside as if the bridge itself shifted in its sleep.

THE MORNING LIGHT crept reluctantly into the bookshop flat, pale through the fog, the kind of gray that made the lantern flame linger longer than it should. Marley sat at the kitchen table, her hand still stained with the night's ink. No amount of scrubbing with soap had erased it fully; the loops of the cursive *C.M.* remained like faint bruises, embedded in her skin.

She heard Damien before she saw him—the solid tread of his boots on the stair, the faint scrape as he pushed the door open. He entered with a stack of papers tucked under his arm, intending to bury himself in records as usual. But the moment he saw her, his stride faltered.

"You didn't sleep," he said, voice taut.

Marley held up her hand. The ink shone faintly even in the dim light. "No. Not well."

Damien's brow furrowed. "What's that?"

She extended her palm across the table. The script curved there, loops dark against her skin. "I woke with it. Ink. Not smudged from my notebook, not anything I remember writing. Look closer."

He set his papers down slowly and took her wrist in his hand, turning it toward the window's light. His thumb brushed the letters as though testing their reality. "C... M..." His voice dropped to a whisper. "Celia Marwick."

Marley pulled her notebook close and opened to the page. The word *Callum* sprawled in ink she had not written, elegant and certain. Beneath it, her own pencil notes crowded, frantic: *Dream of woman on the bridge, 19th-century dress, calling for Callum.*

Damien stiffened. "You're saying you dreamed this—and when you woke—"

"It was already written," Marley finished.

He released her wrist and stepped back, pacing. His hand ran through his hair, a gesture of agitation Marley had come to recognize. "This isn't possible," he muttered. "Ink doesn't appear out of nothing. Your hand doesn't—"

"Then explain it," Marley pressed, her voice sharper than intended. "Explain how I saw her, standing on the bridge. How she looked at me, spoke to me, told me to write. Explain how her words found their way onto my hand while I slept."

Damien stopped pacing, his back to her. His shoulders sagged. "I can't."

Silence pressed heavy between them. Outside, a gull cried through the fog, its voice raw.

Marley closed the notebook gently, her resolve steadying. "This isn't coincidence. Not anymore. The plate, the sycamore, the children's drawings, the voices—now this. She's reaching across."

Damien turned, his face pale, the scholar's certainty stripped away. "You believe it's Celia."

"I know it's her," Marley said. "And she wasn't alone. She called for Callum. She was desperate. It wasn't a ghost story—it was a woman waiting. Her brother's name on her lips."

Damien sank into the chair opposite, folding his hands together as though bracing himself. "If you're right—if this isn't dream but visitation—then the Marwicks buried more than rumor. They buried an entire life, an entire truth. And whatever held them silent is no longer holding."

Marley leaned forward, her voice low. "You've studied this town's records more than anyone. You've seen the gaps. You've felt them. Tell me you haven't always suspected something lived inside those silences."

His eyes flicked to hers, and in them she saw the crack she had been waiting for. He exhaled, long, defeated. "I've suspected," he admitted. "But suspicion isn't belief. And belief—belief makes you vulnerable."

Marley reached across the table and set her ink-stained hand atop his clasped ones. "So maybe it's time we stop protecting ourselves. Maybe vulnerability is the only way we'll hear what's been waiting all this time."

He looked down at their joined hands, the letters C.M. shadowed across her skin. His lips parted as though to argue, but no words came. Instead he sat still, his silence heavier than denial, closer to concession.

The fog pressed harder against the window. The bridge was out there, ribs hidden in mist, holding its breath. And for the first time, Damien didn't call it imagination.

THE FOG DID NOT LIFT that day. It lingered into the afternoon like a guest unwilling to leave, clinging to the rafters of the bridge and the eaves of the bookshop, thick enough that lanterns glowed even with daylight behind them. Inside, Marley and Damien sat across from one another at Clara's old desk, the notebook open between them. The word *Callum* stared up in black ink neither of them could deny.

Damien had been silent for nearly an hour, riffling through ledgers, census lists, and fragments of newspapers spread across the desk, though Marley knew he wasn't really reading. His eyes skimmed columns but never anchored. He was avoiding the thing both of them knew could no longer be avoided.

Finally, Marley broke the silence. "You heard me describe her—the dress, the way she called out, the way she looked at me. You've seen the ink, Damien. You've seen my hand. Tell me you don't believe something deeper is happening."

Damien's hand stilled on a ledger. He didn't look up. "Belief is a dangerous word."

"It's the only word left."

He closed the ledger and sat back, pressing his palms together under his chin. For a long moment he stared at the ceiling as if weighing the structure itself for answers. Then his gaze dropped, raw and unguarded. "I can't explain it away anymore."

Marley's breath caught. She leaned forward, gripping the edge of the desk. "Say it."

He exhaled, shoulders bowing under the weight. "I believe something is happening. Beyond reason. Beyond history. And it terrifies me."

The admission hung in the room like a bell tolling, vibrating in the quiet. Marley felt the air shift with it, felt the fog at the windows press harder, as though listening.

"You don't have to be afraid," she said softly.

"Don't I?" His laugh was bitter, humorless. "I watched Jackie vanish into this same fog because she believed. She let it consume her, Marley. She stopped seeing where the dream ended and the world began. And now here you are— with ink on your hands, with names appearing in your sleep. I should be pulling you away from it. But instead—" His voice faltered. He shook his head. "Instead I'm starting to believe with you."

Marley reached across and set her hand—ink and all— over his. "Then maybe Jackie wasn't broken. Maybe she was closer to the truth than anyone."

His jaw clenched, but he didn't pull away. His thumb brushed unconsciously against the stain on her skin. "Tell me again," he said, his voice quiet. "Everything. From the start of the dream."

So she did. She told him how the bridge had gleamed in moonlight, how the fog had curled like breath, how the woman's gown clung damp at the hem. How her voice had cut through the mist, not with menace but with long-ing. *Callum. Callum, come back.*

Damien's eyes closed as he listened, his brow furrowed. "Callum Marwick," he said when she finished. "The younger brother. He left town in 1889. No record of him returning."

Marley's heart quickened. "Then she wasn't calling into nothing. She was calling to him. To blood."

"Or to betrayal," Damien murmured.

Marley opened her notebook again and wrote in deliberate strokes: *Dream: Woman on bridge calling for Callum. Likely Celia Marwick. Ink on my hand and notebook matches plate initials. Connection between Celia and Callum confirmed.*

She looked up at him. "This isn't madness. It's testimony. She's giving us pieces. And we have to keep following."

Damien rubbed his temples, his rational armor crumbling in the face of mounting evidence. "You realize what this means? If she's reaching across—if she's using you to finish what she couldn't—then you're not just a witness. You're a participant."

Marley's eyes burned, but her voice was steady. "I already was. From the first whisper in the mist. From the first word written when I didn't lift the pen."

The stove popped, flames shifting, the only sound in the room. Damien sat very still, his eyes fixed on her hand again, as though memorizing the stain that refused to fade.

"Then God help us both," he said finally, "because I believe you. I believe her. And that means the story isn't finished."

Marley closed her notebook, the weight of his words anchoring her resolve. She slipped it into her satchel and rose, moving to the window. The fog clung to the glass, shifting like a body behind a curtain. She laid her palm against it, ink pressing faintly against the pane.

"She waited," Marley whispered, almost to herself. "And she's still waiting."

Behind her, Damien whispered the name like a confession: "Celia."

The sound of it seemed to ripple through the fog, answering back with silence that felt alive.

Marley lowered her hand from the glass, turning back to him. "Then we'll finish what she began. We'll write what she couldn't."

Damien's eyes met hers, shadowed with fear and reluctant faith. "And when the bridge decides to answer?"

Marley tightened her grip on the satchel. "Then we'll listen."

The fog pressed harder, the bridge invisible beyond it, but Marley no longer doubted its presence. It was there. Waiting. And now, so were they.

7

AN INTERRUPTED KISS

The night pressed thick around the bridge, fog curling like gauze through the beams. Marley and Damien walked in silence beneath its arch, lantern light casting their shadows long against the damp planks. The air smelled of wet timber and iron, the river moving slow and heavy below.

They had spent the day sorting through more fragments of the Marwick story—ledgers, chapel records, the rubbing of the printing plate now worn soft at the edges from Marley's constant touch. Each clue had pulled them closer, but it was not history that lingered between them now. It was the weight of words left unspoken.

At the midpoint, Marley stopped, resting her hand on the railing where mist beaded cold against her skin. "Do you ever wonder," she said quietly, "why it's us? Why the echoes reach for me—and why you keep standing here beside me, even when every part of you wants to deny it?"

Damien leaned against the opposite beam, folding his arms. His breath clouded in the lantern light. "I've asked myself that every day since you arrived. And I don't have an answer I like."

Marley's gaze met his. "But you're still here."

He looked away, jaw tight. "Because I can't not be. Because if you're right—if the past really is reaching for us—then someone has to stand between you and whatever waits in the fog. And God help me, I'd rather it be me."

Her chest tightened at the rawness of his admission. "That sounds less like duty and more like—"

"Don't," he cut in, sharper than he intended. His hands gripped the railing until his knuckles whitened. "Don't name it. Not here."

Marley stepped closer, the lantern swinging faintly between them. The air pulsed with tension, thick as the fog around them. "Maybe here is exactly where it should be named. Maybe that's what she wanted me to write—what they wanted to be remembered. Not just grief. Not just silence. But love that was never spoken aloud."

Damien's eyes snapped to hers, and for a moment the scholar's mask, the rational façade, all of it broke. What remained was a man carrying both fear and desire, torn between them like two rivers colliding.

"Marley," he said, her name a confession on his lips.

Her breath hitched. She stepped closer still, until the lantern's glow cast both their faces in its circle. He reached out, hesitated, then brushed a damp strand of hair from her cheek. His fingers lingered, light but certain, and her skin burned where he touched.

The world seemed to hold still. The river, the fog, even the bridge itself—all waiting.

Slowly, inevitably, they leaned toward each other.

And then—

A voice.

Thin, urgent, carried in the mist right between them. "Wait for me."

Marley froze, the words piercing her chest like a hand pressed flat against her sternum. Damien's breath caught, his body going rigid. For a moment, neither moved.

The lantern flame sputtered, smoke curling upward.

Marley pulled back, her pulse hammering. "Did you hear it?"

Damien's face was pale in the shifting light. "Yes."

Her throat tightened. She gripped the railing, steadying herself. "It wasn't her usual call. Not Annabelle. Not Celia. This was different."

Damien shook his head, still stunned. "It doesn't matter who it was. The timing—Marley—" His voice cracked. He turned away, staring hard into the fog as though it might offer explanation. "This is what I feared. That the bridge doesn't just echo the past. It interrupts the present."

Marley reached for his arm, her voice low but unyielding. "Or maybe it's reminding us that some promises must wait. That timing matters."

His gaze flicked back to hers, shadowed, conflicted. "And what about us?"

She held his eyes, her hand steady on his arm. "Maybe we're part of the waiting too."

The silence that followed was heavier than the mist. The kiss had been stolen by the echo, but the truth of the moment lingered, sharper for its interruption.

Damien exhaled, slow, as though surrendering to gravity. "Then we wait."

Marley nodded, though her chest ached. Her notebook felt suddenly heavier at her side, as if already demanding the words. *Wait for me.*

The lantern flickered again, and the bridge settled under their feet like a body exhaling.

MARLEY'S HANDS shook as she opened her notebook, the lantern glow catching the graphite smudges on her fingers. She pressed the tip of the pencil to the page, forcing her hand steady, writing as quickly as she could before memory dulled.

January 16. Beneath the bridge. Fog heavy. Damien and I spoke openly—emotions surfacing. As we leaned closer, a voice cut through the mist: "Wait for me." Both of us heard it. Not imagination. Clear. Present. Not Annabelle. Not Celia. A third voice. Unknown.

She underlined the words twice, then set the pencil down, exhaling shakily. The act of writing steadied her pulse, but her body still carried the tension of what had almost been—what had been interrupted.

Damien leaned against the railing, watching her. His face was taut, shadowed by the lantern, but his eyes were no longer hard with denial. They were troubled, conflicted.

"You write even this," he murmured, his tone caught between wonder and fear.

"It happened," Marley said, closing the notebook gently. "If I don't record it, the bridge will erase it. And I can't allow that."

He was silent a moment, then pushed away from the railing. "Marley... if that voice hadn't come, we would have —" He stopped himself, his jaw tightening.

She looked at him, her own breath caught. "We would have kissed."

His throat worked. "And I don't know if that terrifies me more than the voice itself."

Marley stepped closer, her satchel pressing against her hip, her notebook heavy within it. "Why?"

"Because I want it," Damien admitted, his voice breaking raw across the words. He gripped the beam as if holding himself upright. "I want you. But the timing—this place—it's all wrong. The echoes don't just haunt—they interfere. They demand."

Marley's chest ached at the vulnerability in his voice. "So you're afraid the bridge won't let us choose for ourselves."

"I'm afraid of losing myself in it," he said. "Like Jackie. Like Celia. Like everyone who's ever answered when the fog called their name."

She touched his arm, light, deliberate. "You're not them. And I'm not them either. We're here together. That's different."

His eyes flicked to hers, unsteady. "Is it? Or is that exactly how it begins—every time? A vow, a promise, a kiss stolen by the river, and then silence?"

Marley tightened her grip on his sleeve. "Then let us be the ones who finish the story instead of being erased by it."

Damien closed his eyes briefly, the tension in his shoulders pulling taut before easing again. "You make it sound so simple."

"It isn't simple," she said. "But it's necessary."

The fog curled low at their feet, threads of mist winding around their boots as though listening. Marley felt it tugging at her, but she refused to flinch. Instead she opened her notebook again and wrote slowly, deliberately:

The bridge interrupts. The bridge waits. But we choose what we record, what we remember. And memory is stronger than silence.

She shut the book, slid it back into her satchel, and turned to Damien. "We can't undo what we feel. Pretending will only make us weaker. We just have to hold it steady, even when the echoes try to tear it apart."

He studied her for a long moment, then exhaled, surrendering to honesty. "Marley, I've been standing between belief and fear since the first night you told me about the voices. Tonight I crossed a line. I can't go back."

She nodded, her throat tight. "Neither can I."

For a moment, the fog hushed, the river holding its breath. The kiss had been interrupted, but something deeper had been spoken between them, something that could not be unspoken now.

Damien's hand brushed hers, tentative, then withdrew. "Then we wait. Not because the bridge tells us to. But because we choose it."

Marley felt both the ache of restraint and the strength of it. She pressed her palm flat against the satchel where her notebook rested. "Then we wait."

Above them, the bridge beams groaned softly, as if approving or mocking—Marley could not tell. But she wrote the sound into memory all the same.

THEY LINGERED beneath the bridge longer than either intended, lantern light throwing restless shadows against the beams. The fog pressed thick on every side, curling low around the posts as if reluctant to let them leave.

Marley rested her palm against the railing, her notebook safe in her satchel but pulsing in her thoughts. She wanted to capture every moment—every breath between them, every silence broken by voices not their own. But she held back, giving Damien space to speak first.

He finally did, his voice low, hoarse. "I don't know how to carry this."

She turned to him, waiting.

He leaned against the timber, shoulders bowed, hands gripping the edge of the rail. "With you, I feel—" He stopped, started again. "I feel something I thought I buried with Jackie. Something that terrifies me because it's alive. And yet, I can't separate it from the fear that this bridge, these echoes, are leading us into the same ruin."

Marley stepped closer, the lantern between them casting her face in warm gold. "Then maybe that's what makes it real. Wanting and fearing at the same time. It means we haven't surrendered to the fog. We're still choosing."

Damien's eyes flicked to hers, shadowed with longing he could no longer deny. His hand lifted halfway before falling back. "I wanted to kiss you. God, Marley, I wanted it. But when that voice came—when it told us to wait—it was like the river itself reached up and dragged me back."

Her chest ached, but her voice was steady. "And you think that means we shouldn't."

"I think it means timing matters," he said. His jaw tightened. "Not just for us, but for the story unfolding around us. If we move too soon, if we blur our choices with theirs— Celia's, Callum's, Annabelle's—we risk becoming part of their echo instead of breaking free of it."

Marley studied him, her breath visible in the cold. "And if waiting only repeats their silence? If the bridge isn't warning us but testing us?"

His lips curved in a bitter half-smile. "Trust you to turn even a ghost's interruption into invitation."

"Because it is," she said, her voice fierce with quiet conviction. "Everything they left unfinished is pressing against us now. We can't ignore it. But we also can't let it dictate everything. We're still alive, Damien. That matters."

He closed his eyes briefly, as though steadying himself

against the weight of both her words and his own feelings. When he opened them, his gaze softened. "You're right. It matters. More than I want to admit."

The silence between them was heavy, but not empty. It pulsed with what had almost happened, with what might still.

Marley reached for her satchel, pulled out the notebook, and opened to a fresh page. Her pencil hovered for a moment, then she began to write, speaking the words aloud as she pressed them into the page:

January 16, midnight. Beneath the bridge. The echo interrupted us—voice: "Wait for me." The kiss did not happen. Damien admits he feels torn: desire against fear, wanting against timing. We chose restraint. But the silence between us carried more weight than words. Recorded here so it cannot vanish.

She set the pencil down. "Even silence has to be remembered."

Damien's eyes lingered on the page. "You write us into permanence, Marley. Even when I'd rather forget."

"Because forgetting is what the bridge wants," she said, shutting the notebook firmly. "It feeds on erasure. We'll give it memory instead."

He exhaled, the tension in his body easing, though his face still carried the mark of conflict. "Then remember this too: I want you. And I fear you. Both truths live side by side. And until the echoes stop interfering, I can't tell which one will win."

Her throat tightened, but she met his gaze steadily. "Then let's keep both alive. Desire and restraint. Love and fear. Until the bridge is finished with us—or we're finished with it."

The river shifted below, its current groaning against the

pilings. The lantern flame sputtered, then steadied, casting their faces into the same fragile glow.

Damien straightened, pulling his coat tighter. "We should go before the fog decides otherwise."

Marley slipped her notebook back into the satchel, her fingers brushing the ink-stained page where *Callum* still gleamed. She followed him out from under the arch, but with every step she felt the weight of what she carried: the almost-kiss, the whispered warning, the confession carved into the night.

When they reached the road, she glanced back once. The bridge loomed through the mist, ribs dark against the pale fog. For an instant, she thought she saw a figure standing where she had dreamed Celia waited, but when she blinked the image dissolved.

She tightened her grip on the satchel. Every silence, every interruption, every broken moment—they would not be lost. She would record them all.

Even the kiss that had not been.

8

———

THE SÉANCE REENACTMENT

Brookwood loved its festivals. Lanterns strung along Main Street, children in costumes of another century, tables heavy with sugared apples and spiced cider—the whole town leaned into its own history whenever it had the chance. What had begun decades ago as a way to draw tourists each autumn had long since become ritual: a harvest celebration stitched together with dramatized "hauntings" that gave the townsfolk permission to laugh at the fog instead of fear it.

This year, the Historical Society had added something new to the program: a reenactment of one of the séance circles held in the late 1800s, when spiritualism gripped even the most practical of families. Flyers had promised *a theatrical glimpse into Brookwood's mysterious past.*

Marley stood near the town hall steps, notebook in hand, as the crowd gathered. The air was damp, lantern light blurring in the mist, and though the laughter was easy, a hush underpinned the evening—an awareness that Brookwood's past was never just theatre.

At the center of the square, six chairs had been arranged

in a ring around a low wooden table. Volunteers, mostly from the Society, filed in and took their seats. Evelyn bustled past Marley, muttering about "putting on nonsense for the tourists" even as she passed out cups of cider.

Damien joined Marley at the edge of the crowd, his coat buttoned high. "This is history turned carnival," he said dryly.

"Or history remembered," Marley countered, eyes on the stage. "Even mock rituals have roots."

A hush fell as the "medium" for the evening—a young actress dressed in dark lace, veil draped dramatically across her hair—took her place at the table. She spread her hands, rings glinting in the lantern light, and called for silence.

"Tonight," she intoned, "we honor the voices that have walked these streets before us. We call them not in fear, but in remembrance. We ask them to sit with us once more."

The crowd shifted, a ripple of amusement and unease. Marley scribbled quickly in her notebook: *Festival séance, October. Public ritual. Tone theatrical but weight palpable.*

The actress gestured to the circle. "Join hands. Close your eyes. Listen for the echoes."

The volunteers obeyed, their hands linked, their faces solemn in the lantern glow. The crowd hushed further. Fog curled low at their feet.

For several minutes, nothing happened. Then the actress began the scripted chant printed in the program, words borrowed from 19th-century transcripts:

"If you are here, give us a sign. If you are waiting, let us hear your name."

The volunteers echoed her softly.

Marley wrote, underlining the last phrase: *Waiting. Again waiting.*

And then—

One of the participants—a woman Marley recognized as Mrs. Keene, who ran the post office—jerked upright in her chair. Her head tipped back, her mouth opening wide. At first Marley thought it part of the act, until the sound spilled from her throat.

Not English.

Not the chant.

The voice rose high and harsh, words tumbling in a rhythm unfamiliar, syllables knotted in a dialect Marley did not recognize but felt in her chest like the vibration of a struck chord.

The crowd gasped. Someone laughed nervously, but the sound quickly died. The other volunteers shifted uneasily, hands tightening in the circle. The actress faltered, losing her script.

Marley's notebook nearly slipped from her fingers. She had heard fragments of those syllables before—not in town, but in Clara's old journal. She flipped frantically through the worn pages she kept tucked in the back of her satchel until she found it: half a stanza written in Clara's looping hand, untranslated, left like a riddle.

Her eyes darted between the page and Mrs. Keene's trembling lips. The words matched.

Damien's hand closed around Marley's wrist. His voice was low, urgent. "What is it?"

She shoved the journal toward him, her finger pressing to the page. "Clara wrote this years ago. She didn't know the meaning. And now she's speaking it."

Mrs. Keene's voice climbed, raw and insistent, the strange syllables carrying a cadence that shook the crowd into silence. Her body rocked forward, eyes glassy, as if the voice that spoke through her pulled strings from elsewhere.

The actress dropped her hands, her veil sliding from her hair. "This wasn't in the script," she whispered.

Panic rippled through the crowd. Some stepped back, murmuring prayers. A child began to cry. Evelyn dropped her tray of cups, cider spilling across the cobblestones.

Damien stepped forward, his posture firm. "Mrs. Keene!" he barked, his voice sharp with authority. "Enough. Stop this."

But the voice did not stop. It surged louder, words hammering the fog, rising into a wail that cracked on its final note.

And then—silence.

Mrs. Keene collapsed forward against the table, her breath ragged, sweat shining at her temples.

The crowd erupted into chaos—questions, accusations, fear masked as laughter. The actress fled the stage, her veil dragging. Evelyn hurried to Mrs. Keene's side.

Marley clutched her notebook, her pulse thundering. The words she had scribbled in Clara's journal all those months ago now burned with new life.

She wrote in a rush, her hand trembling: *Séance reenactment. Participant spoke in unknown dialect. Matches Clara's journal. Not theatre. Not coincidence. Real.*

Beside her, Damien's face had gone pale. He rubbed his temples, eyes fixed on the table as if it still hummed with the sound.

Marley whispered, almost to herself: "The echoes don't just haunt—they speak."

Damien's jaw tightened. "And sometimes through people who don't ask to be vessels."

The fog pressed closer, swallowing the edges of the lantern light. The festival's laughter had dissolved into uneasy murmurs. And Marley knew, with every line in her notebook, that Brookwood's past was no longer content to be remembered in theatre.

It demanded voice.

THE CROWD SCATTERED in small clusters after Mrs. Keene collapsed, but the square didn't empty entirely. Fear rooted people to the cobblestones as firmly as curiosity. Lanterns sputtered in the fog, their light making the unsettled faces around Marley appear half-stranger, half-shadow.

Marley crouched near the edge of the stage, notebook balanced on her knee, Clara's journal open in her other hand. The lines scrawled in Clara's looping script looked almost alive now, as if they might shift on the page to match the cadence that had just shaken the night.

She whispered them aloud, sounding the syllables: "*Anu... marach... silen...*" The unfamiliar tongue rasped in her throat.

The sound of it drew Damien sharply toward her. He knelt beside her, his hand clamping her wrist. "Don't repeat it," he hissed.

Marley's eyes flashed. "It's here in Clara's journal. She must have heard it years ago. These phrases—they're the same Mrs. Keene spoke tonight. This isn't coincidence."

Damien glanced back at the murmuring crowd. "All the more reason not to speak them into the air. If the echoes are looking for a vessel, don't give them your tongue."

Marley bit back the retort that rose, forcing herself to breathe, then lowered her voice. "But we need to understand. Clara wrote these words, but she left them untranslated. Why? Did she not know? Or did she fear what they meant?"

She scanned the page again. Clara had underlined the

same three words in a darker hand, as though she'd tried to force her future self to remember them. Beneath, she'd scribbled in the margin: *heard at festival—child's rhyme? connected to east bank? investigate.*

Marley tapped the margin with her pencil. "This isn't the first time. Clara heard them here. At a festival. Just like tonight."

Damien's mouth pressed thin. "History repeating. That's how Brookwood works. What we don't resolve returns."

The crowd surged again as Mrs. Keene stirred. Evelyn knelt by her side, fanning her with a folded program. Mrs. Keene's lips moved faintly, words lost under the clamor, but her eyes had the glazed, exhausted look of someone waking from too deep a sleep.

"Let me through," Damien said, standing and pushing past the cluster of neighbors. His voice carried command, and the crowd parted enough for him to kneel beside Mrs. Keene. "It's over," he said gently. "You're safe. Just breathe."

But his eyes betrayed him. Marley saw the tremor in his hand as he helped Evelyn steady the woman. She saw the tightness around his mouth, the fear carefully folded beneath calm.

Marley flipped quickly through Clara's journal, searching for other fragments. Halfway through, she found a longer note:

Voices at the bridge—same tongue. Cannot trace origin. Sounds older than Brookwood itself. Words like plea, like waiting.

Her pencil darted across her own notebook: *Unknown dialect. Phrases repeated across time. Clara heard it, now Mrs. Keene. Possibly pre-settlement? Or ritualistic? Plea of waiting.*

The square slowly began to empty, townsfolk whispering nervously as they drifted into the fog. Only Evelyn remained, fussing with a damp cloth on Mrs. Keene's forehead, muttering about "foolish pageantry gone too far."

Marley approached the table, her notebook clutched tight. Damien looked up at her, the mask of composure slipping now that the crowd was gone. His face was pale, his eyes shadowed.

"You saw her," Marley whispered. "You heard her. The words matched. Damien, this isn't just theatre anymore."

He nodded once, but the gesture was weary, almost broken. "I know. And that's what frightens me. Because if Clara heard the same thing, if it's woven through every generation, then the bridge isn't only echoing individual stories—it's echoing the town itself. And maybe it won't stop until someone answers."

Marley opened her notebook again, the pencil steady this time. *The echoes use vessels. Language is older than the town. Rooted in waiting. Demands reply.*

She looked up, her eyes catching his. "Then we have to be the ones to answer. To record. To translate."

Damien's jaw tightened. "Or to refuse. To keep the line drawn between their voices and our own."

His voice carried conviction, but Marley saw the crack in him—saw the way his hand still trembled as he brushed dust from the table, saw the way his eyes darted back to Mrs. Keene as though afraid she might start again.

He was shaken. Badly.

And for the first time since the bridge had begun speaking, Damien didn't look like the one standing between her and the echoes. He looked like he was standing beside her, already claimed.

Marley shut the journal slowly, her decision clear. She would not let silence claim the night. She would write every word, every syllable. Even if the echoes spoke in tongues no one yet understood.

Even if Damien's fear mirrored her own.

THE SQUARE THINNED as the last of the townsfolk drifted into the fog. Laughter had long since dissolved into uneasy silence, replaced by the hollow shuffle of boots on cobblestone. The lanterns flickered, their light refracted in damp air, and the smell of spilt cider lingered sharp and sour.

Evelyn led Mrs. Keene away, muttering curses at the Society for turning history into "parlor games gone mad." Marley watched them vanish into the fog, the older woman's figure unsteady, her shawl slipping from her shoulders.

Now only Marley and Damien remained at the table. The wood still held the warmth of bodies, the imprint of hands recently joined. The circle looked broken—like a ritual undone halfway through.

Marley sat heavily on one of the chairs and opened her notebook. The words she had scrawled earlier in the chaos stared back at her: *Unknown dialect. Phrases match Clara's journal. Plea of waiting.* She turned to Clara's journal itself, pressing her pencil hard against the margin as she began to transcribe exactly what she'd heard from Mrs. Keene's lips.

"*Anu... marach... silen...*" she whispered as she wrote. "*Vireth... calum... senn.*"

The syllables spilled jagged onto the page, her hand shaking but determined. The sound of them still echoed in her head, almost vibrating in her chest. She paused only when her pencil snapped.

Damien flinched at the sound. He stood nearby, arms crossed, but his stance betrayed him—rigid, defensive, eyes darting as though the fog itself might lunge.

"Don't," he said sharply.

Marley looked up, startled. "Don't what?"

"Don't write it," he said, voice low but fierce. "Don't give it permanence."

She straightened, meeting his gaze. "If I don't write it, it's lost. And then the bridge decides the meaning. At least this way, we have it. We can study it. Translate it."

His jaw clenched. "Or you're feeding it. Every time you press those words into paper, you're carving a path for them. For it. Whatever this is."

Marley closed the notebook with deliberate care, though she kept her hand pressed against its cover. "Maybe that's the point. Maybe Clara understood that the only way to resist silence is to make a record, even of what terrifies us."

Damien's expression cracked. He dragged a hand down his face, exhaling hard. "Marley, I tried to tell myself tonight was nothing more than hysteria. A woman overcome by pageantry, the mind catching fire in a crowd. But it wasn't. I heard the words too. And I've studied enough dead languages to know when something doesn't belong to books."

Marley's chest tightened. "So you admit it."

His eyes met hers—pale, shaken. "I admit it. This wasn't theatre. This was intrusion."

The fog pressed closer, curling around the base of the stage like water rising. A lantern hissed as its wick died, throwing half the square into shadow. Marley's pulse quickened. She lifted Clara's journal again, thumbing the familiar pages until her eye caught another fragment, written in her aunt's distinct hand:

The voice does not belong to us. Yet it seeks us. If I write it, perhaps I will belong less to it. Perhaps words can trap what sound cannot.

Marley whispered the line aloud. Damien's head snapped toward her, his face tightening with something between fear and recognition.

"She thought writing could trap it," Marley said. "That's why she wrote. Not because she wanted to remember—but because she wanted to contain."

Damien's silence stretched long. When he finally spoke, his voice was ragged. "And did it work?"

Marley closed the journal gently, her thumb lingering on the edge. "That's what we're here to find out."

She pulled her own notebook closer, scrawling in quick strokes: *Clara believed writing = containment. Words stronger than sound. Tonight confirmed echoes enter vessels unwilling. Danger. But transcription necessary.*

Damien moved closer, leaning against the railing of the stage, his voice quieter now, stripped of denial. "I thought I could stand beside you without being drawn in. I thought I could protect you by refusing belief. But tonight proved I was wrong."

Marley turned to him. His face was pale in the fog-dimmed light, his eyes shadowed with the strain of carrying both fear and longing.

"You're not just standing beside me anymore," she said softly. "You're inside it too."

He gave a strained laugh, bitter. "God help us both, then."

For a long moment, the two of them stood in silence, lanterns guttering, the fog pressing closer as though to listen. The festival had dissolved, the laughter gone, the town left rattled in its bones.

Marley pressed her palm flat against the notebook, steady in her resolve. "Then we'll write every word. Even the ones that don't belong to us. Especially those. Because silence is worse than fear."

Damien closed his eyes briefly, then opened them, resigned. "Then write. But promise me one thing."

"What?"

"Promise me you'll write even the silences. Even the moments when the words stop. Because sometimes that tells the truth more than language does."

Marley nodded slowly, the weight of his words settling deep. She flipped to a fresh page and wrote one final line for the night: *Silence after the outburst. The crowd broken. Damien shaken. The town unsettled. But the echoes louder than ever.*

She shut the notebook firmly, her hand steady despite the tremor in her chest.

The bridge was waiting. And now, so was she.

9

THE CANDLE RITUAL

The metaphysical shop was tucked into a narrow corner of Market Row, its windowpanes fogged with steam and the faint scent of beeswax drifting into the street. Inside, shelves leaned with jars and tapers, bundles of wicks hanging from hooks like skeins of thread. It was warm, fragrant, filled with resinous smoke and the faint tang of lavender.

Marley had always liked the place, but tonight she entered with a different urgency. In her satchel lay one of Clara's copied recipes—*a blend for bridging memory,* her aunt had called it, scrawled in looping cursive across yellowed paper. The mixture called for wax softened with oil of cedar, pressed thyme, and a drop of honey warmed over an open flame. Clara's margin note had read: *For calling what lingers to the surface.*

The shop owner and specialty candle maker, Hazel Merrow, looked up from his workbench. Her hands were stained with wax. "Marley," she greeted warmly. "You've brought me another experiment, haven't you?"

Marley smiled faintly, pulling the folded recipe from her

satchel. "Something I found in my aunt's notes. I don't know if she ever made it herself."

Hazel adjusted her glasses and studied the page. "Bridging memory, eh? Sounds like Clara. She always had a sense for blending scent with symbolism. Let's see what we can do."

She set to work without hesitation, gathering wax blocks and jars from the shelves. Marley watched as she melted the base wax, added cedar oil that smoked sharp, thyme leaves crushed between his palms, and finally the honey, golden and viscous, stirred into the molten pool. The scent lifted into the room, sharp and sweet at once, earthy but carrying something luminous at the edge.

Hazel poured the mixture into a small glass jar, the wick standing straight in the center. "You'll want to burn this during reflection, not work," she said, sliding the jar across the counter to her. "Candles like these soften boundaries. Good for prayer, dangerous for distraction."

Marley tucked the candle carefully into her satchel. "Thank you. I'll record what happens."

That night, back at the bookshop, she set the candle on Clara's desk. The room was dim, only the fire in the stove and the lantern on the wall to keep the dark at bay. She lit the wick, and at once the scent filled the air—cedar deep, thyme sharp, honey softening the edges.

She opened her notebook, pencil poised. At first, she expected nothing more than calm. But as the flame burned lower, something shifted. Her hand began to move on its own, the pencil scratching across the page faster than her mind could follow.

Words spilled:

Dearest, I have waited by the water, by the sycamore, by the bridge. I have left threads in the mist for you to follow, but still you do not come. They say I am gone, but I remain where I was last whole—where the planks met the river, where the bell should have rung. I belong to you still. I belong to the promise we spoke when the fog wrapped us close.

Marley tried to stop, but her fingers refused. The words flowed with a voice not hers, a hand not her own. The script curved in elegant strokes, unlike her quick notations—fluid, practiced, intimate.

At last her hand slowed. One final line curved across the bottom of the page:

Wait for me. Yours always, Annabelle.

The pencil fell from her fingers. Marley's chest heaved as she stared at the page. The candle flame bent low, guttering in a sudden draft, then righted itself. The scent seemed stronger now, almost suffocating.

She pressed her trembling fingers to the signature. *Annabelle.* The name that had haunted the riverbank, the whispers in the fog. Now written, signed, claimed.

A knock startled her. Damien entered, shoulders hunched against the cold, his scarf damp with fog. He froze when he saw her face. "What happened?"

Marley turned the notebook toward him. "I wrote," she whispered. "But it wasn't me."

His eyes dropped to the page. He read silently, then again more slowly, his lips moving over the words. When he reached the signature, he went still.

"Annabelle," he murmured. His voice shook.

Marley gripped the notebook. "You believe me now?"

He sank into the chair opposite her, his hands trembling as he touched the margin of the page. "I've seen this hand before. This exact hand."

Marley's breath caught. "Where?"

He looked at her, eyes pale, face grave. "In the archives.

On a letter from 1886. The ink was faded, but the script—the flourishes on the capital letters, the looping y's—it's the same. And it was signed *Annabelle Warren*."

The candle flickered sharply, spitting wax.

Marley's heart thundered. She bent over the page, her pencil steady now as she wrote in the margin: *Handwriting matches archival document. Annabelle Warren. Connection confirmed.*

When she looked up, Damien's face was pale with something between awe and dread. "Marley," he said hoarsely, "you didn't just bridge memory. You brought her back to the page."

The flame bent again, smoke curling like script into the air.

THE CANDLE BURNED low between them, wax pooling in the jar like liquid gold, the air heavy with cedar and thyme. Marley's pulse had not steadied. Her hand still tingled from the furious script that had poured through it. She sat back, breathing hard, notebook open before them like evidence neither could deny.

Damien leaned forward, elbows braced on the desk, eyes fixed on the letter. He traced the ink strokes without touching, his expression caught between reverence and dread.

"I remember the first time I saw it," he said at last, his voice quieter than the hiss of the flame. "A letter in the archive, folded between pages of the chapel register. Faded, brittle, half its words lost to water damage. But the hand— this hand—survived. I told myself it was nothing. A fragment of family correspondence. But it bore her name. Annabelle Warren."

Marley's breath caught. "So she's real. She wasn't just a

voice in the fog or a whisper from the bridge. She lived. She wrote."

Damien's gaze flicked to hers, pained. "And now you've written for her."

The words sank into her chest. Marley stared at her ink-stained fingers, curling them into fists. "I don't know if it was possession or... something softer. But it didn't feel like my hand. It felt guided. Urgent."

"Guided," Damien repeated, his tone hard. "Marley, that's what terrifies me. If a voice can use your hand, where does it stop? How much of you remains when the writing begins?"

She looked down at the page again, at the words *Wait for me. Yours always, Annabelle.* Her throat tightened. "But if she trusted me to carry this—shouldn't I?"

Damien pushed back from the desk, standing abruptly. He paced the length of the shop, his boots thudding softly against the boards. "Trust is one thing. Control is another. Jackie believed she was entrusted too. She filled journals until she barely remembered which words were hers. And when she vanished into the fog, no one knew what part of her remained."

The comparison landed sharp. Marley shut her notebook with trembling hands. "I am not Jackie."

He stopped pacing, turning toward her. His face was pale, his eyes dark with fear. "Then promise me you won't let the candle guide you again."

Marley looked at the jar. Its flame leaned toward her as though listening. The scent pressed deeper into the room, earthy and sweet, like memory itself turned tangible. She could almost feel it pulling at her, inviting her to write more.

"I can't promise that," she whispered.

Damien's jaw clenched. "Why not?"

"Because this might be the only way to hear her clearly," Marley said. She rose, standing across from him, her voice low but steady. "The bridge gives fragments. The river gives whispers. The children draw shadows. But the candle—it gave her words. Whole sentences. A letter. A love that survived."

Damien's expression cracked. He turned away, bracing himself against the shelving of old ledgers. His voice came rough. "And what if that love isn't meant for you? What if it drags you into a story that ends the same way hers did—unfinished, cut short, drowned in fog?"

Marley stepped closer, pressing her hand flat against the notebook's cover. "Then at least someone will have written it down. At least she won't be forgotten."

The silence stretched between them, taut as the rafters above. The flame flickered, throwing shadows that bent and wavered like figures caught in half-motion.

At last Damien spoke again, his voice breaking. "Annabelle Warren was engaged to a ferryman's son. That's what the archives suggest. His name was Callum. When she disappeared, he left town within a year. Some said he never forgave himself. Some said he never stopped waiting either."

Marley's breath caught. The dream, the voice on the bridge, the unfinished poem—all of it tangled together. "Callum," she whispered.

Damien nodded, weary. "The name you wrote in your sleep. The name Clara heard in the dialect she couldn't translate. Callum Marwick. Every thread leads back to him."

Marley opened her notebook again despite herself, the pencil trembling in her grip. She scrawled across the fresh page: *Letter signed Annabelle. Handwriting matches archives. Mentions waiting by water, bridge, bell. Addressed to Callum. Confirmed link: Annabelle Warren and Callum Marwick.*

Her hand steadied as the words filled the page. Writing was the only anchor that held against the storm pressing from every side.

Damien rubbed at his eyes, exhaustion carving lines into his face. "You think recording protects you. I fear it's the very thing binding you closer."

Marley closed the notebook softly, but not with regret. "Maybe it's both. Maybe protection and binding are the same thing. Maybe that's the only way memory survives."

The candle sputtered, smoke curling like script in the air. Both of them turned toward it instinctively, waiting, as though expecting the flame itself to speak.

It didn't. But the scent deepened, filling the space until Marley felt it settle in her lungs like a vow.

Damien sat heavily in the chair across from her, his hands covering his face. "God help me, I don't know how to fight this anymore."

Marley reached for her pencil, her resolve quiet but absolute. "Then don't fight it. Read it with me. Record it with me. Because whether we choose it or not, the bridge is writing us into its story."

The flame bent low, then straightened again.

Neither of them spoke.

But Marley's hand hovered over the page, ready, because silence itself demanded transcription.

THE CANDLE BURNED LOWER, its wax spilling into rivulets that clung to the glass like tears. The air was thick now, heavy with cedar and thyme, the sweetness of honey turning cloying, oppressive. Marley stared at the flame too long and felt her vision blur, the edges of the room softening as though painted in water.

She reached for her notebook before she could think better of it. The pencil slid into her hand, her grip tightening. A shiver ran through her fingers—not cold but compulsion.

"Marley," Damien warned, his voice taut. "Don't."

But her hand was already moving. The pencil scratched furiously across the page, faster than thought, faster than she could shape.

I remember the bell that never rang. I remember the promise by the sycamore. I remember his hands, calloused from the oars, the way he swore he would come. I wait still. I write still. Do not let them erase me.

Marley gasped, but the words continued. She felt her wrist ache, her knuckles stiffen, but the pressure would not release until the final line tore itself from the page:

I am Annabelle. I am waiting.

The pencil clattered from her hand, her chest heaving. Sweat dampened her brow. The candle flame bent sideways as if pushed by an unseen breath, then straightened again, steady, defiant.

Damien was already at her side, his hand gripping the edge of the desk, his eyes scanning the page. He read aloud, his voice shaking: "The bell that never rang... the sycamore... the oars..." He stopped, his breath uneven.

"Damien?" Marley's voice was small.

He pressed his palm against the page as if to still it. "I've seen this script before. Not just the letter in the archive— another piece. A chapel ledger, tucked with an unsigned entry. Same hand. Same flourishes. Only one word was clear." His throat worked. "Callum."

Marley's heart hammered. "Then it's her. It has to be her."

Damien dragged a hand down his face, his composure

cracking. "Marley, this is dangerous. You're not just transcribing now. You're channeling. The intimacy of it—" His voice faltered, breaking on the word. "You're giving her your hand, your breath. That's not recording. That's surrender."

She shut the notebook with trembling fingers, but not before pressing her palm flat against the ink, sealing the words into her skin. "Maybe surrender is the only way to understand."

His eyes flashed, fear raw. "Do you hear yourself? You're letting her live through you. Where does Marley end and Annabelle begin?"

Marley met his gaze, steady despite the tremor in her chest. "Maybe that line isn't supposed to be sharp. Maybe the bridge exists to blur it."

Damien stepped back, running a hand through his hair. His face was pale, his eyes stormed with conflict. "You're talking like Jackie now."

"I'm not Jackie," Marley said firmly. "I'm me. But if Annabelle's words are reaching through, if she trusts me to write them—then I will. And you can't stop me."

The silence that followed was thick, broken only by the hiss of the candle. Damien closed his eyes briefly, then opened them, his fear tempered now with something more vulnerable.

"You don't understand," he whispered. "The more you write for her, the more I feel her presence here with us. And the more I feel—" He broke off, unable to finish.

"Feel what?" Marley pressed.

He looked at her then, raw, stripped of his defenses. "The more I feel like she's binding us together. You and me. Through her. Through the waiting. It's not just her love letter, Marley. It's becoming ours too."

Her chest tightened, the truth of it vibrating in her

bones. She reached across the desk, her ink-stained hand brushing his. "Then maybe that's why she chose me. So we wouldn't have to wait alone."

Damien's hand lingered against hers, trembling. His face was shadowed with both longing and dread. "And if she doesn't let go?"

Marley's gaze fell to the flame, burning low but steady. "Then we write until she does."

The candle sputtered once, then steadied. The room seemed to breathe with it, as though satisfied for now. Marley lifted her pencil again, her resolve unshaken. She wrote one final line beneath Annabelle's words:

I am Marley. I am listening.

And when she shut the notebook, Damien's silence was no longer denial. It was belief, heavy and unavoidable.

10

DAMIEN'S DOUBTS

They climbed the narrow stairs to Marley's apartment above the shop without speaking, Marley first with the key caught between chilled fingers, Damien behind her with his coat buttoned but his throat bare to the damp. Fog moved at the windows like a living thing, pressing its pale face against the glass panes each time the wind turned up Main Street. Inside, the stove's small fire ticked and settled; the room smelled faintly of beeswax and cedar—the last breath of last night's candle.

Marley set the kettle on and only then looked back. Damien was still at the top of the stairs, not fully in the room, his posture paused on some private threshold. He held a slim wooden box against his chest, both hands around it as if its contents could shift and spill.

"Come in," she said softly.

He stepped forward, laid the box on Clara's desk, and stood beside it rather than take a chair. The lamplight caught in the lenses of his spectacles; his eyes behind them were older than the morning.

"I should have told you sooner," he said. "Before the

candle. Before the letter." He tapped the box once, a hollow sound. "I've been pretending the past can't ask anything of us we don't offer. That if I refuse it, it will refuse me back. And I was wrong."

Marley crossed to him and waited. He undid the small brass clasp with his thumbs and lifted the lid. Inside lay a sheaf of narrow notebooks, cloth spines faded to a washed gray—three volumes no bigger than a hand, the paper clearly handled, the corners softened by years of being carried and opened and set down again. He didn't touch them at first. He just looked.

"Jackie's," he said.

The name built a pressure in the room without raising the volume. Marley steadied her breath.

"I told you she wrote," he went on. "That she believed the bridge spoke. But I haven't shown you how far it went." His hand hovered and then settled on the topmost volume. "These were under a false bottom in my desk. They've been there for years. I couldn't look and I couldn't let them go."

He opened to a page in the middle—a leaf mottled by time and the ghost of a coffee ring. The handwriting unfurled with a grace unlike Marley's quick field-script: a slower, taught hand, careful with loops and tails. He slid the journal toward her.

The entry was dated in Jackie's neat numerals. Below, a single line:

Not alone.

The third word was underscored hard enough to leave a ridge on the back of the page.

"I told myself it was grief," Damien said. "We had lost a child the winter before. I thought the mind made company out of emptiness. I told myself 'not alone' was a prayer, not a reply."

He turned a few pages. A sketch of the bridge appeared: ribs suggested by light strokes, the span a single sweep. In the margin, another word carried weight beyond ink: *wait.*

"And then," he said, flipping farther, the pages whispering like leaves, "this."

He stopped at a page where the neat hand became a rush. Black ink scudded and thickened—words half-formed, letters trailing as if dragged faster than the wrist could carry. Marley leaned closer. In the run of script a name began and cut off: *Cal*— A dark dot where the pen had been pressed hard. A second attempt beneath it, incomplete again: *Call*—

"She would wake like this," Damien said, voice low. "Ink on her fingers. The pen uncapped. She'd be certain she'd only dreamed. And the book would say otherwise."

Marley glanced at her own hand, at the faint ink that persisted in her palm though she had scrubbed after the candle. The echo landed like a small blow.

"She heard the bell that winter," he went on. "When no one else did. She counted boards from the east bank and wrote the numbers over and over like rosary. She drew the sycamore with its skin half-peeled and labeled it *keeper*. And once"—his mouth tightened—"she wrote a line I refused to read twice." He turned one more page.

She waited beneath the sycamore tree...

It lay there in Jackie's hand, the same sentence Marley had rubbed from copper and carried under her coat, the same breath that had pressed itself into the candle-white letter signed *Annabelle.*

Marley felt the kettle begin to tremble on the hob. She moved to lift it, needing the ordinary anchor, and filled two cups with water over teabags Evelyn had made from chamomile and some bitter herb. When she set Damien's cup beside the journals, his hands remained on the desk instead.

"I thought I could keep you safe by refusing belief," he said, not looking at the tea. "If I did not give the echo a listener, it would pass us by. But I stood with Jackie while she slipped further into the fog of it, and I did what men do when they are helpless—I lectured. I named illusions. I made rules. I kept the door latch polished like a talisman. And she died anyway, Marley. Not because of the bridge—because bodies fail—but she died sure that something unfinished had chosen her and she hadn't finished it."

He finally looked at her then, and what he had been carrying since the first night she heard the mist say her name pushed to the surface. It was not only fear of the uncanny. It was grief's superstition, a private bargain with the universe that if he refused, he might never be asked to fail again.

"I am afraid," he said. "Not of ghosts. I'm afraid of repeating history. I don't know how to stand beside you without seeing the last year of her life. I don't know how to want you without thinking of timing and vows and bridges and the way a voice in fog can make a man set his own desires aside until there is nothing left but timing and fear."

He closed the book as if to hush it. The sound was small. The words in the room were not.

Marley took his hand—not the back of it the way condolences do, but palm to palm. His fingers were cold and strong and slightly inked from turning old pages. The kettle hissed in the quiet like a far-off tide.

"You are not repeating history," she said. "You are telling me the truth in time to change it."

He exhaled, a breath that seemed to fall through him. "I don't know if I can. The moment you told me the candle wrote through you, I smelled Jackie's ink. I saw her wake with a page she didn't recall. I heard that word again—*wait*—and something in me closed like a fist."

She held his hand harder. "Then open it now."

"Marley..." His voice broke on her name.

"I'm not her," she said, as gently as she could. "And you're not the man you were when you were trying to keep her from drowning by telling her water isn't wet. We'll make rules we keep. We'll name the dangers and meet them together. But do not mistake my listening for a willingness to be used up. I intend to live."

The word rang in the small room. It surprised her, the fierceness of it. It surprised him too—his eyes widened and then softened, as if some proof he had been waiting for had presented itself.

"What rules?" he asked, not ironic, only tired.

She let his hand go and reached for the notebook she kept for the practical. She wrote as she spoke, the act itself a way to keep both of them in the same weather.

"Rule one," she said. "I don't write with the candle unless you're here. If the line begins to move without me, you pull me back. Blow it out. Close the book. Call my name until I answer."

He nodded, once, the muscles in his jaw easing.

"Rule two. We count days as well as nights. We do not let the bridge own our hours." She wrote it: *Daylight, errands, bread, laughter.* Simple words that felt like stakes in the ground.

"Rule three," she went on, keeping her voice steady, "you do not protect me by withholding. If you see a page in Jackie's journal that matches what I've written, we face it together the same day."

"I will," he said. It wasn't a promise wrung from him. It was relief shaped into speech.

"And rule four," she said, and this one she didn't write at once; she looked at him while she said it, "we remember that the story is not our master. We are living people. We owe the dead a hearing. Not our lives."

He gave a sound that might have been a laugh if it hadn't broken in the middle. "You think clarity keeps wolves away?"

"No," she said. "But it keeps us from inviting them to supper."

The fire ticked, a log shifting. The fog's face pressed and slid at the window again. Damien lifted the top journal once more, thumbed without opening, and set it down as if practicing the act of letting the past rest in its small, respectful box.

"There's more," he said, and the heaviness of it announced itself before the specifics could. "Before she died, Jackie dreamed of a woman in a winter dress. Not just the word *wait*, not just the bridge. She dreamed of a name she could not say awake. She wrote it as letters forming and unforming. I found pages with *C*. I found *Cal—*. I found *CM* scratched into the pasteboard inside the back cover the way a child carves initials into a desk. I told myself it was grief folding the town's stories into her own. And when you came home from the river with the children's drawing and the smell of water in your coat and the word *Annabelle* on your page, I—" He stopped, then forced the admission. "I began counting the ways I could lose you."

Marley poured the tea, put his cup in his hands, and let the heat do some small portion of the work. "You might," she said, because mercy and lying are poor cousins. "Life may yet do what it does. But it will not be because we let a voice in the fog drive us to the edge of ourselves. It will not be because you kept standing at the door with a polished latch and a rule about belief."

He stared into the steam. "What if wanting you is a risk in itself?"

"Then it is one you name. And one you take. Not because the bridge allows it or interrupts it. Because you do."

He lifted his head at that. The lines at the corners of his mouth were still grave, but his gaze had come back to her from wherever he had been counting.

A quieter thought arrived and found a seat in her, and she knew it would not leave even after he went home to the small house with the lamp he left burning in the front window. She did not offer it to him; she let it be hers a moment first. It shaped itself as a question, not an accusation: Was Damien ready to love someone who listened to the very thing that had terrified his marriage into a vigil? Or did he want, without knowing he wanted it, a version of her he could keep outside the weather?

She lifted her own cup and set her mouth to the heat while the question took the place in her that questions take when they promise to shape a season. She would not write it yet. She would not rush to make it obedient to ink. But it was there, and the honesty of it steadied her.

He closed the journals and returned all three to the little box. He did not latch it at once. His fingers rested on the wood as if testing whether he could have this kind of nearness to the past without leaving it open between them. The moment stretched. The fog shuddered at the pane and recoiled.

"Come with me, then," he said finally. "This afternoon.

To the archives. I'll show you the letter. Annabelle's hand. You should see it with your own eyes."

"I will," she said, and somewhere inside the ache she felt something like gratitude for the shape of the invitation: not a command, not a test, not a lock on a door. A door held open.

He latched the box and tucked it under his arm. When he stepped toward the stairs, he paused, looked back, and—awkwardly, boyishly—touched two fingers to the rim of the candle glass on Clara's desk, now cold. "Tonight," he said, "we leave it unlit."

"Tonight," she agreed.

He went down, careful of the last step that always complained. Marley crossed to the window and laid her palm to the glass where the fog had left its breath. The cold had the clean edge of a blade. She imagined the bridge just beyond the white, bones quiet for now. She turned and wrote the rules on a fresh page in the front of her working notebook, copied out in a slow steady hand that belonged only to her. Beneath them she wrote a last line, small, her pencil lifted lightly between each word:

Comfort offered. Truth heard. Questions kept.

She closed the book and set it beside the cold candle. The fog moved and the day opened its hand.

THE ARCHIVES always smelled faintly of dust and iron—the scent of paper too long pressed together, of ledgers and receipts that no hand had touched in years. The following afternoon, Marley found herself at a wide oak table with Damien across from her, the narrow box of Jackie's journals at his side. His movements were careful, deliberate, as if touching history too quickly might tear it.

He opened a folder wrapped in cloth, laid it gently on the table, and turned the first brittle sheet. "Here," he said. His voice was low, reverent. "The letter I told you about."

Marley leaned closer. The ink was faint but the strokes were familiar—elegant loops, the long tails curling beneath the line. At the bottom, faint but unmistakable, the name: *Annabelle Warren.*

Marley's throat tightened. "It's the same hand. Damien, it's her. What I wrote last night... it's her voice, her shape."

He looked up at her, eyes pale, shadowed. "Do you understand now why I couldn't keep this from you any longer? Why I'm afraid?"

Marley touched the page carefully, her finger hovering just above the script. "Because Jackie wrote like this too. Because she slipped into the same current."

Damien closed the folder, the sound sharp in the quiet. "She didn't just slip. She drowned in it, Marley. And I was beside her the whole time, telling myself she was only tired, only dreaming, only grieving. I thought if I didn't believe, it couldn't claim her. But it did."

Marley studied him, the weight in his shoulders, the bitterness woven with guilt. "You're afraid I'll follow her."

He exhaled, a sound closer to defeat than confession. "Yes. Every time you lift that pencil, every time you let the words guide your hand instead of the other way around, I see her again. Her head bent over the desk, her ink-stained fingers trembling. And I think—God, I think—I'm watching it happen all over."

The words cracked something in her chest. She wanted to reach for him, to undo the wound of memory that drove him to this edge, but she also knew the truth he carried was not hers to erase. It was his to carry, his to speak.

"What were her dreams like?" Marley asked quietly.

He hesitated, his gaze dropping to the grain of the oak. "They began like yours. Whispers in the mist. Faces at the edge of sleep. But then they turned relentless. She dreamed the bridge groaned under a weight it couldn't hold. She dreamed of voices calling names she didn't know. She dreamed of a woman in a gown too heavy for the planks, standing where no one else could stand."

Marley's breath caught. "The same woman I saw."

"Yes." His jaw tightened. "And when Jackie told me, I told her it was grief's theater. That her mind was putting shape to sorrow. I thought I was protecting her from herself. But in truth, I was protecting myself from admitting that something larger was happening."

He pressed his palms flat on the table, the journals between them like a burden. "The night before she died, she dreamed again. She woke with ink all over her hand. A word written three times, hard enough to tear the page." He paused, his voice trembling. "*Wait.*"

The silence after was heavy, filled only by the creak of the shelves and the distant shifting of the building against the wind.

Marley's throat was dry, but she forced herself to speak. "And now you see me waking the same way. Ink on my skin. The same words. The same woman."

His eyes lifted to hers, raw with anguish. "How can I not be afraid, Marley? How can I not feel I've been led back here only to fail again?"

Marley reached across the table, laying her hand over his. "Because I'm not Jackie. And you're not the man you were then. You're not hiding this from me anymore. That changes everything."

He shook his head, though his fingers curled around hers instinctively. "But what if knowing isn't enough? What if the bridge doesn't care what we believe or what we confess? What if it only repeats?"

Her heart ached at the hopelessness in his voice. She tightened her grip. "Then we choose differently. We write it together. We name what it is. Jackie didn't have someone who would record it with her, who would take the ink into their own hands. She was alone. I'm not."

His breath hitched, but he didn't argue. He looked at her hand on his, his thumb brushing the edge of her knuckles as though grounding himself in the present.

Marley's thoughts turned inward, sharp as a blade. Was he here with her because he wanted to be, because he believed in her, or because he saw Jackie's shadow and feared losing again? Was his presence protection, partnership, or penance?

She swallowed the question for now. It would grow, she knew—it had already planted itself in the soil of her heart. But in this moment, Damien's face was too raw, his fear too fragile to confront with more doubt.

"Tell me the truth," she said softly. "Do you believe I'm in danger?"

His answer came without hesitation. "Yes."

"And do you believe I'm strong enough to face it?"

The silence stretched. Then, quietly, "I want to. God help me, I want to. But I don't know yet if wanting makes it true."

His honesty cut deeper than denial ever could. Marley squeezed his hand once more, then pulled her notebook close, flipping to a blank page. She wrote deliberately, her pencil steady despite her racing heart:

Damien fears repetition. Jackie's dreams mirrored mine— bridge, woman, waiting, ink. He carries guilt as if he failed her by not believing. He fears losing me in the same way. Truth: he is shaken, but he is speaking. Comfort is naming what was hidden. Danger lies not in writing but in silence.

She shut the notebook gently, her resolve settling around her like a cloak. "Then let's face the danger together. Even if we're afraid. Especially because we're afraid."

Damien's eyes closed briefly, a long breath leaving him as though she had given him permission to breathe again. When he opened them, the rawness remained, but so did something else—something almost like relief.

THE FOG HAD THICKENED by evening, folding itself around the windows of the bookshop flat until the glass looked painted in milk. The fire in the stove had burned low, the embers a soft pulse of red. Marley sat cross-legged on the rug, her notebook balanced against her knees, while Damien paced in the narrow space between the desk and the door.

He'd been pacing for nearly an hour. His steps were restless, his coat still on, scarf loose at his throat. Every so often he stopped at the window, stared into the fog, then turned back as though what he saw there only sharpened what he was trying to resist.

Marley closed her notebook. "You're wearing a track into Clara's boards," she said gently.

He stopped, exhaled, then sank into the chair across from her. His elbows braced against his knees, his head bowed into his hands. The silence stretched, thick as the fog outside.

Finally, he spoke, voice rough. "Do you know why I push so hard against this? Why I try to smother belief under reason until even I can't breathe?"

Marley waited.

"Because when I stop fighting," he said, lifting his head, "I feel everything I've kept locked since Jackie died. And it's too much."

His face in the lamplight was raw, stripped of its usual sternness. The scholar's distance was gone; what remained was a man frayed by grief and longing in equal measure.

"I loved her," he continued. "God, I loved her. But even before she was gone, I felt her slipping from me—night after night, page after page. I would lie beside her and feel like a stranger, as though the real part of her was already elsewhere, already claimed. And I hated it. I hated the bridge for taking her. And I hated myself for not being enough to keep her here."

His voice cracked on the last word. He pressed his fists against his thighs, his whole frame trembling with the effort of keeping his composure.

Marley moved closer, kneeling beside his chair. She laid her hand on his arm, steady. "You don't have to carry that alone."

He looked at her then, eyes stormed with pain. "But what if I am already repeating it with you? What if you slip the same way, and I am left watching again—helpless, useless, full of love with nowhere to put it?"

The truth of it tore at her, but she held his gaze. "Then you name it now, before silence takes it from you. You don't bury it under reason until it rots inside. You speak it. You give it light."

His eyes glistened. "And what if the light only blinds me to the fact that I'm too broken to stand beside you? What if I want more than I have any right to want?"

Her hand lingered on his sleeve. "Tell me what you want."

He closed his eyes, exhaled as if surrendering. "I want

you. I want the way you see the threads others ignore, the way you refuse to let silence swallow anything. I want to stand with you on that bridge and not fear what waits in the mist. I want to believe we can finish the story instead of being consumed by it."

His words rang with both confession and plea. Marley's chest ached with the weight of them.

She brushed her thumb lightly against his arm, steady. "Then want me. But don't confuse me with her. Don't let the echo of Jackie drown the sound of me."

His head bowed, a breath shuddering through him. "I don't know if I can separate them yet. I don't know if I'm ready."

The admission landed heavy. Marley swallowed against the sting in her throat, pressing her resolve into her voice. "Then let me be patient. But don't mistake patience for silence. I'll keep writing, Damien. I'll keep listening. And if you want to be beside me, you will have to learn the difference between protecting and withholding."

He nodded slowly, the fight draining out of him. His hand lifted, hesitated, then rested over hers on his sleeve. "I don't deserve this grace."

"No one does," she whispered. "That's why it's grace."

The fire popped, a log shifting. The fog at the window pressed harder, then seemed to ease, as if the night itself had been listening.

Damien squeezed her hand once before releasing it, leaning back into the chair with a sigh that sounded like surrender. "I can't promise I won't falter. But I can promise I won't hide anymore."

Marley rose, returning to her notebook. She opened to a fresh page and wrote in slow, deliberate strokes:

Damien confessed: fear of repeating Jackie's fate. Admitted desire tangled with grief. Truth: he wants, but questions his readiness. Comfort offered, but questions remain—his ability to stand in the present without being dragged by the past.

She closed the book, the sound soft but final. When she looked back at him, his eyes were closed, his body sagging with exhaustion.

Marley watched him for a long moment, a quiet question forming in the hollow of her chest: *Is he ready for me—or only ready for what I remind him of?*

She did not write it. Not yet. Some truths needed to breathe in silence before they could be inked.

Outside, the fog shifted, the bridge unseen but present, holding its vigil.

11

THE BRIDGE KEEPER'S DIARY

The morning had the color of pewter. Fog lay close to the river, low and deliberate, like a cat that had decided the bridge was worth watching. Marley crossed the gravel pull-off and stepped into the covered span with her notebook tucked beneath her arm, gloves in her pocket, senses pried open by cold. The interior smelled of wet timber and old iron; somewhere a loose plank had found a rhythm and clicked softly with the slow flex of the river's current.

She had come to measure the bench supports. It was a thin pretext—an archivist's errand—scribbled on the first line of her day's list so she could tell herself she was here for work, not compulsion. After the candle and the letter and Damien's confession, rules had been made and agreed to. Daylight. Bread. Laughter. No candles without a witness. But the bridge had its own kind of invitation, and daylight did not blunt it. It only drew the grain of it into sharper relief.

The benches ran along the inside of the trusses, rough and gray, their iron brackets bolted into the posts like old knuckles. Marley crouched by the first support and traced the seam where the bracket met the wood. The bolt head wore a bloom of rust; beneath it, a thin crescent of darkness suggested a gap. She tapped it with her ring. The sound came back hollow.

She glanced along the length of the bench. Four brackets, equidistant. The furthest one had a different sheen, as if someone had wiped it clean once and time had been slow to reclaim the gesture.

Marley moved to it. The iron felt colder than the others, less furred with salt. She slid a fingernail under the head's edge and felt the give of packed dirt flake away. A tiny circle of brad hole peered back at her like a pupil. The bracket had been unscrewed before. Not recently—long enough ago for grit to fill the threads—but not only by the original builder.

"Don't pretend you're not a door," she murmured, more to herself than to the iron.

She searched her pockets, came up with a coin, and worried it into the slot. The screw resisted, then yielded with a dry squeal like a reluctant truth. She turned it half, then full, then the bracket pivoted a fraction from the post. A darker seam opened, just wide enough to make her pulse jump. She glanced back along the length of the bridge— empty, fog pressed at the far portal like a soft white wall— and pulled the bracket farther out until it cleared the post face.

Behind it, a narrow cavity had been cut into the bench's support rail, a small coffin-shaped recess just big enough for a pamphlet or pocket ledger. Something wrapped in oilcloth rested there, the fabric slick with damp, its edges stuck to the wood as if grown in place.

Marley sat down hard on the bench to keep from sway- ing. For a moment she only listened—to the slow beat of water under the planks, to the far-off gulls, to her own breath making small clouds in the weak light. Then she slid her gloved fingers into the seam and coaxed the parcel free. The oilcloth rasped like a snake's skin.

It was heavier than she expected, and swollen. Water had found it many times; the cloth had done what it could, but time is solvent. Marley laid it in her lap and peeled the layers back, careful not to tear what clung. Inside, a leather cover waited—brown once, now the gray-brown of river stones, the spine softened to the softness of bread. The clasp had corroded long ago; where its tongue had been, a thread of stiffened linen held like a stitched wound.

She breathed once, twice, third time, and loosened the tie.

A diary. Not large—a man's pocket book, the sort that fits a vest—but thickened by damp into something with the heft of confession. When she lifted the front board, the smell rose up—mildew, iron ink, a thin sweetness of old paper that stirred something under her ribs like memory of summer.

She slid on nitrile gloves, their pale shine making her hands look borrowed, and opened to the first page that would let her. Water had blurred the early leaves into unreadable clouds; she turned past them until text gathered again, legible enough to catch. The handwriting was not elegant like Annabelle's; it was blockier, a working hand taught in ledger lines, letters formed the way men formed rope—practical, repeating.

April 7, '86. Bittern nest below the east beam again. Replaced two planks near midspan, countersunk the irons. The girl with the parcels came through at dusk—Miss Warren they call her. Light step, no chatter. Nodded and passed. Fog sharp, from the south.

Marley's chest tightened. She read the name twice, as if the second reading might undo the ache of recognition. *Miss Warren.* Not a rumor, not a folk descendant. A person moving across a page in a hand that had no reason to flatter or haunt.

She turned a leaf.

May 2. Night walkers again, boys from the mill daring each other. Drove them off before the boards could tell on them. I do not keep the bridge for ghosts or game. Warren again, this time later. She waited at the midbeam. I told her the river had its own clocks. She said she knows that and went on waiting.

The entries marched: weather, tar, pitch, names of men who carried sacks of flour, a note about a cart's axle cracking, a little joy when the first swallows nested high in the rafters. Between these, a thin thread ran: the girl at dusk, the girl at midnight, the girl with a parcel or a letter or a ribbon in her hand. Always the bridge keeper saw her. Always he wrote her down.

Marley gave the keeper a name in her head because the book did not offer one yet—*keeper* was what he called himself. She tried on a few: Mr. Hale, Mr. Dyer, Mr. Cobb. None held. He was simply *keeper*, and to have tended this span he would have been someone the town trusted to keep weight from killing them.

She turned carefully, lifting each wet-joined pair with the flat of a thin bone folder, letting the grain separate. A droplet formed at the leaf's corner and fell to her glove. She froze. No candles, she thought. No rituals. Daylight. Work.

A page near the middle had a small rip at the bottom edge, triangular, as if someone had worried at it while thinking. On that page, the keeper's hand had tightened.

September 19. Fog blank as wool. Warren at the sycamore, barefoot, carried a note. Said she had no stamp for it that could reach who it must. Asked if the bridge would carry it in her stead. I told her planks bear weight, not letters. She smiled in a way made me look at my boots and I said I would leave a place. This and no more.

Marley pressed her thumb against the glove to keep it from trembling. She could see Annabelle's smile, though the diary did not draw it. She could hear the dryness in the keeper's voice softening against his own rules. He had cut a place in the bench for a letter. He had left a door.

She looked at the bracket she had opened and the little hollow behind it. Had Annabelle's note once lived where the diary had? Had the keeper traded what he was supposed to keep for what he couldn't bear to lose to the weather?

Outside, a gull scolded the river for being stingy with fish. The sound came in like laughter that had not been invited and made itself at home anyway. Marley turned another page.

October 3. The seventh night of fog. The girl again. I will not write her name for fear I am making a pattern of it. She waited and would not come inside. I told her a man is not measured by the crossing he makes but by the ones he keeps. She said he has kept his, only not yet. I do not like to be made a witness. But I am a bridge, and bridges make witnesses of men.

A faint smear under *seventh* had bled into the fibers, as if a damp finger had passed there while the ink was still wet. Marley touched the air above the word the way one touches the shoulder of a sleeping child without waking her.

Seven. The number sparked against the tangle of other fragments she carried—Clara's underlined phrases, Mrs. Keene's outburst in the square, the copper plate's unfinished poem. Seven nights of fog. The seventh night.

"Show yourself to your own page," she whispered, and moved on.

October 5. Hammer and pitch. Boys again. Drove them off. Warren came later, barefoot. Said the boards know her now. She asked about bells. I said bells ring for the living and the dead but not for the waiting. She said that is a poor rule and I should change it. I said the rope is not mine to pull. She said someone must.

Marley read the line three times. *Someone must.* The chapel bell rope laid in winter of '87 by the Marwicks. A donation to atone for silence. The bell that hadn't rung since. It all hoisted itself inside her like a lantern going up on a hook.

She was not ready to see what she saw next, but she saw it anyway. At the top of the following page, in the keeper's hand, the date had failed; he had begun to write *October 7* and then scored the 7 as if what the number carried had burned him. He wrote *7th* again in the line below and underlined it as if to press its meaning into the wood of the board beneath.

The entry itself was short.

The seventh night. The river took the fog up like breath. She stood midspan with her letter and said it would wait if she could not. Left ribbon. Left print of bare heel in tar. I am no bellman. But the board groaned. Twice.

Marley closed her eyes. The page thinned under her glove where water had eaten it. She tried to imagine the keeper, practical, careful, who believed in planks taking weight and letters being for other men to carry, standing where she stood in a morning not unlike this one and choosing to write *I am no bellman.* Hearing the bridge groan. Twice.

Her throat pulled tight. She had meant to wait, to call Damien before she lifted whatever this was out of its cell. But the rules they had made had not accounted for the way some doors, once cracked, insist on being opened all the way.

She turned the next few leaves, trying to keep her breath from fogging the page. The ink here had bled into wooly shadows. Words rose and then sank again. She could make out *seventh* once, twice, *fog* another time, *girl* and *midspan* like timbers in a flood. The last pages were worse—river ghosts of sentences, salt-sugared and almost.

She did what training had taught her to do. She took out her phone to take reference photographs for transcription later, then slid it back without pressing the shutter. It felt wrong to steal the pages with a machine before she had read them with her own attention. She folded a piece of clean paper into a V to cradle the spine and eased more leaves apart with the bone folder, willing the fibers to be generous.

A sudden gust funneled through the bridge and lifted her hair. Cold ran the length of her neck. She flattened a page with her palm above her glove and looked, because if she was going to believe in echoes then she would live by the rules of witnesses and write what she saw.

October 8. Quiet. No Warren. Seven nights make a shape. A man came to the far mouth and did not cross. I saw him even in fog. A hat in his hands twisted tight. I am a bridge. I am not a judge. I keep the weight.

A shape formed in her mind: a man at the north portal, hat turning in, spine bent around a promise he did not know how to keep. Callum Marwick. The name rose unbidden. She did not write it in the diary; she wrote it in her own.

She took out her notebook and copied the lines exactly, her pencil steady despite the thickening of the morning. Twice she stopped just to listen. Once she thought she heard the briefest tremor of a bell from the direction of the chapel—so faint she might have imagined it. The second time she heard only her own blood.

Her hands had gone numb. She tucked the diary back into its oilcloth for the moment, wrapped it with the care she would give a child in a borrowed blanket, and slid it into the hollow behind the bracket again to keep it from the wet while she decided her next move. She left the bracket cocked, a sign to herself that this was not a closing, only a pause.

When she stepped out into the gray light at the bridge mouth, the world brightened by a degree she wouldn't have been able to prove, only swear to later. She took three breaths so deep the cold burned her teeth and then turned toward town at a half-run, diary in her mind if not under her coat, the words *the seventh night* beating time with her steps.

She found Damien at the archives, as she had known she would. He looked up at her before she could speak and read the urgency in her face with the kind of accuracy that had nothing to do with scholarship. She didn't speak in the middle of the reading room; she held up her notebook and set her finger on the line. He didn't ask questions. He closed the ledger he'd been working in, stood, and followed her into the back room where the old map cases made a low geography of wood and brass.

Only then did she tell him. The bracket. The cavity. The oilcloth and the leather. The hand not elegant but faithful, the entries that counted fog, that named the girl, that refused to name the pattern and then wrote it anyway. The seventh night.

He listened, his face tightening and then going very still. When she finished, he didn't say *you should have called me first*. He didn't say *this is dangerous* or *we should leave it where it was.* He said, quietly, "We'll bring it here. We'll treat it. But first, take me to the page that says *seventh.*"

"Several say it," Marley said. "But one of them underlines it as if the number itself is the lever."

"Then we'll pry with it," he answered, and that was enough for now.

They walked back together—daylight, bread, laughter postponed—and the fog made room for them like a curtain drawn by a careful hand. Marley put her palm to the bench again, slid the bracket aside, and lifted the diary out while Damien held the oilcloth ready. He did not touch the leather with his bare skin; he used the corners of the cloth the way a man uses a flag to carry a child from a fire.

On the near plank, preserved in tar so faintly even Marley might have missed it once, the crescent of a heel showed where a bare foot had turned years and years ago. She didn't show Damien. Not yet. It felt like a privilege the page had given her alone.

They set the diary down between them on the bench, the river breathing under their bodies through old wood, and opened to the page that had carved a notch in Marley's breath. The keeper's hand, the scored seven, the underlined *seventh night.* Damien leaned in. His finger hovered above the strokes without touching. His expression changed in the way men's expressions change when their grief learns a new tense.

"Seventh," he said softly, as if the bridge would hear him and correct him if he read it wrong. "Again and again."

The fog stroked the doorway, patient as ever. And in the wet hush of the span, Marley had the sense—not frightening, only sure—that the bridge knew the difference between a passerby and a reader, and had decided, for now, to offer itself to the latter.

. . .

THEY SPREAD the diary on the conservation table in the archives' back room, a square of muslin beneath it and blotter paper at the ready. The little lamp on the corner hummed, its beam set low and raked across the surface so that smudged ink threw shadows big enough to read. Marley slid on fresh nitrile gloves. Damien did the same, his movements careful in the way of a man who understood that reverence is a kind of knowledge.

"Let's begin where the hand strengthens," he said, adjusting the lamp a fraction. "These mid-fall entries hold together."

Marley nodded. "He uses 'Warren' first, then 'the girl.' After that—" She tapped the margin with a gloved finger. "—he begins to write her name."

Damien tilted the lamp again. The page sharpened, valleys and ridges of the old fibers turning into legible terrain. "There." He pointed. "A looped *A* that isn't his usual. A concession to affection."

They read aloud—quietly, as if the walls should be kept from listening too closely.

October 12. Fog held off till after supper. Annabelle by the midbeam, letter in her hand. I said the young man won't come on a night that eats lamps. She said he will know when to look by the light my waiting makes.

Marley's chest pulled tight. She scrawled the line into her own notebook in her quick, tidy hand, then underlined the verb: *waiting makes*. The bridge as instrument. Waiting as a kind of lantern.

Damien turned a page with the bone folder, easing fused corners apart. The next entry wavered in places; a wet thumb had once dragged across it and taken a few letters swimming. He read slowly, offering possibilities when ink thinned.

October 14. River up from last rain. Annabelle again. Bare feet. Said leather weighs when you mean to promise. She walked the length once and stood. I said a bridge is a place for moving. She said this bridge keeps. I said that is not a task for wood. She smiled.

Marley felt that smile like warmth she did not own. "Always waiting," she murmured. "Always for someone who never came."

Damien's mouth tightened, but he did not correct her. He turned to the page marked by a corner crease and a brownish tide line. The date had bled, but the keeper's blocky hand remained.

October 17. Seventh night of fog in a circle of weeks. The girl again, and no footfall from the north mouth. She said a promise does not break; it delays. I told her delay is a trick of men. She said she knows and stays anyway.

He looked up at Marley, the lamp making panes of light in his eyes. "Seventh again," he said. "He's marking more than weather. He's counting a ritual he doesn't want to own."

Marley traced the phrase on her page—*seventh night*—and wrote beside it: *pattern, not accident.*

They worked down the leaf, then forward, each turn revealing another variation on the same scene: a woman with a letter or ribbon; a bridge keeper who believed in pitch and load but not in longing; a night pierced by a figure who refused to let darkness decide the limits of her vow.

October 20. Cart lost a wheel near the southern sill. Helped them lift. Annabelle came near midnight. I told her the plank seams grow slick when breath turns to frost. She said the bridge knows her feet now and will not shoulder her off. She waited. He did not come.

Marley exhaled, the words landing like small stones in her chest. "There it is," she said softly. "Plain. *He did not come.*"

Damien nodded once, slow. "And still she returns."

They kept reading. Some entries were only a line: *Annabelle—night—no crossing.* Others held small details that made the figure particular: a sprig of rosemary tucked into the bench near midspan, a thread pulled loose from a hem and tied around a nail, the scuff of a heel in tar Dane had noted and circled with a neat pencil line later, ashamed of the sentiment (or proud of it). The keeper's reluctance softened gradually; where he first wrote *the girl*, he drifted into using *Annabelle* without apology.

On one leaf the ink had bloomed into feathery splotches. Damien lowered the lamp until the fibers themselves cast shadows, then leaned close, reading the gaps the way a fisherman reads a current. "You can see the long downstroke of the *y*," he said. "And here—'Annabelle —', then a name—lost."

"Callum," Marley whispered before she could stop herself. The room seemed to tilt, as if the river had turned in its sleep beneath the floorboards.

Damien looked at her but did not scold. "We won't force it onto the page," he said gently. "Let the page give what it will."

She nodded, chastened, and wrote in her notes only: *Annabelle names a you.*

They turned another page. The paper here was puckered, the edges ruffled like a scallop shell. The keeper's hand pressed hard, as if he had argued with himself about writing at all.

October 23. Rain before dawn. Seventh night again if you count from first frost. Annabelle walked bare. I told her the board I replaced near the third beam might give. She said a promise does not weigh a board the same. I told her a promise breaks men. She said I've seen men do that without help. She waited. He did not come.

Marley closed her eyes. The pattern of it—returning and returning—felt like the ache that builds when a bell is rung and the sound searches the air for somewhere to go.

"'Seventh night' repeats," Damien said. "Not just once in a season. Recurrent sevens. He's mapping circles." He was quiet a moment, then added, "Where I grew up by the coast, sailors kept a habit of counting the seventh wave as the one that would take you under if you forgot to brace. Superstition becomes measure when the body believes it."

"Which means the keeper had started to believe," Marley said. "Even as he resisted. He names it so often the resistance becomes its own ritual."

They smiled at each other—grim, shared—and bent back to the page.

Midway through the book a blot of iron gall ink had eaten a hole through both leaves. Marley peered through the tear at the next page, the lamp lifting the thin borders of ruin into a delicate crown. Damien folded a square of thin Japanese tissue, slid it beneath the wound to support it, then coaxed the page over with the bone folder's flat.

He read the surviving corners, stringing fragments into sense. "... *seventh ... sycamore ... bell ...*" He swallowed. "There's more, but I won't guess."

Marley wrote what she heard, then lifted her head to watch Damien's face as he tried to call back letters from a century ago with nothing but light and patience. The steadiness of him in this work, hands exact, breath held when needed, made something in her unclench. Even weighted with fear, he could do this—meet the page on its own terms.

The next entry was mercifully clear.

October 25. Cart from the mill at dusk. Boys again. Drove them off. Annabelle at midnight. She stood where the boards remember her. I told her not to give the river a reason to know her name. She said the river already does. She waited. He did not come.

Damien's jaw tightened. He looked away for a moment, as if the plainness of it had pierced something he kept braced. Then he bent again. "There," he said, tapping the lower margin. The keeper had added a line in faint pencil later, a private footnote to his own entry: *She is not foolish.*

Marley copied that too. The kindness of it broke her a little.

They paused to rest their eyes, drinking water from paper cups Evelyn kept by the back-door desk. When they returned, the light had changed by a degree that made the ink on the next page bolder. A small mercy.

October 27. Fog from the south again, heavy. Seventh night since last clear. Annabelle came. Asked if wood remembers the weight of waiting. I told her there are depressions in every board I have ever set. She said then she is not the first. I said the bridge does not confess to me. She waited. He did not come.

Marley felt the repetition become revelation. "He recorded her refusal to stop," she said. "And in doing so, he made her waiting into fact."

Damien nodded. "He is what bridges make of us— unwilling witnesses until we speak."

They reached a cluster of pages where the ink had been scoured into ghosts. Damien switched the lamp off and on again, set it lower, brought a small mirror from a drawer and threw light across the surface at so shallow an angle that letters appeared as glossy ridges. "Raking gloss," he said, slipping into the calm of a teacher. "The iron gall etches, even when the pigment lifts. See?"

Marley leaned in. The word *seventh* lifted in relief from the page like a watermark, repeated three times down the margin as if the keeper had written the number itself when he could not make more words. Between them, shallow grooves formed the lighter strokes of *night*.

He wrote while he was weeping, Marley thought, catching at herself. Or while the page was wet. She wrote instead, tidy: *keeper writes SEVENTH down margin when text fails. Compulsion—noting a cycle.*

Another entry, barely legible, yielded under Damien's patience and a soft, narrow beam:

October 29. Wind cut. Lantern out in a gust. Annabelle waited without light. She said if he cannot see her, he can feel her waiting. That is not science. I do not hold with it. She waited. He did not come.

And then, turning again, they found it—the line that felt like the hinge for all the rest, intact and plain.

November 1. The seventh night of this run. Annabelle said a vow ripens at seven. I told her rot does too. She laughed and left a ribbon at the third beam. I left it there, God forgive me.

Marley pressed her gloved fingers against her own sternum, breath brief and precise. The ribbon. She had held it, damp and cold, after the vision under the bridge in her earlier storm—though the storm was still ahead of them by the calendar of this book. The diary told her what she would find before she found it, and yet the finding had already been lived. The bridge had its own times.

Damien had gone still. "A vow ripens at seven," he repeated. "There's your ritual. Not conjure; custom. And a custom becomes a cage if no one names it."

Marley's pencil moved before she could think: *Seventh*

night = turn of vow. Repeated cycles. Keeper witness, complicit in small mercies (ribbon left). Pattern holds: 'She waited. He did not come.'

They read to the end of the legible run. The last clear entry in that cluster took on the tone of a man who knows the limit of his craft and sets it down so that he can sleep.

November 4. Rain. Swallows gone. Boards will need tar before freeze. Annabelle came. I said this keeping is not made for love. She said then I will keep it myself. I am not a bellman. I am a bridge. Seven nights make weights. Tonight I will not write if she waits. I am tired of writing no.

The page after had melted into wool. The next page held only two words, pressed hard and underlined once as though they were all the diary could bear.

Seventh. Quiet.

Damien stepped back from the table, exhaling. He rubbed a gloved thumb against the edge of one leaf, then removed his glove and set his bare fingertips to his brow as if staunching a small, interior bleed. "All these lines," he said quietly, "and his restraint becomes the loudest thing in the room."

Marley looked down at her notebook. She had written *She waited. He did not come.* seven times, each line a copy from a different date, the repetition forming its own kind of column. She drew a bracket beside the list and wrote: *testimony.*

When she looked up, Damien had recovered himself. He adjusted the lamp once more and returned to the task. "We'll capture raking images tomorrow," he said, practical again. "Interleave with fresh blotter. Humidity chamber, then flatten. For now, we read."

They bent to it again. Evening crept into the windows; the fog pressed its face to the glass. The diary gave what it would. The keeper kept confessing in the only way he knew how—by trying not to confess and failing. He wrote a woman into permanence by refusing to call her foolish, by writing her walks as part of the work of the bridge.

And when the lamp buzzed once and steadied, Damien found a small pencil note hidden at the very bottom of a page, a private instruction from the keeper to his future self or to whatever reader might someday lift the oilcloth and listen. He squinted, then smiled—a tired, human curve.

"Read it," Marley said.

He did. "*If he will not come, then let it be written that she did.*"

Marley's throat closed around a sound that was not yet a sob. She wrote it down, exactly, and drew a box around it with a steady hand. The bridge had made a witness of a man who had not asked to be one. Now it had made witnesses of them. And the night beyond the windows, thick with its soft, white listening, kept the shape of their breaths while they read the word *seventh* again and again until it stopped sounding like a number and started sounding like a door.

BY THE TIME the courthouse clock tolled five dull notes through the fog, the diary lay opened to its worst places— the leaves the river had nearly eaten, the entries where iron gall had browned, migrated, and blurred the words into wool. Damien drew the raking lamp lower until its beam skimmed the page at a razor angle. The ink, what was left of it, lifted in gloss. The dry valleys showed as shadow.

"Don't chase meaning," he said softly, the teacher in him steadying both of them. "Find letters. Then words. We let sense come last."

Marley nodded and leaned in. He slid a sheet of Mylar over the page and set glass weights along the edges, then took a very fine-tipped archival pen and traced only what light made certain: the long spine of an *l*, the belly of an *o*, the forked tail of a *y*. On a second sheet, Marley copied each found letter in pencil, building a parallel page of fragments. Their hands moved in a careful duet, never quite touching the diary itself.

Damien angled the beam a fraction more. "There," he murmured. "See that shallow groove? No pigment left, but the iron bit the fiber."

Marley followed the faint channel with her eyes until the groove met a cluster of darker scratches—letters written while the page was damp, strokes thickened where the nib dragged. She could make out *sev*—. Her pulse jumped. She forced it down. Letters first.

They worked the line inch by inch. The scratches resolved into *seventh n*—. A drop-out in the middle. Then the last strokes surfaced as if from silt: *ight*.

"'Seventh night,'" Damien said, not triumphant. Just sure. He lifted the Mylar and penciled the phrase on the transparent overlay as if placing a window where the page remembered.

They turned to the facing leaf. This one had suffered a spill that had fanned outward and dried in delicate tide lines. Under the low lamp, salt shimmered. Damien fitted a small mirror between page and light so that the beam bounced back at an even shallower angle. Letters leapt to life where flat light had seen none.

"*Seventh* again," Marley breathed. "There—three lines down."

Damien traced the ghost strokes. "And again in the margin," he said, tapping gently beside a column of short verticals—seven hash marks with a diagonal slash through them. "He's tallying. Not days, I think—runs. Sequences of nights inside longer weeks."

"Se'nnight," Marley said, half to herself.

He glanced up, surprised into a smile. "Exactly. A word fallen out of fashion by his time, but not out of use. *This day se'nnight*—one week hence. He's trying not to give the thing a ritual name, so he writes the old measure instead. Practical superstition."

They bent back to the leaf. The phrase returned with insistence—as a heading, in the margin, tucked after notes on tar, woven into weather: *seventh night wind south... seventh night bell quiet... seventh night—Annabelle walked without lamp.* Each time the hand tightened as if the keeper heard himself making a pattern and resisted while making it.

Damien opened a fresh notebook and drew a grid as if he were diagramming a song. At the top he wrote columns: *Date / Wind / Water / Annabelle / North Mouth / Keeper's Note.* As Marley called letters and words, he filled the cells. The work steadied them both; making a table was a way of telling fear it could wait its turn.

"*October 12—fog holds off, Annabelle at midbeam, letter in hand—seventh night?*" Marley read, watching the grooves resolve.

He set it down. "No explicit 'seventh' here. But two nights later—" He slid to the next page. "—we have it three times."

She followed his finger to the row: *Oct 14 / south / river up / Annabelle barefoot / no crossing / 'seventh night' in text + margin.*

A few leaves later, where the page had bubbled with old damp, the words broke into syllables. Damien lowered the lamp until they were almost working in dark. He whispered letters as he found them, and Marley wrote, building the phrase the way a person stones a path across a stream.

"S... e... v... e... n... t... h," he said. "Pause in the nib. Then n... i... g... h... t."

"Again," she said, a steadiness in her even when her heart kicked. "It's everywhere."

He sat back, flexing his cramped hand. "Everywhere the page can still speak, it says it." He drew a bracket down a column of dates, October into early November. "And always with her." He didn't have to say Annabelle's name. It rang between them.

Marley cupped her hands around her paper cup of water, warming her fingers. "He tried not to write a ceremony," she said, "so the ceremony wrote itself in his refusals. Seven as a gate. Seven as a vow's hinge."

Damien's eyes lifted to hers. "And on the seventh, something always... intensifies." He gestured to a line where the keeper had pressed so hard the page embossed: *Board groaned. Twice.*

They returned to the worst page of all—the one the river had almost claimed. Beneath the lamp, the surface looked like linen left out in frost. Damien set a black cloth beneath it to kill the bounce of the white muslin and brought the mirror down so low his knuckles brushed the blotter. The smallest change in angle turned mush to script.

"Read to me," Marley said, pencil poised above her own clean sheet.

"*Seven—*" he began, then stopped. "No. That's *several.* Sorry." He adjusted a hair's breadth. "All right. *Sev—seventh...*here." He traced the ghost strokes. "*Seventh night...*" He squinted at the next words, then grinned, sudden, boyish and fatigued. "*...and I will not write no.*"

Marley copied it in full, her breath catching on the last word. "It killed him to set that down," she said.

"Because he understood what witness does. Once you write *no* enough times, the absence becomes a fact the world has to carry."

He lifted the mirror, blinked the sting from his eyes, and turned the page. The next entry had survived in islands of legibility. Between them, the keeper seemed to have used pencil over ink as if arguing with what he'd already written. Damien read the ink first, then the graphite, weaving the two into one voice.

"*Seventh night again, if counted from first frost,*" he said. "*Annabelle asked if wood remembers weight. I told her every board bears a print. She said then I am not the first to wait.*"

Marley circled *not the first* in her notes. "Others before her," she said quietly. "A lineage of waiting impressed into the planks."

Outside, rain ticked once against the window. The weather had turned while they worked. A cold damp rose from the floorboards as if the river had pushed a little closer to hear.

"Two more," Damien said, voice rough with concentration. "I think we can pull two before the paper begs for rest."

He eased a brittle corner over with the bone folder and found a surprise in the gutter: pencil math. Seven short verticals, slashed, then seven again. Below them, a single word, hard-pressed and underlined: *bell.*

"Counted sevens," Marley murmured. "And when the last mark is made, he writes *bell.*"

"Or writes what he cannot ring," Damien answered. "I am no bellman," he read a leaf later, where that phrase returned. "He keeps saying it like a refusal and an apology."

They moved through one more leaf of ghosts. Light,

mirror, breath held—the ritual of reading. Damien stopped suddenly, his finger hovering over a faint diagonal stroke near the lower margin. "Do you see that?"

Marley leaned so close her hair brushed his sleeve. The stroke became the tail of a letter. Then a second tail. Then the suggestion of two initials cramped into the corner where a man might hide a private truth.

"C... M," she said, barely voicing it, terrified of wanting it to be what it was.

"It could be anything," he cautioned gently. "A flourish. A tally. The ink's fled."

"But the grooves—" She traced air above them. "They look like a *C* and an *M,* side by side. A witness naming a man at last and then thinking better of it."

He set his hand over hers for a moment, steadying the reach. "We write what we can prove," he said, though his eyes were not unlit by the possibility. "For now, we mark: *initials?* And we keep going."

They did. Rain found its confidence and pattered in earnest on the sash. In the pool of lamplight the page yielded one final line without need of tricks, as if deciding to speak plain before they put it to bed:

Seventh night. Wind south. Annabelle walked without lamp. He did not come.

No flourish. No metaphor. The sentence lay like a beam across a span—weight-bearing, unadorned. Marley wrote it, each word landing with more certainty than the last.

Damien eased the lamp upright and turned it down. The page went matte. The diary looked smaller when the light let go of it, like a thing that has given what it could and now asked for rest. He and Marley interleaved the leaves with fresh blotter, slid the volume into a clean tray, and covered it with muslin. The rhythms of conservation—

humility, patience, order—replaced the fever of deciphering.

"I'll set the humidity chamber in the morning," he said, voice returning to its practical register. "A few hours at fifty-five percent will relax the crumpled fibers. Then we flatten under boards. We'll get more text if we let the paper breathe."

Marley nodded, grateful for the language of care that did not demand belief to function. "And then we return to the seventh nights," she said. "Map them against wind, against tides, against the chapel ledger."

"And against your journal," he added quietly. "Dreams, voices, the candle. If there's cadence, we'll find it."

Thunder—distant, almost polite—rolled somewhere out over the bay. Both of them looked toward the sound. A filament of memory tightened in Marley's chest: the vision she hadn't yet had by the calendar of the diary—the downpour beneath the bridge, the lace ribbon wet in her hand. Time folded oddly here; sometimes the page told tomorrow like it was yesterday.

Damien saw the look pass through her and went still. "Not tonight," he said. Not command. Request. "We've done enough for one day."

She let the request sit between them. The rain had gathered itself now, a steady percussion. She could already hear the bridge absorbing it, plank by plank, beam by beam—the way wood learns a storm by heart.

"One more thing," she said, reaching for her notebook. She drew a small box and wrote a single sentence inside it, the keeper's pencil verdict they had uncovered just before the worst of the smudges: *If he will not come, then let it be written that she did.* She shaded the box's edges until it looked like a nailed placard. "We carry this forward," she said. "Every seventh night. Every time the town says myth. We answer with that."

Damien's throat worked. He nodded. "We will."

They packed the tray and turned off the lamp. The back room fell to a silver dim. Rain ran down the window like script undeciphered. At the door to the street he paused, his hand on the latch, then looked back at her with a weariness that had softened into resolve.

"If the forecast holds," he said, "tomorrow will be more than fog. It will be weather. Don't shelter under the bridge alone."

"I won't," she said, because promises given in doorways tend to hold. "Call me when the barometer drops. We'll go together."

He managed the ghost of a smile. "It's already dropping." He lifted the tray with the diary as though it were a child sleeping. "Seventh nights," he added, half to himself, and the way he said it sounded less like dread and more like a measure they could dance by without falling.

Marley watched him go into the rain, the tray under his coat, his hat low against the wind. When the door closed, she stood with her palm on the wood and felt the weather lean against it from the other side. Then she opened her notebook one last time and copied their makeshift table into a clean hand, adding a final column he hadn't drawn: *Bell (heard/not heard)*. She left the cells empty—for now.

Outside, the downpour found its voice. The bridge waited, timber remembering a hundred storms, a thousand footfalls, and the insistence of a phrase the page had said again and again until even wood could not forget it: *the seventh night.*

12

———————

RAINFALL MEMORIES

The storm began like a warning in the distance, a low rumble rolling from the coast toward the valley. By midafternoon, the wind had pushed the fog into tatters, and rain came down in hard, slanted lines. Marley was already on the footpath toward the bridge when the clouds split open entirely, loosing sheets that soaked her coat in minutes.

She pulled the collar up, clutched her notebook under her arm, and quickened her steps. The bridge loomed ahead, its timbers darkening as the rain sank into them. She crossed the threshold and stepped beneath the shelter of the roof, breath shallow, heart pacing to the thunder.

The interior was dim, boards dripping with rivulets. Water hammered the roof overhead, drumming like a hundred fists. The smell of wet pine and tar rose sharp and earthy, wrapping around her like a cloak.

She shook the rain from her hair, pressed her back against one of the posts, and closed her eyes to steady herself. For a moment it was enough just to listen—the sound of the storm engulfing the bridge, the muted roar of the swollen river below. But soon a different rhythm threaded through the din: the creak of planks shifting under a step that was not hers.

Marley's eyes flew open.

No one stood in the span. Rain sheeted down beyond both portals, sealing the bridge in silver curtains. The sound had come from within.

Her notebook slipped slightly in her hand. She drew it close against her chest and moved to the center of the span. The planks beneath her feet felt alive, as though remembering too many crossings.

Thunder cracked. In its wake, she thought she heard the echo of a woman's voice, faint as mist: *Wait for me.*

Her breath faltered. She steadied herself, setting the notebook on the bench. "Annabelle," she whispered. "If you're here, I'm listening."

The boards responded with a subtle tremor. Then the air shifted.

It began as a shimmer at the edge of her vision, a brightening of the rain as though light moved through it in unseen shapes. Marley blinked. The bridge darkened around her, its grain dissolving into shadow, and she felt her body sink, not physically but as if her mind slipped beneath the surface of water.

The storm dimmed. The drumming softened. And when she opened her eyes again, she was not standing in her own hour.

The bridge was new, timbers pale and sharp-edged, iron bolts bright as coin. Lanterns burned at either end, their flames wavering in the damp. Beyond them, fog pressed in, thick and waiting.

And there—halfway down the span—stood a woman.

Marley's heart stopped, then surged. Annabelle.

She was barefoot, the pale arches of her feet pressed against the damp planks, toes gripping as though testing the bridge's strength. Her gown was pale green, hem darkened by rain, sleeves clinging to her arms. In her hand she held a folded letter, the paper already blotched with wet. Her hair, long and dark, clung to her cheeks in strands.

She moved slowly, deliberately, her eyes fixed not on Marley but on the northern mouth of the bridge. She raised the letter once, as though showing it to the fog, then pressed it to her chest.

Marley felt herself drawn forward. She wanted to speak, to call Annabelle's name, but her throat held silence. The air around her felt too fragile for sound, as though one word would shatter the vision.

Annabelle reached the midspan. She paused, lifting her face to the storm. Rain streaked her cheeks, indistinguishable from tears. She whispered something Marley could not hear. Then she pressed the letter into the seam of the bench, her fingers lingering as if asking the wood to keep it safe.

Lightning flared outside the portal, throwing the woman into stark silhouette. In that flash, Marley saw the depth of Annabelle's waiting—the sorrow carved into her mouth, the defiance in the set of her shoulders.

Thunder rolled. Annabelle turned toward the north again, waiting.

Marley strained to see through the fog, desperate for a figure to emerge. But the portal stayed empty. Only the storm moved.

Minutes—or moments, time had no measure here—passed. Annabelle's hand dropped to her side. She lifted the hem of her gown slightly, stepped to the rail, and rested her palm on the beam. "Seventh night," Marley heard her whisper, faint but distinct, carried through the boards.

Then the vision cracked like glass.

The lanterns guttered out. The planks blurred. Marley felt herself pulled backward, as though the bridge itself exhaled and expelled her from its memory.

She staggered, gasping, and dropped to her knees on the wet boards of the bridge as it stood in her own century. Rain poured around her, plastering her hair to her face. The sound of the storm returned in full, hammering the roof like fists.

Her hands pressed against the boards for balance—and met mud. She lifted them. Her palms were streaked brown, as though she'd been kneeling in wet earth.

A shiver ran through her. Something else clung to her fingers.

She looked down. In her right hand she held a length of lace ribbon, damp, knotted at one end, the pattern delicate but worn. It had not been hers when she stepped onto the bridge.

Her chest rose and fell in sharp breaths. She clutched the ribbon to her chest, shivering not from cold but from the weight of proof. The vision had not left her empty-handed.

Lightning split the sky again. This time Marley whispered into the storm, voice shaking: "Annabelle, I see you."

The bridge groaned beneath her in reply.

THE RAIN SOFTENED to a steady downpour, more curtain than fist, and Marley forced herself upright on the bench. Her palms stung where grit had pressed into them. She stared down at the ribbon lying limp across her lap.

It was pale cream once, now the color of aged bone. The lacework was fine but fraying, the knotted end darkened as if it had been carried through water again and again. When she pinched the fabric between her fingers, it released a faint, mineral scent—damp stone, iron, the tang of river.

She laid it across her open notebook. Ink had already begun to run on the last page from where the storm had soaked through her coat. She tore the sheet free with steady hands, folded it to keep the ink from staining the ribbon, and turned to a fresh leaf.

Her pencil felt heavy, as though the storm itself pressed down on it. She wrote anyway, large and deliberate:

Vision during downpour—bridge transfigured. Annabelle present in pale green gown, barefoot. Letter clutched. Placed letter in bench seam. Whispered "seventh night." Waiting for someone who never arrived.

She paused, touched the damp ribbon again, and added beneath:

Physical evidence: lace ribbon retrieved upon waking. Mud on hands, though no soil present on planks at time of storm.

Her handwriting began to slant as she quickened. She pressed harder, filling the page with the urgency of witness:

Lanterns in vision—two, both ends, flame. Bridge new. Keeper's entries corroborated (ribbon, midspan, vows, waiting). Confirmed: not imagination alone. Bridge remembers. Bridge delivers.

The last sentence underlined itself in the pressure of her hand. She let the pencil fall, flexed her aching fingers, and stared at what she had written. The page trembled slightly on her lap; whether from her hands or the bridge itself, she couldn't tell.

A draft ran the length of the span, carrying the scent of rain-wet earth from the banks. Marley looked at her mud-caked palms again. The streaks had already begun to dry into patterns, ridges forming in lines that almost looked like script. She raised one hand close to the lamplight. In the grooves of her skin, she swore she saw the faint outline of an *A*.

Her pulse leapt. She rubbed her palm across her coat, smearing the impression until it blurred. "No," she said under her breath. "Not here. Not yet."

She turned the ribbon in her hands again, lifting the knotted end. The knot was precise, not careless, pulled tight enough to resist untying without effort. She thought of Annabelle pressing it around her wrist, or fastening it to a letter. A token meant to be kept, not discarded.

Her eyes burned. She pressed the ribbon flat between the pages of her journal, like a leaf preserved in autumn. She wrote beside it: *Artifact. Possible link to November 1 entry: ribbon at third beam. Keeper left it. I hold it now.*

The storm began to ease outside, thunder rolling away across the hills. The bridge creaked once, long and low, as though relieved of a weight.

Marley sat back, spine against the post, and closed her eyes. The vision replayed itself with brutal clarity: Annabelle's wet gown clinging, her bare feet pale against the wood, her lips shaping words Marley could only half-hear. The way she stood waiting, eyes fixed on the far mouth, as if the act of staying were more vow than any words spoken.

Marley whispered into the dim: "What did you wait for, Annabelle? What did he fail to keep?"

No answer came. Only the drip of rain through the seams of the roof, falling onto the planks in steady rhythms.

She opened her eyes and forced herself to look outward. The river was swollen, carrying branches and foam. The world beyond the portals looked blurred, as if her sight were still caught between times. She breathed slowly, deeply, anchoring herself back to her own body, her own moment.

After several minutes, she shut the notebook firmly and tied it with its cord. The ribbon inside felt like a living vein pressed between the covers, pulsing faintly against her hands. She slid the journal into her satchel, her fingers lingering on its spine as if to test whether the weight of it had changed.

Only then did she rise. Her knees were stiff, her coat heavy with rain, but her resolve had hardened. She touched the beam where Annabelle had placed her letter in the vision. Nothing waited there now but slick wood and a faint line of moss. Still, Marley pressed her palm against it as though to answer: *I saw you. I carried it forward.*

The storm thinned into mist. She stepped out from the shelter into the gray light of late afternoon. Rain clung to her lashes, but beneath it her eyes were sharp. She turned toward town, each step heavy with water and vow, the notebook close against her side.

Behind her, the bridge groaned once more, low and resigned, as though it knew what it had surrendered and what it had delivered.

BY THE TIME Marley reached the edge of town, the storm had waned to a steady drizzle. Water streamed down the gutters, carrying pale leaves and grit. The lamps had already lit up; each globe along Main Street glowed through the mist like an anchored star. Marley kept her satchel pressed against her side as though it might be wrested from her if she let her grip loosen. Inside, the ribbon lay folded between notebook leaves, heavier than its weight should allow.

She had almost reached the bookstore flat when Damien appeared out of the haze. He was bareheaded, rain plastering his hair to his forehead, his scarf half-unwound. He looked as though he had run the entire way from the archives.

"Marley." His voice cracked her name. He caught her by the elbow, scanning her face with sharp, searching eyes. "I went to the bridge when the storm broke. You weren't there. For God's sake, what happened?"

She swallowed, suddenly aware of the mud dried on her hands, the damp weight of her coat. "I was there. I—I saw her."

Damien's jaw set. He steered her beneath the awning of the bookshop and pressed her against the door, not unkind but with urgency that brooked no delay. "What do you mean, *saw her*?"

Marley unfastened her satchel with trembling fingers. She pulled out the journal, opened to the page where the ribbon lay pressed like a fragile bone, and held it out.

Damien stared. His hand hovered above the lace but didn't touch. "Where did you get this?"

"It was in my hand when I came back," Marley said. Her voice was low, steadying itself by force. "I was under the bridge when the storm hit. The boards—Damien, they shifted under me, they carried me somewhere else. I saw Annabelle. Pale green gown, bare feet, letter in her hand. She pressed it into the bench seam. She whispered 'seventh night.' And when I woke, this ribbon was in my palm."

The silence stretched long enough that the rain's rhythm seemed to mark it into increments. Damien's eyes fixed on the ribbon as though it were a live ember. Finally, he said, "Marley... if what you're saying is true, then the bridge is no longer echoing in dreams alone. It's crossing the barrier in waking hours. It's... delivering."

She touched his wrist, forcing him to meet her gaze.

"This isn't imagination. This isn't grief's trick. This is evidence."

His face twisted. "Evidence of what? That you're being pulled the same way Jackie was? That the bridge is patient enough to wait until you're standing in the rain and then take more from you than it has any right to?" His voice sharpened. "This is exactly how it began with her. Night visions, artifacts that couldn't be explained. And then—" He broke off, the end of the sentence too dangerous to speak.

Marley refused to let the silence win. "And then you ignored it. You told yourself it wasn't real, and that's what left her alone. I'm not her, Damien. Don't confuse the two."

He flinched at her words, but his hand came to rest on the open journal. He traced the edge of the page near the ribbon, careful not to touch the lace itself. His expression shifted from fear to something like despair. "Do you know what this means for me? To see her handwriting in the archives, to hear Jackie murmur in her sleep, to watch you now, with this ribbon in your hands—" He exhaled, a harsh, broken sound. "It feels like the bridge is pulling all the threads together and knotting them around my throat."

Marley closed the journal, placed it firmly back in the satchel, and covered his hand with hers. "Or it's knotting them into something that can finally be untangled. We're not victims here, Damien. We're witnesses. That ribbon isn't a curse—it's a message. Proof Annabelle lived, proof she waited. The bridge gave it to me so the story wouldn't rot in silence."

His eyes searched hers, storm-dark and rimmed with a fear he couldn't mask. "And what if the story doesn't want to end? What if it keeps demanding new witnesses until it swallows us all?"

"Then we write louder than it echoes," Marley said, her

voice fierce. "We carry forward what Annabelle left, and we refuse to be quiet."

The awning dripped steadily, the rhythm marking the stalemate between them. Damien's shoulders sagged, his fight guttering like a lamp starved of oil. He pressed the heel of his hand against his eyes, then lowered it slowly. "You terrify me," he admitted. "Because I believe you. Because the ribbon is real. And because I don't know if I can lose to the bridge twice."

Marley's heart ached, but she did not release his hand. "Then don't think of it as losing. Think of it as keeping your vow. To Jackie. To Annabelle. To me."

His grip tightened once, desperate. Then he let go, stepping back into the rain as though he needed the cold to steady him. "Tomorrow we'll return to the bench where you saw her. We'll look for what the boards remember. But Marley..." His voice softened, strained. "Promise me you won't go alone again."

She nodded, though inside she knew the bridge would call her regardless of his pleas. Still, she said the words he needed: "I promise."

He lingered, watching her as though to memorize her standing there, hair wet, journal pressed to her chest, ribbon hidden but undeniable. Then he turned into the mist, leaving her with the sound of the river rising and the knowledge that her evidence had become his fear.

Marley climbed the stairs to her flat. She laid the satchel on the desk and untied it once more. The ribbon gleamed faintly in the lamplight, its knot tight, unyielding. She traced it with one finger and whispered, "We see you, Annabelle. We'll carry you forward."

The bridge groaned faintly in the distance, as if answering across the rain-soaked night.

13

THE SILVER BUTTON

The rain had thinned into a mist by morning, leaving the ground slick and shining as though the earth had been polished. Marley walked the river path with her satchel at her hip, notebook inside, ribbon pressed between pages. Damien followed a pace behind, silent but present, his eyes scanning the wet ground the way a man reads the fine print of a contract.

The river ran fast beside them, its current swollen from the storm. At the foot of the path where the bank curved inward, the gravel gave way to mud. Marley slowed. Something small gleamed faintly against the dark soil.

She crouched, brushing her hair back from her damp cheeks, and dug with her gloved fingers until the object came free. A round disc, no bigger than a coin, silver dulled by tarnish but catching enough light to betray itself.

"A button," she said softly. She turned it over in her palm. The face was engraved, faint but clear enough: two initials intertwined in a deliberate flourish. *C.M.* bound to *A.W.*

Damien crouched beside her, eyes narrowing. "Where exactly was it?"

"Here," she said, pointing to the impression in the mud. "Half-buried. As though the storm unearthed it."

He reached, hesitated, then touched it with the corner of his scarf rather than his hand. "Interlaced initials. This was no ordinary fastening. It was made to be remembered."

Marley's pulse quickened. She turned the button again, tracing the groove of each letter with her eyes. "C.M. and A.W." She spoke them aloud, letting the syllables anchor themselves. "Callum Marwick. Annabelle Warren."

The names rang with the weight of recognition. She pulled her notebook from her satchel and flipped to the census records she had copied weeks before. Her pencil underlined the entry she'd nearly memorized:

Marwick, Callum, 22, laborer.

Warren, Annabelle, 19, domestic servant.

She held the page beside the button, the written names mirroring the carved letters. "It's them," she whispered. "They were bound even in their clothing. A token worn against the body, holding their vow."

Damien's jaw tightened. He straightened slowly, his boots sinking a fraction into the mud. "Or a grave good. Something left where memory ought to lie undisturbed."

Marley rose with him, button still in her hand. "You think we're trespassing."

"I think," he said carefully, "that when storms unearth relics of the dead, it is not always an invitation. Sometimes it is a warning."

She turned the button once more, then pressed it between the leaves of her notebook beside the ribbon. "Or it's evidence. Another thread proving Annabelle was more than rumor. Every object draws the pattern tighter."

Damien's gaze lingered on the closed notebook, unease written plain across his face. "Evidence for you. But for the families who lie in this soil, for the ones who still live with their names... it may be disruption. We don't yet know if the bridge is asking to be remembered—or commanding us to stop."

Marley exhaled, rain-damp air searing her lungs with cold. "I can't stop, Damien. Not now. Not when Annabelle's initials are carved beside his. It means she was not waiting in vain. He pledged himself to her. The story has proof."

"And if proof is what lured Jackie down that path?" he asked sharply, then faltered, his voice catching on the name. "What if each artifact is bait?"

Marley looked toward the bridge, its pale frame ghostly in the thinning mist. The river between here and there seemed louder now, the current speaking in tones she almost understood. She touched the notebook against her chest.

"Then I'll write it all," she said firmly. "Every name, every mark. If Annabelle and Callum are asking for witness, we won't betray them by silence."

Damien's face darkened, torn between fear and reluctant conviction. He glanced back toward the river, then at the place where the button had lain in the mud. "We'll mark the coordinates," he said finally, voice low. "And we'll return it here when we've finished our work. No artifact should be kept from its ground forever."

Marley nodded, though her grip on the notebook only tightened. She knew the button was more than soil, more than memory. It was a vow made solid, initials carved into silver so that even time could not separate them.

The mist rose again, drifting across the river like pale

fingers. Marley stepped closer to Damien, her words a whisper against the fog.

"Annabelle's story is surfacing, piece by piece. If the bridge carries echoes, then this—" she touched the note-book—"is how we make them stay."

The button's weight pressed against the page like a heartbeat.

And the river, relentless, kept speaking as though it had waited a century for someone to finally listen.

THE ARCHIVES SMELLED FAINTLY of glue and dust—comforting scents that had grown familiar to Marley, though today her nerves made them sharp. She and Damien carried the button in together, wrapped in clean muslin. The day outside was gray, but the electric lamps hummed steady, their light falling over the long oak tables.

Marley untied her satchel and laid her notebook open. The ribbon pressed between its leaves seemed to breathe against the paper; the button sat beside it, a small circle of tarnished silver. Both artifacts glowed with a weight dispro-portionate to their size.

She turned to the census copies she had made weeks earlier. Her finger traced the rows. "Callum Marwick. Annabelle Warren. The initials match exactly."

Damien hovered behind her, his hands tucked into his coat pockets as though to keep them from trembling. "Initials aren't proof. Half the county bore names that could bend toward those letters. We cannot bind a century of soil to two marks on a button."

Marley's jaw tightened. She slid the button closer, pressing her pencil into the grooves of the engraving until the lead traced the letters onto a scrap page. The C and the

M interlocked with the A and the W like vines twined on a trellis. She pushed the rubbing across the table toward Damien.

"This wasn't casual," she said. "This was deliberate—two names joined, carried on clothing. A vow made visible."

Damien didn't touch the paper. He bent close enough to see, his shadow stretching long over the table. "Or it was mourning jewelry, a token worn after they were gone. You don't know which way time cut."

Marley flipped through the census sheets until she found the household records she had copied from 1880:

Marwick, Callum—22, laborer. Warren, Annabelle—19, domestic.

She tapped the page. "Together in the same entry year. Young. Working. Breathing. This was before the bridge's seventh nights claimed her. That button proves connection —not myth."

Her voice rose, echoing in the high-ceilinged room. Damien flinched, then set a hand on her notebook as if to ground her. His touch was gentle but his eyes carried unease.

"I believe you've found something," he said. "But I worry what kind of something it is. Objects carry residue, Marley. Families used to bury personal tokens with their dead so memory would stay sealed. When storms uncover them, they aren't always meant to be lifted into light."

Marley pulled the notebook back toward her, pressing her palm flat over the button. "And when they *are* meant? When they're gifts from the bridge, testifying what it remembers? If Annabelle's ribbon came into my hand, and now Callum's initials rise from the mud, then both voices are calling for witness. If we ignore them, we let them sink again."

Damien's mouth pressed tight. He turned away, walking to the shelves where boxes of records lined the wall. "I've seen how witness consumes. Jackie kept a drawer of scraps—pressed flowers, copied poems, an old key she swore belonged to a vanished house. Each piece pulled her further from me until nothing I said could match the weight of what she thought she carried." His shoulders sagged. "Artifacts can be anchors—or they can be chains."

Marley rose from the table and joined him. She laid her hand on the shelf beside his, not touching but near. "I'm not Jackie. I'm not collecting scraps to disappear into them. I'm mapping a pattern. Every artifact we find ties Annabelle's name tighter to Callum's, tighter to the bridge's memory. This button isn't a chain—it's a clue."

He turned, meeting her gaze. Fear warred with reluctant belief in his eyes. "Then prove it's a clue. Find the name carved somewhere else. Find the initials in ink or stone. Don't just hold the dead's clothing as if it speaks. Make the page match the soil."

Marley nodded, accepting the challenge. She returned to the table, pulled the census rubbings, the diary fragments, Clara's journal notes. One by one she spread them across the wood until the button lay in the center like a keystone. "C.M. and A.W. We have the record of their existence. We have the bridge keeper's testimony. We have Annabelle's ribbon. And now—this."

Her pencil tapped each artifact. "That's not accident. That's structure."

Damien stood back, arms crossed, his face shadowed. "And if the structure you're building is a mausoleum?"

Marley didn't answer. Instead, she drew the initials on a clean page and circled them hard enough to nearly tear the paper. Beside them she wrote: *Callum Marwick + Annabelle Warren. Vow in silver.*

She slid the page beneath the ribbon and closed her notebook with finality.

"This story isn't finished," she said quietly. "But it's speaking louder every day. The bridge doesn't want silence anymore."

Damien looked at the button once more, his expression torn, then turned toward the window. Beyond the glass, mist curled along the river, hiding the bridge's silhouette. His shoulders rose and fell in a long breath, but his voice came low, almost a plea.

"Then promise me, Marley—promise me we'll tread as if every step disturbs the ground of the dead."

"I promise we'll tread as witnesses," she said. Her fingers traced the satchel strap at her hip, feeling the press of the button within. "But witnesses must write what they see. And I won't stop writing."

Damien closed his eyes. For a moment, the room filled only with the sound of the river moving unseen through the mist outside, carrying the weight of stories not yet surrendered.

EVENING LIGHT PRESSED against the tall windows of the archives, muting the room in shades of ash and blue. The button sat between them on the oak table, its tarnished face catching the lamplight like a single, watchful eye. Marley stared at it as though it could still speak, while Damien kept a wary distance, arms folded tight across his chest.

The silence between them stretched too long. Finally, Damien broke it. His voice was low but sharp, the kind of edge honed by fear.

"Marley, do you know what you're holding?"

She turned toward him, her fingers brushing the button's ridged initials. "Proof. Proof that Annabelle and Callum weren't just names buried in ledgers. They were bound, Damien. This button ties them together."

"Or it ties you to them," he shot back. His eyes flicked from her hand to her face. "Objects like this—mud-stained, unearthed after storms—they don't surface without reason. Families buried them, or lost them in moments that should remain private. When we disturb what soil has claimed, we invite more than memory."

Marley's jaw tightened. She closed her notebook over the button as if shielding it from his suspicion. "You're saying I should put it back in the mud and pretend it never appeared. You want me to walk away from evidence when the bridge itself seems determined to give it."

His fists clenched at his sides. "I'm saying you might not realize what evidence costs. You think this is a breadcrumb trail to a story that needs finishing. I see it as a grave marker pulled loose, a nameplate pried from a coffin. My wife began exactly this way—carrying tokens, telling herself they were messages, not warnings. Do you know where that path led her?"

The raw edge in his voice startled her, but she forced herself not to flinch. "Damien, I'm not Jackie. And this isn't the same path."

"You don't know that," he said, stepping closer, his expression tight. "She believed she was building a bridge for the lost. But the bridge was only too glad to use her belief as mortar. When I see you holding that button as if it's sacred, I see history repeating itself."

Marley rose from her chair, her satchel still open on the table. She pressed her palm over the notebook, grounding herself. "This isn't history repeating. It's history surfacing. We can choose how to respond. You can live in fear of being consumed again, or you can stand with me and help name what Annabelle and Callum left behind."

Damien's face softened for half a second—an old ache flickering through his features—but then hardened again. "And what if naming it is what keeps it alive?"

She met his gaze, unwavering. "Then silence has already failed. Because Annabelle keeps walking that bridge, Damien. Because Callum's vow is pressed into silver, waiting for someone to witness. I won't dishonor them by pretending not to hear."

The lamplight wavered as a draft threaded through the room. Marley thought of the button, the ribbon, the diary— each artifact an echo made solid. The bridge wasn't just speaking through visions and dreams anymore; it was placing proof in her hands.

Damien rubbed his temple, his voice heavy with strain. "Marley, if we keep drawing these echoes into daylight, we might be binding ourselves to their unfinished vow. These aren't just clues. They're invitations. And invitations from the dead don't end well."

Her throat tightened, but she forced her voice steady. "Maybe that's exactly what we need to risk. To accept the invitation. To see it through to its end. Because if no one does, then Annabelle waits forever. Callum waits forever. And the bridge never lets go."

His eyes darkened, storm brewing behind them. "And if by answering, you're the one who doesn't come back?"

The question hung in the air like a tolling bell. Marley closed her notebook, slid the button and ribbon deeper into its pages, and tied the cord. She slung the satchel over her shoulder, her decision plain.

"Then at least I won't have stayed silent."

Damien's hands fell to his sides, helpless. He looked at her as though torn between dragging her back from the path and stepping onto it beside her. His voice dropped, hoarse and quiet. "You're going to break me in half."

Marley's heart ached, but her conviction did not falter. "No. I'm going to carry them forward. And if you choose, you'll walk with me."

The rain outside had begun again, faint at first, then steady. The sound of it filled the room, echoing the river's voice. Damien finally lowered his gaze, the fight gone from his posture, though not from his eyes.

He whispered, almost to himself: "The bridge doesn't stop once it begins. You know that, don't you?"

Marley touched the satchel strap, feeling the weight of silver against the weight of lace. "Neither do I."

The button, hidden but present, seemed to pulse like a heartbeat between them.

14

JAZZ MEMORIES IN A MINOR KEY

The church basement smelled faintly of coffee grounds and brass polish. Folding chairs were arranged in a half-circle around music stands, each cluttered with penciled notes and worn charts. The Brookwood Jazz Ensemble rehearsed here every Thursday evening, a ritual almost as steady as Sunday service. Marley had never attended before, but Evelyn had insisted she come—"Music tells the truth faster than words," she'd said—and so Marley sat in the back row, notebook balanced on her knees, the silver button and lace ribbon locked in her satchel at her feet.

The saxophonist was a tall man named Royce, a machinist by day and musician by night. He warmed the reed with care, his long fingers quick and practiced. The first pieces ran smoothly, the rhythm section steady, the trumpets bright if a little sharp. Marley tapped her pencil against her notebook, trying to focus on the interplay of instruments instead of the low hum of the bridge still moving through her thoughts.

Halfway through the set, the director called a break and

handed out a new arrangement—"Autumn in New Orleans," penciled neatly at the top. They shuffled pages, adjusted lamps clipped to stands, and began again.

But a few bars in, something shifted.

Royce's eyes half-closed, and his horn bent away from the chart. The written melody fell aside, replaced by something slower, more haunted. The first notes curled like smoke, low and trembling, rising with a plaintive ache that cut straight through the chatter of the room.

Marley froze.

She knew this song. She had heard it in her dreams, threaded through the visions that woke her in sweat and silence. The same ascending phrase, the same falling resolution that never quite landed, leaving the listener suspended, longing for the next note.

Royce kept playing, unaware of the others watching him. The drummer softened instinctively, adjusting to his lead, brushes tapping like a heartbeat. The pianist found chords beneath him, tentative but sure, until the entire ensemble was pulled into the melody he carried.

Marley's hand tightened on her notebook. Her pencil trembled, tracing the shape of the notes as if she could capture them on paper. The melody wound higher, then dipped, a cry woven into brass. She closed her eyes and saw Annabelle again—not walking this time, but standing at the bridge's midspan, her arms lifted as though calling across the water. The horn became her voice, sharp with yearning, deep with loss.

When the final note faded, the room held silence so complete it felt reverent. The director blinked, cleared his throat, and tapped his stand. "Royce, that wasn't on the page."

Royce looked down, startled, as if waking from a trance.

He shrugged, wiping the reed with his thumb. "I don't know. It just came to me."

The words rippled through Marley, chilling her more than the rain ever could. *Just came to me.* The melody from her dream, breathed into life without sheet or memory. She scribbled in her notebook, her letters jagged with urgency: *Dream melody—played by Royce. Not written. He says it came to him.*

She looked up and found Damien watching her across the room. His expression was taut, already reading her reaction. He didn't shake his head this time. He didn't mouth denial. Instead, his gaze slid to the old clock against the far wall, where its brass pendulum swung steady and patient.

The director tried again. "Royce, you mean you improvised it? Or you had something in your head?"

Royce shook his head, still dazed. "No. Not improvised. Not something I've heard. It felt... older. Like it belonged in the room already, waiting for someone to blow it out."

The other musicians muttered among themselves. Marley pressed her pencil harder into the page until the tip snapped. She didn't move to replace it. Her chest felt tight, lungs filling with music that wasn't hers.

Damien rose quietly from his seat near the door and approached. He bent close to her ear, his whisper nearly lost in the murmur of the room. "The rhythm."

She turned, breath catching. "What about it?"

He gestured toward the horn, still cooling in Royce's hands. "The phrasing. It matched the lantern's pulse."

Marley's eyes widened. The lighthouse lantern—the same one that beat through the fog at night, guiding ships, keeping time with echoes. She replayed the melody in her mind and realized he was right. The rests fell where the lantern's glow faded; the long notes surged where the beam swept across the water.

She shivered. "Then the song isn't only Annabelle's. It belongs to the bridge. To the light."

Damien's mouth tightened, but he didn't argue. He looked instead at Royce, who was carefully re-aligning his sheet music as though embarrassed by what had just passed through him.

The director cleared his throat again, trying to regain authority. "Let's—let's take it from the top. Stick to the chart this time."

But when they began again, the melody sounded hollow, like bones without flesh. The haunting phrase lingered in the room anyway, impossible to silence, as if the air itself remembered.

Marley closed her notebook with shaking fingers. She leaned toward Damien and whispered, "You heard it too. Tell me you heard it."

His eyes were shadowed, his voice low. "I heard it. And it terrifies me."

She pressed her palm to the satchel strap across her chest. Inside, the ribbon and button pressed their silent testimony. Now the melody joined them, intangible yet undeniable. Another proof. Another echo.

The horn's last note still rang in her bones as she whispered back, "Then it means we're closer."

Damien didn't answer. His silence carried both warning and surrender.

The lantern of the lighthouse, though unseen, seemed to blink in her memory, matching the rhythm of the music note for note.

.   .   .

THE ENSEMBLE SHUFFLED awkwardly after the failed attempt to play the chart as written. Trumpets squeaked; the drummer tapped half-hearted fills, but the haunting strain Royce had breathed into the room still lingered like smoke. The director clapped his hands once, sharp. "All right, settle down. One more run-through, then we break."

Royce hesitated. His reed squealed when he tested it. The man's usual confidence was gone, replaced with an uneasy stillness. Marley leaned forward from her chair in the back row, unable to stay silent.

"Royce," she said, her voice clear enough to cut through the muttering. "That melody—where did you hear it?"

Heads turned toward her. Outsiders didn't usually speak during rehearsals. But Royce only blinked, running a thumb along the brass keys. "Nowhere. Like I told you, it just came to me. As if it were sitting in the horn all this time, waiting."

"Do you dream of music?" she pressed, notebook balanced in her lap. "Do you ever wake with a phrase in your ear?"

Royce shook his head. "Not usually. But tonight—" He frowned, searching. "It felt like déjà vu. Like I'd known it once, long ago, but forgot until now."

Marley scribbled in her notebook, her hand nearly tearing the paper: *Royce claims déjà vu. Music already in horn. Phrase waiting. Not his own.*

Damien moved beside her, his posture taut, his eyes scanning the room. He leaned close, voice pitched low. "Listen to the phrasing again. You caught the melody. Now hear the rhythm."

She stilled her pencil.

Damien tapped the beat softly against his leg: long—pause—short—short—long. His eyes stayed locked on hers. "That's the lantern. The lighthouse signal. One sweep, dark interval, two flashes, another sweep. It matches exactly."

Marley's stomach dropped. She heard it now, as clearly as if the horn still played. The rhythm of light across the bay had become music in Royce's lungs. She wrote quickly: *Lantern signal = melody rhythm. Bridge voice through light, translated by horn.*

When she looked up again, she saw unease ripple through the ensemble. The trumpeter whispered to the drummer, who muttered back, "Sounded like a dirge." A trombonist rubbed the slide with his sleeve as though wiping something off more than condensation. Even the director shifted uncomfortably, tapping his baton against the stand without calling for another start.

Royce shrugged, but his brow was furrowed. "I can play it again, if you want. But I don't think it'll be the same."

"No," Damien said quickly, too quickly. The sharpness of his tone made half the musicians look up. He tempered it, lowering his voice. "Let it lie for now. Music like that—when it comes unbidden—it's better not to press."

Marley bristled. "Better not to press? Damien, that's exactly what we should do. If the bridge is carrying its rhythm into sound, then this is our first living witness." She looked at Royce. "Please. Try again."

Royce hesitated, the horn half-raised. His eyes darted between Marley's insistence and Damien's warning. Around the room, the other players shifted, sensing something uncanny at work. The drummer whispered, "Feels like playing at a funeral."

Marley's voice softened. "Not a funeral. A message. If you don't play it, the silence swallows it."

Damien cut in, firm. "And if playing it keeps it alive when it should rest?"

The clash of their words thickened the room's air. Royce lowered the horn, caught between them, sweat standing out on his brow. "I don't know what's in that tune, but I'll tell you—it didn't feel like mine. Felt like... someone else was breathing it through me."

Unease tightened the circle. The pianist muttered, "You're giving me chills, Royce." Another nodded. "Like we weren't alone in the room."

Marley's heart pounded. She knew they *hadn't* been. Annabelle's presence threaded the melody, the bridge's echo stitched into every phrase. She rose from her chair, clutching her notebook. "That's because you weren't alone. Royce played what the bridge remembers. And we all heard it."

The director cleared his throat, visibly unsettled. "All right, that's enough talk. We're here to rehearse, not chase ghosts. Let's return to the chart—page thirty-six." His baton clicked nervously against the stand.

The room tried to obey. Instruments lifted. Notes stumbled. But the melody Royce had pulled from the air lingered, ghosting every bar they tried to play. Nothing sounded right.

Marley sat down again, her pencil scratching furiously. *Room unsettled. Musicians admit not alone. Damien: fear of keeping melody alive. Royce: 'someone else breathing through me.' Confirms Annabelle's voice.*

Damien leaned toward her, voice low but urgent. "Write all you want, but mark this clearly: the bridge doesn't just haunt—it *uses*. The lighthouse beats its pulse into men. The horn gave it voice. That is not proof of safety. That is proof of reach."

She looked at him, defiant. "And if reach means it wants to be heard? If silence is the real danger?"

His jaw clenched. "Or if sound is the lure."

Around them, the ensemble stumbled through the written chart, but no one's ear could forget the phrase that hadn't been on the page. The melody had entered the room like a seed, and already it was growing in the silence between notes.

Royce set his horn down after the final bar, shaking his head. "Doesn't matter what we play. That tune's stuck now. Can't get it out."

Damien's shoulders stiffened. Marley only gripped her notebook tighter, her heart racing.

The lantern out on the bay continued its sweep, unseen in the night, its rhythm pulsing steady. She felt it in her bones.

THE REHEARSAL COLLAPSED in on itself. The musicians packed away their instruments quickly, their chatter strained and fragmented. No one joked as they usually did, no one lingered over coffee in the side kitchen. Chairs scraped louder than necessary. Cases clicked shut with a kind of finality that belonged more to fear than fatigue.

Royce kept his horn in his lap, staring at it as though it might betray him a second time. The director muttered something about "fatigue and sloppy intonation" but his voice betrayed how unsettled he was. He dismissed the group earlier than usual, and the ensemble filed out into the misted night like mourners leaving a service.

Marley stayed seated in the back row, notebook still open. She began drawing the melody on the page, not with formal notation but with the curves and breaks her memory insisted on. Ascending, aching, a long pause like a held breath, then the fall that never resolved. She wrote beneath it:

Melody heard in dream—confirmed through Royce. Rhythm = lighthouse lantern. Echo has breached music.

The page looked stark, alive. She pressed her pencil harder, etching the phrase as if that would pin it to the earth.

Damien stood nearby, his coat already buttoned. He watched her write but did not approach until the last musician's footsteps had faded upstairs. Only then did he step close, his voice low, almost accusing.

"You should have stopped him."

Marley looked up, startled. "Stopped him? Damien, that melody is proof. For weeks I've been haunted by it in dreams, and tonight it surfaced in waking sound. How can I ignore that?"

"Because it isn't proof of safety," he said sharply. "It's proof of danger. You saw how they reacted. Every player in that room felt something enter with that tune, and none of them wanted it. They left like a funeral had just finished. Is that what evidence looks like to you?"

Marley shut her notebook with a snap, but her voice stayed calm. "It looks like witness. They felt it because it was real. That's the whole point—this isn't fantasy spun out of sleep. It's shared. Documented. And now it's written." She tapped the cover of her notebook.

Damien's expression tightened. He paced a few steps, then turned back. "I watched Royce's face, Marley. That wasn't inspiration. That was possession. Something borrowed his breath and pushed it through brass. That rhythm—it wasn't human. It was mechanical, relentless, the very pulse of the lantern. It's the bridge teaching us how it beats."

She rose to her feet, meeting him eye to eye. "And if that's true, then it's communication. The bridge is showing us its pulse, its language. Don't you see? Every artifact, every dream, every vision—they're building a vocabulary. And tonight it spoke through music."

His voice cracked, ragged. "You think I don't see? I see too much. I see how the bridge is weaving you tighter into its story. The ribbon, the button, now a song you can't stop humming. It's pulling you piece by piece. And if you let it, one day it won't give you back."

The air between them was taut as wire. Marley held her ground. "I won't let fear silence me. If Annabelle waited all those nights, if Callum carved vows into silver, if Royce breathed a melody not his own—then we owe it to them to keep listening. I'd rather risk being drawn too close than turn my back on them."

Damien's hand balled into a fist at his side. For a moment it seemed he would argue again, but instead he exhaled, shoulders sagging as though the fight itself had drained him. "You terrify me," he said softly.

Marley touched her satchel strap, feeling the familiar weight of ribbon, button, and journal pressing against her side. "And yet you're still here."

He closed his eyes. When he opened them, something had shifted—fear remained, but beneath it lay reluctant loyalty. "Because I can't bear to leave you to it alone. But don't mistake my presence for agreement. Every step forward feels like trespass. Remember that."

She nodded, accepting both the warning and the vow laced into his words. "Then walk with me anyway. Write it down if you must. But don't look away."

The sound of rain began again overhead, pattering against the church's roof. Marley reopened her notebook, ignoring Damien's weary sigh. She sketched the lantern's pulse in jagged lines, marking where the horn's notes had aligned. Beside it she wrote: *Echo through music. Echo through light. Next: where melody meets word.*

Her pencil faltered for a moment, then she added a final line, bold and certain: *Annabelle is teaching us her song.*

She closed the book and met Damien's eyes once more. "That's not danger, Damien. That's history demanding to be heard."

He turned away, pulling his scarf tight around his neck. "Or it's a haunting demanding to go on forever."

Together they left the basement, stepping into the misty night. From across the bay, the lighthouse's lantern swept the fog, pulsing its rhythm into darkness. Marley heard the phantom melody thread itself through the sweep, the same aching phrase that Royce had carried, the same one from her dreams.

She whispered into the night as though Annabelle herself might be listening: "I hear you."

And the bridge, silent but present in the fog, seemed to hum the answer back.

15

THE BAKERY CONNECTION

The bell above the bakery door chimed with a soft, tinny ring, and the scent of warm bread rolled over Marley and Damien as they stepped inside. Morning sun slanted across the counters, catching on jars of jam and rows of golden loaves. The place was already busy: a young mother balancing a toddler on her hip, an older man ordering his usual rye, two teenagers laughing over muffins. Yet beneath the hum of routine, the shop carried something quieter, an oldness Marley couldn't name.

Evelyn had insisted they stop here—"Stories rise where ovens have burned longest," she'd said—and so they came, notebook tucked under Marley's arm. Damien looked skeptical but hadn't protested.

Behind the counter stood Mrs. Ruth Bennett, the owner, flour streaked across her apron. She was a sturdy woman with silver in her braid and the same no-nonsense eyes Marley remembered from town meetings. She rang up the customers briskly, wiped her hands, then glanced toward Marley.

"You're the one always at the archives," she said. It wasn't accusation, but neither was it idle curiosity.

Marley nodded. "And sometimes under the bridge."

Mrs. Ruth Bennett studied her for a beat too long. Then she waved them toward a small table by the window. "Sit. I'll bring coffee."

They obeyed. The table wobbled slightly, worn from years of elbows and sugar spills. Damien set his satchel beside him, already uneasy. Marley opened her notebook, pencil poised.

When Mrs. Ruth Bennett returned, she set down two steaming mugs and lowered herself into the third chair. Her hands clasped together on the table, flour dusting her knuckles. She leaned forward, her voice lowering.

"I can recall my great-grandmother working this bakery. She told us stories—ones you don't share with customers. About a girl named Annabelle."

Marley's pulse quickened. "Annabelle Warren?"

The woman nodded slowly. "A slip of a thing. Nineteen, maybe twenty. Worked deliveries on foot, back when the wagons were too costly for small orders. She carried baskets of bread and flour up and down the streets, no matter the weather. Folks liked her. Said she sang while she walked."

Marley's pencil flew. *Annabelle—delivery girl, bakery, sang as she walked.*

Mrs. Bennett's voice lowered further, as though the ovens themselves might be listening. "One night she left with a basket for the north side. Never came back. Next morning, they found the basket near the covered bridge. Loaves still wrapped, tin of flour dented, but no Annabelle."

The words struck Marley like a bell. She looked up. "The bridge again."

The baker nodded. "Always the bridge."

Damien shifted uncomfortably in his chair. "Stories grow in the telling. Children vanish in storms, and families place them at the nearest landmark. Doesn't mean she was taken by the bridge."

But Mrs. Bennett wasn't finished. She rose, disappeared into the back room, and returned carrying a round flour tin, dented but intact. Its metal was dark with age, its lid scratched with lines that at first seemed accidental. She set it on the table between them.

"This was the tin from Annabelle's basket. My grandmother kept it, though no one liked to touch it."

Marley leaned forward, breath catching. The scratches weren't random. They formed a shape—circular, with branching lines, like roots or veins radiating outward. She flipped through her notebook until she found a copied sigil from Clara's journal. She laid the page beside the tin. The shapes matched.

Her pencil scrawled furiously: *Flour tin = sigil. Same as Clara's notes. Proof of Annabelle's ties to lineage?*

Damien bent closer, his brow furrowed. "I've seen this mark before," he murmured. "In the healer's ledger. Green Healer lineage. They etched symbols into tools, vessels— meant to carry energy through daily use."

Marley's chest tightened. "You're saying Annabelle was part of the lineage."

"I'm saying she might have been touched by it," Damien said, his voice tight. "Delivery girl or not, this mark isn't acci- dent. If she carried it, she was carrying more than bread."

Mrs. Ruth Bennett crossed herself unconsciously. "We were warned never to use that tin. Said it still carried some- thing. I only kept it because I couldn't throw it away."

Marley traced the lines of the sigil with her eyes, shiver- ing. Annabelle wasn't just a vanished girl—she was woven into the same current Clara had studied, the same echo that now pulsed through the bridge. The sigil tied her to something older, something dangerous.

Damien sat back, unease written plain across his face. "If Annabelle was of the lineage, then this isn't only a ghost story. It's a disruption of ancestral work. And meddling with it could be... costly."

Marley closed her notebook, but her voice was firm. "Then it's even more important to finish the story. If Annabelle was silenced because she bore that mark, then we write her name louder."

Mrs. Bennett's eyes darkened, the lamplight catching the flour dust on her skin. "Careful, child. Some names don't like being called back."

The tin sat between them like an omen, its sigil faint but undeniable. Marley could almost feel it humming beneath her fingertips, as though Annabelle herself had etched it into the metal for her to find.

MARLEY LIFTED the flour tin gently, turning it so the light caught the faint grooves of the sigil. The lines shimmered against the dull metal, more deliberate with every shift of her hand. It wasn't just scratches from use; the symmetry was undeniable.

She pulled her pencil from the spiral of her notebook and began sketching. The outer ring, nearly perfect despite age. The spokes radiating inward. The inner knot, twisted like vines or braided rope. With each stroke she compared it to the copied image from Clara's journal. They aligned almost seamlessly.

"It's not random," Marley murmured, her pencil scratching steadily. "It's a sigil. One of the Green Healers'.

Look—Clara drew the same pattern, only hers was beside notes about binding memory into objects."

Damien's hand pressed against the edge of the table. He leaned in, his voice low, measured. "Binding memory. You mean sealing intent into everyday tools. That was the Healer way—hiding power in flour sacks, cooking pots, water jugs. So the work wasn't confined to altars but lived in the rhythm of daily life." His eyes narrowed at the tin. "If Annabelle carried this on her deliveries, then every step she took was carrying their current through town."

Marley's heart quickened. "Maybe that's why she sang while she worked. Not just habit—ritual. Song to weave intent into the bread, into the people she delivered to."

Damien's unease sharpened. He rubbed the bridge of his nose, a habit she recognized when he wrestled with something too large to dismiss. "Marley, do you realize what this means? Annabelle wasn't just a girl who vanished. If she bore the lineage—if she *practiced*—then her disappearance wasn't chance. It was disruption. And what you're doing now, tracing her steps, isn't uncovering harmless stories. It's stirring the ovens cold with ghosts still waiting to rise."

Mrs. Bennett's eyes, dark and grave, fixed on Marley. "He's right about one thing. My grandmother said Annabelle was different. Called her a bringer. Said she carried warmth into homes that had none. Bread tasted sweeter when she delivered it. But when she disappeared, so did that warmth. Ovens burned flat for weeks. Families whispered she had taken the yeast of the town with her."

The words hung heavy. Marley's pencil slowed. "Taken the yeast," she repeated softly, writing it down. "The life that leavens. The breath that makes bread rise. They were speaking of spirit."

The baker leaned closer, her flour-streaked hands knotting together. "Child, don't fool yourself into thinking every spirit wants remembering. Some linger because they were never laid right. You open that door, you may not be the one to close it."

Marley set the tin back down, but her eyes stayed on the sigil. She felt its pull as surely as she had felt the ribbon's weight and the button's engraving. "If Annabelle was silenced, then forgetting her isn't peace—it's injustice. Memory is what she asked for."

Damien straightened, his voice firm. "And what if memory isn't what she asked for? What if she's bound because someone *else's* vow tied her to the bridge? What if uncovering her work only tightens the knot?"

Marley bristled, but before she could reply, Mrs. Ruth Bennett spoke again, her tone sharper than before. "You two speak of Annabelle as though she's waiting for you to rescue her. But what if she waits for something else entirely? My grandmother said the bridge took her on the seventh night, when her song echoed loudest. That wasn't a call for witness —it was a warning. And every year since, people have heard footsteps when ovens cool too fast. Always the bridge. Always the night."

Marley scribbled, her handwriting jagged. *Seventh night again. Sigil. Song. Flour tin as vessel.*

She looked up, determination flashing in her eyes. "Then the pattern is clear. The bridge doesn't just echo voices—it carries rituals forward. Annabelle's work isn't gone. It's been waiting."

Damien's voice dropped, almost a plea. "Waiting to be finished—or waiting to consume whoever dares to touch it?"

The tin gleamed between them, its sigil faint but undeniable. Marley pressed her palm over it, feeling the cool metal against her skin. It felt less like an object than a conduit, a vessel meant to hold breath, memory, song.

Mrs. Bennett recoiled slightly. "Don't touch it too long. It's been cold for a century, but a cold oven can flare hot when stoked. Some fires aren't meant to be relit."

Marley pulled her hand back, but her gaze stayed locked on the tin. She thought of Annabelle carrying it through rain-dark streets, singing as she went, weaving unseen threads into the town's bread. A girl bound by lineage, by vow, by silence.

She wrote a final note across the page: *Annabelle was not only waiting. She was working. And the bridge still carries the song of her labor.*

Damien saw the resolve in her eyes and shook his head slowly. "You're already too deep."

Marley closed the notebook with care, her voice quiet but steady. "Then let's make sure we go deeper with our eyes open."

The bakery's ovens thudded as fresh loaves shifted in the heat. The sound was ordinary, yet it seemed to echo with something older, a heartbeat from Annabelle's vanished steps.

THE BAKERY HAD EMPTIED. The morning rush had thinned to silence, save for the muffled thud of the ovens in back and the faint scratch of Mrs. Ruth Bennett wiping flour from the counter. The flour tin remained on the table between Marley and Damien, its etched sigil faint but undeniable, like an eye that refused to blink.

Damien leaned forward, his voice pitched low, taut as a string about to snap. "Marley, listen to me. If Annabelle was tied to the Green Healers, this changes everything. Their lineage wasn't just about herbs and blessings. They worked with memory, with binding. Every object was both vessel and vow. And vows... vows never die easily."

Marley met his gaze without flinching. "Then Annabelle's disappearance wasn't just a tragedy. It was an interruption of purpose. If she carried this sigil, if she sang her work into the town, then silencing her wasn't fate—it was erasure. And the echoes we're finding are her pushing back against that silence."

Damien's hand pressed hard against the table. "Or it's the lineage itself, demanding payment for what was broken. Annabelle might not be calling for witness at all. She might be bound by someone else's oath, someone else's ritual unfinished. If you keep dragging her name forward, you may be stepping into the very vow that drowned her."

The words struck like cold water, but Marley didn't retreat. She opened her notebook again, flipping back to the census record, the diary fragments, the sketch of the button's initials. Her fingers trembled as she laid each page beside the tin. "You keep speaking of danger, of vows unfinished. But look at this. Every thread points to Annabelle. The bridge, the diary, the ribbon, the button, the melody, and now this sigil. They're not random. They're converging. And if they're converging, then it means Annabelle *wanted* to be remembered. She left the pattern for us to follow."

Damien's eyes darkened. "You speak as though she chose it. As though she wanted to be bound. But what if she didn't? What if every token you clutch was left not as invitation but as shackle? The Green Healers weren't naive—they knew memory could be a cage. They etched marks like these to trap what should not be loosed."

Mrs. Ruth Bennett's voice cut across their rising tension. She stood with her hands braced against the table, her flour-streaked apron dusting the air with each motion. "Enough. You two argue as though truth is yours to bend. But truth has weight, and Annabelle's truth was heavy even in my grandmother's telling. She said the girl carried bread like it was sacrament, but the town whispered of more—of healing, of blessings that clung to crust and crumb. And when she vanished, people said it was the bridge's hunger that took her, not God's will. The Green Healers' work was powerful, but power draws teeth as surely as sugar draws flies."

Marley's throat tightened, but she forced the words out. "Then that's why we have to write it. To free her from being only a whisper, a caution, a ghost. If Annabelle's story is bound in these objects, then recording it gives her voice again."

Mrs. Bennett shook her head, her braid swaying. "Or it gives the bridge her voice again. And that voice is not one you want in your ear when the mist thickens."

Damien seized on her warning. "You see? Even her own bloodline tells you. The ovens went flat when Annabelle vanished. Families whispered she took the yeast of the town with her. That wasn't absence—that was curse. Something broke when she disappeared, and I will not let you carry that break into us."

Marley looked at him, her chest aching at the fear in his voice. "You can't protect me by silencing her. That's what was done before, and it left her lost. We're not repeating that. If it breaks something, then maybe it breaks the silence. Maybe that's the cost."

Mrs. Ruth Bennett's eyes narrowed. "Child, costs don't pay themselves. If you light a cold oven, you'd better be ready for what rises. Some loaves come out burned black."

The weight of her words pressed into the room like a

third presence, thick and undeniable. The tin seemed to hum faintly under Marley's palm, as though echoing the warning—or agreeing with her resolve.

Damien pushed back his chair abruptly, the scrape loud in the quiet shop. His voice shook, stripped of its usual measured calm. "Marley, I've lost one woman I loved to the bridge. I won't stand by while it takes another. If you keep pulling Annabelle into light, I may not be able to follow you there."

The statement hit her harder than she expected, but she refused to yield. Her voice steadied, quiet but firm. "Then don't follow me out of fear. Walk with me because Annabelle's story deserves witness. If you can't, I'll write it alone."

Silence fell, broken only by the low hiss of the ovens.

Mrs. Bennett gathered the tin back into her arms, cradling it like something fragile yet volatile. She glanced from Damien to Marley, her voice final. "You've both heard enough. If you keep stirring the ghosts, don't say you weren't warned. Annabelle's name is older than your notebooks, older than your griefs. Be careful, or it will bind you both before you know you've spoken the vow."

With that, she turned and carried the tin into the back room, leaving them with the smell of bread rising and the echo of her warning.

Marley stared after her, notebook clutched to her chest, heart hammering. Damien stood stiff, his breath uneven, torn between fear and love.

Neither spoke. But between them, Annabelle's presence pressed heavier than ever, as though she had been sitting at the table all along.

16

BRIDGE DREAM #2

Rain fell in silver sheets across the bridge, the kind of rain that blurred sky and earth into one endless gray. Marley stood at the edge of the planks, the boards slick beneath her bare feet. She knew it was a dream even as she breathed the cold air, but the dream had a density to it, as if each drop carried weight.

Callum Marwick appeared first. He stepped from the shadows at the far end, his dark coat plastered to his body, hair soaked against his brow. His face was young—sharper in its lines than the portraits Marley had pieced together from census records, but alive, vivid. He walked with purpose, one hand clutching a folded sheet of paper, the other reaching outward as though toward someone unseen.

His lips moved, but the roar of rain smothered the sound. Then the words sharpened, cutting through the storm as if the bridge itself carried them to her.

"I vow before heaven and earth—Annabelle, my heart is yours."

The words rang against the beams. He lifted the paper

higher, voice breaking. "I wrote the vow to seal it. To give you proof when all else fails."

From the misted middle of the bridge, Annabelle emerged. She wore the pale green gown Marley had seen before, its hem heavy with water, clinging to her ankles. Her bare feet left no trace on the planks. Her arms reached toward Callum, trembling with urgency.

"Come to me," she cried. Her voice was wind, desperate and fierce. "Callum, the vow is ours. The bridge cannot break it."

He surged forward, rain hammering his shoulders, but just before he reached the midpoint his body jolted as if against an invisible wall. He stumbled back, chest heaving. He tried again, running this time, his hand outstretched— but the air itself resisted him, an unseen barrier forcing him away. His palms pressed flat against nothingness.

"I can't," he choked, his forehead dropping against the barrier though Marley saw only mist. "Something holds me."

Annabelle's arms stretched wider, her eyes brimming with grief. "It is only fear. Push through, Callum. Push through."

But his body shook with the force of resistance. His paper vow fell from his hand, whipped away by the storm, vanishing into the river below. He cried out as though part of himself had been torn.

Marley wanted to scream, to run forward, but she remained rooted at the edge, her throat sealed by the dream.

Callum's voice broke again, the rain mingling with his tears. "I would cross, Annabelle. I swear it. But something— someone—won't let me."

Annabelle collapsed to her knees on the planks, hands

reaching, face twisted with anguish. "Then I will wait until the seventh night. I will wait until the vow breaks or binds."

The storm howled louder. The planks beneath Marley trembled. Callum pounded the invisible barrier, his knuckles raw and bloody, but it did not yield. Annabelle's wail pierced the rain, a sound so deep Marley felt it in her chest.

And then they both turned—not toward each other, but toward her.

For a breathless instant, their eyes locked on Marley. Annabelle's gaze burned with pleading, Callum's with despair. Their voices, though torn by storm, joined in unison:

"Write what we cannot."

The world fractured.

Marley jolted awake in her bed, her body wracked with sobs. Her pillow was damp beneath her cheek, and her chest ached as if she had been the one pounding against invisible walls. Her hand clutched something crumpled and wet. She opened her fist slowly, trembling.

It was a page—torn from Clara's journal. The ink was smeared, the edges ragged, as if ripped in haste. She didn't remember tearing it. She didn't remember opening the journal at all.

She spread it flat on the blanket. The words blurred, half-washed away by water. But she could make out fragments: *seventh night... vow... bridge will not yield.*

Her sobs quieted into shallow breaths. She pressed the page to her chest, tears slipping down her face.

She whispered into the dark, her voice breaking: "Annabelle. Callum. I saw you."

The rain outside her window had stopped. But the

sound of it still pounded in her ears, echoing like a vow too heavy to silence.

MARLEY SAT UPRIGHT in her bed for nearly an hour, the torn journal page spread across her knees like a fragile relic. Her breath came shallow, each inhalation pulling the damp ink's scent deeper into her chest. She traced the words over and over with her fingertip: *seventh night... vow... bridge will not yield.* The rest blurred into water stains, as though the dream's rain had seeped into the waking world.

She didn't remember tearing the page, but the jagged edge told the truth of her hand. The realization unsettled her more than the vision itself. The bridge was no longer just giving her glimpses—it was *using* her body, her actions, to draw out its testimony.

By dawn, she couldn't hold the weight of it alone. She found Damien in the kitchen, already awake, his shoulders tense as he stood over a steaming kettle. He turned as she entered, his face softening slightly but never losing its shadow of caution.

"You didn't sleep," he said.

"No." She held the page out between them. Her hand shook. "I dreamed again. Callum was there. Annabelle too. And..." She swallowed, trying to force the words past the knot in her throat. "I woke with this in my hand."

Damien set the kettle aside, drying his hands slowly before taking the paper. He studied the torn edges first, then the blurred ink. His jaw tightened as he read.

"The seventh night," he murmured. "Always the seventh. And the vow." He looked at her sharply. "Tell me everything."

Marley recounted the dream in halting detail—the rain,

the vows shouted into the storm, Annabelle's arms outstretched, Callum's desperate pounding against the invisible barrier. As she spoke, her voice broke, but she forced herself through, describing how both had turned to her, their plea echoing: *Write what we cannot.*

Damien listened without interruption, though his hands trembled slightly as he held the page. When she finished, he exhaled through his nose, setting the paper gently on the table.

"Marley," he said, his tone grave, "this isn't just dream residue. It's transference. The bridge is drawing you deeper. You didn't just see their vow—you enacted it. Your hand tore this page, your body carried its mark into waking. That's more than vision. That's possession."

She bristled, hugging her arms around herself. "Or it's proof that Annabelle and Callum are giving me their words. I asked for evidence, Damien. This is it. Their vow is unfinished, and I've been chosen to record it."

"Chosen?" His voice rose, sharp with alarm. "That's the language Jackie used before the bridge swallowed her. She said she was chosen to finish the story, chosen to carry the vow forward. And it killed her, Marley."

His words sliced deep, but she shook her head, refusing to yield. "This isn't Jackie's story. It's Annabelle's. And I can't ignore what they gave me. Callum couldn't cross. Something held him back. That means the vow broke—or was broken. And Annabelle has been waiting ever since."

Damien's face was pale, haunted. He pressed his palms to the table, leaning close. "And if you step into their vow, what if you become the bridge's answer to that broken bond? What if it isn't Annabelle who waits for you, but the vow itself, hungry to claim another witness?"

Marley clutched the page, pulling it to her chest. "Then

let it claim me as witness. I won't let silence bury them again. I saw their eyes, Damien. They looked at me as if I was the only one left who could carry them forward. I can't turn away from that."

He dragged a hand through his hair, his composure fraying. "You talk like it's duty. But duty to whom? To two lovers who may have been bound in ritual neither of them chose? To a bridge that feeds on vows left undone? Or to yourself—because you can't let go of the idea that you were meant to solve what no one else could?"

His words stung, but she held steady. "Maybe it's all of those. Maybe it doesn't matter why. What matters is that Annabelle's arms are still reaching, Callum's vow still echoes, and no one else has listened. I *will*."

The kettle whistled, shrill and sudden. Damien snatched it off the flame, pouring water into two mugs as if the motion might steady him. His hands shook as he slid one mug toward her.

"Drink," he said. "And promise me this—you'll at least record everything. Don't trust memory alone. Don't let the bridge keep pieces that you can't put back together."

Marley nodded, though her resolve didn't waver. She opened her notebook and carefully taped the torn page into its center. Across the margin she wrote in bold strokes: *Dream #2. Callum vows in storm. Annabelle waits. Invisible barrier. Seventh night. Page torn by my hand.*

She pressed her palm flat against the page, feeling the ridges of ink beneath her skin. It was more than memory now. It was testimony, fixed in her own script.

Damien sat across from her, his mug untouched. His eyes were fixed on her notebook, his silence heavy. Finally he spoke, his voice low.

"I'm terrified you're writing yourself into their vow."

Marley looked up, meeting his gaze. Her cheeks were still wet from earlier tears, but her voice was steady. "Then let the record show that too."

The morning light spilled through the window, pale and cold. The torn page fluttered faintly as though stirred by an unseen breath. Marley pressed it flat again, her heart pounding.

She had carried Annabelle's ribbon, Callum's initials, the melody in Royce's horn. Now she carried their vow, torn from her aunt's journal without her conscious will. Each piece deepened the pattern. Each piece bound her closer.

And somewhere in the mist over the bridge, Annabelle and Callum still waited—unable to finish what had begun.

THE JOURNAL PAGE lay spread open on the kitchen table, taped into Marley's notebook, its ink-stained fragments looking more like wounds than words. The silence between her and Damien thickened until it felt like a third presence in the room. Marley tried to steady her breathing, but the memory of Annabelle's wail and Callum's desperate pounding returned with such force that her chest ached.

Her grief broke loose. Tears ran hot down her cheeks, unbidden, as she pressed her forehead into her hands. "Damien, I could feel them. Not just see, not just hear— their pain poured into me like I was standing there with them. Annabelle reaching, Callum swearing, and both of them turning to me like I was their last chance. How am I supposed to ignore that?"

Damien circled the table and crouched in front of her, his hands on her knees. His voice was rough, more plea than argument. "Marley, listen to yourself. That's not empathy— it's entanglement. The bridge is wrapping itself around you, pulling you into vows that aren't yours. It doesn't matter how much compassion you have, it doesn't matter how much you ache for them—you don't belong to their story."

She shook her head violently, her sobs making her words uneven. "But maybe I do. Maybe I've been drawn here, now, because no one else can bear it. My aunt heard pieces, Clara tried to record them, but she never finished. I'm finishing what she couldn't. What Annabelle and Callum couldn't."

Damien gripped her knees tighter, as if trying to anchor her. "And what if finishing it means losing yourself? Jackie believed the same thing—you know she did. She thought she was chosen, that she was meant to finish a story no one else could. And she never came back from it. She lost herself, Marley. I lost her. I can't lose you too."

Her tears blurred his face, but she didn't look away. "This isn't about being chosen. It's about responsibility. If Annabelle's voice keeps finding me, if Callum's vow literally tears itself into my hands, then refusing to record it is betrayal. What's more dangerous—bearing witness or letting the silence devour them again?"

Damien dropped his gaze, his shoulders sagging with exhaustion. "You think bearing witness is harmless. But what if writing it down *is the act* that seals you into their vow? Words aren't neutral. Vows are forged in words. You put pen to paper, you might be forging your own bond to them."

The truth of his fear hit her, but grief outweighed hesitation. She pushed his hands away gently and lifted the notebook. The torn page stared back at her like an unfinished sentence demanding completion.

Her voice steadied, even through tears. "Then let it bind me. If the cost of silence is Annabelle's eternal waiting, if the cost of fear is Callum's vow dissolving into the river, then I would rather risk myself than leave them unheard."

Damien rose, pacing to the far side of the room. His fists clenched and unclenched, his breath uneven. "Marley…" He broke off, turned, and his face looked raw. "I don't know if I can walk this with you. Every step you take toward the bridge, every word you write—it feels like standing at Jackie's grave again. I can't go through losing another woman I—"

He stopped himself, the unspoken word hanging heavy in the air.

Marley's sobs softened into tremors. She stood slowly, clutching the notebook to her chest, her voice low but clear. "Then don't walk with me out of fear. Walk with me because you know it's the only way forward. Because silence isn't safety, Damien—it's surrender."

His eyes glistened, though he blinked the tears back. He pressed his palm against the wall, as if bracing himself against a weight too heavy to name. "You terrify me," he whispered.

She stepped closer, until her breath brushed his shoulder. "And yet you're still here."

The torn page crackled faintly as if stirred by unseen wind. Marley opened the notebook again, took her pen, and beneath the blurred fragments she wrote in bold strokes:

Dream #2, testimony complete: Callum vows to Annabelle in rain, unable to cross. Invisible barrier holds him. Annabelle waits, arms outstretched. Seventh night binds their fate. Both command: Write what we cannot.

The act steadied her, even as it shook Damien. He turned, his jaw tight, his eyes torn between love and terror.

"Then God help us," he said. "Because you've just bound yourself to them."

Marley closed the notebook, pressing it to her chest. Her tears still fell, but her voice was resolute. "No, Damien. I've freed them to speak."

Outside, the morning sun broke through low clouds, streaking across the mist that lingered over the river. For a moment the light glinted like silver on water, and Marley felt the bridge watching, waiting, carrying her words into its endless echo.

17

THE CAFÉ OWNER'S STORY

Evelyn kept the café lights low on storm days— habit or superstition, Marley couldn't tell. The afternoon sky had gone the color of bruised slate, and the windows wore a slick of rain that blurred Main Street to a watercolor of umbrellas and parked trucks. Inside, the place was quieter than usual. The espresso machine exhaled in slow, weary breaths. A single table of high school kids argued over a chessboard in stage whispers, and a couple in raincoats huddled over scones as if sharing a secret.

Evelyn waved Marley and Damien toward the far corner banquette—Evelyn's corner, where a crossbeam dipped low and the wallpaper's fern pattern had been scrubbed thin by years of elbows. Marley slid into the seat with her notebook already open, the ribbon and button tucked in their usual pocket, the torn page from Clara's journal pressed between leaves. Damien sat opposite, rain freckling his glasses, his jaw set in that quiet, wary way Marley now understood as love precariously balanced against fear.

Evelyn set down three mugs without asking what they

wanted. The coffee was darker than usual, spiced with something Marley couldn't place. "Warmer," Evelyn said, as if that explained it. She wiped her hands on her apron, glanced toward the door to be sure no one else was coming in, and then hooked a chair with her foot and sat facing them like a woman readying herself to carry a weight.

"You asked before," Evelyn said, eyes on Marley. "About the bridge bride. About what's told and what's kept."

Marley held her pencil still over the page. "I did."

Evelyn's gaze shifted to Damien and back, measuring the room around her the way a sailor measures wind. "I wasn't sure I'd answer. Some names are louder when they're spoken. But storms press on old places. They bring up silt." She took her glasses from her apron pocket, set them on, and leaned in. "This is what my great-aunt told me. I was a child. She made me promise to keep the bones of it straight."

The café hummed—a spoon clink, a milk steamer's sigh —but all of it felt a layer distant as Evelyn began.

"Her name was Annabelle Warren. She worked in town. You know some of that." Evelyn's mouth softened. "She had a voice on her, honey-sweet with a rasp like she'd laughed too much as a girl. Delivered bread from Bennett's, carried flour tins under her arm, sang to babies she passed in doorways. Folks said you could taste it in the loaves the days she'd done the rounds."

Marley's pencil moved: *Annabelle—sang, deliveries, warmth carried.*

Evelyn's gaze drifted toward the windows, where the rain beat faster. "The night I'm telling you about was a thunder night, the kind that drops the whole sky on your head. The river ran high and hard. People stayed in. But the chapel light burned—Reverend Snell was in a temper about the

Marwick boy and the bridge, said he'd pray the town back into sense if it broke his knees to do it." A thin smile. "Prayers don't much like being ordered, but men try anyway."

"Callum," Marley said quietly.

Evelyn tipped her chin. "Mm. Callum. My aunt said rumor had run hot for weeks—that Annabelle waited nights on that bridge and Callum wouldn't come. Some said his family had other plans for him. Some said he'd promised to meet her and didn't. Some said the bridge itself laid a hand on men who didn't keep clean company with their vows." Evelyn shrugged, palms up. "I won't tell what I can't know. I'll tell what the bells know."

Damien's eyes flickered—there it was again, the old muscle twitch of disbelief and desire to believe wrestling in his face. He folded his hands on the table, knuckles pale.

Evelyn took a slow drink and set her mug down with care, as if not to startle the story. "Annabelle went to the chapel that night. Not to pray," she added, a ghost of humor returning. "She'd done enough of that on the bridge. She went to the bell. My aunt said her own mother—my great-grandmother—was bringing broth to a sick neighbor on the lane and saw the chapel door stand open, light pouring across the gravel, rain hammering the steps. And over it all —clear as a heartbeat—the smallest sound of a rope moving through a hand."

Marley's pencil stilled. She could see it: the door blown wide, the nave smelling of wet wood and wax, the bell rope hanging like a question from the tower, its end knotted with old, polished oil.

"Annabelle had climbed the belfry before the storm set its teeth," Evelyn said. "Most girls wouldn't, not in a dress, not with thunder threatening to split you. But Annabelle—

Annabelle had business. She'd found the lever no man would give her." Evelyn's eyes shone now, not with tears but with that bright glint of a woman telling a true thing that still makes her breath hitch. "She took the rope in both hands and rang that bell like a vow. Not a funeral toll. Not a Sunday call. A naming."

The air around the banquette seemed to change pressure. Even the chess players at the other table glanced over, distracted without knowing why.

"How many times?" Marley asked, voice low.

"Seven by my aunt's count," Evelyn said. "Seven clean strikes that cut through rain and wood like brass learns to do. Some said she matched the lantern's sweep. Some said she drove the storm off its mark. But what stuck was this: on the seventh ring, lightning laced the sky like a net." Evelyn's fingers drew a tremor through the air. "The bell swung back and did not come down again."

Damien swallowed audibly. "What do you mean 'did not'?"

"I mean," Evelyn said, "the rope slackened as if hands had let go. The sound died in mid-air. And from that night to this one, the bell of St. Bartholomew's hasn't answered a pull."

Marley felt the gooseflesh lift along her arms. She saw Annabelle in the dream of it—hands braced, muscles humming, mouth set around a name. She heard the seventh note cut the air. And then that rope, suddenly light. That silence, heavy as water.

"Where was she?" Damien asked, too quickly, as if speed could keep meaning from catching up.

Evelyn's mouth flattened. "Gone. The belfry was empty when Hicks the sexton stumbled up, swearing over the smoke smell and the crack of lightning. No scorched beam.

No burned rope. No girl. My aunt said the men combed the yard with lanterns until their arms shook, the river path until their boots sucked mud, and the bridge until sunrise made them look like ghosts on their own feet. They found a scuff in tar, heel and half a toe near midspan, same spot the keeper once marked with pencil. They found the ribbon you already know about, or one sister to it—caught under a third beam nail. They did not find Annabelle."

Silence. Even the espresso machine seemed to hold its steam.

Marley knew she should ask careful questions now, librarian-precise: who told whom, what year, what diary note corroborated—but the picture had her throat caught. "Evelyn," she managed, "why ring the bell?"

Evelyn's smile was tender and dangerous. "Because bells are the oldest text most towns can read. Because a vow is a bell if you strike it hard enough. Because if a man won't cross to you and a bridge won't carry the weight of what you're owed, you pull a rope the whole valley must hear."

Marley wrote: *Bell as vow. Seven rings. Rope slack. Bell silent since.*

Damien leaned back, pinched the bridge of his nose, and looked up at the café's tin ceiling as if answers might be stamped there. "The year?" he asked.

"Eighteen eighty-seven," Evelyn said. "A late summer storm that felt like a season changing its mind. Some say it was Autumn's first muscle. Some say it's when Brookwood learned what it would and wouldn't speak aloud."

"Your great-aunt was sure," Damien said, dry with effort; he needed one place to set his skepticism down and Evelyn had left him few.

Evelyn tipped her head. "As sure as women get when men don't write it down for them."

The words landed in Marley's bones. She looked at Damien and saw him register it, too—the old truth in Evelyn's tone, that bent the line between superstition and record into a circle that only witness could close.

Evelyn reached into her apron and came up with a folded napkin. She smoothed it flat with the palm of her hand, then drew a quick circle with the tip of a pencil, seven short lines like rays. "My aunt would trace this on my palm when thunder rolled," she said. "Said seven nights make a shape, and the seventh night makes a door. She told me, 'If you hear a bell that isn't ringing, close your windows and be still.'" Evelyn slid the napkin across the table. "I think you're past the point of closing windows."

Marley stared at the little sun of lines, the circle that refused to be only a circle. She wrote the shape into her notebook beside the words *seventh night* until the page looked like a field of small suns and small doors.

"What happened after?" she asked, lifting her eyes. "To the town? To the families?"

Evelyn sat back, a woman who had carried her portion of telling and now expected them to carry theirs. "People did what they always do. They cooked. They married. They died. They made stories where there weren't records and records where they feared stories. They stopped ringing the bell. And when someone went missing near the bridge—a farmhand, a mother who'd just lost a child, a boy dared too far by other boys—folks would say the night had seven in it."

Damien's mouth opened and closed, a fish in air. The rational part of him pushed up—Marley could see it—and then slowed back, not vanquished but winded. "I'll check the vestry log," he said finally, rough. "And the town ledger. If the bell went quiet in '87, there'll be complaint letters, repair requests, donations withheld, sermons about it. Men get tidy when silence starts to cost."

A flare of relief flickered through Marley. Evelyn had given them the story; Damien would go fetch the paper bones of it. Between them, maybe the truth would stop being only fog.

Evelyn's attention softened. She reached across and covered Marley's hand for a heartbeat. "You keep good notes," she said. "That much I trust. Keep them kinder than the town kept Annabelle."

Marley squeezed back, hard. "We will."

The chess players knocked over a knight and laughed with embarrassed relief; someone opened the door and let the rain's fresh, metallic scent in with the draft. Evelyn stood, collecting empty mugs, putting her glasses away as if she were sheathing a knife. She turned at the last moment, one more thing to lay on the table.

"My aunt used to say the bridge remembers the weight of a woman's waiting longer than it remembers the steps of the man who made her wait," she said, voice gone quiet. "If the bell won't ring, you find other ways to make noise. But noise draws lightning."

She left them with the weather and their pages. Damien had already pulled his phone from his coat to type a note— "parish minutes, 1887"—and Marley, hand steady now, wrote Evelyn's last sentence under everything else and boxed it in ink: *Noise draws lightning.*

She underlined *seventh* again, hard enough to etch the paper.

Outside, thunder stitched itself thinly through the rain, like a seam being tested. Inside, the café's low lights held. And in the margin beneath the napkin sun, Marley added the question that had tightened in her since Evelyn spoke: *If a bell is a vow, what does a silence become?*

She didn't expect the bridge to answer out loud. But she had learned—by ribbon, by button, by song—that it would answer somehow.

DAMIEN DID NOT WAIT. By the time they left Evelyn's café, his mind was already turning like the cogs of one of the old mills upriver. Marley could see it in his stride—the sharp, clipped pace, the way his jaw clenched whenever thunder rattled through the valley. He was a man caught between disbelief and the ache to prove something false with his own hands.

They cut across Main Street beneath the storm. The rain had softened into a steady curtain, soaking the cobblestones and muting the town's colors to shades of gray. The chapel loomed ahead, its steeple stark against the turbulent sky, the weather vane spinning in erratic jerks.

Inside, the nave smelled of wet stone and extinguished candles. Damien moved straight to the side aisle, where a narrow door opened to the vestry. Marley followed, her notebook clutched close, the napkin Evelyn had sketched still folded between its pages.

The vestry was cramped: shelves sagging with hymnals, ledgers, and brass candlesticks tarnished with neglect. Damien dragged a stool under the highest shelf and pulled down a stack of records, bound in cracked leather. Dust plumed around him.

"Here," he said, flipping open the cover of one ledger, his voice clipped with purpose. "Parish accounts, 1880s."

Marley perched on the arm of a chair, her pencil poised. Damien's fingers traced down the neat columns of ink, line after line of donations and expenditures. And then his hand stilled.

"August 1887," he read aloud. His voice had shifted—it carried the weight of something undeniable. "'Repair of east guttering—five dollars. Purchase of linens—two dollars. Note: the bell rope frayed, replace immediately.'"

He looked up at her, his eyes sharp. "They noted it. The rope was damaged."

Her breath caught. "The night Evelyn said Annabelle climbed it."

He turned the page with care, his hands trembling despite his steady tone. The next month's entries rolled on—candles, hymnals, firewood. But the line for bell maintenance remained empty.

Damien pressed his lips together, flipped another page, then another. He read quickly now, skimming down the years. "No mention. Not in '88, '89, or '90. Nothing for repairs, nothing for ringing. Look—" He jabbed at a line from 1891. "'Use of horn in place of bell for wedding procession.' They stopped using it. Entirely."

Marley's heart hammered. "So Evelyn's story was right. The bell has been silent since that night."

Damien closed the ledger, his fingers lingering on its worn cover. "Silent by choice," he said grimly. "The sexton could have repaired the rope. They chose not to."

She leaned forward. "Because it wasn't just a rope breaking. It was Annabelle's disappearance."

Damien's silence was answer enough.

They carried the ledgers to a long oak table. Rain tapped at the stained-glass windows overhead, streaking the colors into blurred shadows across the wood. Damien opened another book, older, this one a bound collection of vestry minutes. The ink was faded, but his eyes moved with the precision of a man trained to pull meaning from fragments.

"Here," he whispered. "'Meeting of the vestry, September 1887. Reverend Snell opened with prayer. Discussion: the bell of St. Bartholomew's no longer sounds. Sexton Hicks reports rope intact yet clapper unresponsive. Multiple attempts unsuccessful. Reverend advises suspension of bell use until matter discerned.'"

Marley's pencil nearly tore through the page of her notebook. *Bell intact—clapper unresponsive. No ring since August storm. Suspension ordered.*

Damien's face tightened. "It doesn't make sense. A bell doesn't just... stop. Not unless the clapper is removed, or the frame shifts. But here they say the clapper wouldn't strike. As if the air itself swallowed it."

He turned another page, flipping through to December of the same year. "'Parishioner complaints regarding absence of bell at Advent. Reverend insists silence to remain until further guidance.'"

His hand dropped. He sat back hard against the chair, staring at the stained glass. "They kept it silent deliberately. For years."

Marley whispered, "Because Annabelle rang it last."

Neither spoke for a long moment. Rain filled the silence. Marley looked down at her notes—the sketches of Evelyn's sun with seven rays, the torn journal page with its vow, the sigil etched into a flour tin—and saw them aligning. The bridge, the bell, the vow. Always sevens, always silence where sound should be.

Damien finally pushed the ledger away, his voice low, rough with conflict. "Marley, I can't deny it anymore. Evelyn's story matches the records. The bell hasn't rung since 1887.

But that means... that means Annabelle's disappearance wasn't just town gossip. The church itself folded silence over it. They documented the absence but never the cause."

Marley's grief and resolve flared together. "Then we have to. We can't let her vanish twice—once from the bridge, and once from the record."

He met her eyes, fear dark in his own. "And if writing it down doesn't free her, but binds you instead?"

Marley pressed her palm flat over the notebook, steadying her hand. "Then let it bind me long enough to speak her name."

Thunder rolled overhead, long and low, as though the sky itself agreed—or warned.

THEY SPREAD the books the way people spread maps before choosing a dangerous road—slowly, with a care that masqueraded as caution but was really appetite. Rain smeared color down the stained glass; the vestry smelled like wet wool and ink. Damien drew the long oak table under the lamp and set the parish ledgers to one side, the vestry minutes to the other. From a lower shelf he hauled up the *Harbor Master's Weather Register, 1879–1913* and a slim, hand-copied *Lighthouse Keeper's Log: Excerpts.*

"Dates," he said, not looking at Marley. "If there's a pattern, it's going to sit right where men refuse to see it—in the dates."

Marley opened her notebook to a clean spread and ruled six columns: *Name / Date / Weather / Emotion-Trigger / Evidence / Notes (7th?)* The act steadied her hands. She wrote *Annabelle Warren* in the first row, the pencil's point digging a little deeper into the paper at the last letter of the surname, as if underlining could keep a woman from slipping.

"August 1887," Damien said. He had the vestry minutes open, one finger pressed to the line about the bell's suspension. "Thunderstorm."

Marley recorded it. "Trigger?"

He hesitated, and she answered for both of them. "Vow." She added *bell rung; seventh peal; chapel rope slack; bell silent after*. In the last column she wrote *seventh—yes*.

Damien reached for the bridge keeper's diary they'd been conserving—today wrapped in muslin and interleaved with blotters, but one copied page free on the table. He skimmed the faint lines they'd traced with overlays. "Two nights prior he wrote *seventh coming* and *Annabelle at midbeam, letter in hand*. And the morning before that: *board groaned—twice*."

Marley marked the notes, then drew a small sun with seven short rays in the margin—the shape Evelyn's great-aunt traced for storms.

"Next," she said.

Damien pulled the deaths-and-missings ledger from the town clerk's shelf—a practical, brutal book that recorded both what ended and what never turned up again. He turned pages with the efficiency of a man who feared what he would find and couldn't afford the luxury of slow dread.

"October 1894," he said finally. "Jacob Dunn. Farmhand. *Disappeared at dawn; last seen near river path after an altercation at Barnaby's*." He checked the weather register. "Barometer fell to 29.3. 'Sheets of rain; standing water on Main.'" He flipped the *Herald* bound volume to that week and found the line in police notices: *Traces discovered: scrap of jacket lining, wet as if pulled; footprints along path leading to water, then none*. His jaw shifted. "And here"—he tapped the bridge keeper's thin hand—"*seventh night counted from first frost. Lantern south. No crossing.*"

Marley wrote, adding in the *Emotion-Trigger* column: *rage; fight over broken engagement.* The word *seventh* planted itself again in her notes like a stake.

They built the table in that careful, relentless way the two of them had learned: he would pull documents, she would cross-check and fix the bones into the page. Names bloomed across the left-hand column with the implacable calm of a roll call, each accompanied by the weather's voice and some human spark that could be mistaken for coincidence until you had six, then nine of them.

"June 1903," Damien read, softer. "Rachel Henshaw. Widow. Lost her daughter, Lena, on Thursday. *Seen walking at night with child's shawl.* Weather: *slow rain, river high; fog.* Keeper's note—" He swallowed. "*She asked if wood remembers weight. I told her every board bears a print.*"

"Emotion: grief," Marley said, and wrote it, the pencil's pressure leaving the faint bruise of graphite beneath the page. In *Evidence* she added: *shawl found snagged at third beam nail; footprints to water; stop.* In *Notes: seventh—yes (counted from death).*

"September 1921," Damien went on. "Rebecca Proctor. Sweetheart of Aaron Wright, lost in France. *Letter delivered that he will not come home alive.* That night—storm. The lighthouse log—" He flipped the slim book and found the crabbed hand. "'Double sweep due to maintenance anomaly; cadence irregular'." He glanced at Marley. "Two flashes —your horn's rhythm."

Marley wrote *grief + vow unkept (letter)*, then added *ring discovered in silt below north mouth*—the note had come from a church ladies' minutes in which the ring was described anonymously and then never spoken of again. In *Notes: seventh—implied (tallies in margin).*

They kept going, the rain stitching steady on the glass.

"May 1955," Damien said, his voice gone flat to save itself. "Michael Arnett. Sixteen. *Dared to walk the top rail.* Weather clear at dusk; sudden squall at ten. Hazard note in the keeper's hand: *Boys taunting. Lady on bridge seen by two at long distance.*"

Marley wrote *pride / fear (peer dare)*, then paused with the pencil above *Evidence.* "Anything?"

Damien shook his head. "Just this. His mother testified she heard a bell 'that wasn't ringing.' The minutes record it as 'hysteria'." He pushed the book away as if it had dirtied his hands.

Marley wrote that phrase exactly: *bell that wasn't ringing.* She boxed it.

"July 1969," Damien said. "Cora Vale. Wedding the next day. Storm at midnight. Disappearance near the bridge." His mouth tightened. "The lighthouse: 'Fog thick; light's lens halos; rotation sticks and frees—pattern stutters.'"

Marley wrote *vow—anticipation / fear (eve); veil ribbon found; third beam again.* Then under *Notes: seventh (counted from banns?)* She looked over her column, at how often *seventh* had settled there like an old coin gathering thumb grease.

The names marched closer to them. Marley didn't ask him to read the last one; he did without her prodding, his voice the lowest she'd heard it.

"October 2006," he said. "Jackie Hawthorne." He didn't look at her. "Storm. Barometer low. Fog. Lighthouse normal." His mouth pressed. "*Journal entries prior: dreams, voices, ink on hands; candle ritual attempted.*"

Marley's pencil paused above the page. "Emotion?"

He stared at the table, at his knuckles white against the wood. "We'd argued," he said, almost too quiet to hear. "I told her I couldn't follow if she kept collecting pieces. She walked out with her notebook. I... I waited. I thought waiting would keep her safe." He finally looked up, not at Marley but at the empty air above the ledger, as if Jackie's name lived there. "It didn't."

Marley wanted to touch his hand, but the table was a border neither of them could cross just now. She wrote *love / fear / rupture (argument)*. In *Evidence* she set down the single line they had always been careful with: *notebook recovered, last page blank; wax on page edge.* In *Notes* she wrote nothing, because some words are not yours to put in ink for other people.

They sat back. The table of names stared up at them, brutal and orderly. Weather bled across it. So did vows. The column of *Emotion-Trigger* read like the spine of a life: *vow, rage, grief, grief again, pride, fear, love broken.* Under *Notes* the little suns—Evelyn's sevens—shone again and again. It wasn't a pattern that let anyone off the hook. It was the kind that accused.

Damien rubbed his temple. "Men will say coincidence. That grief and storms share a bed in every town, that boys do foolish things near water, that lovers run." He blew out a breath. "But the sevens. The bell. The third beam. The lantern's stutter. It's too much order for chance."

Marley copied the table a second time more neatly, as if a fair hand could bind it to the page as a thing the town would be forced to see. When she finished, she looked at Damien. "It's not just storms," she said. "It's storms and *intensity.* Vows spoken or broken. Emotions that feel like bells. The bridge keeps time not with the clock, but with the heart at its loudest."

He nodded, eyes on the window where the rain came slant again. "Which means..."

"Which means the next seventh night after a vow or rupture is the dangerous one," she finished. She flipped to the page where they'd tallied the bridge keeper's sevens beside weather. "We're three nights from the seventh since the séance. Four since the candle. Two since the jazz." She hesitated and added, softer, "One since my dream."

Damien's chair scraped back. "Then we stay away."

Marley shook her head. "Then I go with my eyes open."

He came around the table as if proximity might change her mind. "You just laid out a list of names that ends with Jackie. You want to set yours under it next?" His voice frayed. "Marley, I can't lose—" He stopped himself the way he always did at that precipice. "I won't watch the bridge write itself on your skin."

She stood, the notebook between her hands like a shield and a prayer book. "Do you think I want to be brave?" she said, not angry—something past that. "Do you think I don't hear Evelyn's warning ring in my head, or feel your fear in my bones? I do. But I also heard them tell me to write what they cannot. And this—" she tapped the table of names "—is writing. Out loud. And if a seventh night is a door, then leaving it closed is not safety. It's complicity."

He flinched as if she'd struck him, then looked, unexpectedly, like a man who had reached the end of the argument he knew how to make. He leaned on the table, breathing as if he'd run. "You're going to go."

"Yes."

"Then I'm going with you." It came out before he could take it back. Fear made the edges of it sharp; love dulled that sharpness a second later. "I will not let you walk into that alone."

They stood like that for a beat—the table between them; the names a demand; the rain a witness. Somewhere above them the bell rope hung in its shaft, the clapper inert in air that remembered the last strike. A small draft found the vestry and made the rope in the corner sway at the gentlest touch. Damien and Marley both looked up. The motion was nothing. It was everything.

"We plan," he said, gathering himself back into a man who trusts process when the heart won't obey. "No candles. No music. We observe. We document. We bring Evelyn's napkin and your notebook and nothing violent. We anchor ourselves to the ordinary."

"Evelyn said noise draws lightning," Marley murmured, glancing at the little suns she had sketched. "We keep our noise on paper."

He managed half a smile that didn't reach his eyes. "On paper," he agreed. Then, quieter: "And if the lighthouse stutters, we leave."

Marley almost promised. She almost said *Yes, I'll go when you say.* Instead she said, "We read what happens, and we don't blink."

He nodded because there was nothing else left to do that wasn't lying. He closed the vestry minutes and capped his pen. Marley closed her notebook and slid it into her satchel. The lamp hummed. The stained glass threw bruised color onto the ledgers and then faded as the cloud thickened.

On their way out, Damien paused in the nave and looked up the length of the sanctuary to the dark mouth of the belfry. "Hundred and thirty-eight years," he said softly. "If she rang it for a vow, maybe she got the silence as the answer."

Marley followed his gaze. "Or the silence is the unanswered part." She touched the pew's smooth back—so many hands over so many Sundays sanding rough wood down. "Either way, the bell and the bridge are keeping the same time."

Outside, the rain had become a sheer veil. They crossed the churchyard, and the river's voice—the one Marley now knew as well as her own—came up through the wet air. At the gate, she stopped and opened her notebook once more and, under the table of names, wrote a single line: *When vows break, water answers. When water answers, the bridge opens its mouth.* She closed the book and slid the pencil behind her ear.

Damien took her elbow, not to steer but to say *I know the risk you're taking and I'm taking it, too.* The tension between them—the ache, the argument, the love—stretched like the span of the bridge itself: it could hold a miracle or a fall, and there was no way to know until they stepped into it.

"Three nights," he said. "We keep to daylight until then."

She nodded. "We try."

They walked into the rain. The lighthouse swept its unseen rhythm beyond the mist. Behind them the bell that would not ring hung in its tower, not sounding—and yet, somehow, in Marley's chest, keeping time.

18

TOWN MEETING AND SUSPICION

The town hall smelled like lemon oil and wet wool. Rain had driven half of Brookwood under its roof, and the rest came anyway, because meetings like this were their weather: pressure building along the ridges until thunder had to roll. The historical board had claimed the dais where, in another century, magistrates tried poachers and men who stole rope. Now there were microphones, a plastic pitcher of water with sweating sides, and a banner tacked crookedly on the wall: **BROOKWOOD HISTORICAL SOCIETY—KEEPERS OF THE RECORD.**

Marley sat in the second row with her satchel at her feet, notebook on her knees, the ribbon and the silver button enclosed in muslin and wrapped twice. She had not brought the flour tin. She had considered leaving everything at home, but she knew what these nights were like: facts evaporated in warm rooms when people felt embarrassed by their ghosts. You needed the weight of objects in your lap to remember why you didn't stand up and apologize for caring.

The board filed in—Chairwoman Edith Tuller, with her tidy gray bob and a voice that made people correct their posture; Harold Fenwick in a blazer and three other stalwarts whose names moved through town files like dependable punctuation. The clerk plugged in the little red light on the recorder. A murmur ran through the room, a tide catching on broken shells.

"Thank you for coming," Mrs. Tuller said, gaveling once, not because anyone was rowdy but because the sound was part of the ritual. "We've added a special item to tonight's agenda in response to community concerns." Her gaze slid over the crowd and then, without blinking, landed on Marley. "It pertains to the use of the archives and the handling of sensitive, sometimes painful material."

There it was—the word that towns used when they were afraid: *sensitive*. Marley's pencil found its balance against the paper. She didn't write. She listened.

Lorraine, one of the board members, leaned toward the mic, smile thin. "We understand there's been a great deal of interest, some might say fixation, on certain local legends— the covered bridge, the so-called 'bridge bride,' the bell at St. Bartholomew's." She flicked her eyes to Evelyn, who had taken a seat along the back wall, arms crossed, expression unrepentant. "We admire civic curiosity. But there's a line between scholarship and sensationalism. And frankly, we're hearing that line has been crossed."

A rumble ran through the audience—agreement and discomfort braided together. Someone coughed into a fist. Evelyn's mouth hooked at one corner, but she didn't speak.

Harold Fenwick cleared his throat, leaned in. "We're not saying the young lady has bad intentions." He nodded toward Marley with a paternal benevolence that made Marley's jaw tighten. "But removing artifacts from their contexts—buttons, ribbons—publishing insinuations in that community blog about patterns of disappearances—"

"I've never published anything," Marley said before she could stop herself. Her voice carried farther than she meant it to. Heads turned. She felt heat rise to her face, the kind that came from a thousand small shames finally adding up to boldness. "I've written in my notebook. I've shared with the archivist. I've asked for permission every time I looked at a ledger."

Mrs. Tuller's smile was kind but edged like a paper knife. "Ms. Taylor, you'll have time to speak." She turned back to the board. "We are concerned, as custodians of the record, about the current vogue for—" she searched for the term, found it with relish—"*romanticizing myth.*"

The phrase only needed to be said once and it found its stone to land on. *Romanticizing myth.* Marley watched it, like a thrown thing, arc through the room, turning heads, relaxing shoulders, giving people something tidy to hold instead of the messy ache they all felt whenever thunder rolled and someone didn't come home.

Marley slid her hand into her satchel and touched the muslin-wrapped bundle as if to remind herself (and maybe Annabelle) that she wasn't here to be scolded into smaller shapes. She kept her palm on the fabric and steadied her breath.

Mrs. Tuller went on. "There has been... activity." She looked down at the sheet the clerk had typed for her. "A séance reenactment that got out of hand. Jazz rehearsals being disrupted by... unusual improvisations. A candle ritual in a private home that resulted in certain claims. And the archives—our archives—have seen unprecedented requests for access to vestry minutes, weather logs, and private diaries. We are not opposed to research." She smiled. "We are opposed to superstition parading as scholarship."

A man in the back—one of the commercial fishermen—

said, not quietly, "Storm weeks are storm weeks. Don't need a ghost for that." There were nods, the practical kind. Another voice, older, said, "And what harm, Mrs. Ashcroft, if a girl writes what she sees? We all write our grief somewhere." The room murmured. The fisherman shrugged, already conceding—he'd said his thing; he didn't need to climb a hill he hadn't chosen.

Marley lifted her notebook to the edge of the seat in front of her and wrote in a tight, even hand: *Accusation: romanticizing myth. Response: pattern ≠ romance. Vow ≠ superstition. Record ≠ spectacle.* She underlined each, then forced herself to look up. If she lived only on the page, they would accuse her of that too.

Mrs. Tuller folded her hands. "We appreciate the energy Ms. Taylor has brought to the archives." The word appreciation did not hold warmth. "We have also received complaints from families distressed by rumors traveling faster than facts. We are not a town that thrives on Gothic invention. We are a town that keeps its ledgers balanced."

Evelyn's laugh was soft and shaped like *good luck with that.* Mrs. Tuller ignored it.

Professor Edmund Ashcroft leaned back, laced his fingers over his stomach. "Stories belong in their place," he said. "Church bells ring on Sundays, not on storm nights. Bridges carry wagons and tourists, not—" he waved a hand —"portents. I don't mean to scold. But we've got schoolchildren drawing ladies in veils on their spelling tests." His smile tried to make it a joke. "Let's keep our heads."

Marley pictured the child's drawing from weeks ago— the lady standing on the bridge. She wondered if Arthur had ever looked a child in the eye when they told him something that scared them, and said, *I believe you, and we will be careful.* She doubted it.

"Point of order," Lorraine said, enjoying herself now. "We're not simply airing concerns. We're proposing—" she glanced at Mrs. Tuller for the precise phrasing—"a temporary suspension of Ms. Taylor's independent access to the archives pending review of her methods."

A shift in the room's temperature—shoulders straightening, bodies leaning forward the way they do when someone pulls a chair out from under a person and you don't know yet if they'll catch themselves. Evelyn swore softly. The clerk adjusted his glasses, regretting the meeting already.

Mrs. Tuller nodded, tone smooth. "This is not a censure. It's a pause. Ms. Taylor may, of course, request materials through the board."

Through you, Marley thought. Through the sieve that keeps what makes you uncomfortable from reaching daylight.

She rose before she had decided to. The notebook stayed in her hand like a flag that wasn't for waving but for anchoring. "May I speak now?"

"Two minutes," Mrs. Tuller said.

Marley turned—first to the crowd, because they were the ones she was writing for, then to the dais, because the rules liked to be fed. "I was invited to Brookwood to write," she said. "I've baked bread with your bakers, watched jazz rehearsals in your church basement, walked your bridge in fog and in full sun. I have not published anything. I have not posted a single rumor." She lifted the notebook. "I have *recorded* what your records already know."

The phrase rolled out of her before she could tidy it. She let it stand.

"I asked for vestry minutes," she said, voice steady. "They told me the bell was silent after a thunderstorm in 1887. I read the harbor master's weather log. I read the lighthouse keeper's notes about lantern stutters and double sweeps. I read the bridge keeper's diary where he wrote 'seventh night' in a hand that shook. I did not make the pattern. It made itself."

A flutter of conversation, quickly shushed. Marley saw Lorraine's smile thin further, saw Professor Ashcroft's chin lift as if to clear the air of the word *pattern*.

"I know what 'romanticizing myth' means," Marley said, gentler now, because she had learned her tone mattered more than her facts. "It means we're afraid of feeling too much in public. It means we'd rather keep grief behind hedges and Sunday best." She looked at the back row, at the fishermen and the high school kids and the woman who shelved books at the library. "I'm not asking you to believe in ghosts. I'm asking you to let the records breathe."

Someone clapped once, awkwardly. It was Evelyn. Marley didn't turn; she didn't dare break the thin wire she was walking.

Mrs. Tuller rapped the gavel, polite, corrective. "Thank you, Ms. Taylor. We appreciate your... passion."

Passion. Another word that let people pat you on the head and put you in the corner where children sleep while grown-ups make decisions that look like kindness and feel like amputations.

Marley sat. Her hands trembled a little; she flattened them on her notebook until they steadied.

Mrs. Tuller inhaled. "We'll take comments from the floor before the board votes. Please keep them brief. Remember we're neighbors." The last sentence carried both plea and threat.

Three people stood in a row. The first was Mr. Barlow, who had run the hardware store since before Marley was born. "I've lent Ms. Taylor maps," he said. "She returns them better than she got them—notes on the margins I can actually use. She's careful." He sat, uncomfortable with his own speech.

A woman Marley recognized from the historical walking tours rose next. "My great-grandmother wouldn't say the bridge's name," she said, clasping her purse so hard the leather creaked. "But she would wake the children on storm nights and count to seven. Ms. Taylor didn't teach me that. The town did. Let her read." She sat before her voice could break.

A third stood—young, one of the teenagers from the chessboard. He shoved his hands into his hoodie and blurted, "My little sister draws the lady on the bridge because she saw her once at dusk and nobody believes her. Maybe Ms. Taylor does." He sat down as if he'd sprinted.

The room held those statements warily, like birds startled by their own wings. Mrs. Tuller thanked each speaker and looked relieved when no one else stood.

Lorraine resumed her smile. "We all love a good story," she said, "but we must love our town more. I move we adopt the temporary suspension."

Professor Ashcroft seconded it, his eyes sliding past Marley to some comfortable place where water was simply water and chairs stayed put beneath anyone who sat. Mrs. Tuller looked satisfied in a way that made Marley's teeth ache.

"All in favor?" Mrs. Tuller said, lifting her hand.

Hands rose on the dais—Lorraine's, Professor Ashcroft's, two more, the fifth, Fenwick, hesitantly opposing—

Marley felt Damien shift beside her. He had been silent since he took his seat halfway through the meeting, sliding in soaked from the chapel like a man who had run because he suddenly couldn't bear not to. She had felt his presence even before she saw him—the way the air changes when someone who knows your edges sits down.

His chair scraped back.

Mrs. Tuller paused, brow knitting. "Sir, public comment has closed."

He didn't head toward the floor mic. He walked straight down the aisle toward the dais, the way a man walks when he has already decided he will either regret something or regret having left it unsaid. Several people murmured; someone hissed, "Damien," half warning, half surprise. Evelyn's mouth went soft in a way that meant *Finally.*

Marley's throat tightened. She had not asked him to come. She had not asked him to stand. But when he reached the front and turned to the room, rain dark in his hair and his eyes alight with something fiercer than fear, she knew what was about to happen.

Mrs. Tuller lifted the gavel. "Sir—"

"I'm the town archivist," Damien said, voice clear as the bell that wouldn't ring. The red light on the recorder threw a small circle on the table's edge. "And I object."

The room inhaled together, the way people do when they expect lightning to find them. The gavel hovered in Mrs. Tuller's hand. Marley's fingers tightened on her notebook until the cardboard bent.

She had been alone in so many rooms like this. She was not alone now.

The board's hands, half-raised for the vote, wavered.

Damien looked at Marley once—only once, the way you look at a person at the edge of a span and say without speaking, *I'm right here*—and then he turned back to the board to make the case that would either open a door or slam it.

The gavel fell. "Proceed," Mrs. Tuller said tightly.

But that belongs to the next breath.

. . .

Damien didn't need the mic. His voice carried with the clarity of a man who'd spent years reading to rooms that only half wanted to listen.

"I'm the archivist," he repeated, calmer now that the first breach was made. "If there's fault here, it's mine before it's Ms. Taylor's. The records in question—vestry minutes, the harbor master's weather ledger, lighthouse logs—are municipal holdings. They exist to be examined." He let the sentence rest. "By the public."

A shift ran through the rows—some bristling, some relieved, some simply surprised to hear procedure spoken like prayer. Mrs. Tuller's smile cooled. Lorraine's pen clicked twice, a small metronome of disapproval.

Damien turned slightly, not to Marley but to the room that had made him, that had watched him shelve their grandparents' photographs and the minutes of their births and budgets. "The accusation on the table is that Ms. Taylor is 'romanticizing myth.' I can't speak to anyone's taste for romance, but I can speak to method." He lifted a hand, counting off without theatrics. "She filed request forms. She wore gloves when handling fragile paper. She returned every item on time, with interleaving sheets where they were missing. She logged her notes. She did not publish. She did not remove anything from the building."

Professor Ashcroft leaned toward his mic. "She removed a button."

Damien didn't flinch. "Which the river removed first. She brought it to me wrapped in muslin and asked how to record it without claiming provenance we can't prove." He let the ledger on the dais see his palm—empty. "It's in the archive safe until the board decides whether it belongs in municipal custody or back in soil. That's not sensationalism. That's stewardship."

A soft murmur of approval stirred near the back. Mr. Barlow nodded once to himself, as if a ledger line had just balanced. Evelyn sat forward, elbows on her knees, eyes bright. Marley felt something loosen in her chest that she had kept cinched for months.

Mrs. Tuller steepled her fingers. "No one questions your diligence. We question scope. We're seeing a surge of... imaginative interpretations." Her gaze flicked to Marley and back. "Storms and sorrows happen in every town."

"Right," Damien said. "Which is why we keep weather registers and minutes. So we don't have to rely on imagination." He reached into his coat and produced a thin folder, the sort he carried when he couldn't bear to arrive at a room naked of paper. He didn't slap it down—he set it carefully on the edge of the dais as if the table might bruise. "Parish minutes, September 1887: *The bell of St. Bartholomew's no longer sounds. Sexton reports clapper unresponsive. Suspension of bell use until matter discerned.* Harbor log that week: *barometer fell, thunderstorm of exceptional duration.* Lighthouse log: *rotation stutter, double sweep for maintenance.* These are not folktales. These are ink."

Lorraine smiled without softness. "Ink can be misread."

"Which is why you let more than one pair of eyes read it," Damien said, and for the first time a blade showed under his voice. "And why you do not punish the person who has done precisely what a citizen is supposed to do— bring the records into conversation with our living memory." He looked past the dais to the rows. "You remember, some of you. Not because you want to, but because thunder feels the same in your bones as it did in your fathers'."

A fisherman in the back shifted, embarrassed to be so accurately seen.

Mrs. Tuller tapped the gavel once, a polite correction. "Mr. Hawthorne, this is not a seminar. We have a motion."

"And I'm responding to it," he said, but he gentled the edge. "Suspend her access and you signal that the archive is a vault for comfort, not a laboratory for truth. The word 'myth' has been used to sweep inconvenient experience into the corner for a long time—particularly women's accounts. The materials at issue are not hearsay. They're ledgers kept by men who loved neat columns." He glanced down at the folder. "They record a bell that fell silent on a storm night in 1887 and did not ring again."

Professor Ashcroft sniffed. "So the clapper jammed. A mechanical failure doesn't make a ghost."

"No one said it did," Damien answered. "What it makes is a datum—one that aligns with weather, with testimony, with the bridge keeper's repeated notation of the 'seventh night.' The responsible response to alignment is not to close a door. It's to keep looking."

A gray-haired woman in the third row—the librarian who shelved the mysteries—lifted a hand. "Let him finish," she said when Mrs. Tuller started to interrupt. "We're listening." It was not a challenge. It was a reminder.

Damien inclined his head to her, then to the board. "I'll make this plain. I have advised Ms. Taylor to be cautious. I will continue to do so." His throat worked once; he swallowed whatever else wanted to rise. "But my caution is not grounds for your censure. It's my conscience, and it belongs to me. The records belong to all of us."

Lorraine leaned in. "And what of the families who've asked not to have old grief stirred? We have a duty to the living as well as the dead."

"We do," Damien said. "Which is why we observe handling protocols, anonymize where appropriate, and refuse spectacle. Ms. Taylor has done all three. The harm here would be in pretending our ledgers don't already whisper what our grandmothers said out loud in kitchens." His voice went softer. "Shutting your eyes does not make thunder stop."

A rustle of agreement. Evelyn gave a single, sharp nod. The teenager from the chess game yesterday was here with his sister; the girl, all elbows and big eyes, had drawn a small circle on her program and added seven little lines. Marley saw it and nearly laughed from the place in her where relief meets fear.

Mrs. Tuller regrouped. "If we allow this... inquiry to continue unfettered, we expose the town to—"

"To what?" Damien asked, but without heat. He had the patience of someone who had cataloged whole estates of brittle paper. "To the possibility we'll learn something we didn't write down the first time? That's what archives are for. Not to ossify what we wish were true, but to test it against what was."

Professor Ashcroft drummed blunt fingers on the dais. "You're getting philosophical, Hawthorne."

"I'm getting specific," he said. "Here is a proposal: no suspension. Instead, a supervised research plan like we use with graduate fellows. Appointment hours. Sign-out logs. A copy desk where any notes taken from primary sources are left overnight for review before they exit the building." His tone stayed even. "If the board's concern is process, tighten process. If the board's concern is fear, name it as fear and don't pretend it's policy."

That last line landed. People shifted as if a draft had

found a crack and gotten in. Lorraine bristled. Professor Ashcroft looked briefly at his hands.

From the back, a voice Marley knew—a member of the firehouse board—said, "Seems workable." Another—Mr. Barlow—added, "We already do the log for maps." The room did the math of civic compromise in a murmur that sounded, to Marley, blessedly ordinary.

Mrs. Tuller saw the ground move under her feet and reached for a new foothold. "Even with supervision, we can't condone... narratives that make a spectacle of private pain."

"Neither can I," Damien said. He hesitated, and Marley knew what was coming because she had seen him wrestle it every night since she'd met him. He could leave the next sentence out and be safer for it. He didn't. "My late wife's name is in those ledgers." A hush fell that was almost a kindness. "If anyone has cause to fear 'romanticizing myth,' it's me. I would benefit from closing the door. But I won't. Because the alternative is to pretend the records we keep are just furniture." He let out a breath. "They are not."

Evelyn had gone very still, hands knotted in her apron as if to keep from clapping. Marley didn't move. She couldn't. The room's focus had settled into a steady beam; she felt warmed by it and flayed by it at the same time.

Damien finished simply. "Let the records be examined. Let us be the kind of town that can bear to look."

Silence. Not hostile—considering. Mrs. Tuller, to her credit, heard where the room had shifted. She conferred with Lorraine and Arthur in a quick whisper that sounded, to Marley, like paper tearing. Then she faced the hall.

"Mr. Hawthorne proposes a supervised plan," she said. "Limited hours, note review, sign-outs. The board retains discretion over fragile items." She swallowed her original motion like a pill without water. "We will entertain that as a substitute."

"Second," Professor Ashcroft said, surprising himself or pretending not to be surprised.

"All in favor?" Mrs. Tuller asked.

Hands rose—Lorraine's last, like a cat hopping a puddle it would rather not acknowledge. A smatter of applause made it to life and died under Mrs. Tuller's glare, but the sound had been made.

Marley's breath left her as if a strap had finally been loosened on her ribs. She looked at Damien, and he didn't look back—deliberately, perhaps—because the thing that had just happened was not between them, or not only; it was between a man and the town that had paid him in salary and grief and asked him now to spend both.

Mrs. Tuller tapped the gavel. "We will reconvene in two weeks to review compliance." She stacked her papers, no longer tidy. "Next item."

The room exhaled. People began to rise, scrape chairs, murmur to neighbors. Evelyn passed Marley in the aisle and squeezed her shoulder hard enough to leave the good kind of bruise. Mr. Barlow nodded on his way out, a ledger-line made human. The teenager grinned at Marley without quite meeting her eyes; his little sister held up her program sun and whispered, "Seven."

Marley smiled at her, then sat again because her knees did not entirely trust the floor. The muslin-wrapped bundle in her satchel felt heavier and safer all at once.

Damien returned to the second row. He didn't sit right away. He stood beside her, hands in his pockets, gaze somewhere neutral—a hymn board, the crooked banner, a scuff on the polished floor. "You'll have to leave your notes overnight," he said. "I wasn't bluffing."

"I know," she said. Her voice was softer than she meant it to be. "Thank you."

He nodded, still not looking. She knew why—he was holding himself together with the same thread he'd used to cross the aisle. If he turned to her now, the knot might give.

"Don't make me regret it," he said, and there was more in it than policy.

"I won't," she said, and there was more in that, too.

When the meeting adjourned, the hall spilled its people into the damp, humming evening. The rain had thinned to a sheen that made the streetlamps into smeared coins. Marley stayed behind to drop her notebook at the copy desk according to the new rule that was not yet a rule but would be by morning because a thing becomes policy here the instant enough hands have touched it. She wrote her name on the log, the date, the time, the contents: *notes; census copies; bell minutes; lighthouse excerpts.* She slid the book into the tray. The clerk nodded like a priest who'd just taken a confession he respected.

Damien waited for her in the vestibule, hands braced on either side of the doorframe like a man who has just held a weight and isn't ready to lift another. When she joined him, he released the wood and gave her a single, taut smile that said *We survived the first part* and also *This isn't over.*

"No," she agreed aloud, answering the thing he hadn't said. "It isn't."

They stepped into the cooled air. Somewhere upriver, thunder rumbled like a cart on planks. The bridge was only a cut of darkness against darker trees, but Marley could feel it holding its own meeting, the kind that keeps minutes in water and writes 'seventh' in the bones of anybody foolish enough to listen.

They turned toward Main Street. They did not yet know

what would be waiting at the bookstore door—an envelope with no return address, a sentence that would make the night feel like a hand tightening on a throat. For now there was only rain, and the small miracle of a room that had, for a few breaths, chosen inquiry over comfort.

"Two weeks," Damien said.

"Three nights," Marley answered.

They didn't have to explain which measure mattered more.

THE STREETLAMPS HUMMED WITH MOISTURE, their light smeared in the fog that had crept down from the river. Damien walked Marley back toward the bookshop, his silence heavy, his shoulders drawn up as if he were expecting more thunder. The town had thinned out after the meeting, but the air still carried the static of too many words said and too many swallowed.

At the shop's stoop, Marley reached for the door—and froze.

An envelope had been tucked between the handle and the frame. The paper was off-white, thick, the kind that didn't belong in a town where most notes were scribbled on café napkins or hardware store receipts. Her name wasn't written on it. No return address. Just the fold, neat, deliberate.

Damien saw her hesitation and stepped closer. "Marley?"

She pulled it free, her fingers damp with mist. The flap wasn't sealed. She unfolded it.

The handwriting was bold, blocky, each letter pressed into the page as if the writer wanted the pen to bite through:

STOP DIGGING, OR THE BRIDGE WON'T BE THE ONLY THING BURIED.

Her throat went dry. The words seemed to echo, as though the bridge itself had spoken them through the hand of some coward who hid behind paper.

Damien snatched the note from her fingers, scanning it. His jaw tightened; the muscle along his cheek jumped. "Damn it." He crushed the paper, then immediately smoothed it again, unwilling to destroy the evidence. "Someone wants you frightened."

Marley reached for it, her hand brushing his. "And succeeding," she admitted, though her voice was steadier than her stomach. "But frightened isn't the same as silenced."

Damien gave a sharp, incredulous laugh. "Don't you understand what this means? This isn't just whispers at Evelyn's counter anymore. This is a threat."

"Which means we're close to something." Marley slipped the note back, flattening it against her notebook pages. "Close enough that someone decided paper and ink were safer than leaving the truth exposed."

"Or close enough that someone's dangerous," Damien shot back. His voice was low, but urgent, stripped of patience. "I defended you in there tonight. I stood up and told them you were doing legitimate work. I gave them a reason to let you keep digging. And this"—he jabbed a finger toward the folded paper—"is the thank you. You're marked now, Marley. Don't tell me you don't feel that weight."

She did. The weight pressed cold against her chest like the damp ribbon she still kept in her satchel. But she had learned—through rain, through dreams, through vows whispered across centuries—that weight was not always the same as warning. Sometimes it was responsibility.

"I feel it," she said quietly. "And I'll carry it."

Damien's eyes narrowed. "You think it's that simple? You carry it, and what—Annabelle is free? Callum crosses the planks at last? You don't even know what the end of this looks like."

Her voice caught, but she pressed on. "Neither did Clara, and she still wrote. Neither did Annabelle, and she still waited." She lifted the note between them like a shard of mirror. "If this is meant to bury me, then it tells me one thing: the bridge is ready to be unearthed."

He raked a hand through his hair, rain scattering from the motion. His rational façade—the archivist, the steady one—was fraying again, thread by thread. "You can't romanticize threats into destiny. Whoever wrote that could be sitting in the back row of town hall, or on the board, or one of the old families who think their secrets should stay rot behind ledgers. They don't care about Annabelle, Marley. They care about control."

She stepped closer, her voice softening but not yielding. "Then control is exactly what I refuse to give them."

They stood like that, the fog thickening, the river's hum seeping into the street like a bass note. Marley folded the note into her journal, pasting it in with a strip of tape. She wrote above it in quick, firm script: *Anonymous threat, received after town meeting. Intent: silence. Response: record.*

Damien watched, his face a knot of anger and awe. "You're unbelievable."

She closed the book and looked up at him. "And you're still here."

The words lingered between them, heavier than the note. He turned away first, down the street where the lamps blinked against the fog, then back. His voice was rough. "Because if you're going to walk into the fire, someone has to carry water."

She touched her satchel, where the ribbon, the button, and now the note rested together. "Then we walk."

The mist curled low, swallowing their silhouettes as they stepped inside the bookshop. Behind them, on the stoop, the moisture beaded where the envelope had been, as if the warning itself had left a stain on the wood.

And upriver, though no hand pulled its rope, the chapel bell swayed once in the draft, silent but heavy, a motion unseen by all but the bridge.

19

______

DAMIEN'S DAUGHTER SLEEPWALKS

The phone shattered the gray at 4:11 a.m., a small violence in Marley's dark room. It rang once, twice—by the third she was upright, her brain already assembling only one reason Damien would call at this hour. She fumbled the screen to life.

"Marley," he said, breathless, the sound of wind in the open line. "It's—she's—" He swallowed, words snagging. "The bridge."

"I'm on my way."

She didn't ask which bridge. There was only one that called the town by its bones. Marley dragged jeans over cold legs, shoved her arms into a sweater, jammed bare feet into boots. The notebook went into the satchel by muscle memory; the pen found its spiral like a homing bird. Outside, fog hugged the street, drawn low and dense by the river's breath. She ran, breath stitching in little white threads, every step a syllable: *be—there—be—there.*

The road to the covered bridge bent through alders that held the fog in their branches like wool. The moon had washed out, but the lighthouse's distant sweep pried a faint gleam into the mist, a slow pulse like a sleeping heart. Marley cleared the last bend just as her skin prickled with the sensation she had learned to both dread and answer— the bridge was *aware*.

Damien's figure surfaced from the fog near the north mouth, a dark line against the paler dark, one hand lifted not to warn her back but to anchor himself to something that wasn't moving. He turned when he heard her boots on the wet boards; the look on his face made the world narrow to him and the span that held him.

"Where?" she asked. Her voice was a whisper that pretended, for his sake, it could keep the air steady.

"Midspan." He pointed. "She's... she's speaking."

Marley followed his hand. There—halfway down, where the third beam nail had caught more than one ribbon— stood a small, pajamaed figure. The fog thinned just enough to reveal bare calves, the hem of a sleep shirt, hair mussed by a pillow then by damp. One hand hung slack; the other clutched a scrap of paper so tight the knuckles blanched.

The child's lips moved. Her voice, soft as the turning of a music box key, drifted back along the planks:

"...count to seven at the gate..."

Damien flinched as if struck. "She won't answer me," he said hoarsely. "I tried her name—I didn't shake her—but she keeps saying—" He broke off, the rest climbing his throat and sitting there like a stone.

"Let me," Marley said. "We'll go slow."

They moved into the covered shadow, each step deliberately placed and quiet. The wood sighed under their weight. Up close, Sophie's face carried the open, unfocused calm of a sleepwalker: eyes half-lidded, pupils drowned in the dark, mouth shaped around someone else's cadence. She stood facing the west window, toward the place where the lantern would sweep if fog hadn't eaten its beam.

"Sweetheart," Marley murmured once they were within arm's reach, the old universal word that a child recognizes even when a name doesn't land. "It's cold. We're here."

Sophie didn't turn. Her voice, trance-clear, lilted again:

"If I wait and you are late,

count to seven at the gate.

When the river hushes stones,

carry me by vow and bones."

Marley felt the verse in her blood before her mind found it. It was the poem from the little music box—the one whose melody had a seam of sorrow stitched into it so cleanly that you didn't feel it until it tugged. The lid had carried the words on a tiny brass plaque, and the cylinder's pins had done the rest. The first time she'd wound it, she'd sworn she heard a voice under the tune, like breath in the mechanism. Now those lines had walked out of the box and into a child's mouth.

"It's the music box," Marley whispered to Damien, her skin chilled. "She's reciting the verse."

He swallowed hard. He was holding himself together with both hands; she could see the old training in him—do not startle, do not pull—but underneath it a father's fight or flight bucked and broke. "I don't—how would she—"

"I don't know." Marley kept her voice level. "But we're going to bring her back."

She eased closer until they were almost shoulder to shoulder. Gently, she placed her hand over the child's free hand and the crumpled paper. Warmth. The smallness of that hand, the dampness of fog pressed into skin. The girl's lips continued, softer now, like a candle guttering:

"Turn the key and let me hear,

low as rain against the eaves..."

"Shh," Marley breathed, not to hush but to fold herself into the rhythm. "Hear us now. We're here."

Damien shifted to the other side, his breath shaking. "Honey," he said—the name he had used when she was teething, when fevers came, when nightmares sent small feet down hallways. "Look at me."

Sophie's eyes didn't fix. They lifted a fraction, the way a bird's will when you stand too close, seeing you and not seeing you. The paper in her hand rasped as Marley eased it loose a millimeter, then another.

"Marley," Damien warned, but she shook her head.

"I won't take it," she promised. "Just... read with her."

The paper freed by degrees, like a splinter pulling itself from skin. When it finally slipped into Marley's palm, the girl didn't react. The note had been written in a childish hand but guided by something older—each letter carefully shaped, the lines straight as if a ruler had been laid along them. And it wasn't just the music box verse. Below it, in smaller words, lay lines Marley recognized from the bridge keeper's diary, not as he'd written them, but as if they'd been translated into a child's mouth: *Seventh night. Midbeam. Letter in hand.*

Marley's heart hammered. She lifted the paper for Damien to see. He looked, swallowed once, and made a sound that carried every year of his life in it.

"Okay," he whispered to his daughter, voice breaking. "Okay. Enough now."

He reached—slow, slow—and rested his fingers lightly on her shoulder. The girl swayed and stilled, her body adjusting around the touch as if remembering weight. Her lips moved again. For a moment Marley thought another fragment of verse would come—but instead Sophie's mouth formed a name so soft the fog seemed to drink it.

"Annabelle," she said.

Damien closed his eyes. He kept his hand steady by force. "We're going home," he said. "Let's step back."

Marley shifted her stance, ready to brace. Moving a sleepwalker can be a delicate thing—a wrong pressure, a wrong word, and you can yank a person too fast out of their own skin. She knew this because grief had sent her walking once, long before Brookwood, down a street whose name she couldn't remember now, and someone had touched her like a shout. She would not let that happen here.

"Back," she murmured. "One step."

The girl obeyed, heel sliding on wet plank, body not fully inhabited but yielding. Damien mirrored the motion, guiding without steering. Another step. Another. Marley took the paper and slid it into her sweater cuff, leaving both her hands free.

At the north mouth, the bridge released them. The difference was palpable—the way air felt when the shadowed ribs of the span were no longer holding it up like a throat. The fog thinned to a veil clinging to the alders; the lantern's distant beat regained its faint reach.

The girl blinked as if surfacing. Her pupils tightened. She looked straight at Damien, saw him, and the bones of his face seemed to rearrange around relief and terror.

"Daddy?" she said, and her voice belonged to this morning again, not to 1887. "What are we doing out here?"

"You were sleepwalking," he said, kneeling to bring his eyes level with hers. His hands couldn't decide whether to touch her shoulders or the sides of her face; they hovered, then settled on her hair. "It's early. You're cold."

Sophie wrapped her arms around herself. "I dreamed I was on the stairs," she said. "I heard a song. Like a box."

Marley swallowed. "Do you remember the words?"

The child frowned, thinking. "Something about a key," she said. "And seven." She yawned—an ordinary, sloppy yawn that broke the bridge's spell more effectively than any ritual could. "Can we go home?"

"Yes," Damien said. He lifted her into his arms, not because she needed carrying but because he needed to carry. She curled against him, trusting the old architecture of his chest and arms. He looked over her head at Marley. Whether he meant to or not, he let the panic show.

"How?" he said. "How did it reach her?"

Marley glanced back into the bridge's mouth. The midspan was a suggestion in fog, the third beam just a darker idea of wood. "You left the notebook at the copy desk," she said softly. "You did everything right."

"I've never—she's never—" He shook his head once, as if trying to fling water from his hair. "This is my fault."

"It isn't." The answer came too fast, the way one pulls a friend back from a drop. "The bridge doesn't need permission. It took Annabelle's bell. It took Jackie's pages. It will take whatever is tense enough to carry current."

"Which includes my daughter," he said, a new anger under the fear. "No. No." He tightened his hold, as if his ribs could become a gate. "I won't—"

"I know," Marley said. She did not say *You can't stop it by saying no*. She said, "We'll learn how to outwait it."

Sophie stirred, mumbled something into his coat that sounded like "lantern," then fell heavier in his arms as drowsiness reclaimed her. Marley stepped close, took the cuffs of the sleep shirt and pulled them over small, cold wrists. She couldn't do more than that and knew it; the help-lessness made her want to set the world alight and call it kindness.

They walked toward Damien's place. He shrugged out of his coat and tucked it around her. She sighed. Her hand loosened; Marley eased the paper fully from her cuff and unfolded it in the wash of the dome light.

The lines sat there, impossibly plain: the music box poem in a child's careful block print, and beneath it the bridge keeper's phrases copied like homework. A small smear of graphite darkened the corner, the universal mark of a left-handed writer dragging her hand as she worked.

"When did she write this?" Damien whispered. "We keep the pencils in the kitchen drawer. Did she..." He trailed off, all the small logistics of fatherhood colliding with the large terror of the bridge. "I locked the door last night."

"She didn't need the door," Marley said. "She had a verse."

He flinched again, anger and despair rising in him like stormwater. "Don't—please don't make poetry of this right now."

"I'm not." Marley folded the paper and slid it into an enve-lope from her satchel, labeling it with the time and place because that was how she won small wars. "I'm making record."

He closed his eyes, breathed once, then again—and when he opened them, the archivist had reassembled himself enough to stand beside the father. "Thank you," he said, the words sounding like they'd been dragged across gravel. "For coming."

"Always."

"I thought I cursed her," he said abruptly, not looking at Marley. "By loving you. By saying yes to more after Jackie."

He lifted his hands and let them fall, empty. "Maybe the bridge punishes greed."

"Greed?" Marley's laugh was soft and incredulous. "For wanting more life?" She shook her head. "No. The bridge doesn't punish love. It preys on loneliness. On vows that missed the hand they were meant for. That's not you, Damien. That's the town's old debt, not yours."

He pressed his thumbs into his eye sockets, then dropped his hands and looked at her the way people do when they want to believe the thing that will save them and are afraid to touch it. "If it's an old debt, why does it ask new payments?"

"Because no one has settled the account." She turned toward the span, where fog rolled and rested as if the bridge were breathing. "Yet."

The lighthouse swept, faint and far. The seventh night was coming like a tide no wind could turn. Marley felt the clock of it inside her; so did Damien, she knew, because he glanced instinctively toward the unseen lantern as if it were a wristwatch.

"We'll keep her with someone tonight," he said, practical surfacing because a plan is a human against the dark. "My sister. Locks. Alarms."

"And we'll leave messages with Evelyn," Marley added. "In case we're at the bridge when—" She didn't finish. They both knew what she meant.

Damien nodded, jaw tight. He looked smaller in that moment, narrowed to the outline of a man who would pick up anything to block the path to his child. Marley reached out and touched his sleeve. He didn't pull away.

"Three nights," she said. "We count. We prepare. We go anyway."

The word *anyway* hung there, fragile and necessary. He nodded once.

Sophie dreamed without sound, the way a safe house does. The fog opened before them, closed behind.

When they reached his house, the porch light was a small gold coin in a gray palm. He carried his daughter inside. Marley waited on the stoop, the anonymous threat from the night before prickling under the skin of the wood, and listened to the house accept its sleeping child back into its rooms.

She opened her notebook and wrote across a new page in a hand that shook and still steadied: *Pre-dawn. Sleep-walking to midspan. Child murmurs music box verse. Holds note: poem + keeper's phrases. Spoke "Annabelle." Removed safely. Evidence sealed.*

Then, smaller, beneath the tidy facts, the sentence that was not a datum but a vow: *We will not let the bridge learn her name the way it learned Annabelle's.*

She closed the book. The fog pressed its cool palm to her face and let her go.

THE FOG HADN'T LIFTED, even as dawn threatened the horizon. It clung to the bridge's ribs, to the bark of the alders, to the figures standing in the aftermath of something neither parent nor chronicler had words ready to hold.

Marley leaned against the railing just outside the covered span, her fingers still damp with the paper she had coaxed from the girl's hand. She unfolded it again, this time slowly, reverently—as if any wrong angle might make the words vanish. The graphite lines shimmered faint under the lantern's pulse from across the water. She read, aloud enough that Damien heard, though her voice quavered:

"Count to seven at the gate,
If I wait and you are late.
When the river hushes stones,
Carry me by vow and bones."

Her throat closed on the last line. She had seen these words before, not scrawled in a child's pencil but etched in brass, polished to shine inside the lid of a little music box. That box had been wound, once, in Evelyn's café storeroom months ago. Its tune had been haunting enough then; now, held in Damien's daughter's sleep-soft mouth, it was unbearable.

She lowered the note and added, almost in disbelief, "It's the same verse from the music box."

Damien's breath cut short, ragged. "The one you found with Evelyn?"

"Yes." Marley steadied herself, clutching her satchel to anchor her trembling hands. "But this—this is in her writing. I'd swear it. The block letters, the way the 's' curves back too far. She wrote it, Damien. Or something wrote through her."

His gaze locked on the paper as if it were a weapon pointed at him. "That box was in storage. Locked. She's never seen it."

"I know." Marley pressed the page flat against the rail, tracing the lines with her fingertip, needing to feel their physicality. "Which means she pulled them from the same source we've been tugging at—dreams, echoes, whatever this bridge and this town are breathing into us."

Damien shook his head hard, like a man trying to break water out of his ears. "No. It's not the same. I'm an adult—I made the choice to step into this. You—you chose. But her?" His voice cracked. "She's a child, Marley. She didn't invite any of it."

Marley closed the note, folded it once, then twice, her chest tight. "Maybe she didn't invite it. But something did. Something old that knows the names, the vows, the songs." She tucked the paper carefully into her notebook, writing the date in quick, sharp script: *Pre-dawn, 19th. Poem from music box. Written in child's hand.*

Damien's face twisted at the sight of her pen moving. "You're recording it? Now? After what just happened?"

"Especially now." Her voice was steady, though her knees wanted to give. "Because if we don't, the town will swallow it like it swallowed Annabelle. Like it swallowed Clara's notes, Jackie's pages. We can't let this disappear into whispers."

He turned away, pressing both palms against the damp railing as if it could hold him upright. His daughter's small figure rested in the back seat of the car, curled under his coat. She hadn't stirred since he carried her out.

"She said Annabelle's name," Damien murmured. The words were raw, stripped of armor. "You heard her."

Marley nodded. "I did."

"That's not just words on a page," he said, still facing the river. "That's the bridge calling her by name. I've lived here long enough to know what that means. It never lets go of what it names."

Silence stretched. Marley stepped closer, resisting the instinct to fill it with platitudes. Instead, she opened her notebook again, flipping to where she'd copied the original brass inscription months ago. She set the two versions side by side—the delicate engraving she'd transcribed, and the jagged pencil scrawl just pressed into her hand.

"Look," she said. "The words match, but not exactly. The music box verse ended with 'low as rain against the eaves.'

This one—" she tapped the graphite letters—"ends with bones. Vows and bones."

Damien turned his head, his eyes catching hers at last. They looked hollowed, cavernous with fear. "So it's changing."

"Yes." She felt the chill of the truth settle against her ribs. "Evolving. Rewriting itself through each vessel."

He laughed once, harsh. "Vessel. That's my little girl you're talking about."

Marley flinched, but didn't look away. "I know. That's why we need to understand what it wants. Because if we don't—if we just slam the archive doors, burn the ribbon, throw away the button—the bridge will keep reaching. For her. For you. For me."

Damien's fists tightened on the rail. "Don't you dare put her in the same breath as us."

"She already is," Marley whispered. The words hurt her throat, but she forced them out. "You heard it. I heard it. Annabelle's name from her mouth."

For a long moment, the only sound was fog dripping from beams onto the water below. Then Damien turned away from her, shoulders heaving. When he spoke again, his voice was broken glass.

"When Jackie was sick, she dreamed too. Of the river, the bridge, storms. She'd wake shaking, clutching the sheets. I told her it was fever. I told her it was imagination. I couldn't admit then what I admit now—that it was the same thing. The same damn echo. And now—" His voice faltered. "Now it's touching my daughter."

Marley's chest hollowed at his confession. The threads of his past—his lost wife, the hidden echoes he'd kept buried—were unraveling in front of her, raw and undeniable. And with them, the truth: this wasn't just her investigation. The bridge had always had Damien, too.

She touched his arm, tentative. "Then we won't let it take her. We record, we map, we learn the pattern before it writes her deeper into it."

He pulled his arm back sharply. "You think words will hold it? Ink on paper? That's your answer to everything—record it, write it down, tape it into a notebook. But Annabelle was recorded. Clara wrote until her hands blistered. And still the bridge kept them." His voice dropped to a whisper jagged with despair. "What makes you think we can keep her?"

Marley swallowed, the note heavy in her pocket like a second heart. "Because this time, we know it's coming."

Damien's silence was a wall she couldn't scale. He turned and walked toward the car, his figure half-swallowed by fog. He opened the back door, checked his daughter's breathing, adjusted the coat around her. Marley followed, the paper burning against her ribs, her notebook clutched tighter than ever.

When he looked up at her again, his eyes had the hollow, hunted look of a man who already feared the end was written. "If this kills her," he said quietly, "then every record you've kept will be nothing but an obituary."

Marley met his gaze. "Or a testimony."

Neither word comforted him. He shut the car door softly, as if sound itself might wake the bridge's hunger.

HE TURNED SHARPLY THEN, as if the act of loving his daughter had burned him. "You should go," he said.

Marley shook her head. "Not until we talk."

He laughed once, without humor. "Talk? About what?

That my daughter just recited a verse from a cursed music box she's never seen? That she said Annabelle's name like she's known it her whole life? That she wrote down the keeper's phrases in her own hand? You want me to talk about that, Marley?"

"Yes," she said, her voice rising despite herself. "Because pretending it didn't happen won't protect her. You tried that with Jackie. It didn't work."

The air cracked between them. Damien's face tightened, a flash of grief so sharp it looked like anger. "Don't you dare." His voice dropped to a growl. "Don't you dare use her name like that."

Marley's hand trembled around her notebook. "I'm not using her. I'm learning from her. Jackie's dreams, Clara's notes, Annabelle's letters—they're all connected. If we stop, if we bury this, then the bridge will keep taking what it wants. But if we record—if we see the pattern—then maybe we can break it."

Damien's eyes were dark, hollowed with exhaustion and fear. He stepped closer, lowering his voice to keep from waking his daughter. "You think ink and paper will stop this? That scribbling in a notebook makes you stronger than the thing that's been swallowing names for over a century? This isn't evidence, Marley. It's a curse. And you're dragging us deeper into it every time you put pen to page."

She met his fury with her own steadiness. "No. Evidence is the only thing we *do* have. The bridge speaks in fragments —dreams, verses, artifacts. If we don't write them down, we lose the thread. And if we lose the thread, then your daughter standing on those planks tonight becomes just another rumor. Just another ghost story whispered over coffee. That's not enough, Damien. Not for her. Not for Annabelle."

His hand slammed against the doorframe, not at her but near enough that the sound rattled the glass. The quilt on his daughter shifted with the echo. He froze, horrified at himself, and stepped back, pressing his palm against his forehead. "God," he whispered. "I can't—"

Marley set her notebook down on the table with deliberate calm. She reached out, touching his arm lightly. "You're scared. I am too. But fear doesn't erase what we saw. It doesn't erase the words she spoke. You can either let that fear bury you, or you can help me dig through it."

He stared at her, his chest heaving. The fight in him was real, but so was the collapse. He looked at his daughter again, then at Marley. "If this kills her..." His voice cracked. "If this kills her, I won't survive it."

Marley's own eyes burned, but she didn't look away. "Then we won't let it. We record everything. We map every echo. We find the pattern before it writes her name in stone. That's how we protect her."

He shook his head, torn between belief and dread. "You make it sound like we have a choice."

"We do." She picked up her notebook again, her voice steady. "The choice to remember instead of deny. To testify instead of bury. That's the only choice that's ever mattered in this town."

The silence that followed was thick, fragile, like glass stretched too thin. Finally, Damien sagged into the armchair across from her, burying his face in his hands. His voice was muffled, broken. "God help me, Marley, I want to believe you."

She leaned forward, resting her notebook on her knees, her own fear tucked inside the act of writing. "Then start here," she whispered. "Believe that she came back tonight because we were there to hear her. That's not a curse, Damien. That's evidence. And it's proof we're not too late."

The old clock on the mantle ticked steady, marking time that felt both fragile and eternal. Outside, the fog thickened against the window like a second curtain. And beneath it all, the river's hum carried a rhythm both warning and promise—reminding them that the bridge was still listening.

20
___

HEARTS AT ODDS

The house had quieted, but the quiet wasn't peace —it was brittle, like glass stretched too thin, ready to shatter at the slightest sound. Damien's daughter was upstairs, asleep again in her bed, the quilt tucked to her chin. He had checked on her three times in as many minutes before coming back down. Now he stood at the kitchen counter with his hands pressed flat against the wood, staring at nothing.

Marley sat at the table, notebook open, the folded slip of paper she'd taken from the bridge resting on its page. She had copied the verse twice already, one in her usual careful script, one in a sharper, hurried hand as if rewriting it might fix it in place. The lamp above the table cast a small pool of light, but the edges of the room were shadowed, heavy.

Finally Damien broke the silence. His voice was low, but the restraint made it rough. "It stops now."

Marley lifted her eyes from the page. "What stops?"

"All of it." He turned, his face drawn tight with exhaustion, fear, and something harder underneath. "The journals, the ribbons, the bakery sigils, the séances. The bridge.

Whatever story Annabelle Warren is begging you to finish —it ends here. Before it takes more."

Marley closed the notebook slowly, the weight of his words pressing against her chest. "Damien—"

"No." He came closer, leaning across the table so the light caught in his eyes. "You saw her tonight. My daughter. On those planks, repeating words she never should have known. You saw the paper in her hand. Do you think I care if it's evidence or a curse? Do you think it matters? It could have pulled her straight into the river." His hands gripped the chair back between them until his knuckles whitened. "I will not risk her because you're chasing someone else's ghost."

Marley held his gaze, but her own voice shook with urgency. "This isn't just chasing ghosts. This is history repeating itself. Annabelle waited, Callum couldn't cross, Clara wrote until the ink blurred, Jackie dreamed until it consumed her. And now your daughter is being pulled into the same echo. You think walking away will save her? It won't. It'll leave her defenseless."

"Defenseless?" His laugh was sharp, bitter. "She's defenseless because we keep feeding the thing that wants her. Every time you write another page, every time you follow another whisper, you give it more shape. More presence. Maybe if you stopped—if you burned those notebooks —maybe it would wither back into the fog where it belongs."

Marley slammed her hand down on the notebook before he could reach for it. "Burning the record doesn't erase the truth. It just blinds us to it. The bridge won't vanish because we stop looking. You know that. You've known it since the first night you admitted Jackie's dreams weren't just fever."

The name landed like a blow. Damien stiffened, his jaw tightening until she thought it might crack. "Don't bring her into this," he said, voice low and dangerous.

"She's already in it," Marley whispered. "So is your daughter. So are you. This isn't about me chasing some romantic tragedy, Damien. It's about ending it before it takes more from all of us."

For a long moment he just stared at her, breathing hard, the chair between them a fragile barrier. His hands trembled once before he clenched them tight.

"I don't care about Annabelle Warren," he said finally, each word weighted like stone. "She's been dead a hundred years. My daughter isn't."

Marley swallowed, her throat aching. "And that's exactly why we can't stop. Because Annabelle's story isn't finished. Because unfinished stories keep writing themselves into the living. Into her. Into us. If we don't finish it, Damien, then your daughter will carry it next. You can lock every door, but the bridge doesn't need keys."

His shoulders sagged, then stiffened again. He turned away, bracing both hands against the counter as though the wood might hold him up where his belief couldn't.

The clock ticked in the silence. Marley picked up her pencil, almost against her own will, and wrote at the bottom of the page: *He wants to stop. I can't. The story isn't done. The bridge knows it. So do I.*

The scratch of graphite sounded like defiance. Damien's head turned at the noise, his eyes catching the movement. The look he gave her was raw, torn between admiration and fury, between the part of him that had stood beside her in the archives and the part of him that would burn it all down to keep his daughter safe.

"Marley," he said finally, voice quiet but unyielding, "if

you make me choose between her and Annabelle's ghost, you will lose."

She shut the notebook with a snap, meeting his gaze without flinching. "Then pray we don't have to choose. Because the bridge is already trying to make that choice for us."

The words hung in the air like storm clouds waiting to break, neither of them moving, neither willing to back down. Upstairs, a floorboard creaked softly—just the shifting of a sleeping child, but both of them froze, listening, fearing it might be more.

The sound passed. The silence returned.

And with it, the fragile thread of trust between them frayed further, stretched taut by grief, by fear, by love—and by the bridge's relentless echo.

Damien pulled away from the counter and began pacing the kitchen, his footsteps quick, sharp, the way a man walks when he's too full of fire to sit still. Every few strides, he glanced up the stairs as if to confirm his daughter was still sleeping. His hands flexed open and shut at his sides.

"Do you hear yourself?" he snapped, rounding on Marley. "You're talking about finishing a dead woman's story like it's some noble quest. But what it really is? An obsession. And obsessions don't end well. Not for Clara. Not for Jackie. And sure as hell not for my child."

Marley rose from her chair, notebook still in hand. "It's not obsession, Damien. It's continuity. Clara wrote because she had to. Jackie dreamed because she couldn't stop it. And now your daughter—"

"Don't," he cut in, his voice cracking like a whip. "Don't put her name in the same sentence as theirs."

Marley's tone softened, but she didn't retreat. "She's already there. The bridge pulled her in tonight, not me. She spoke Annabelle's name, recited words from the music box she never saw. That's not me dragging her into it—that's the story already inside her. And if we don't follow it to its end, then she'll keep carrying pieces of it until it swallows her whole."

Damien's face twisted, a man straining against grief, against fury, against the terror of losing the one thing he couldn't replace. "Do you even hear yourself? You sound like you're saying it's inevitable—that she's doomed unless you scribble enough in that damned journal of yours."

"I'm saying it's inevitable unless we *understand it*," Marley shot back, her own anger sharpening now. "Unless we stop treating this like a superstition we can smother under silence. The bridge isn't a ghost story, Damien—it's a pattern. And patterns can be broken. But only if we're willing to see the whole of it."

He laughed then, a harsh, bitter sound. "A pattern? You think this is some puzzle you can solve with ink and intuition? This isn't your aunt's riddles in the margins of a journal, Marley. This is my daughter's life."

"And Annabelle's death," Marley said firmly. "And Callum's vow. And Clara's silence. It's all tied together. If you think walking away will protect her, you're wrong. You'll just be giving the bridge one more unsolved disappearance to feed on."

Damien slammed his palm against the table so hard that the lamp rattled. His daughter stirred upstairs, and both of them froze until the house settled again. When the quiet returned, his voice was low, trembling with restraint. "You don't get it. I've lived here my whole life. I've seen what happens when people poke at things that should stay buried. They go missing. Or worse, they lose themselves while they're still breathing. My wife—" His breath caught. "I won't let that happen to her. To my daughter."

Marley clutched her notebook tighter, her knuckles white. "And what about you? You've already lost yourself once, Damien. You've been walking around half-buried since Jackie died, pretending silence is protection when it's really surrender. But tonight—tonight you saw it for what it is. Silence doesn't protect. It devours."

His chest heaved, his eyes flaring with both fury and hurt. "Don't you dare presume to tell me how I grieved my wife. You weren't there. You don't know what I did to keep from breaking."

Marley took a step closer, her voice low, urgent. "I know because I've seen you breaking anyway. Because I see you now, Damien—terrified that history is repeating itself, and desperate enough to think you can shut it out by shutting me down. But it's too late for that. The bridge already knows her name. The only choice left is whether we face it or hide from it."

He shook his head, his hands balling into fists. "Facing it isn't bravery—it's handing it more lives. I can't let you risk her because you feel some pull to a woman who died before either of us was born."

Marley's voice softened again, a tremor of grief threading through her anger. "It's not just Annabelle, Damien. It's every woman who was silenced. Clara. Jackie. And now your daughter. Don't you see? The bridge has been waiting for someone to speak. And if we don't—if I don't— then the silence wins. And it won't stop with her."

The words hung heavy, filling the kitchen like fog. Damien's breathing was ragged, his jaw clenched. His eyes flicked once more toward the stairs, toward the small life sleeping above them, and when he looked back at Marley his expression was fractured—equal parts rage and despair.

"You're asking me to gamble my daughter's life on your faith in ink and echoes," he said, his voice breaking. "And I can't. I won't."

Marley's throat tightened, but she held her ground. "And I'm telling you the real gamble is pretending we can walk away. We can't, Damien. Not anymore. The only way out is through."

The silence that followed was suffocating. He turned from her, pacing again, gripping the back of the chair until his knuckles blanched. She opened her notebook, pressing her pencil to the page, the act itself a vow.

The sound of graphite scratching filled the air between them like a third presence. Damien turned sharply at the noise, his eyes blazing, but Marley didn't look up. She wrote: *He wants to end it. I want to finish it. The bridge stands between us.*

She closed the book with a snap, the sound like a gavel. "I'm not stopping, Damien," she said quietly, but with steel in her tone. "Not when we're this close."

His chest rose and fell, fury trembling under his skin, but he said nothing. The kitchen light flickered once, as if the house itself absorbed the strain. Upstairs, his daughter shifted, murmuring in her sleep—a sound that froze them both in place.

And in the silence that followed, their fragile trust stretched thinner still, one heartbeat away from breaking.

THE HOUSE SEEMED to shrink around them, walls bowing inward beneath the weight of everything unsaid. The clock ticked too loudly. The lamp hummed. Upstairs, Damien's daughter shifted again in her sleep, the soft creak of her mattress a reminder that she was still there—still safe, for now.

Damien moved to the window, bracing his hands on the sill, staring out into the fog that lapped against the glass. His reflection looked like a stranger, hollow-eyed, wild around the edges. "I can't do this," he muttered. "Not like this."

Marley stayed by the table, notebook pressed against her chest as though it were armor. Her voice was calm, but the tightness in it betrayed the storm inside her. "Do what, Damien? Face what's happening? Admit that it's bigger than us?"

He spun around, his face lit with a fury she had rarely seen from him. "No. Drag my daughter through it. Let you keep writing every cursed word that slips through that bridge until it decides she belongs to it too. That's what I can't do."

Marley's hand trembled on the notebook, but she held it steady. "You think shutting the book stops the story? It doesn't. The bridge is already writing her in, Damien. The only way to change the ending is to *see it through*."

His voice rose, jagged, as though pulled raw from his chest. "You sound like Clara. You sound like Jackie. Always reaching, always believing you could outwit it with ink and conviction. And where did that leave them? Clara vanished into her pages. Jackie into her dreams. And you—" He broke off, running a hand through his hair. "You'll end up the same. And I can't watch that happen again."

The words sliced deeper than he intended, but he didn't pull them back. Marley flinched, her breath hitching. For a moment, her resolve wavered under the weight of his grief. Then she stepped forward, her voice cutting through the silence like a blade.

"Maybe Clara and Jackie didn't fail," she said. "Maybe they kept the thread alive long enough for me to pick it up. For us to pick it up. You keep calling it obsession. I call it survival. Because if we walk away now, Damien, then the bridge wins. And it won't stop at Annabelle. Or Callum. Or Clara. Or Jackie. It'll take her, too. Your daughter. Because unfinished stories don't die—they feed."

He shook his head violently, his fists clenched at his sides. "You don't get it. You think this is about Annabelle's story, but it's not. It's about mine. About hers." He gestured upstairs, his hand trembling. "She's all I have left. I won't risk her for your... your *compulsion*."

Marley's chest burned with anger and sorrow. "And I won't abandon the truth just because it terrifies us. If we do nothing, Damien, she'll still be at risk. At least if we face it, we have a chance to stop it."

They stood only feet apart, the air between them taut, humming with everything unspoken. For a moment, Marley thought he might close the space—bridge it with an embrace, or even with fury. Instead, Damien stepped back, shaking his head.

"Then maybe we can't do this together," he said, his voice low but final.

The words hit her harder than a shout would have. Marley's fingers tightened around the notebook until the spiral cut into her palm. "You don't mean that."

He looked at her, his eyes torn and blazing all at once. "I do. Because if staying with you means dragging her deeper into this, then I choose her. Every time. I'll burn every journal, every archive, every cursed note if that's what it takes to keep her safe."

Marley's throat closed, but she forced the words out. "And if burning the truth means she gets lost anyway? What then, Damien? What if protecting her the way you think you can is exactly what hands her over to the bridge?"

He turned away, unable—or unwilling—to answer.

Silence settled again, heavy as stone. Marley opened her notebook one last time and pressed her pencil against the page. Her hand shook, but she wrote anyway: *Tonight the choice tore us apart. He wants to end it. I have to finish it. The bridge waits between us.*

She closed the book, the sound sharp in the quiet kitchen.

Damien still stood at the window, his reflection fractured by fog. He didn't turn when she moved toward the door.

On the threshold, Marley paused, her heart breaking with every breath. "You can lock every door, Damien," she said softly. "But you can't lock out what's already inside the walls."

She left then, the night swallowing her, the fog curling around her shoulders like the very story she refused to let go of.

Inside, Damien leaned his forehead against the cold glass, his reflection staring back at him with eyes that no longer looked like his own. Upstairs, his daughter stirred again, murmuring in her sleep—one word, soft, fragile, carried through the cracks of history:

"Annabelle."

And downstairs, the fragile trust between Damien and Marley splintered, the soundless fracture echoing louder than any bell.

21

ANCESTRAL PAINTING FOUND

The antique shop smelled of beeswax polish and old cedar, the kind of scent that clung to pieces which had outlived their owners. Rain pattered faintly against the front windows, streaking the display of glass jars and pressed tin signs with a sheen that made them shimmer. Marley had come for nothing more than a lamp repair—something mundane, something steady—but when the dealer emerged from the back with a canvas wrapped in brown paper, she knew routine had just surrendered to the extraordinary.

"Thought of you the moment this came in," Mr. Whitcomb said, sliding the package onto the counter with a reverence he rarely showed even his most prized clocks. His fingers lingered on the twine. "From the Marwick estate, in fact. They've finally cleared the old place after decades of it sitting locked."

Marley's pulse quickened at the name. "Marwick?"

He nodded, reaching for a pocketknife. "The family auctioned the furniture and silver off last month, but a few unsorted boxes ended up in my hands. This was in the attic, unframed. Wrapped tight in oilskin."

The knife sliced clean through the twine, the paper crackling as it fell away. The canvas within was old but surprisingly well-preserved, the paint dulled yet intact.

Marley's breath left her in a rush.

A woman stood at the center of the canvas, poised on the covered bridge in a green dress that shimmered even in faded pigment. Her hair was dark, pulled back simply, her gaze cast outward as though expecting someone—or waiting. The brushwork wasn't masterful, but the figure held an undeniable gravity, the kind of presence that froze the room.

Whitcomb cleared his throat softly, his eyes flicking between Marley and the canvas. "Unsigned. Could've been done by a local hand. But the detail in the background—you'll notice it, I think."

Marley leaned closer, her fingertips hovering above the paint. Behind the figure, the valley unfolded. The river curved wide, but where Brookwood's cluster of homes and shops now stood there were only a few scattered farmsteads, fenced fields, and a dirt road. No gas lamps. No chapel steeple. No town square.

Her chest tightened. "This is before Brookwood was Brookwood," she whispered. "Before incorporation."

Whitcomb gave a satisfied nod. "Exactly. Which dates it to at least the 1880s, maybe earlier."

Her gaze returned to the woman, to the dress. The shade of green was familiar, like the gown she had seen in her dream—the dream where Annabelle walked barefoot with a letter in hand. The resemblance was undeniable. Marley's throat tightened as though the paint itself was speaking.

The shop door opened, bells jangling, and Damien stepped in from the rain. His coat was soaked through at the shoulders, his expression tired but alert. When his eyes fell on the canvas, he stopped cold.

"What is this?" he asked, his voice low.

Whitcomb gestured at the painting. "Estate clearing. From the Marwick attic. I was just showing Miss Taylor."

Damien moved closer, his steps slow, deliberate, like a man circling a wound he already knew was his. He stood beside Marley, his jaw tightening as he studied the image. "That's the Marwick bridge," he said, almost to himself. "The way it looked before they reinforced it." His gaze sharpened on the woman's dress. "And that color—family records mention it. A green gown Callum had made, custom for her."

Marley turned to him sharply. "For Annabelle?"

His throat worked. He gave the faintest nod. "For Annabelle Warren. The records said she wore it the last night anyone saw her."

The words landed like a stone dropped in still water, sending ripples through Marley's chest. She looked back at the canvas—the waiting woman, the unbuilt town, the green gown—and the air seemed to hum, as though the bridge itself had been painted into permanence.

Whitcomb, oblivious to the storm between them, carefully propped the canvas against the counter. "I'd keep it myself, but something about it feels... unsettled. It belongs in your hands, I think." He gave Marley a small, almost apologetic smile. "Or in yours," he added, glancing at Damien.

Damien's jaw worked, but his eyes never left the painted figure. "No. It belongs with her." He jerked his chin toward Marley. "She's the one piecing this together."

Marley felt the heat of his words, the reluctant admission of trust, though it was threaded with fear. She crouched down, her face level with the painted woman's, and whispered under her breath, "Annabelle, you're still here."

The shop's silence deepened. Outside, the rain softened. And in the canvas's faded strokes, Marley felt the pulse of the story rising again, another fragment drawn into her hands.

MR. WHITCOMB FETCHED a wooden easel from the back and cleared a corner of the counter, making room as if he were preparing a chapel. He lifted the canvas with both hands, reverent, and settled it into the cradle. The shop's front lamps threw a low, amber wash across the paint; the surface woke under it—varnish gone to honey, craquelure like fine frost.

Marley stepped in close. The old habit returned—she set her notebook on the glass case, tugged a stub pencil from behind her ear, and began to read the picture the way she'd learned to read ledgers and weather logs: with patience and a willingness to be surprised.

The woman in green stood a half-step left of center, one hand resting near the rail, the other at her side. The gown was not fashionable frippery; even in oil it had the honest weight of something sewn for use, not parade. The tone of the pigment—a green with the memory of leaf-shadow in it —pulled the eye the way the river pulled mist. The painter had laid it in thin, disciplined strokes; in places the ground showed through—warm umber under the sleeves where the light caught, a darker underpaint along the hem that suggested damp.

"Barefoot," Marley murmured. The toes were hinted more than drawn, pale stains against the plank's brown, but once she'd seen them she couldn't unsee them. "Look—no shoes."

Damien had come to her shoulder. "Like your dream," he said, not a challenge this time—more a statement that admitted how tired he was of coincidence.

Marley nodded, tracing the line of the hem without touching it. "And here—" She leaned, squinting. "Do you see that? The right hand—"

Damien angled his head. The knuckles were only a handful of warm strokes, but against them lay a narrow strip of paler paint. Not a folded letter precisely—more the suggestion of paper, of edges, of something carried that had weight only because the story gave it weight.

"Could be anything," Whitcomb offered, ready to defend or dismiss depending on what the moment required.

"Or it could be a letter," Marley said softly, the pencil already moving over her page—*bare feet, letter edge—painter implies, not declares.* She looked past the figure to the span itself. The roof trusses were simpler than the current bridge's, a hint of diagonal brace where there would later be a lattice; the visible ribs told a builder's eye somewhere near the painter's shoulder. Outside the far mouth, the hillside rolled away clean of houses—just fields stitched by low stone fences, a cluster of poplars, a single bold sycamore anchoring the near bank with a flare of pale bark.

"The sycamore," she said, almost to herself. The same tree from the printing plate's unfinished poem; the same tree where the path bent and grief paused to consider water. The painter had set it slightly off true—stylized, a little larger than scale—but unmistakable.

Damien touched the easel's side, steadying the canvas as if the past might sway. "There's no chapel spire," he said. "No lamp posts. No town green. If that's the sycamore at adult size, we're before incorporation by at least a handful of years." He slid his phone from his pocket, scrolled, and brought up a scan Marley recognized—the 1881 survey plat she'd helped him flatten on the archive table months ago. He zoomed, then held the screen a breath from the paint. "Same bend in the river. Same angle of the west pasture fence." He tipped the phone, matching horizon to horizon. "It's the right vantage—whoever painted this stood on the east abutment and looked west."

Mr. Whitcomb whistled softly. "That would put the painter almost in the road."

"Or on the rail," Damien said, half a smile in the corner of his mouth despite himself. "Which would be a very Callum thing to do."

Marley's pencil hesitated. "You think he painted it?"

Damien didn't answer immediately. He stepped around to the back of the canvas and peered along the stretcher. "Mr. Whitcomb, may I?"

"Gently," Whitcomb murmured, but he relaxed his hands.

Damien tipped the painting forward a fraction, enough to let the upper edge catch the light. The stretcher bars were rough pine, keyed at the corners with small wedges. Along the top rail, in faint graphite, someone had written a line in a hand unpracticed but careful: *For A.W.*

Marley's breath snagged. "Initials," she whispered. "Annabelle Warren."

"Could be anyone," Mr. Whitcomb said, habit making him cautious even when belief wanted in.

Damien's voice went quiet. "The Marwick house inventory I saw at the executor's office last week—the attic list included 'oilskin roll—bridge, girl in green—gift for A.W.' The same entry page mentions an order Callum placed at

Sargent & Bird, the art supplier—tubes, brushes, canvas, and one 'emerald green'." He tapped the stretcher's corner with one fingernail. "Supplier's stamp, right there."

Whitcomb leaned in despite himself. The ink was ghosted now, but the oval still read: **SARGENT & BIRD, ARTISTS' MATERIALS.**

"It doesn't prove his hand," Damien said, but the admission was threaded with a reluctant wonder. "But it brings him close."

Marley's pencil moved again—*verso pencil: For A.W.; supplier stamp; estate list = 'gift for A.W.'* She shifted, angling her body so the canvas caught a raking band of light from the display lamp. Pentimenti rose where the light skimmed the brushwork—corrections under the final strokes. The hem had been painted twice; the first line fell higher, cleaner. The painter had lowered it, deepening the shadow, making room for bare feet. The hand at the rail had once curled into an empty fist; now fingers rested, softened, open.

"He changed his mind," she said. "About how she stands. About what touches."

Damien nodded, not taking his eyes from the face. The features weren't photographic—no eye glint, no show-off detail—but the mouth was particular, the set of the jaw held a look that was almost familiar from Marley's dreams: resolve and almost-tremble, a readiness for the next thing even if the next thing was ruin.

"Whoever painted her knew her," he said. It wasn't an assertion—it was grief recognizing itself across mediums. "Knew how she stood when she waited."

Marley let her eyes travel to the rails. Seven posts were visible between the figure and the frame of the far mouth. The painter had rendered them with more care than the rest —tiny notches where old rope had once rubbed, a darker seam along the third beam nail. She drew a small sun in her margin, seven rays, as she always did when the number showed itself.

"There," she said, pointing at the third post. "Nail mark. Exactly where we find the ribbons. He saw it too."

Whitcomb rubbed his jaw. "It's odd," he said, "how a thing can be ordinary until you learn where to stand."

Damien's mouth tightened—approval of the sentence, sorrow at how true it was. He looked again at the background. "No bell tower," he repeated. "Which would put us at least a year before St. Bartholomew's finished raising theirs. That narrows the window." He slid his phone back into his pocket as if the device, clever as it was, had nothing left to add. "There's another note in the executor's file—a letter fragment from Callum's father. He scolds him about 'frivolities' and paints, says a Marwick's hands belong on ledgers and beams, not canvases. He mentions the gown, disapproving, and a portrait painted 'in the place that tempts fools.'"

"The bridge," Marley said.

Damien inclined his head. "So even if the painter wasn't Callum, the house knew the canvas."

Marley moved closer to the edge where the water lay in gentle planes of slate and bottle glass. The paint there was livelier—faster strokes, wet-on-wet that had captured the river's habit of absorbing every color and giving back only itself. In the glossy hollows she could make out a suggestion of reflection—the green of the dress, a smear lengthened by the current. And—only if she let her eyes lose focus—a faint vertical opposite, as though a taller figure stood just out of frame and the water knew before the painter did.

She shivered. "He put absence in," she said, half to Damien, half to the woman in the paint. "Or the river did."

Whitcomb busied himself with the ritual of propriety—finding a cloth to polish a thing that wasn't dusty. He had no language for a river that painted itself; he needed the weight of a rag.

Damien glanced sideways at Marley and then away, as if the intimacy of her seeing made him nervous. "There's something else," he said. "Marwick ledgers for the year before incorporation include a charge to a Miss Beatrice Gray for 'instruction in drawing, one quarter.' She boarded three months in town—stayed above the bakery, of all places. Stories say she sketched people for practice. We have two of her landscapes in the archive." He paused. "But none of them have faces as... felt as this."

"So maybe she taught him," Marley said. "And he painted her." The possibility made her lightheaded—not because it was proof, but because it gave all the fragments a room to share: the printing plate with *She waited beneath the sycamore tree...* in his hand, the ring that would be found later, the ledger with *emerald green*. "A gift for A.W.," she repeated softly, as if reading it might carry it more safely.

She bent, careful, to look along the lower edge. A tide line revealed itself—faint, ochre staining where water had once wicked up the canvas. Flood, she thought. Or storage in a damp place. In the craquelure the tiniest grit winked, catching light like sand.

"This was near the river for a time," she said. "Or the river found it even in the attic." She wrote: *flood mark; silt in cracks—kept near water?*

Damien's hand hovered above the paint, then fell. "The house stood high," he said, eyes narrowing, the archivist returning in him with the comfort of facts. "But there was a summer when the barn flooded." He exhaled through his nose, a humorless near-laugh. "You were right, Whitcomb. This belongs to her."

Whitcomb had already wrapped string around a piece of cardboard for a makeshift corner brace. "I'll make a crate before you go," he said, bustling because bustling kept the uncanny in its place. "And I'll write 'HANDLE LIKE A HEART' in red on both sides, if you'll forgive me the poetry."

Marley smiled without moving her mouth much. She didn't dare let the feeling spread; it would become tears if she did. "Forgiven."

Damien, without touching Marley, came to stand as if he were touching—close enough that their shoulders felt each other's heat. "You see the horizon line?" he asked, quieter now. "It sits lower than the painter's eye. He was taller than her." He glanced at Marley. "It's a small thing, but it reads like somebody trying to take the exact place he stood and keep it."

Marley let herself picture it: a man on the rail, heartbeat where the paint is thin, counting the posts—one, two, the third with the nail—and the woman in the green dress half-turned, mouth set in that particular resolve. A wind. An hour when vows feel like bells. She imagined him thinking, *If I can get this right, time will obey me.* She knew better; still, she loved him a little for trying.

She jotted, *horizon below—painter taller—keeps place.* Then she stopped writing because writing was too small for the ache the canvas made in her. She simply looked and let the ache be a kind of prayer.

Behind them, rain thinned to a beaded mist on the glass. The shop had gone very still, as shops do when a thing inside them is older than the lease.

"I'll notify the board," Damien said at last, voice resigned to its old work. "Provenance: recovered from the attic of Callum Marwick's family home, oilskin-wrapped. Executor log matches. We'll document the verso inscription and the supplier's stamp before you take it." He hesitated. "And I'll note that the archivist has recommended the piece be studied—closely—for symbolic elements that tie to known artifacts and testimonies."

Mr. Whitcomb grinned despite himself. "That last bit is new language for a man who doesn't like ghosts."

Damien didn't return the smile. His eyes were on the woman in green. "I don't like losing."

Marley turned a page in her notebook, made a small box, and wrote, *Addendum: if the painter was Callum, then he tried to hold her there—and we are the ones she asked to carry her forward instead.* She traced a tiny ring in the margin beside the initials A.W. and C.M., not knowing yet how literal that ring would be.

"Wrap it," she said finally, stepping back because if she didn't, she wouldn't. "Before I start reading more into it than it gave us."

Mr. Whitcomb moved to obey, fetching oil paper and twine. Damien didn't move. He held the easel steady as the paper slid up around the sides, the image disappearing fold by careful fold, until the woman in green was a secret again, breaths older than anyone in the room and somehow still warm.

When the last knot was tied, Marley laid her palm against the paper where the figure's heart would be. The thump she felt was only her own, echoed back through oil and board. She let it count to seven, then lifted her hand.

"Call the executor," she said to Damien, turning practical before the ache could climb her throat. "Confirm the attic list, the supplier invoice, the 'gift for A.W.'"

He nodded. "I will." He met her eyes, and for the first time since the night on the bridge, neither of them looked away. "And then we decide where to hang it until we understand what it's saying."

"Somewhere the town can see," Marley said. "And somewhere the river can't reach."

Damien's mouth twitched into something almost like a smile. "Those two places are rare in Brookwood."

Marley lifted the wrapped canvas with Whitcomb's help. It was heavier than she expected, as if paint accumulated weight with years. Or as if stories did. She felt it in her forearms and, deeper, where her fear had lived lately—now sharing space with something steadier. Not certainty. Not yet. But the sense that each fragment was beginning to look for its neighbor.

"Let's take her home," she said. And though she meant the canvas, both men heard the other meaning, too.

They carried the canvas out together, Marley at the front, Damien steadying the back, the rain now little more than a mist that clung to their coats. The paper wrapping darkened in patches where drops struck, but Whitcomb had tied the knots tight, and the canvas was safe within. The town street was hushed, lamps gleaming through fog, storefronts shuttered early as though Brookwood itself sensed that something had been disturbed.

Damien set the painting carefully in the back of his truck, laying a folded blanket beneath and another across the top. He stood still for a moment after, hand resting on the bundle like a man lingering over a grave.

"You're certain it was in Callum's house?" Marley asked, her voice low, as if afraid the painting might overhear.

"I've seen the executor's notes myself," Damien said. "Attic storage. The inventory's sparse, but the description matches exactly. Callum Marwick's hand was all over those ledgers, neat and stubborn. If he had a portrait painted, it makes sense it would end up there. And if he painted it himself..." He trailed off, his expression tightening.

"Then it was meant for her," Marley finished. "For Annabelle."

They climbed into the truck, the engine coughing before it caught. Damien pulled onto the road, the tires hissing over wet gravel. The windshield wipers squeaked a slow rhythm, but Marley barely noticed. Her eyes drifted again and again to the rear window where the bundled canvas rested.

"The sycamore tree was there," she murmured. "Not the chapel. Not the square. Just the tree and the bridge. Almost like he wanted to keep her waiting in the same place forever."

Damien's hands tightened on the wheel. "Or like he knew that's where she would be lost."

They rode in silence for a few moments, the fog pulling close around the beams of the headlights. Then Marley spoke again, softly but with resolve. "You said the Marwicks mentioned the gown in records."

He nodded once. "A shipping receipt. 'One gown, satin, green.' His father annotated the ledger with his usual bitter-ness—'wasteful.' That word shows up next to nearly every-thing Callum touched. Paints. Ribbons. The bakery's flour. He wanted his son a banker, not an artist. Not a lover."

"And yet here she is," Marley said. "Green satin, standing on the bridge, outlasting them all."

The truck turned onto the lane toward Damien's house. The bridge's shape loomed in the distance, its ribs faint through the mist. Marley's stomach knotted. For an instant she thought the canvas might hum in the back, as though paint remembered footsteps.

Inside, they propped the painting on the dining room table, the paper wrapping peeled back like a bandage. The lamp light caught the green once more, and the figure on the bridge seemed to take a breath.

Marley drew closer, unable to resist. She traced the outline of the horizon with her eyes. The valley looked young, as though the land itself hadn't yet decided what stories it would bear. The river lay quiet, but she imagined it already knew.

Damien stood opposite her, arms folded, expression unreadable. "Do you know what it means, Marley? Really? Not just that it's Annabelle in paint, but why it's here, now? Why after all this time it finds its way back into your hands?"

She shook her head slowly. "Not yet. But it feels like one more piece placed exactly where it belongs. The ribbon. The button. The poem. And now this." She pressed her palm to her notebook, which lay open beside her. "It's not just fragments anymore. It's beginning to look like a life."

Damien exhaled, the sound equal parts awe and frustration. "And if piecing together her life costs us ours?"

Marley lifted her eyes, steady. "Then it will be worth it. Because no story deserves to end alone on a bridge."

For a moment he looked as though he might argue, but the fight drained from his shoulders. He rubbed a hand across his face, weariness etched deep. "I don't know how much more of this I can shield my daughter from," he said. "If the bridge keeps pulling, it won't just be you it wants."

"I know," Marley whispered. "That's why we can't stop now."

They fell into silence again, both staring at the painted figure—her dress, her bare feet, her waiting. The house ticked around them: pipes shifting, a clock on the mantel marking time.

Finally Damien spoke, his voice softer than before. "The records say Callum's mother found him in the attic once, staring at this very canvas. She told him to put it away. That was the last time anyone saw him paint."

Marley's chest ached. "So this was his confession. Or his vow."

Damien nodded grimly. "And maybe his failure."

Marley reached for her pencil, scrawling the thought before it could fade: *The painting as vow. The bridge as witness. The woman as eternal wait.*

When she looked up again, the canvas no longer seemed like just a relic. It was a mirror. A reminder that love unfinished did not die—it echoed.

Damien turned down the lamp, leaving the figure half in shadow. "Tomorrow, we'll take it to the archives," he said. "Photograph it. Cross-reference with the estate lists. Do this properly."

"And tonight?" Marley asked.

He hesitated, eyes flicking toward the bridge outside. "Tonight we don't look out the window."

But even as he said it, Marley knew she would. And when she did, she thought she saw the faintest shimmer at the bridge's midpoint—as though paint and memory and mist had begun to trade places.

The figure in the canvas, the woman in green, was not just a portrait anymore. She was watching. Waiting still.

22

MASON JAR MESSAGE

The riverbank had softened from days of rain, the kind of damp that left moss luminous and earth pliable. Marley had come alone in the early morning, mist still clinging low along the planks of the bridge. She carried her notebook, a trowel, and the kind of restless urgency that had followed her since the painting was unwrapped on Damien's table.

She paused at the third beam, where ribbons once tied had left their faint indent. The river whispered its long song beneath, steady as breath. She crouched, her palm brushing damp soil where weeds tangled. That was when she saw it— a glass rim breaking the surface, like something that had waited for her hand.

Her breath caught.

The earth gave way easily under her trowel, wet soil slipping aside until the object was free. A mason jar, its lid rusted, its glass fogged with years of seep and cold. Across the lid, in careful script etched with something sharp, were words that stiffened her spine:

For Her Eyes Only.

Her hands trembled. She wiped the jar against her coat, smearing mud but revealing the etching more clearly. Each letter was deliberate, scratched deep enough to last.

Marley sat back on her heels, rainwater seeping into the knees of her jeans, her heart drumming in her chest. For her eyes only. She turned the words over in her mind, weighing whether the message was meant for Annabelle herself or for the one who would come after. Either way, the jar had waited.

The seal had cracked with age, and when she twisted, the lid gave with a sigh, as though it had held its breath for decades. Inside, folded and nearly disintegrating, was a piece of paper. She drew it out gently, the edges breaking like petals, water stains blooming across its surface.

She laid it flat against her notebook, tracing the words with her eyes. The ink had faded, but the hand was still legible—curves and angles particular, a script too tender to be impersonal.

Dearest Annabelle,

If you love him as I know you do, go with him. But do not return. The vows you dream of are not welcome here. He is not welcome here. I beg you, take this and leave before the seventh night. Do not look back.

The page ended abruptly, the lower corner torn. Marley's breath grew unsteady. The note had not been written by Callum—it carried a tone of warning, not devotion. Someone had cautioned Annabelle to run. And the insistence—*do not return*—burned through the paper, urgent even in its faded state.

Her pencil scratched quickly across the margin of her journal, copying line for line before the paper could crumble further. Her hand shook, but she steadied it, whispering the words aloud as she wrote them: "Do not return... the seventh night."

Behind her, footsteps crunched on wet earth. She turned. Damien stood at the base of the bridge, his coat collar up against the chill, his expression taut as he saw what she cradled.

"You found something," he said.

She nodded, lifting the paper. "Buried in a mason jar. Marked for her eyes only."

Damien crouched beside her, his gaze narrowing on the fragile sheet. He didn't touch it—his hands stayed clenched on his knees—but his eyes moved line by line, darkening as he read.

"This isn't the story we were told," he said.

Marley shook her head. "The records say she ran away, alone, spurred by grief or scandal. But this—" She tapped the margin where she'd copied the warning. "This says she was told never to return. That someone wanted her gone, not lost."

Damien's jaw tightened. "Or silenced. To rewrite her story before it was finished."

The fog pressed closer, thickening the air around them, as though the bridge itself leaned in to hear. Marley felt a shiver crawl up her spine but forced herself to look Damien in the eye. "This letter changes everything."

And in the silence that followed, the river seemed to confirm it.

MARLEY SPREAD the letter on the dining table that night, a makeshift preservation station cobbled together with blotting paper, tissue, and the steady patience of her hands. The paper was fragile, its fibers separating at the folds, but the words clung stubbornly, refusing to vanish. She bent low over it, her breath shallow, as though one sigh might erase it entirely.

She traced the etched script again—*Do not return... seventh night*—and the weight of it pressed heavier than anything she'd uncovered yet. Not just a memory fragment, not an echo, but instruction. Warning. And betrayal all at once.

"I don't understand," she said finally, her voice hushed in the lamplight. "The official record says Annabelle fled— alone, in disgrace. But this..." Her finger trembled against the words. "This sounds like someone forced her to leave. Someone who knew she wanted to elope, but forbade it."

Damien stood opposite her, arms braced against the table, his eyes on the brittle sheet. He hadn't spoken for minutes, just studied, his jaw tightening every time his gaze passed over the line about the seventh night.

"It's a contradiction," he said at last, the archivist in him surfacing, though his tone carried an edge. "And Brookwood doesn't like contradictions. The board filed Annabelle's case under 'runaway, presumed dead.' End of story. Neat, efficient, tragic enough to be whispered but never probed."

Marley shook her head. "But the jar was marked *For Her Eyes Only*. Someone cared enough to bury this. To keep her secret safe, or maybe to keep it waiting for the right eyes." She pressed her palm to her notebook, where she'd recopied every word in careful script. "I think it was meant for me."

Damien's mouth pressed into a line. "Or it was meant for her. And she never found it."

The thought chilled her. She sat back, staring at the

warped glass of the jar now empty on the counter. "Why bury it if not to be found? Letters are meant to be read."

"Or hidden," Damien countered. His voice grew darker, more taut. "This could've been planted to mislead. Family politics. Healers. Someone who didn't want Annabelle or Callum crossing the boundaries laid for them."

Marley's chest tightened. "But then the words *do not return*... It's more than a warning. It's exile."

Damien leaned closer, his finger hovering over the stains at the edge of the letter. "Water damage. The ink's bled here, see? But the handwriting's consistent with the period. And the phrasing—it's plain. Not poetic like Callum's letters. Not lyrical. More like an elder's voice. A parent. Or a patriarch of the town."

She looked up sharply. "You think this came from his family?"

"I think it's possible." He met her eyes, and there was sorrow in the steadiness of his gaze. "The Marwicks had reputation to protect. A son courting a delivery girl, a healer—worse, a Warren—it would've been scandal. They could have ordered her away."

"And blamed her after she was gone," Marley said bitterly.

The lamplight flickered, a draft whispering through the old house. For a moment Marley thought she heard the bridge's groan outside, though the river lay quiet in the night. She forced herself to keep her focus on the letter.

"It means everything we thought we knew is wrong," she said. "Annabelle didn't run away because she wanted to. She was told to leave. Forced. And if she tried to come back..." Marley's voice cracked, her imagination filling in the silence with shadows too sharp to name.

Damien straightened, dragging a hand through his hair.

"This is what terrifies me, Marley. Every piece we uncover, every artifact—ribbons, buttons, plates, paintings—it rewrites her story. And each time, the truth is darker, closer to us, less controllable." His eyes flicked to her journal, to the sketches and fragments she had gathered. "You're building a narrative no one in this town has ever wanted told."

She lifted her chin. "And maybe that's why it has to be told. Because silence has never set her free."

His mouth opened, then closed again. He turned, pacing the length of the room, his steps uneven. "If this letter is real—and I believe it is—it undermines a century of Brookwood's history. It means Annabelle wasn't the girl who abandoned love. She was abandoned by those who should have defended her."

Marley's throat burned. "Then we're not just solving a mystery, Damien. We're undoing a lie."

He stopped at the window, his reflection dim in the glass. "And lies don't die quietly."

For a long moment neither of them spoke. The house creaked around them. The jar caught the lamplight, its glass clouded, its etching *For Her Eyes Only* gleaming faintly like a dare.

Marley finally broke the silence, her voice steady despite the tremor in her hands. "I'm going back to the bridge tomorrow. If there was one jar, there may be others. Maybe she left more messages. Maybe she tried to leave a trail."

Damien turned from the window, his face pale but resolute. "Then I'm coming with you. Because if the past is going to fight back, I won't let you face it alone."

And though he spoke with conviction, Marley saw in his eyes what he would never admit—that each step deeper into Annabelle's truth was one more crack in the fragile ground beneath them both.

THE NIGHT WORE on with the sound of rain on the roof, each drop like a quiet metronome to the thoughts that refused to rest. The letter lay between them on the table, fragile as ash, yet heavier than stone. Neither Marley nor Damien touched it again. It was as if their hands knew better than their minds—the paper belonged to the past, and to disturb it further might invite the weight of all it carried.

Marley closed her notebook carefully, pressing her palm against the leather cover. "This changes everything," she said again, the words firmer now, like she was trying to nail them into the air so they couldn't be ignored. "Annabelle wasn't weak. She wasn't reckless. She was exiled."

Damien didn't answer. He sat in the chair opposite, shoulders bent forward, his hand rubbing the back of his neck. He looked older than the hour before, shadows deepening the lines at his temples.

"You're quiet," she said.

"I'm thinking." His voice was rough, as though thought itself had scraped it raw. "I've spent my life protecting Brookwood's records. I've defended the board, the archives, the family names. And now—" He gestured at the letter, a quick flick of his hand as though it burned. "Now I have to admit the records were never truth. They were construction. Story dressed as fact."

Marley leaned toward him, her tone sharpening. "Then you see why this matters. Why I can't stop. Every artifact we uncover pulls Annabelle closer to her true self, the one they erased. If we stop now, we're complicit in that erasure."

His eyes met hers, blue-grey like the river when a storm

rolled in. "And if digging any deeper puts you in her place? If it repeats?"

Her chest tightened, not just at the warning but at the naked fear in his voice. "You think the past is that strong?"

"I think the past never left," he said flatly. "It's here. In my daughter's sleepwalking, in your visions, in the way this town reacts when you so much as ask a question." He leaned forward, his hand flat on the table. "The note isn't just a contradiction in history. It's a warning still alive. Someone once said, 'Do not return.' Maybe that command didn't stop with Annabelle."

The lamp crackled faintly, its flame flickering as if to underline his words. Marley swallowed hard. "So what, Damien? We stop here? We let the lies stand?"

He closed his eyes briefly, exhaling through his nose. "I want to protect you. That's all."

The tenderness in the words collided with the iron of his fear, and Marley felt herself split between wanting to reach across the table and wanting to push it farther away. "Protecting me by silencing Annabelle again?" she asked softly, the edge of accusation threading through her tone.

His jaw clenched. "Don't twist my words."

"Then hear mine," she said, her voice steady even as her hands trembled. "I didn't come here to rewrite Brookwood's records for the board. I came because something—someone —called me to this bridge, to this story. Every ribbon, every button, every dream, every word—it's all been leading to this. I can't walk away now. And I won't."

The silence that followed was thick as fog. Damien stared at her, the battle plain in his face—duty against desire, fear against trust. Finally he pushed back from the table, rising to his feet.

"You remind me of her," he said, voice low.

Marley blinked. "Of Annabelle?"

"No." His gaze softened, though it didn't lessen. "Of my wife. The way she couldn't let go of the visions. The way she insisted the truth was worth more than her own safety. And I lost her." His throat tightened, the confession clawing out of him. "I can't—Marley, I can't lose you too."

Her breath caught. For a heartbeat, neither moved. Then she stood as well, closing the space between them until only the table edge separated them. "You won't," she said, though even as she spoke it she knew it was a promise she couldn't guarantee. "Because I'm not chasing death, Damien. I'm chasing truth. And I need you beside me, not standing in my way."

He looked down at the letter once more, the frail paper that had unraveled everything. His hands curled into fists at his sides.

"The board will bury this if they learn of it," he said finally. "They'll call it forgery, dismiss it as hoax, lock it away where no one sees. That's how they've always kept order."

"Then we don't let them," Marley replied. "We keep it safe. We keep finding more. We build so strong a case the truth can't be denied."

Damien's lips parted as though to argue, but no words came. Instead, he closed his eyes, breathing hard, as if surrendering to the fact that the battle had already been lost. Not to her, but to Annabelle. To the voice of the past that neither of them could silence.

When he opened them again, the fear was still there, but so was something else—an unspoken resolve that terrified and steadied Marley in equal measure.

"We're in this together," he said at last.

Marley's chest loosened, relief and dread tangling. She nodded once. "Together."

The letter lay between them still, ink faded, water-stained, its warning echoing louder now than it ever had in Annabelle's own time. *Do not return.* But here they were, returning anyway.

And outside, the bridge waited in the mist, its silence louder than bells.

23

———

TRUTH IN THE LEDGER

The Brookwood Historical Society always smelled faintly of dust and lemon oil, a fragrance born of constant battles between neglect and care. On that damp October morning, the air was heavy with the perfume of paper after rain. The building's stone steps glistened, and Marley's boots squeaked against the old wooden floorboards as she followed Damien inside.

He held the door for Marley and then led her toward the back, to the room where boxes of ledgers, maps, and deeds filled the shelves like forgotten sentinels.

Marley trailed her fingers along spines as they passed—years carved into leather, cracked labels barely legible. Her pulse quickened with that familiar electricity: the sense that answers lay somewhere in these bindings, waiting to be coaxed out.

Damien pulled a key from his pocket, fitting it into a locked cabinet with well-practiced precision. The door creaked open to reveal a row of oversize books, their bindings stiff with age. "Burial records," he said. "Kept by the society before the chapel took over full registry. Dates from the 1870s through the early 1900s. Few people bother with these anymore."

Marley's heart beat harder. She stepped forward, scanning the row until her eyes landed on one bound in dark brown calfskin, corners reinforced with brass that had long since tarnished. Stamped faintly into its spine: **Burials – 1880–1890.**

"That's the one," she whispered.

Damien lifted it carefully, as if cradling something brittle as bone, and set it on the long oak table in the center of the room. The weight of it landed with a solid thump, the sound reverberating through Marley like a drum. She pulled out her notebook, poised her pencil, while Damien eased the covers open.

The first pages were routine—columns ruled by hand, names inscribed with meticulous script, dates of interment, remarks penned by clerks who had long since turned to dust themselves. Damien turned page after page, each one heavy, the paper thick with rag content, made to last centuries.

Then Marley saw it.

Her hand darted out, stopping his. "There."

Her eyes locked on a single line midway down the page. The name had once been inscribed in the same neat hand as the others: **Annabelle Warren.** But where the ink should have been permanent, a knife had cut. The name was violently scratched out, strokes deep enough to tear the paper. The gouges split through the letters, leaving jagged scars.

Marley's throat tightened. "They erased her," she breathed.

Damien leaned closer, his face grave. "No," he said slowly. "Not erased. Condemned."

Beside the obliterated name, faint but unmistakable, was a mark drawn in ink darker than the rest. A circle bisected by two crossing lines, simple yet deliberate.

Marley's hand shook as she copied it into her notebook. "The Green Healer's Circle," she whispered. She recognized it instantly from her aunt's journals, from the sigils she'd traced in margins and found carved in beams. A mark of belonging, of power—and of judgment.

She looked up at Damien. "This isn't just a burial ledger. It's a sentence. Someone marked her as one of them. And then struck her out."

Damien's expression was taut, the archivist's calm cracking at the edges. "Which means Annabelle's disappearance wasn't only about forbidden love. It may have been punishment. Silencing. An erasure by more than rumor—by decree."

Marley's chest heaved, the weight of the discovery settling on her shoulders. She pressed her hand against the page, hovering above the ruined name as though she could feel the pain of it echoing up through the parchment.

"Annabelle wasn't lost to accident," she said, her voice low but steady. "She was targeted. And the Green Healers knew."

Damien closed his eyes briefly, and when he opened them again, the blue in them had hardened. "Then this was bigger than Callum Marwick. Bigger than romance. Annabelle was silenced because of what she was, or what she carried."

The ledger between them seemed to pulse with its own gravity, the scarred line daring them to keep reading, daring them to risk pulling Annabelle further from the shadows where Brookwood had left her.

Marley tightened her grip on her pencil. She knew now:

the bridge had never been just about love. It had always been about power. And power, once stolen, demanded to be reclaimed.

MARLEY COULDN'T TEAR her eyes away from the violence of the gouges. The knife had not simply scratched Annabelle's name; it had carved into the parchment with rage. She imagined the hand that had done it—a clerk or elder perhaps—pressing down until the nib or blade nearly broke, each stroke a refusal to let Annabelle rest.

Her fingers hovered just above the scarred letters, trembling. "This isn't just erasure," she whispered. "It's execution on paper. They didn't want her to be remembered, not even in death. They wanted her to be nothing."

Damien leaned over her shoulder, his breath slow and uneven. "Brookwood prided itself on keeping order," he said. "No scandal, no unrest, no trace of shame. If someone defied them—or defiled them—they cut them out." His eyes narrowed on the sigil. "But this mark... it wasn't random. Someone wanted it clear. Annabelle wasn't forgotten. She was branded."

Marley opened her notebook, sketching the circle with deliberate precision. The lines intersected cleanly, symmetrical in their finality. "The Green Healers' Circle," she said again. "In my aunt's journals, it shows up beside rituals of protection, secrecy... but also exile. Once marked, there was no return."

She swallowed hard, remembering the mason jar's letter: *Do not return.* The phrase now thrummed like a chorus in her bones, tying the jar to the ledger, the ledger to the bridge. Every thread pulling tighter.

Damien's hand pressed flat against the table, knuckles

whitening. "If this is true, then Annabelle wasn't just a lovesick girl. She was a threat. To their families, to their power, maybe even to the healer circle itself."

Marley turned to him, her eyes fierce. "And they silenced her."

He flinched as if the words were a blow. "You're suggesting a conspiracy, Marley. That Brookwood's founders didn't just cover up a romance gone wrong—they orchestrated her disappearance."

"Not suggesting," she said. "Seeing." She pointed to the torn page. "This is proof. Someone went out of their way to mutilate her memory. That doesn't happen by accident. That's intent."

Damien's jaw clenched. He stepped back, pacing the narrow aisle between shelves. "Do you know what you're saying? If this ledger is ever shown, it implicates half the families still living here. Names, bloodlines, reputations. People will fight this. They'll bury it again."

"Then let them fight," Marley shot back. "Because silence is complicity, Damien. If Annabelle was punished for love—or for power—then every whisper we've heard, every voice in the mist, every dream has been her begging to be remembered."

He stopped pacing, turning toward her with eyes clouded by a storm of doubt. "And if uncovering this tears the town apart? If the descendants of those who struck her out decide you're the next to be silenced?"

Marley's pencil snapped in her hand, the sound sharp in the stillness. She dropped it, her breath harsh, and looked at him squarely. "Then I'll keep writing with the pieces. With buttons and ribbons and ledgers and songs. You can bury flesh, Damien, but you can't bury echoes. And she will not go quietly again."

For a long moment, he said nothing. He only looked at her, and something in his expression faltered—the certainty, the historian's shield. His shoulders slumped, and when he finally spoke, his voice was low and reluctant, as though pried from the deepest part of him.

"You're right."

The words hung between them, startling in their nakedness. He pressed a hand to his temple, sighing. "God help me, you're right. This isn't about a failed romance. It's about silencing. About control. Annabelle's story was rewritten to keep power intact. And now we're unspooling it, thread by thread."

Marley felt the burn of tears at the corners of her eyes, not of grief but of vindication. "So you see it now. She wasn't weak. She was strong. Too strong for them."

He nodded grimly. "And they couldn't allow that."

The ledger lay open still, its wound exposed. Marley traced the mark again, committing it to memory, as if memorizing the scar could keep Annabelle alive.

But as she did, she saw something else. At the bottom of the page, faint and nearly obscured by ink bleed, were two initials: **C.M.**

Her breath caught.

"Callum Marwick," she whispered.

Damien leaned closer, following her gaze. His lips parted in disbelief. "He signed the page..."

"Or tried to," Marley murmured, her pulse hammering. "But the ink was blotted, almost erased. As though someone didn't want his protest seen."

They looked at each other, the weight of the discovery pressing down.

This was no longer just Annabelle's story. Callum's silence, too, had been forced.

And the ledger, once meant to mark endings, had just opened a door they couldn't close.

THE LEDGER REMAINED open between them, the candlelight trembling across its scarred page, turning the gouged lines into shadows that seemed to move on their own. Marley's notebook lay filled with copies of every letter and symbol, but she kept glancing back at the original, as though fearing it might vanish the moment her gaze broke.

Damien lowered into the chair again, his face pale, his hands still gripping the table edge. For a long moment, he didn't speak. He stared at the scratched-out name, at the circle beside it, at the faint initials almost lost in the bleed. Then, slowly, he exhaled.

"It's all here," he said at last, voice hoarse. "The ledger was meant to keep record, to guard the truth, but someone turned it into a weapon. Annabelle Warren wasn't just erased—she was condemned. And Callum... he tried to resist, but they smothered even his ink." He leaned back, pressing his palms over his face. "God, Marley. This isn't just a love story. It's a purge."

The word landed like a stone in Marley's chest. "A purge," she repeated, tasting its bitterness. "That means there were others."

Damien's hands dropped from his face, and though his features were tight, his eyes betrayed the admission. "Yes. If Annabelle was marked with the healer's circle, then she wasn't alone. She was one of them. And if she was silenced, so were others. Maybe not killed—but erased. Cut from records. Shamed into shadows. Their memory stolen so the families could preserve the illusion of purity."

Marley shivered. "The bridge isn't just haunted by one woman. It's haunted by everyone silenced with her."

Damien swallowed hard. "And we've been walking over their bones without ever knowing."

For the first time since they'd begun, Marley saw the scholar in him falter completely. He wasn't just shaken—he was broken open. His loyalty to the archives, to the town's curated memory, to the stories he had defended for years—it all cracked in the glow of that one marred page.

She reached across the table, resting her hand over his. "You see it now," she said softly. "This isn't just about Annabelle and Callum. It's about power. About a whole community rewriting its own history to bury the inconvenient. And if we keep going, Damien, we may find it goes deeper than even this ledger can show."

He didn't pull away. His hand twitched beneath hers, and for a heartbeat he looked at her with something raw—gratitude, fear, and the faint glimmer of trust. "You're right," he said. "I can't deny it anymore. The conspiracy's undeniable. Annabelle was silenced because she carried something larger—love, lineage, power, maybe all of it. And the town's been living on the lie ever since."

Marley tightened her grip on his hand. "Then we owe it to her to bring the truth back. To bring them all back."

Damien drew in a shaky breath. "And in doing so, we risk becoming the next names scratched out."

The words sent a chill through her. She withdrew her hand, picking up her pencil again, her jaw set. "Then let them try. I'll write until my hands bleed if I have to. Annabelle will be remembered."

He closed the ledger gently, almost reverently, as though laying a body back to rest. The sound of the cover shutting echoed in the quiet room. "We'll copy it," he said. "But the book stays here. If the board learns what we've uncovered, they'll destroy it. Or us."

Marley nodded, though the weight of it pressed heavier on her chest. They weren't simply uncovering a forgotten love—they were prying open the town's oldest wound. And Brookwood would bleed for it.

She looked once more at the closed ledger, her fingers twitching as if they longed to pry it open again. "This isn't the end," she whispered. "It's only the beginning."

Damien rose, gathering his coat, his movements stiff but resolved. "Then be ready, Marley. Because once we carry this truth out of here, Brookwood will never look at us the same again."

Together, they walked out of the archive room, the echoes of their footsteps swallowed by the silence of shelves that had held their secret for over a century.

And as the door shut behind them, the ledger sat alone in the dark, its scarred page humming like a wound that had finally been touched.

24

BRIDGE DREAM #3 – THE DEPARTURE

The dream came like snowfall—silent, inevitable, shrouding everything in pale, unyielding stillness.

Marley stood at the edge of Brookwood, though it wasn't the Brookwood she knew. The streets were narrower, the houses fewer, their lamps glowing with the faint yellow of oil rather than the hum of electricity. Winter clutched the town in its skeletal grip. The trees were bare, branches clawing at a sky the color of slate.

And there—moving through the snow with slow, barefoot steps—was Annabelle Warren.

Her dress was green once, Marley knew, though now it hung in tatters, hem frayed and soaked from the frost. Her hair clung to her damp cheeks, wild strands plastered to skin as she clutched something against her chest—a letter, edges blackened where flame had eaten it. The ashes drifted from her fingers, scattering into the snow like shadows trying to take root.

Marley wanted to call out, but her throat sealed. She could only follow, her steps leaving no mark in the snow, as

Annabelle drifted past shuttered windows and toward the bridge.

The closer they came, the louder the river below roared, a fury beneath the silence of the town. The bridge loomed, black beams slick with ice, lanterns swaying though no wind stirred. Annabelle's bare feet left prints on the planks, each one darker than the last, as though the boards themselves drank her sorrow.

She stopped midway across, turning her head as if to listen for someone who should have been there. "Callum," she whispered. The name was carried off by the mist, swallowed before Marley could catch its echo.

Annabelle drew a deep breath, her body trembling as she pressed the burning letter tighter to her chest. Then, with sudden finality, she ripped it in two, feeding the rest of it to the flame cupped in her hand. The fire licked her fingers but she did not flinch. When the last scrap vanished into smoke, she let out a sound that was neither sob nor scream—just a raw exhale of loss.

At the base of the bridge, she knelt, setting down a small wooden box. Marley recognized it instantly: the music box. Its carvings were the same—delicate ivy winding around the lid, the faint outline of initials half-hidden by time. Annabelle lingered with her hand upon it, her lips moving in words Marley couldn't hear, her breath misting in the icy air.

Then she stood, her green dress whipping about her ankles though no wind blew, and she walked away from Brookwood. Away from the bridge. Away from the life she had been promised.

Marley wanted to chase after her, to beg her to stay, to ask her why she was leaving the box. But her feet refused to move. She remained rooted to the planks, watching the figure of Annabelle diminish into the white, her bare feet disappearing into the snowfall until she was nothing more than a memory etched into the mist.

The river swelled, the bridge groaned, and the music box began to play. Not its usual melody, not the delicate tune Marley knew. This was slower, fractured, the notes dragging as though weighed down by grief. Each chord bent low, twisting into something mournful, aching.

Marley clutched her ears but the sound seeped through her bones. It was Annabelle's song—slowed, broken, unfinished.

When she woke, her pillow was damp with tears, her fingers clutching the air as though they had tried to grasp the wooden box. On her bedside table, the music box sat closed, silent. She reached for it, her hands shaking, and wound it gently.

The song spilled into the room.

Slower. Sadder. Just as it had been in the dream.

Marley's breath caught in her chest. She pressed her palm over her mouth to keep from crying out, her eyes locked on the box as though it might open on its own.

Annabelle hadn't just walked away in Marley's dream. She had left a piece of herself behind.

And now, the bridge had carried that sorrow into Marley's waking world.

MARLEY SAT at her small desk long after the dawn had turned the sky a watery gray. The journal lay open, its spine worn from constant handling, pages crowded with notes that straddled the line between dream fragments and historical records. Her hand trembled as she scrawled the latest entry across the ruled lines:

Annabelle burned her letter. Bare feet on the bridge. The music box left at the base. Song changed—slower, heavier, like mourning in melody.

The graphite smeared beneath her palm as she wrote faster, afraid the images would slip away if she lingered. She pressed her lips together, hearing again the scrape of Annabelle's bare feet across the icy planks, the crackle of fire devouring the letter, the way her hand lingered on the box before she turned away. Each detail weighted her like a stone.

Her eyes shifted to the real box sitting on the table. She wound it again, though her stomach tightened at the sound. The melody spilled out—hesitant, dragging, notes pulled down like branches under snow.

It was no longer just an object. It was alive in its own way, echoing Annabelle's grief through time.

Marley closed her eyes, tears prickling as she tried to understand. Why would Annabelle leave the box behind if it was so precious? Why leave it at the bridge, the very place that now seemed to hoard her memory like a jealous keeper?

Her pencil scratched furiously, trying to force sense onto the page:

Possibility 1: She left it for Callum. A promise.

Possibility 2: She left it as a marker, a vessel of memory, to be found later.

Possibility 3: She had no choice—was forced to leave it behind.

The more she wrote, the more questions multiplied. She rubbed her eyes, smearing graphite onto her skin. Her mind replayed the image of Annabelle's face—stoic, resigned, but beneath it, something burning. A woman who had chosen love, and in that choice, had been condemned.

The knock on her door startled her. She shoved the journal aside, hastily closing it before Damien stepped into the room. He looked exhausted, his hair damp from the mist outside, his coat still clinging with drops of rain.

"You didn't come by the archives this morning," he said softly. "I was worried."

Marley gestured to the desk. "I couldn't sleep. I had another dream."

Damien's expression darkened, the lines at the corners of his mouth tightening. He crossed the room and stood over the desk, his eyes falling on the music box. "Something happened."

She nodded. "It's changed."

Before he could ask, she wound the box again. Together, they listened as the song filled the room—notes that once lifted now dragging, their cadence broken, slowed, mournful.

Damien's face shifted, disbelief clouded by recognition. "That's not possible," he said, though his voice lacked conviction. "Mechanisms don't just... change. Not without tampering."

Marley leaned forward, her gaze sharp. "I didn't touch it. Damien, I swear to you. This is exactly how it played in my dream. Annabelle left it at the bridge. And now..." She gestured helplessly toward the box as the melody stumbled through its grief. "Now it plays her sorrow."

He sat down heavily in the chair beside her desk, running a hand through his hair. For a long moment, he said nothing, his jaw working as though grinding against a thought he didn't want to release.

Finally, he whispered, "Tell me everything."

So she did. She described the snow, the bare feet, the torn letter, the flames. She described Annabelle's whisper of

Callum's name, the resignation in her walk, the way she left the music box as though planting a seed for someone to find. As Marley spoke, she watched Damien's face harden, his rational armor fraying until his hand pressed to his forehead, eyes closed.

When she finished, silence stretched between them. The box wound down, the final note hanging brittle in the air before it died.

Marley's voice cracked as she asked, "What does it mean, Damien? Why leave it behind?"

He looked up at her, blue eyes bleak. "Because she knew she wasn't coming back."

The certainty in his tone pierced her. She shook her head, refusing to let it be final. "Or because she wanted us to find it. Because she wanted someone to finish what she couldn't."

Damien leaned back, his chair creaking under the weight of his body. He looked older suddenly, wearier, as though the dream had drained him too. "You're asking me to believe that the bridge itself carried her message across time. That this box is more than wood and brass—it's her grief, still alive."

Marley pointed to the journal. "I'm not asking you to believe me. I'm asking you to see. Every echo we've uncovered—every ribbon, every letter, every mark in the ledger—has been leading us here. Annabelle isn't just a ghost. She's history refusing to stay buried."

Damien rubbed at his eyes, then let his hands fall with a sigh. "And what if history doesn't want to be uncovered? What if she's warning us?"

Marley's lips pressed into a thin line. She picked up her pencil again and wrote in the margin of her journal, pressing hard enough to tear the page:

Not warning. Inviting.

She turned the book so Damien could see. "If she wanted to warn us away, she wouldn't leave signs. She wouldn't change the song. She wouldn't call my name in dreams. Damien, she wants us to finish her story."

He stared at the words, then at her, and she saw the fear in him deepen. But beneath it was something else—acceptance. He didn't want to believe, but belief had already lodged itself inside him, and it was growing roots.

"Then God help us both," he muttered, "because if Annabelle's pulling us into her story, there may be no way to walk back out."

Marley wound the box again, the mournful notes filling the room, and whispered, "Then we won't walk back. We'll walk through."

And for the first time, Damien didn't argue.

THE ROOM SEEMED SMALLER with the music box between them, its sorrowful notes lingering even after the winding ran down. The silence that followed was heavier than any melody—an airless hush that pressed on Marley's chest until she thought she might choke.

Damien leaned forward, elbows on his knees, his head bowed into his hands. The lamplight caught in his hair, tracing the silver that had crept in at the temples. He looked less like the confident historian who had guided her through archives and more like a man cornered by his own ghosts.

When he finally spoke, his voice was rough, the words strained through his throat. "I can't deny it anymore. Not the voices, not the dreams, not this." His gaze lifted, blue eyes raw. "That song isn't just different—it's deliberate. It's

Annabelle's way of reminding us she's still here. Of pulling us into her grief."

Marley drew in a slow breath, the confirmation both vindication and terror. "So you believe me now," she whispered.

"I believe the evidence," Damien said, his hand tightening into a fist against his knee. "And every piece points to the same truth: Annabelle wasn't just abandoned or forgotten. She was erased. And now... she won't let us rest until the story is told."

Marley turned toward the box again, her fingers brushing its carved lid. The wood felt warm, as though it pulsed faintly with life. "She left it for us," Marley murmured. "For me. So the music would change when the time was right."

Damien shook his head, his mouth tightening. "No—she left it because she couldn't carry it where she was going. The bridge took it. The bridge took everything. And now it's using us as its mouthpiece."

His words cut her, but she refused to let them stand. "It's not the bridge. It's her. She's using it, yes, but not to hurt us. To finish what was stolen."

"Marley," Damien said sharply, "every step we take into this story pulls us closer to whatever destroyed her. You think it's just about remembrance? Then why does my daughter sleepwalk to that cursed bridge? Why are threats sliding under our door? Annabelle's story isn't just tragic— it's dangerous. And if we keep following her, she could take us too."

Marley's throat ached. She wanted to argue, to drown his fear with her certainty, but the image of Annabelle's torn dress and burned letter seared into her mind. Damien wasn't wrong about the danger. Still, she couldn't turn away.

Not now. Not when Annabelle's echoes had carved their way into her own life so completely.

She steadied her voice. "You're right—there's risk. But the greater risk is silence. If we stop now, she stays erased. And Damien—maybe your daughter's walking because Annabelle knows she'll be heard. She isn't trying to curse us. She's trying to finish what she started."

He stared at her for a long time, chest rising and falling in uneven rhythm. Finally, he closed his eyes and leaned back in the chair. "I want to believe you. God, I do. But every time I start to... I see my wife's face. I hear her dreams before she died. The same voices, the same calling. And I can't shake the thought that Annabelle's story isn't just a plea— it's a trap."

The confession hit Marley like a physical blow. She reached across the table, her hand closing over his fist. His knuckles were cold, tense, but he didn't pull away this time.

"Then we face it together," she said firmly. "If it's a plea, we'll answer. If it's a trap, we'll spring it. But we can't keep living in this half-space where we pretend it's all coinci- dence. We've already crossed the line. The music's changed. The story's changed. And so have we."

Damien opened his eyes, meeting hers. Something shifted there—a resignation, but also resolve. "You're right," he whispered. "We can't go back."

For the first time, Marley saw him fully admit it—not just with words, but with the quiet surrender of a man who had fought too long against the tide. His belief was no longer reluctant. It was carved into him now, just as the ledger's scars had carved Annabelle out.

The lamp flickered, casting their shadows onto the wall —two figures leaning toward each other, bound by a story not their own.

Marley pulled her journal closer, her pencil poised. "Then we record everything. No more hesitation. Every dream, every vision, every echo—until Annabelle has her voice back."

Damien exhaled, a long, weary sound. "And until we find out what it costs."

Outside, the wind rattled the shutters, the river groaned beneath the bridge, and somewhere in the quiet heart of Brookwood, the echoes of Annabelle Warren stirred, carrying her sorrow into the living.

And Marley and Damien, whether ready or not, had just promised to carry it with her.

25

THE CHILD'S VOICE RETURNS

The house was quiet, the kind of quiet that feels weighted, like a held breath. Damien stirred at the faint rustling from down the hall, his body already tense, ears sharpening for any sound that didn't belong. He lay still for a moment, then pushed himself upright, heart hammering in his chest.

Marley, who had fallen asleep in the armchair with her journal across her lap, blinked awake at the movement. "What is it?" she whispered, her voice rough from sleep.

Damien lifted a hand for silence. There it was again—his daughter's voice, soft and laced with the peculiar clarity of sleep.

"Say it... ring it... call him home."

The words floated down the hallway, oddly rhythmic, as though part of a chant.

Damien's blood ran cold. He was on his feet before he realized it, moving toward the sound with long, urgent strides. Marley followed, her bare feet padding quickly against the wood floor, her journal clutched tightly to her chest as if she might need to record every syllable.

They found her standing by the bedroom window, her nightgown brushing her ankles, hair mussed with sleep. Her eyes were closed, her lips moving in steady cadence.

"Say it. Ring it. Call him home."

Damien crouched beside her, careful not to wake her suddenly. His hands hovered just shy of her shoulders, fear warring with the instinct to shake her awake. "Sweetheart," he whispered, his voice breaking. "You're dreaming. Wake up, please."

But she didn't stir. Instead, her hands rose slowly, as if she were tugging on an invisible rope, mimicking the pulling of a bell cord.

Marley's throat tightened. "The chapel bell," she breathed.

Damien's eyes snapped to hers, the recognition cutting him deeper than he wanted to admit. "Don't," he warned. "Don't say it."

But Marley stepped closer, her gaze fixed on the girl. "It's a ritual, Damien. Don't you see? Annabelle wasn't just waiting on the bridge—she was waiting for the bell to ring. She needed someone to call him home."

Sophie's hands moved again, tugging, tugging, her lips whispering the refrain like an invocation.

"Say it. Ring it. Call him home."

Damien felt the ground shift beneath him, as though the very air of the house was no longer his own. "This isn't a game," he said sharply, more to himself than to Marley. "This is the same pattern, the same voice that dragged my wife into her nightmares. And now it's come for my daughter."

Marley, however, was already scribbling the words into her journal, her hand shaking with urgency. "It's not dragging—it's directing. Don't you hear it? These are instructions. A ritual Annabelle never finished. If we follow it—if we reenact it—maybe we can release her."

"Or bind her," Damien snapped. His daughter's voice rose slightly, insistent now, and he gathered her into his arms. Her head lolled against his chest, lips still moving. "Say it. Ring it. Call him home."

Marley reached out, brushing a strand of hair from the girl's damp forehead. "Damien... she's not afraid. Look at her. She's calm. Peaceful. If this was some curse, she wouldn't look like that."

Damien shut his eyes, clutching his daughter tighter. "She's a child," he whispered. "She shouldn't look like anything except asleep."

Sophie's voice faded then, her body relaxing as she slipped back into true slumber. Damien laid her carefully onto the bed, pulling the blanket over her shoulders with shaking hands.

Marley lingered at the doorway, her journal open to the fresh scrawl of words. "Say it. Ring it. Call him home," she murmured, tasting the cadence aloud for the first time. "Damien, this is what Annabelle wanted. Not just love—not just memory. Completion."

He turned on her, his face pale, his eyes rimmed with exhaustion and fury. "Completion? Do you hear yourself? You're talking about dragging my daughter into a ritual we don't understand. You're gambling with something we can't control."

Marley met his gaze, steady despite the pounding of her heart. "No. I'm listening to the one voice Brookwood has tried to silence for over a century. And I think your daughter just gave us the key Annabelle was waiting for."

The words hung heavy between them, the air taut with both fear and inevitability.

Damien's shoulders sagged, his strength drained. He turned back toward his sleeping child, brushing her hair with trembling fingers. "If you're wrong..." His voice cracked. "If you're wrong, it won't just be Annabelle's story that ends. It'll be ours."

Marley closed her journal with a snap, determination flaring in her chest. "Then we can't afford to be wrong."

Outside, the wind shifted, carrying with it the faint echo of a bell that hadn't rung in over a hundred years.

MARLEY SAT at the kitchen table long after Damien had retreated to his daughter's bedside. The lamp hissed softly, casting a thin cone of light across her journal. On the page, she had written the words again and again until they blurred into a chant:

Say it. Ring it. Call him home.

Each repetition steadied her hand even as it quickened her pulse. The phrase was too precise, too deliberate to dismiss as a fragment of childish dreaming. It carried weight —the rhythm of an unfinished act. Annabelle's act.

She flipped back through her journal, scanning past entries with a scholar's urgency, looking for connections. Notes on the séance, the altered music, the ledger scratched through, the bell that hadn't rung since 1887. Each clue felt like a separate shard until now.

Marley circled the words, then drew a line to an earlier entry: *The chapel bell was the last sound Annabelle heard.*

Another line to: *Music box—song slowed after dream. Marker of transition?*

Another line still: *Letter burned in dream, but left behind a vow.*

She leaned back, tapping the pencil against her lips.

"Say it. Ring it. Call him home." The phrase wasn't just eerie —it was instructional.

The "say it" could mean the vows Callum and Annabelle never completed, spoken aloud but never bound. The "ring it" clearly pointed to the bell, silenced since Annabelle vanished. And "call him home"—that had to mean Callum, kept from crossing in Marley's dream, forever trapped on the far side of absence.

The pattern unfolded in her mind like ink bleeding into water. The echoes weren't random. They were fragments of a ritual interrupted, scattered across generations, waiting for someone to weave them whole.

Damien returned quietly, his face pale but resolute, shoulders still heavy with the weight of fatherhood. He lowered himself across from her, his hands clasped tightly as though bracing against a storm.

"She's asleep again," he murmured. "Peaceful." His voice faltered, and for a moment the fear behind his composure showed. "But she was tugging the rope, Marley. Like she was at the bell. How do I keep her safe from something I can't touch?"

Marley slid her journal toward him, the page filled with her scribbles and connecting arrows. "By finishing it. Damien, I think Annabelle was trying to complete a ritual— a calling home that was never completed. Every clue fits into this. The music box, the vows, the bell, even the letters. They're not separate—they're steps."

He frowned, scanning the page. "You're suggesting Annabelle staged her own... rite? Some binding of voice, of love? And we're supposed to finish it?"

Marley's eyes gleamed in the lamplight. "Not supposed to. Chosen to. That's why the echoes have been leading us here. That's why your daughter spoke those words. She's not cursed, Damien—she's conduit. Annabelle's reaching through her because she knows we'll listen."

Damien shoved the journal back toward her, agitation flashing across his features. "You make it sound almost holy. But what if it isn't? What if it's dangerous? A ritual left unfinished could be unfinished for a reason. Maybe it was never meant to be completed."

Marley leaned forward, her voice steady, fierce. "Or maybe Annabelle died because it wasn't. What if she vanished because no one said it, no one rang it, no one called him home? Don't you see? The silence was the curse."

He looked away, his jaw flexing. For a long while, the only sound was the wind rattling the windowpanes, the river muttering in the distance.

Marley softened. "I know you're afraid. I am too. But Annabelle trusted someone would come along who could listen. Who wouldn't flinch. Damien, I think that someone is us."

He rubbed his temples, exhaling hard. "If we even consider this—what would it look like?"

Marley turned the journal back toward herself, pencil in hand, sketching hastily. "The vows—spoken. We have Annabelle's letters, the ring, even the music box. That's 'say it.'"

She scribbled again. "The bell—we have to find a way to ring it, even if the rope's long gone. That's 'ring it.'"

Finally, she underlined the last phrase. "'Call him home.' That's the crossing. Annabelle couldn't bring Callum across the bridge, but maybe we can. Symbolically, ritually. With the objects, with the words."

Damien watched her, torn between disbelief and reluctant awe. "You're planning a reenactment."

"Not just reenactment," she corrected. "Completion."

He pushed back from the table, pacing the room, his shadow restless against the walls. "Do you realize what you're suggesting? That we meddle with whatever force swallowed Annabelle whole? That we invite it back?"

Marley stood, meeting him in the center of the room. "Not invite. Release. If Annabelle has been trapped in repetition all this time, don't we owe it to her to let her rest?"

Damien stopped, his chest heaving with a mixture of anger, fear, and something else—something like acceptance. He pressed his hands against his face, then dropped them with a weary groan.

"You won't stop, will you?"

"No," Marley said simply. "Because she hasn't stopped. And until she does, neither can I."

The music box sat between them on the table, its carvings catching the lamplight. Marley wound it once more, the slowed notes spilling out like a heartbeat.

Damien stared at it, then at Marley. "Then God forgive me... because if we're wrong, I've just allowed my daughter's voice to drag us all into Annabelle's unfinished night."

Marley lifted her journal, pressing it to her chest. "Then let's make sure it doesn't stay unfinished."

The melody faltered, stretched thin, then ceased—leaving only the sound of their own breathing, heavy with the weight of what they were about to attempt.

THE NIGHT PRESSED close against the windows, a heavy curtain of silence broken only by the low hum of the river beyond. Damien sat rigid at the table, hands clasped so tightly the knuckles blanched white. Marley leaned forward across from him, her journal spread open like a map, the words and arrows connecting threads of the mystery: *Say it. Ring it. Call him home.*

They had circled the same debate for hours—his fear circling her conviction, her insistence hammering against his walls of doubt. But there was no denying it now. Every piece, every echo, every vision had driven them here.

Damien exhaled, his voice rough. "If we do this, there's no turning back. You understand that, right? Whatever waits at that bridge—it won't let us walk away a second time."

Marley met his eyes, steady. "We were never meant to walk away. Annabelle's story doesn't let go. It asks. It insists. And tonight... it demands."

Her words struck something in him, loosening the knot he'd held since his daughter's voice carried those haunting instructions through the dark. He closed his eyes briefly, and when he opened them again, the resistance was gone. Only resolve remained—resigned, reluctant, but undeniable.

"Then we prepare," he said at last.

Marley's heart jolted. She seized her pencil, scribbling across the journal page. "We'll need the vows—spoken aloud. The music box, the letters, the ring, the ribbon. And the bell."

At that, Damien flinched. The chapel bell—silent since Annabelle vanished—loomed in his memory like a sentinel. "The bell's rope rotted decades ago. Even if it could still swing, no one's heard it in over a century."

Marley's eyes sparked with determination. "Then we'll climb. If Annabelle could pull it in a thunderstorm, we can do it now. It has to be part of it, Damien. Her words were clear: *ring it.*"

He pinched the bridge of his nose, muttering. "Climbing a bell tower in the middle of the night... God help us."

Marley leaned across the table, her hand brushing his, grounding him. "Not God. Annabelle."

He looked at her then, and for a flicker of a moment, the shared weight between them felt almost unbearable. He nodded, pushing to his feet. "Fine. Then we gather what we need."

THE HOUSE GREW restless with their movements. Marley fetched the ribbon, still faintly damp from her vision, folded carefully into the pages of her journal. Damien unlocked the small drawer where the music box rested, its carvings etched deep with sorrow, the slowed song coiled inside like a waiting spirit.

On the mantle, the ring—Callum's promise engraved with *C.M. to A.W. Forevermore*—gleamed faintly in the lamplight. Marley cupped it reverently, her chest tightening at the weight of its history.

"The letters," Damien murmured, producing the mason jar and the torn pages of Annabelle's unfinished vows. He placed them beside the other relics.

One by one, the table filled with objects, each carrying a fragment of a story long severed. Together, they formed something whole. Something ritualistic. Something dangerous.

Marley stood back, staring at the collection. "This is it. These are the pieces Annabelle left behind. Now all that's missing is us."

Damien lingered, his eyes fixed on the music box. "You really believe this will set her free?"

"I believe it's the only way forward," Marley said softly. "And I believe she chose us to finish what she couldn't."

He swallowed hard, then nodded.

. . .

THEY PACKED CAREFULLY, Marley wrapping each relic in cloth as though preparing offerings. The journal stayed in her hand, ready to record every detail.

By the time they stepped outside, the air had thickened with mist, curling low over the ground, clinging to the path like memory made tangible. The bridge loomed ahead, its silhouette stark against the swollen clouds.

The river whispered beneath, carrying with it a chill that sank into bone.

Marley tightened her grip on the satchel. "We'll begin at the bridge. Place the objects where she left them. Speak the vows." She glanced at Damien, steady. "Then you and I will climb the chapel tower and ring the bell."

Damien let out a bitter laugh. "I never thought my life would come to reenacting a century-old tragedy."

Marley's eyes softened. "It isn't reenactment. It's release."

He didn't answer, but his silence carried no refusal.

AT THE BRIDGE'S ENTRANCE, Marley paused, the mist folding around her like a cloak. She thought of Annabelle—barefoot, gown torn, letter clutched to her chest—standing here on her final night. The thought sent a shiver through her, but she steadied herself with a whispered promise.

"We'll finish this for you, Annabelle."

Damien moved closer, his presence solid beside her. "And if this takes us under too?"

Marley turned, meeting his gaze in the dim light. "Then at least we'll go telling the truth."

The river groaned beneath them, the wood of the bridge creaking as if stirred by footsteps long past.

Together, they stepped onto the planks, carrying the past in their hands and the future in their resolve.

For the first time, both of them fully accepted the same truth: the ritual would be completed. And whatever it summoned, whatever it demanded—it would not let them leave unchanged.

26

A HIDDEN PROPOSAL

The mist still clung to the bridge when they returned home, as though the night itself didn't want to loosen its hold. Damien carried the satchel of relics with the kind of care reserved for fragile things—not because the items themselves were breakable, but because of the weight they carried. He set it on the dining table, his shoulders taut, his jaw working as though he were bracing for another blow.

Marley stayed near the doorway, reluctant to break the silence. Her journal was pressed tight to her chest, her mind still replaying the cadence of her niece's voice. *Say it. Ring it. Call him home.* The phrase still throbbed in her ears, a demand she couldn't escape.

Damien finally eased the satchel open. One by one, he laid out the pieces: the ribbon, the letters, the faded vows, the mason jar. Then he set the music box before them, its carved wood catching the lamplight.

It had been their most constant companion—changing songs, slowing rhythms, carrying with it echoes they couldn't explain. And yet, Damien looked at it now as though it were an adversary, something to be confronted rather than cherished.

"We've wound this thing a hundred times," he muttered, brushing his thumb across its etched surface. "Played it backward, forward, slow, fast. But what if it's never been about the song at all?"

Marley's brow furrowed. "What do you mean?"

He leaned closer, tracing the ornate design with his fingertip. "These carvings... they're not just decorative. Look here."

He tilted the box so the light revealed an almost imperceptible seam in the wood along the bottom edge. It wasn't part of the original grain—it was something cut, purposeful.

Marley's breath caught. "A hidden compartment."

Damien didn't answer. He retrieved a small screwdriver from the drawer, working the seam gently until the panel shifted with a soft click. The air between them seemed to still, charged with anticipation.

When the panel lifted free, a velvet-lined cavity revealed itself. Nestled inside was a ring.

Marley's hand flew to her mouth, stifling a gasp.

It was delicate yet solid, the gold dulled by time but the engraving still sharp. *C.M. to A.W. Forevermore.*

Damien stared at it, the weight of the discovery pressing into him like stone. He didn't touch it at first—didn't dare. The initials burned in the dim lamplight: Callum Marwick to Annabelle Warren. Forevermore.

A vow sealed in metal. A promise buried in silence.

Marley's voice was hushed, reverent. "He meant to propose."

Damien nodded slowly, his throat tight. "And he never had the chance."

They both sat there, the ring between them, as though

Annabelle herself had stepped into the room. Marley's eyes shimmered with unshed tears. "It was never about running away alone. She was waiting—for this. For him."

Finally, Damien lifted the ring from its velvet cradle. It was heavier than he expected, as though the years of grief had settled into its gold. He turned it over in his palm, tracing the inscription with his thumb, feeling the depth of each etched letter.

When he looked at Marley, his expression was raw, stripped of the shields he usually wore. He held the ring out to her, hand trembling. "You should be the one to return it."

Marley's breath caught. "Me?"

"Yes." His voice cracked, but he didn't falter. "Because she chose you. All of this—the visions, the words, the dreams. You're the one Annabelle trusted to carry her story through. Not me. Not anyone else. You."

She hesitated, her hand hovering over his. To accept the ring felt like more than just taking an artifact. It felt like taking Annabelle's final plea into her bones.

When her fingers finally closed around the band, the metal was warm, almost pulsing with life. A shudder rippled through her, sorrow and release braided together so tightly she couldn't separate them.

She bowed her head, the tears spilling freely now. "Forevermore," she whispered, the word tasting like both grief and completion.

The air in the room shifted, softer somehow, as though even the echoes leaned in to listen.

Damien leaned back heavily, exhaling a long, ragged breath. He rubbed his face, his voice low. "Then that settles it. We finish what they couldn't. We return what was lost."

Marley held the ring to her chest, the weight of it pressing against her heart. For the first time, she felt not just

Annabelle's sorrow—but her longing, her hope, her refusal to be forgotten.

It wasn't only a mystery anymore. It was a covenant.

And Marley knew, as sure as the bridge still stood in the mist, that Annabelle's forever had found its way into her hands.

THE RING LAY in Marley's palm as if it had always been there, as though time itself had been waiting for her hand to complete its circle. Its gold was tarnished, its inscription softened by decades of silence, yet when she touched it, warmth spread up her arm like a current, steady and unrelenting. She had held relics before—ribbon, letters, scraps of history—but nothing had carried this much immediacy.

This wasn't just evidence. It was intimacy.

Her breath trembled as she whispered the inscription again, her thumb brushing the delicate engraving. *"C.M. to A.W. Forevermore."* The phrase struck her chest like a bell, vibrating down into the deepest chambers of her being.

Marley had always been a collector of words, a keeper of echoes. But this wasn't ink on parchment or a voice carried through fog. This was permanence hammered into metal— a vow so solid it refused to vanish even when their bodies did. She clutched it tighter, her heart tightening with both awe and unbearable grief.

Damien, watching her, leaned against the table as though his legs couldn't bear the weight. His face was half in shadow, but his eyes reflected the same pull she felt—an ache so personal it seemed to break through the boundary between past and present.

"You feel it too, don't you?" Marley asked softly, not daring to lift her gaze from the ring.

He hesitated, his jaw working. "Yes. And it terrifies me."

She looked up at him, startled by the honesty in his voice. Damien was a man who built walls out of logic, who patched his fear with skepticism. To hear him admit terror was to glimpse the fracture running through his carefully constructed defenses.

"What terrifies you?" she pressed gently.

He swallowed hard, then rubbed the back of his neck. "That when I gave it to you... it was like setting down a weight I didn't know I'd been carrying. I've fought this every step—rationalizing, warning, denying. But the moment I handed it over, I realized I didn't want to carry it anymore. I wanted *you* to."

Marley's chest tightened. "Damien..."

He cut her off, his voice ragged. "Do you understand what that means? I've been clinging to my fear as if it would protect us. Protect my daughter. But fear doesn't protect—it strangles. I see that now. And handing you that ring..." He exhaled shakily. "It was a release. Not just of the metal. Of the story. Of the silence."

Marley blinked back tears, her voice trembling but sure. "Then we're both carrying it now. Not just me. Not just you. Us."

Her words steadied something in him, though his posture remained taut, as if waiting for the next blow. "You don't know how long I've dreaded becoming part of this. But now... it feels inevitable. Like it always would've come to this moment."

She nodded, still cradling the ring. "It did. Every clue, every voice, every dream led us here. Annabelle's story was never just about her. It was about us finding her—and maybe finding ourselves in the process."

Damien's eyes darkened, flickering with both yearning

and warning. "And what if the cost is too high? What if Annabelle's forevermore becomes our nevermore?"

Marley reached across the table, setting the ring gently between them as though it were an altar. Her fingers brushed his, grounding him. "Then at least we'll face it together."

The silence stretched between them, heavy but not empty. The ring sat gleaming in the lamplight, a tether to the past that bound them in the present.

Finally, Damien let out a broken laugh, shaking his head. "You make it sound like destiny."

Marley's lips curved faintly, though her eyes were wet. "Maybe it is. Or maybe it's just love refusing to die, demanding someone bear witness. Either way, we're chosen."

Damien's gaze lingered on her, and for a moment, the air between them thickened with something more than history —an undercurrent of unspoken feeling, fragile yet fierce. He didn't speak it, not yet, but it hung there, as undeniable as the ring.

Marley picked it up again, holding it to her chest. The sorrow weighed heavy, but beneath it pulsed a strange release—as though Annabelle herself had sighed through her bones, grateful to finally be seen.

She closed her eyes, whispering a promise: "I'll carry this, Annabelle. I'll carry you."

Damien exhaled, long and low, the tension draining from his frame. He reached across, resting his hand lightly over hers, over the ring. His voice dropped to a near whisper.

"And I'll carry you, Marley."

Her eyes opened, meeting his. The words weren't meant only for the dead.

For a long moment, they sat in silence, the ring between them like a heartbeat. Neither moved to break the spell, because both knew that when they did, the next step would begin—the act of returning the ring, and with it, perhaps, Annabelle's final release.

The echoes had drawn them here, but it was no longer just Annabelle's story. It was theirs too, intertwined, inescapable, and edging toward something that terrified them both as much as it compelled them forward.

And Marley knew—just as Damien did—that from this moment on, nothing would ever be the same.

THE RING PRESSED into Marley's palm with a weight that was far more than gold could ever carry. It wasn't just a relic. It was grief, love, promise, abandonment, and hope—compressed into a band meant for a finger that never wore it. She sat in silence, fingers curled around it, as though loosening her grip might unravel the fragile tether connecting her to Annabelle's heart.

Tears welled and spilled, but she didn't wipe them away. For once, she let herself feel it fully—every echo of sorrow that pulsed from the metal into her bones. This wasn't a haunting meant to torment. It was a cry for remembrance, a plea to be finished.

Damien watched her, his chest tightening at the sight. He wanted to reach for her, to steady her trembling hands, but he didn't move. He knew this wasn't his moment to take. It was hers.

Finally, Marley lifted her gaze to him, her voice shaking but clear. "This isn't just about Annabelle anymore. It's about promises broken and promises kept. About love that refused to be buried, no matter how much time tried to silence it." She pressed the ring against her heart. "She waited for this moment. And now it belongs to us to finish it."

Damien nodded slowly, his throat thick. "Then we'll finish it. But not blindly."

He pushed the music box closer, its hidden compartment now bare, as though it too had surrendered its secret. His fingers lingered over its carvings, tracing them like a map. "The bridge was always the center. Every vision, every clue—it draws back there. But if we're going to return this ring, it has to be done right. Not dropped, not abandoned. Returned as it was meant to be given."

Marley caught the flicker of pain in his eyes, the shadow of his late wife's memory surfacing, uninvited. She reached for his hand and held it, anchoring them both. "Then we'll learn what that means. We'll find the right place, the right words. We won't let it slip away half-done."

For a long moment, their hands stayed joined over the table, the ring resting between them like a pulse.

LATER, Marley spread her journal across the desk, carefully sketching the shape of the bridge, its beams, and the path beneath. She drew small circles at its base, where the iron box had once been discovered, and another where the mist always seemed to cling longest. She was no cartographer, but her lines carried intention.

Damien leaned over her shoulder, pointing. "Here. This is where the old foundation stones meet the river. My grandfather used to say there was a hollow built into the beam to keep small offerings safe from storms."

Marley looked up at him, startled. "Offerings?"

He nodded grimly. "Superstition. People used to leave

trinkets, prayers, coins—tokens for safe passage. He said the bridge wasn't just a structure. It was a threshold." His voice dropped, hushed by the gravity of the memory. "Maybe that's where the ring belongs."

Marley's breath caught. "A threshold." She wrote it in her journal, underlining it twice. "Not just wood and stone. A place between. That's where Annabelle stood. That's where Callum meant to join her."

She closed her journal with resolve, lifting the ring again. The sorrow that had nearly crushed her before softened now into something else. Release. As though Annabelle had wept through her and was now exhaling relief.

"She's closer," Marley whispered, her hand trembling. "I can feel it."

Damien's face hardened, though not in denial. In protection. "Then we prepare carefully. We'll take the music box, the ribbon, the vows. And this—" He nodded toward the ring. "We'll return them, all together. The ritual, the voices—they've been pointing to this from the start."

Marley nodded, but her eyes never left the ring. "We need the bell too. It isn't enough to return what was hidden. We have to ring it into being, call him home. That's what she waited for."

The mention of the bell made Damien's stomach twist. His late-night confession about his wife's dreams clawed at him now, whispering warnings. But he didn't argue. He couldn't—not anymore.

Instead, he leaned closer, his voice low. "Then promise me this. If we do it, we do it together. No wandering off, no brave solo acts. Together, Marley. Or not at all."

She met his eyes, fierce and certain. "Together. Always."

.   .   .

THE HOUSE GREW quiet around them, but inside the silence pulsed something undeniable. The echoes no longer felt scattered, half-seen fragments. They were aligning, pressing them toward a single moment.

Marley slipped the ring into a small pouch, knotting the cord tight before tucking it close to her chest. She whispered, almost unconsciously, "We'll bring you home, Annabelle."

Damien exhaled, as though he'd been holding his breath since the compartment had opened. His shoulders loosened, though the lines of fear didn't fade. "And once we do, maybe the echoes will finally let this town breathe again."

Marley reached across, closing her hand over his. "Maybe they'll let *us* breathe again too."

Damien's fingers tightened around hers, neither letting go. And in the quiet lamplight, with the relics of a forgotten love spread before them, both understood that the act of returning the ring would test not only the strength of Brookwood's ghosts—but their own hearts as well.

27

COMMUNITY MEMORY CIRCLE

The old town hall smelled faintly of cedar and lemon oil, as though the wood itself had soaked up a century of polishings and prayers. Marley had spent the morning dragging chairs into a wide circle, the legs scraping against the floorboards in a rhythm that sounded almost ceremonial. She had no pulpit, no platform, no grand speech prepared. All she had was a conviction: Brookwood's story could no longer be carried by a handful of whispers. It had to be spoken aloud.

She placed a small table at the circle's center, draping it with a cloth embroidered with ivy leaves, faded but sturdy. On it she set the music box, the ribbon, the old letter fragments, and finally—the ring, still wrapped in the pouch she carried close to her heart. She arranged them not as relics, but as offerings, invitations.

When Damien arrived, his brow furrowed at the sight. "You've turned this into a kind of altar," he murmured, half-wary, half-moved.

"It's not an altar," Marley said softly. "It's a gathering

place. These aren't relics—they're voices. If we're asking others to share, the echoes need to be here too."

Damien didn't argue. He simply nodded, taking a chair beside her. His presence steadied her more than she wanted to admit.

The townsfolk trickled in slowly, curiosity written on their faces. Mrs. Bennett from the bakery arrived with her apron still dusted in flour, wiping her hands nervously. Evelyn from the café entered carrying a thermos of coffee, her sharp eyes darting to the items on the table as though expecting them to stir. Royce, the saxophonist, leaned against the doorway before sliding into a chair, restless fingers tapping his knees. Others followed—shopkeepers, teachers, elders—some Marley knew by name, some only by sight.

They filled the circle with a hush that felt deeper than silence.

Marley stood, her journal clutched at her side. "Thank you for coming," she began, her voice steady but reverent. "I asked you here tonight because I believe the bridge's story isn't mine to uncover alone. It belongs to all of us. To this town. To those who came before, and those who still wait."

Her words settled into the space, and for a moment no one moved. Then Mrs. Bennett shifted, her apron rustling. "You mean Annabelle."

Marley nodded. "Yes. Annabelle Warren. And Callum Marwick. And perhaps others we don't yet know. Their voices have echoed for generations, and I believe some of you have heard them too."

Evelyn gave a sharp laugh, more brittle than mocking. "You think people will just admit that?"

Marley met her gaze, unflinching. "I think they're tired of carrying it alone."

The silence deepened again, heavy with the weight of unspoken truths. Then, from the far side of the circle, an older man with weathered hands raised his voice. "My grandmother used to say she saw a woman in green at the bridge when she was a girl. Swore she was waiting for someone. We never spoke of it outside the family. Folks would've called her touched."

A ripple moved through the circle—gasps, murmurs, quick glances exchanged.

Evelyn's shoulders stiffened, but her jaw softened. "My great-aunt told a story too. About the chapel bell. Said she heard it ring when no one was near it. Claimed it was Annabelle calling. I laughed it off for years." She shook her head. "But lately... I've heard it in my sleep. Like it's waiting for me to answer."

Marley's heart pounded, but she kept her tone calm. "That's why we're here. To put the fragments together. To stop pretending we haven't all felt the bridge watching us."

Royce leaned forward, his restless hands stilling. "That tune I played the other night—the one that came out of nowhere. My uncle once whistled it when he thought no one was listening. He said it was a song his grandmother used to hum, but he never told me where it came from." He met Marley's gaze, his eyes unnerved but earnest. "It wasn't mine. It never was."

The room shivered with recognition.

Mrs. Bennett pressed a trembling hand to her mouth. "All these years... we thought we were imagining it. Or worse, that we'd be cursed for speaking it aloud."

Marley's voice softened, breaking through the tremor in the air. "You're not cursed. You're connected. Annabelle's story isn't a haunting—it's a thread. And together, we can follow it back."

Her words loosened something in the circle. More voices followed. A schoolteacher admitted to dreaming of the bridge as a child, of standing barefoot in the snow with a letter clutched tight. A young mother whispered that her daughter sometimes sang lines of a lullaby she herself had never learned. An elder confessed to avoiding the bridge his whole life, not from disbelief, but because he felt its pull too strongly.

The circle became a living river of confession, each voice flowing into the next, until the silence that once held them captive gave way to a hum of shared recognition.

Marley's journal lay open on her lap, her pen racing to capture every word. The stories overlapped and tangled, yet together they formed a pattern clearer than any archive could provide.

At her side, Damien sat still, his gaze sweeping the circle with growing intensity. He saw it now—what Marley had insisted from the beginning. This wasn't obsession. It wasn't hysteria. It was memory, communal and unresolved.

He leaned close, his voice low but weighted with awe. "It was never just you, Marley. This isn't just your journey."

Marley looked at him, the candlelight flickering across his face. "No. It's Brookwood's."

And in that moment, Damien understood—finally, fully —that the echoes weren't only meant to be solved. They were meant to be healed.

THE HUM of voices inside the circle grew, no longer tentative but insistent, as though a dam had broken. What had been secret for decades, tucked into bedtime stories or whispered only to the closest of kin, was now spilling into the open air of the town hall. Marley, seated with her journal open on her knees, felt like a conductor who hadn't planned a symphony but found herself leading one anyway.

An elderly woman in a plum-colored shawl leaned forward, her voice quaking but strong. "When I was a girl, I woke to find my sister standing at the window, pointing toward the bridge. She said, 'She's out there again, waiting.' I thought she was dreaming, but the next morning, her footprints were outside in the frost. Bare feet, leading to the fence. We never spoke of it again."

Gasps rippled through the circle. Marley's pen scratched furiously across the page. Bare feet. Again. The detail echoed Annabelle's last walk from her vision—snow, feet unshod, a letter clutched in her hand.

Evelyn shifted uncomfortably, her usual sharpness blunted. "My mother kept a tin on the mantel, said it belonged to her grandmother. I once opened it when she wasn't looking. Inside was a scrap of lace ribbon, dirt still clinging to it. She snatched it back and told me it was never to be spoken of. But I've seen that same ribbon in dreams since. Wrapped around my wrist, as though someone tied it there."

Marley glanced at Damien, her eyes bright with recognition. She had held Annabelle's ribbon herself. What Evelyn described was no invention—it was confirmation.

Royce, the saxophonist, leaned forward, his voice uncharacteristically raw. "I dream of music sometimes. Not jazz, not anything I know. It's slower, almost like a hymn. And in the dream, there's a woman swaying on the bridge. She's not dancing, exactly. More like... waiting, holding herself to a rhythm only she hears. When I wake, I can't shake the notes."

"You played them the other night," Marley murmured, more to herself than to him.

Royce's eyes widened. "Then it's not just mine. It never was."

Marley's pen moved faster, the page filling with phrases —*bare feet, lace ribbon, hymn at the bridge.* She circled each, drawing lines between them, sketching a web. The pattern was there, if only she could bring it into focus.

From the far end of the circle, Mrs. Bennett raised her hand, fingers trembling. "I once heard my father say our oven doors rattled during a storm, but not from the wind. He said it was Annabelle passing by, looking for warmth she never found. He warned us not to speak her name at night. But I've whispered it, when I thought no one would hear." Tears glistened in her eyes. "And each time, I swear I heard a voice answer back."

The townsfolk shifted uneasily. Marley steadied her own breathing. "What did the voice say?"

Mrs. Bennett closed her eyes, recalling. "'Wait.' Always just that one word. Sometimes faint, sometimes sharp. But always 'Wait.'"

A shudder passed through Marley. She wrote it down with a firm hand, her mind flashing to the night of her interrupted kiss beneath the bridge. That same whisper had cut through her moment with Damien. Wait. The echo was no longer confined to her alone.

Damien sat still beside her, his jaw tight, eyes scanning each speaker. He wasn't scribbling notes as Marley was—he was absorbing, weighing, resisting the urge to call it hysteria. But with every overlapping story, every repeated phrase, his skepticism eroded further.

Another voice broke in, a man in his thirties, his face pale. "My little boy—he's only four—he sometimes wakes at night and says, 'She's cold, she needs shoes.' He's never even heard these stories. We don't talk about the bridge at home. But he says it like he knows her. Like he's seen her."

The circle froze in collective silence. Marley's pen stopped mid-scratch. Her heart hammered. *Bare feet.* The detail returned again, unprompted, from the mouth of a child too young to carry town folklore.

Marley leaned forward, her voice urgent but gentle. "What's his name?"

"Elliot."

She nodded slowly, as though speaking to herself. "An echo finds its way to the ones still open. Children hear what adults try to silence."

Damien shifted, his protective instincts bristling. "Marley—"

But she pressed on. "Don't you see? These fragments aren't random. They overlap, they connect." She pointed to her journal, the lines spiderwebbing across the page. "Bare feet. Ribbon. Waiting. Music. Shoes. A voice saying 'Wait.' They're all parts of the same night. Annabelle's night."

The murmurs grew louder, some voices trembling, others firm. Evelyn muttered, "Maybe she's never left because we've never finished listening."

Royce leaned back, shaking his head. "Or maybe we've never finished saying what needed to be said."

The plum-shawled woman whispered, "She waited for him. We've all been carrying it, every generation since. The unfinished vow."

The words struck Marley like a bell. *Unfinished vow.* She underlined it in her journal three times. The phrase vibrated through her bones, aligning with the ring hidden in its pouch, the bell long silent, the music box's altered song. Every voice tonight was pointing to the same truth:

Annabelle's story was never resolved. And until it was, Brookwood itself remained unfinished.

Marley looked up, her voice breaking the growing hum. "This isn't just about Annabelle and Callum. It's about us. Every time we've hushed these stories, every time we've buried them under silence, we've kept the wound open. Tonight is proof: we're all part of the same echo. The bridge isn't haunted—it's holding what we refuse to release."

The room stilled, each face reflecting fear, grief, and something harder to name—relief.

At Marley's side, Damien finally exhaled, his voice hushed but resolute. "You're right. It isn't just your burden. It isn't just Annabelle's either." His gaze swept the circle. "It belongs to Brookwood. And if we're going to heal it, we can't keep pretending it isn't ours to carry."

The circle sat in charged silence, but something had shifted. The fear no longer pressed down. Instead, a fragile thread of resolve wound through the room, binding them together.

And Marley, with ink smudged across her fingers and her journal brimming with their confessions, realized she had been right all along. Annabelle's story was never meant to be solved in solitude. It was meant to be carried into the light—together.

THE CIRCLE of townsfolk sat in near-silence, their confessions hanging in the air like a suspended chord. The crackle of the old wood stove in the corner, the faint drip of rain outside the window, even the whisper of wind through the cedar trees seemed hushed, deferential. The stories had been told. The fragments—once scattered, hidden, or denied—now rested together, forming something larger than any single voice could have carried.

Marley sat with her journal balanced on her knees, pages full, her pen hovering but not moving. For the first time that night she wasn't rushing to capture words. She was listening, but not just with her ears—with her whole being. The rhythm in the room had shifted, and she didn't want to break it.

Mrs. Bennett dabbed at her eyes with her apron. "I never thought I'd say her name out loud. Annabelle. It always felt dangerous, like opening a door best kept shut. But maybe it was the silence that cursed us, not the speaking."

A murmur of agreement rippled through the circle. Evelyn, whose skepticism had once cut sharp as glass, folded her hands together and whispered, "We've all carried pieces of her, haven't we? Bits of her ribbon, her songs, her walks in the mist. We've been haunted not by a ghost, but by the weight of what was never finished."

Marley exhaled, her gaze moving over the faces around her. "Annabelle's story was left incomplete. But what I see tonight is that she hasn't been waiting alone. Every one of you has been keeping vigil in your own way. That's what the bridge echoes. Not only her grief, but ours. The whole town's."

Royce shifted, his restless hands clasping still for once. "If that's true, then finishing it isn't just about her. It's about us finally letting go."

The elder in the plum shawl leaned forward, eyes gleaming despite her years. "No, not letting go. Carrying it together. Not leaving her at the bridge, but walking her home."

The words struck Marley like a flame catching dry tinder. *Walking her home.* She underlined the phrase in her journal, circling it until the page nearly tore. That was the truth at the center of all of it. Annabelle had been abandoned at the threshold, stranded between memory and forgetting. And every generation since had lived with the hollow ache of her unfinished journey.

A tremor of recognition passed through Damien. He had sat quietly for most of the evening, his usual need to interrogate or dismantle Marley's convictions subdued by the tide of voices around them. Now he straightened, his jaw working as if forming words he'd resisted too long.

"You're right," he said finally, his voice cutting into the stillness. Every head turned toward him. "All of you. For months I thought this was Marley's obsession. That maybe she'd gotten too deep into her aunt's journals, too lost in dreams. But tonight I see it. This isn't just hers. It isn't just Annabelle's. It's Brookwood's wound. And if we don't face it, if we don't finish it—then it will keep living through our children, through us."

He looked toward Marley then, and the weight of his gaze carried both fear and surrender. "This town is part of Annabelle's story. Which means we're part of her healing. All of us."

The circle breathed in as one, and in that inhalation something shifted. It was subtle, invisible, but undeniable: the collective realization that what had been hidden in shadow could no longer stay there. The echoes were no longer fractured whispers—they were one voice, rising.

Mrs. Bennett clutched her apron tighter, nodding. "Then we help her finish it. Whatever it takes."

Evelyn pressed her lips together, then added, "And we finish it for ourselves. So our children aren't standing at windows in the night, whispering to someone they can't see."

Royce muttered, "So the music can belong to the living again."

One by one, heads nodded. Even those who hadn't spoken aloud shifted forward in their chairs, the body language of surrender.

Marley closed her journal softly, as if sealing a pact. "Then we do this together. Annabelle's story isn't just history—it's our inheritance. And maybe... if we bring her home, the bridge will stop echoing. Maybe it will finally rest."

The stove popped, sending a spark of embers against the grate, and someone—no one could later say who—whispered, "Amen."

The word lingered like a benediction.

Damien reached across the narrow space between them, his hand brushing Marley's. It wasn't a grasp, not yet—it was a touch of solidarity, of recognition. She met his eyes, saw the fear still there but tempered now with something steadier: commitment. He was no longer standing apart from the mystery. He was stepping into it with her, and with all of Brookwood.

Marley felt her throat tighten, but she forced the words out, clear and strong. "This is no longer Annabelle's wait. It's Brookwood's vigil. And together, we'll end it."

The circle held its silence, not empty but full, as if the town itself exhaled. In that silence, a shift occurred—imperceptible to the outside world, but inside that room, undeniable.

Brookwood had moved from whispers to memory. From memory to recognition. And now, from recognition to resolve.

Damien looked around at the faces lit by the stove's glow, and for the first time since the bridge had begun to stir, he felt something beyond dread. It wasn't relief, not yet, but something steadier. A glimpse of what healing could mean—not just for Marley, not just for Annabelle, but for them all.

Brookwood itself had been wounded. And now, at last, Brookwood itself had chosen to heal.

28

THE BRIDGE REVEALS

The sky above Brookwood shifted into the lavender hues of late evening, when day's last breath mingled with the dark approach of night. The covered bridge loomed ahead, its timbers soaked in shadow, its ribs groaning faintly as if recognizing the weight of footsteps drawing near. Marley walked with Damien at her side, the air between them taut with reverence and dread.

She carried the small satchel close to her chest—the ring, the locket, the ribbon, the music box—all wrapped carefully in cloth. Each relic seemed to thrum faintly, as if aware they were being carried home. Every step toward the bridge felt heavier, but also strangely inevitable, as though the earth itself guided them to this moment.

Damien had insisted on caution, his lantern swinging low in one hand, the other occasionally brushing her arm in reassurance that was as much for himself as for her. "If we're wrong," he murmured as they reached the threshold, "we may stir more than just memory."

Marley nodded, though her grip on the satchel tightened. "If we don't, the echoes will never end." Her voice was quiet but firm.

The bridge's entrance swallowed them whole, the dim light stretching long shadows across warped planks. It smelled of cedar and river mist, of iron nails rusted with age. They reached the center, where years before, the iron box had been unearthed. Damien set the lantern down carefully, its golden glow flickering across the carved initials still etched into one of the beams.

"This is where it begins," he whispered.

Marley knelt and untied the satchel with deliberate slowness. First, she drew out the ribbon, still faintly damp from that night in the rain. She laid it across the beam like a path. Next came the locket, its clasp broken but its weight unyielding, as though it clung to secrets it had never released. She placed it beside the ribbon.

The ring came third. Her fingers lingered on it longer, reluctant to let go. "This was never worn," she said softly. "But it was promised." She set it gently atop the locket, where it seemed to rest as if it had always belonged there.

Finally, she lifted the music box. Its carvings gleamed faintly in the lanternlight, and when she wound it, the altered song spilled into the air—slower, mournful, aching. The notes hung above the wooden beams, vibrating in resonance with something unseen.

Damien's breath caught, his hand brushing instinctively to the railing. "It feels... warmer," he whispered. He wasn't wrong. The air, which had carried a damp chill, now seemed to rise in temperature, curling around them like breath against skin.

Marley's eyes fixed on the mist that slithered through the open slats of the bridge. It didn't hover idly as before. It thickened, pooling, then drawing upward in a deliberate shape. Her pulse thundered in her ears.

The mist gathered form—slender shoulders, a fall of hair, the green impression of a gown that fluttered though no breeze stirred. Then came the outline of a face, indistinct at first, then painfully clear.

Annabelle.

Her figure shimmered, half-translucent, yet so undeniably present that Marley's throat closed. Annabelle's hands reached outward, palms open, eyes brimming with an emotion beyond words.

Damien staggered back, his lantern rattling against the floorboards. "God help us..."

Marley didn't move. Her tears blurred the vision but did not break it. She knelt lower, as though in prayer. "We brought them back," she whispered. "The things you left unfinished."

The music box continued its lament, each note shaping the moment into something both unbearably fragile and unshakably eternal.

Annabelle's lips parted. The voice was faint, more wind than sound, but Marley heard it: "Thank you."

And then, as the music slowed into its final bars, Annabelle's figure shimmered once more. The mist thinned, unraveling like threads pulled from a seam. The gown dissolved into air, the face into silvered shadow, until only emptiness remained.

The air cooled, the warmth receding, leaving behind only silence. The lantern flame stilled, no longer flickering.

Marley collapsed onto her heels, her chest heaving. Her hands trembled as she reached for the music box, its song now silent, its presence hollow, as though its purpose had been fulfilled.

Damien crossed the narrow space and sank beside her, his voice hoarse. "She's gone."

Marley shook her head, clutching the box to her chest. "No. She's free."

The bridge creaked softly above them, but for once, it did not echo.

THE SILENCE after Annabelle's figure dissolved was so profound that Marley swore she could hear the beat of her own heart echoing against the wooden planks. The bridge, once alive with murmurs and shifting mist, now seemed inert—just timber and iron, stripped of its voice. For a moment, she dared to believe it was finished.

But belief was fragile, and Damien's hand tightening on her shoulder reminded her of that. His grip wasn't steady—it was desperate, as though he feared that if he let go, the air itself might pull her into the void Annabelle had just vacated.

"Marley," he rasped, his eyes darting to the railings, to the shadows between the beams. "It doesn't feel right. It's too quiet."

Marley clutched the music box to her chest, her knuckles white. "Quiet can mean peace," she whispered. "Isn't this what we wanted? To set her free?"

He shook his head, jaw rigid. "Peace doesn't come like this. Not here. This bridge—" He gestured sharply to the structure around them. "It's been feeding on echoes for generations. You can't starve something overnight without consequence."

Marley forced herself to breathe. The planks under them no longer trembled, the mist no longer swirled, but doubt crept into her chest like rising water. She pressed the music box against her ear. Nothing. No phantom hum, no trembling note. Only wood and silence.

"She thanked us," Marley murmured, as much to herself as to Damien. "I heard it."

Damien's face softened for a heartbeat before hardening again. "I don't doubt what you heard. But what if it wasn't goodbye?" His voice dropped to a near growl. "What if it was permission—for something else to come through?"

Marley's stomach twisted. She set the music box back onto the beam and forced herself to stand. Her knees wobbled, but she held her ground, scanning the length of the bridge. Her eyes lingered on the exact place Annabelle's figure had risen, where the lantern light still clung to the mist-thinned air.

"I can test it," she said suddenly.

Damien straightened, alarm flashing in his eyes. "Marley, no—"

She lifted the music box and wound it once, just enough for a single note to shiver into the air. The sound was thin, almost hesitant, but it carried down the length of the bridge like a stone skimming water. Both of them held their breath, waiting.

Nothing answered.

The box clicked softly as the spring settled back into stillness.

Damien exhaled a ragged breath and pressed a palm to his forehead. "You'll drive me mad."

Marley hugged the box close again, her lips pressed into a thin line. "If it truly ended, the bridge won't answer. But if it hasn't, then we need to know."

He turned toward her, his expression torn between fury and fear. "And what if the test wakes something worse? What then?"

Marley met his eyes, unflinching. "Then at least we won't be blind."

For a moment, neither of them spoke. The lantern crackled faintly, its oil nearly spent, and the night outside pressed against the slats, thick and restless.

Damien broke the silence first, his voice lower, more vulnerable. "When she appeared... for the first time, I didn't want to run. I wanted to believe. But the warmth—it wasn't natural, Marley. It felt like standing too close to a fire you can't see. Something inside me says this bridge isn't finished with us yet."

Marley sank back to her knees, resting her forehead against the cold wood of the central beam. "Maybe it isn't. But if it wants something, it's not us—it's her. Annabelle was waiting for her story to be told. And now, at least part of it has been."

Damien crouched beside her, his eyes shadowed. "You think the echoes will stop now? That the town will suddenly heal because she said two words?"

"I think," Marley said slowly, lifting her head, "that healing isn't sudden. It's layered. Like these planks." She pressed her hand against the beam. "One laid over another, supporting what came before. Tonight was just one layer. There will be more."

He let out a bitter laugh. "And each one risks tearing us apart."

Marley turned to him, her expression fierce. "Or it brings us closer to the truth. To her freedom. To ours."

Her words hung heavy between them, more intimate than any kiss could have been. For a moment, Damien looked as though he might argue—but then his shoulders slumped, surrendering not to agreement, but to exhaustion.

"Then we prepare," he murmured, voice ragged. "We

watch the nights. We listen for the silences. And if the bridge calls again..." He swallowed hard, the words scraping like stone. "We answer together."

Marley nodded, tears threatening again. Together. Always.

As they gathered the relics—placing the ring back into the pouch, the ribbon folded gently, the music box sealed shut—Marley felt a strange stillness settle over her chest. Not relief. Not certainty. But resolve.

When they finally stepped off the bridge and back into the open night, the mist parted for them easily, as though granting passage. The river below gurgled in its eternal rhythm, indifferent to ghosts and vows.

But Marley glanced back one last time, and for the briefest flicker, she swore she saw a figure still standing in the center. Watching. Waiting.

She didn't tell Damien.

Not yet.

THE SKY HAD ALREADY SURRENDERED to twilight when Marley and Damien lingered on the far end of the bridge, hesitant to leave. The lantern Damien had set on the railing sputtered in the cooling breeze, its flame bowing to the night. Sunset bled across the river in ribbons of orange and violet, staining the mist that curled low along the water's edge. Every part of the scene felt suspended, as though the world itself was holding its breath.

Marley clutched the music box to her chest, the weight of it pressing into her ribs. She could still feel the warmth from when Annabelle's figure had manifested—a lingering heat, like an ember buried deep beneath ash. Damien stood a step behind her, his eyes fixed on the bridge's center, unwilling to look away. His entire posture spoke of bracing: for danger, for revelation, for something he couldn't name.

"Look at the sky," Marley whispered. "It's like it's watching too."

The last bands of sunlight slid behind the trees, and for a moment the entire river valley dimmed. The shadows rushed in quickly, devouring the colors until only the dusky blue of night remained. The lantern flame caught this transition, flaring higher for a heartbeat before steadying.

And then the air changed.

It was subtle at first: a warmth brushing Marley's cheek, though the evening had grown cold. The scent of wet earth and old wood thickened, interlaced with something floral—honeysuckle, perhaps, though far out of season. Damien muttered a sharp curse under his breath, gripping the railing until his knuckles blanched.

"She's not done," he said.

Marley's breath caught. At the bridge's center, where they had placed the relics beneath the central beam—the ring, the ribbon, the locket, the music box—the mist stirred. It rose like breath from the planks, coiling upward, translucent at first but thickening with every second.

Shapes took form within it. The curve of a shoulder, the outline of a gown. Slowly, inevitably, a woman's figure emerged. Her dress was the pale green Marley had seen in her dreams, its hem tattered and damp. Her hair, long and loose, shimmered faintly as though caught by a light source unseen.

Annabelle.

She stood with her head bowed, her arms at her sides, and the lantern flame stretched toward her as if pulled by gravity. Marley's throat constricted, her body trembling with awe and grief. She wanted to call out, to cross the planks and kneel at Annabelle's feet, but something in the apparition's bearing warned her against it.

Annabelle lifted her face.

Her eyes were pools of sorrow, but there was no malice there—only longing, centuries-deep. When she raised her hands, Marley saw the ribbon looped around one wrist, the locket clutched tightly in her palm, the faint glow of the ring at her finger. The relics they had returned now adorned her, completing the circle of her unfinished story.

"She took them," Marley breathed.

"No," Damien whispered hoarsely. "They were always hers."

The music box in Marley's hands vibrated faintly, though she had not wound it. A soft melody escaped its seams, slower and fuller than before, each note like a bell struck in velvet air. The song wrapped around Annabelle's figure, steadying her form, anchoring her against the river's restless pull.

Then Annabelle's voice, faint but clear, crossed the span. "Callum."

The name fractured Marley's heart. The sheer ache in that single word was unbearable, carrying centuries of waiting, of love unfulfilled. The mist beyond Annabelle shifted, and for a brief flicker Marley thought she saw another shape—a man, tall, broad-shouldered, his hand extended toward her. But the mist swallowed him again, leaving only Annabelle on the planks.

Tears streaked Marley's cheeks. "She was waiting," she whispered, more to Damien than to herself. "Always waiting for him."

The lantern flame guttered violently, then steadied. Annabelle's figure swayed, her gaze sweeping from Marley to Damien and back again, as though acknowledging them both. Then she lowered her arms, clasped the relics to her chest, and gave a single nod.

It was not a farewell of despair, but of release.

A sudden warmth rolled across the bridge, enveloping Marley and Damien both. For an instant it was almost unbearable, a furnace of emotion—grief, love, longing, devotion—searing through their bones. Marley gasped, clutching the music box tighter, but even as tears burned her eyes, she felt something loosen deep inside her.

And then the warmth faded.

Annabelle's figure dimmed, the edges of her gown unraveling into mist, her hair dissolving like strands of smoke. Her eyes lingered last, steady and sorrowful, before they too thinned into the evening. The relics dropped silently onto the planks where she had stood, no longer glowing, simply objects once more.

The bridge exhaled. Marley swore she heard it—the long, creaking sigh of wood released from a century of tension. The mist lifted, not entirely, but enough to reveal the river glinting beneath, silvered by moonlight. For the first time in months, the bridge seemed to rest.

Damien released the railing and stumbled back, dragging both hands over his face. "It's done," he said, though his voice was raw, uncertain.

Marley bent to gather the relics, her hands trembling. She cradled them gently, as though they were still living things. "No," she said softly, her voice resolute. "It's not done. But she is free. That's the difference."

They stood there together, silence settling over them like the weight of snowfall. The lantern flame flickered its last and guttered out, plunging the bridge into darkness save for the moonlight.

Marley turned to Damien. His face was pale, streaked

with sweat, his eyes hollowed by fear and awe. Yet in his expression she saw something shift—a surrender, not to despair, but to the reality he had resisted for so long.

"We'll finish it," he said at last. "Whatever it costs. We'll finish her story."

Marley reached for his hand. This time, he did not pull away.

Behind them, the bridge creaked once more, softer now, like the final echo of a lullaby.

And then, at last, it was still.

29

A SOUL REUNITED

The first toll came like a breath caught in the throat of the town.

Marley woke all at once, as if someone had snapped a thread inside a dream and everything in her body remembered being alive. The room was dark, the window a rectangle of deeper black. For a heartbeat she thought she'd imagined it—some leftover echo of the music box threading itself through sleep. Then the sound gathered itself and rolled again, fuller, older, impossibly distant and close all at once.

The chapel bell.

It did not clang. It did not shatter the night like an alarm. It arrived the way tide takes a shoreline—steady, deliberate, inevitable. Marley pushed the blankets aside and sat upright, heart hammering the rhythm she had learned to trust: listen first. Then move.

In the hall she heard Damien's door open. A second later his shadow filled her doorway, hair mussed, shirt pulled on backward in his haste. "You hear it," he said, not a question.

She was already on her feet. "It hasn't rung since—"

"Since 1887," he finished, voice low, reverent and frightened in the same breath.

They did not waste time with coats. Cold chased them through the house and out onto the porch, the pre-dawn air knife-sharp, full of the metallic taste of river and cedar. The bell's next note drifted over the rooftops. It was wider than sound had any right to be, as if the night itself were a bowl and someone had run a finger around its rim.

Light flicked on in windows up and down the street. Doors opened. People stood in thresholds and on steps, half clothed, fully awake, their faces turned toward the hill where the chapel sat like a keeper from another century. Marley had seen fear in those faces before; tonight she saw something else, something older—recognition.

"Marley," Damien said softly.

She followed his gaze to the narrow bedroom window at the end of the hall where, a lifetime ago, his daughter had stood sleep-talking to a bell only she could hear. Tonight the room remained dark, the small mound in the bed still. The thought touched Marley with a strange peace. The bell did not wake the child. It woke the town.

They moved, their feet finding the old path without speaking. The bell tolled again as they reached the square, its note traveling through Marley's ribs and out her spine, a vibration more than a noise. Evelyn emerged from the café with a blanket around her shoulders. Mrs. Bennett stepped out of the bakery doorway, dusted in flour even at this hour, as if the oven had asked to witness too. Royce stood on the corner with his hands in the pockets of a coat too thin for winter, head bowed like a man hearing a prayer he didn't know he remembered.

"It's real," Evelyn murmured, a tremor in her voice that wasn't fear. "It's really ringing."

"Who's up there?" someone whispered.

"Maybe no one," Mrs. Bennett said, crossing herself out of old habit. "Maybe finally no one."

Another toll rolled out—lower now, as if the bell were settling into a rhythm older than the town that had built walls around it. Damien's hand brushed Marley's elbow, not guiding, simply present. Together they climbed the hill.

The chapel looked smaller than its history, a wooden spine against the sky. Its door, usually locked, stood slightly ajar. The smell of dust and old hymnals and wax pulled at Marley's memory, though she hadn't spent a childhood in pews. Tonight everything felt familiar anyway: the way the floorboards moaned under their weight, the way silence pressed a palm against the throat of the space between tolls.

A length of frayed rope dangled in the narthex, not where a hand could reach it but higher, stiff with age, swaying almost imperceptibly. Damien lifted the lantern he'd brought, aiming the beam up into the bell loft. Dust motes gathered and spun like a slow galaxy.

"No footprints," he said, crouching. "No fresh scuffing on the stairs." He looked up again, jaw tight. "But the wheel's moving."

Marley followed his gaze. High overhead, the bell rocker nudged, paused, nudged again—the motion dazed, as if awakening from a long sleep. Each time the clapper kissed bronze, the sound moved through them and out into the world. She imagined the waves traveling—over the green where the memory circle had gathered, down Water Street, out across the river to the bridge itself.

"Say it. Ring it. Call him home," Marley whispered, the phrase rising unbidden. It didn't feel like an instruction now. It felt like an answer.

Damien lowered the lantern and looked at her. He didn't

try to push back this time. The fight in him—necessary for months, maybe necessary for survival—had burned down to its useful coal: caution without denial. "If the bell is the answer," he said, "then it isn't to us. It's to them."

The next toll resonated and then thinned, as if stretched over distance. In the space that followed, Marley heard something else, something not in the chapel: the river, churning louder than it should at this hour, and the soft, hollow thud of water against wood.

"The bridge," she said. "She'll be waiting there."

"Or he will," Damien answered, and in the saying of it they both understood. Annabelle had reached for Callum through time. If this was reunion, it would not happen in a bell tower but at the threshold they had honored and disturbed, repaired and unsettled: the covered bridge.

They ran.

Past Evelyn, who didn't stop them, only called, "Bring her home," as if the command could belong to anyone. Past Hazel and past Mrs. Bennett, who pressed a hand to her chest and whispered a blessing neither of them heard. The hill fell away beneath their feet and the path along the river rose to meet them. Marley's breath lashed her lungs; the bell's penultimate note rolled through the trees like weather. She did not count tolls—she was long past needing proof— yet she knew, the way one knows when lightning will split a cloud, that the next would be the last.

They reached the bridge mouth as the final note unfurled. It did not slam shut. It leaned against their bodies and the old timbers and the river's back, and then it dissolved into a hush more complete than quiet: an ending that knew itself as an ending.

Inside the bridge, nothing moved. No mist curled from the planks. The air felt newly used, like a room after prayer.

Damien lifted the lantern and its small circle of light slid forward along the floor, across the marks where wheels and shoes had written their centuries.

"Here," Marley said, her voice lifting into a thread.

At the foot of the beam where they had laid the ring and locket and ribbon and music box the evening before, something rested—no spectral glow, no impossible shine. Simply a parcel. Small, wrapped in oiled paper darkened by time, sealed with a blob of wax cracked like old lacquer. It was not dramatic. It was deliberate. It was waiting.

Marley went to her knees before her mind could decide for her body. The lantern's light gilded the edges of the package. Her fingers trembled but did not touch. She could feel Damien's presence behind her—close enough to catch, far enough to let her move—but she did not look back.

She read the faint lines impressed in the wax. The seal wasn't a family crest but a simple impression: two letters entwined as if they had always been one stroke. C and A, carved clumsily, lovingly.

Her breath left her in a sound that wasn't a sob and wasn't a laugh. It was the sound a lock makes when a key it has never met slides home.

Damien knelt beside her, lantern low. "What is it?"

"An answer," she said, and the certainty in her voice surprised her.

The bell tower fell silent behind them. No echo returned from the river. Somewhere in town a dog barked once and stopped, as if the night had asked for the courtesy of completion. Marley slid her fingers under the oiled paper, feeling the texture of old fibers, the way time had made the edges soft. She didn't open it. Not yet. Some things deserved to be seen in the same light that had kept them alive.

"Let's take it to the archive," she said quietly.

Damien's head snapped toward her. "You don't want to know—right now, here—?"

"I do," she admitted. She let her palm rest against the parcel the way she had once rested it against the central beam. "But the bridge gave it to the town, not just to us. The archive is where Annabelle's story lives now. It's where it belongs."

He held her gaze a long moment, the lantern warming his features, softening them. Then he nodded, a single, deep movement. "All right."

She lifted the parcel as if it were an infant, as if the letter inside—because she knew that was what it was—could feel the way hands chose to hold it. The oiled paper creaked once, a whisper of its own, and then went quiet. She stood, the weight of the package no burden at all.

Behind them the bridge settled, its wood exhaling a breath Marley felt in her bones. They stepped out into the open air. The sky over Brookwood had shifted from black to a blue so dark it was almost tender. Somewhere, far off, a rooster misread the hour. The town was waking to the fact of itself.

"What if it's not his?" Damien asked as they started down the path, the parcel cradled between Marley's hands. The question came like habit, one last defense offered up to the night.

Marley smiled without mirth. "Then Annabelle still made us walk to find out. Either way, the walking is the point."

He gave a surprised huff of breath. "You sound like my grandfather when he talked about that bridge."

"He was right," she said. "It's a threshold. You don't live on a doorway. You pass through."

They reached the square as the first, thinnest seam of

dawn cut the eastern roofs. Evelyn, Hazel, and Mrs. Bennett were waiting. The baker pressed a warm towel into Marley's free hand with a tenderness that made Marley's eyes sting. "For the dew," she said, as if this were an ordinary midwife's errand.

Marley wrapped the parcel more carefully. The warmth of the cloth seeped through the old paper and into her wrists, up her forearms. She felt steadier. She felt like a keeper being kept.

Damien unlocked the archive door, the old key turning with the satisfying resistance of good work. Dust and the faint sweetness of aging paper greeted them. The ledgers waited on their shelves. The ledger with Annabelle Warren's name scratched out waited too, no longer a wound to hide but a scar to learn from.

They carried the parcel to the long table under the front window and set it down. The room took it in the way a church takes in a prayer.

The bell did not ring again.

Marley placed her hands flat on the table, on either side of the parcel, and bowed her head. She did not pray—not in any word she'd learned in childhood—but she made a promise: to open it with the town as witness, to read each line out loud, to place what was inside where any hand, in any year to come, could lift it and feel the weight of truth.

Through the glass she could see the bridge, small in the distance, already part of the morning. It did not look haunted. It looked like work finished well.

Damien stood across from her, eyes on the parcel, then on her. The look there was a strange blend of exhaustion and awe, a kind of love that had not yet dared name itself. "Whatever it says," he murmured, "thank you for bringing it home."

Marley touched the bloomed wax seal with the tip of her finger, the embossed initials cool and real beneath her skin.

"Not home," she said. "To where it belongs."

And Brookwood, as if agreeing, let the last of the night go.

THE ARCHIVE SMELLED of lamp oil and wood polish, a kind of air that held both reverence and the heaviness of things not often disturbed. Marley had known it mostly as a place of whispers—old records pulled from shelves, parchment leaves turned by careful hands. Tonight, though, it felt alive, humming with the residue of the bell's tolls.

She set the parcel on the oak table beneath the tall front window. The wax seal, cracked but still intact, gleamed faintly in the weak dawn light. She rested her fingertips there as though it might vanish if she let go.

Damien closed the door behind them, turning the key with deliberate finality. He stood for a moment with his hand still on the lock, staring at the grain of the wood. His shoulders rose and fell with the kind of breath taken only when the air itself feels uncertain.

"I can't believe it," he whispered finally. "For years—decades—the bell stood silent. And now this."

Marley looked at him, the lantern's low flame catching in the dark pools of his eyes. "It wasn't silence," she said softly. "It was waiting."

She opened her journal, the pages crowded with her looping handwriting, fragments of dreams and visions, sketches of sigils, quotes she had pieced together from Clara's notes. She smoothed a blank sheet with the edge of her hand, uncapped her pen, and wrote across the top: *The Bell's Gift.*

"You're recording it already?" Damien asked, not judgment but awe.

"If we don't, someone will try to explain it away tomorrow. That's how history dies—one dismissal at a time." Her pen scratched. *Parcel found beneath central beam, after final toll of chapel bell. Wax seal: entwined letters, C and A. Oiled paper intact.*

Damien came to stand opposite her. He did not sit. He looked at the parcel as though it might open of its own accord. "C and A," he repeated. "Callum and Annabelle."

His voice broke on the second name, and he caught himself quickly, jaw tightening, as if emotion were a weakness to be corrected. Marley studied him. For all the hours they had spent side by side on the bridge, in dreams, in archives, there were still walls he did not lower easily.

"You've always known," she said gently.

His head snapped up. "What?"

"That this was bigger than rumor. Bigger than ghost stories for tourists. You've always known there was truth here, Damien. It's written all over you. The only thing you've doubted is whether you could bear the cost of naming it."

For a moment he said nothing, the silence of the room wrapping them in its old cloak. Then he placed both hands on the table, leaning over the parcel. His fingers were scarred, the knuckles darkened by years of use, but they trembled. "When my wife..." He stopped, swallowed hard. "When she was alive, she told me about dreams. About bells. I thought they were her imagination, part of her gentleness. But when she died, I buried those stories with her because I couldn't face the possibility they were real."

Marley felt the words cut through her chest as though they were her own. She had not known this detail—he had kept it from her, perhaps from himself.

"And now?" she asked.

"Now I'm terrified," he admitted. "Because this—" He gestured at the parcel. "This is proof. It's real. And if it's real, then all the pain, all the waiting, all the unfinished promises —they were never imagined. They were lived."

Marley let the pen rest. She reached across the table, placing her hand lightly over his. He didn't pull away. For the first time since this journey had begun, she felt his fear not as resistance but as shared ground.

"Maybe that's what the bell was for," she whispered. "Not just to call Annabelle and Callum together. But to make us remember."

Damien's eyes flicked up to hers, searching. "Remember what?"

"That love leaves marks, even when it's broken. That we can't keep pretending those marks aren't part of who we are."

The words seemed to still him. Slowly, he withdrew his hand, dragging it down his face as though wiping away a weight. When he spoke again, his voice was steadier. "We need to open it."

Marley nodded. "But not here. Not yet."

He blinked, startled. "Why not?"

"Because the bridge gave it to the town. The archive will hold it, but the first reading—" She hesitated, feeling the shape of conviction settle in her chest. "The first reading needs witnesses. Evelyn. Mrs. Bennett. Royce. The circle we gathered."

Damien exhaled slowly, as if releasing something he had held for years. "A community memory."

"Yes," Marley said. "Annabelle's story was never just hers. It belongs to all of them. To all of us."

The lantern hissed softly, its flame drawing low.

Marley closed her journal with a gentle thump. She slid the parcel toward the far end of the table, placing it beneath the ledgers as though tucking it into bed. The wax seal gleamed once more before the shadows folded over it.

Neither of them moved for several minutes. The silence was not empty but full, the kind of silence that stretches between notes of a song. Outside, the first faint light of morning pushed through the window, outlining Damien's shoulders, the sharp line of his jaw, the weariness etched there.

Finally he spoke. "When the bell rang, I thought of my daughter."

Marley looked up sharply. "Why?"

"Because it sounded like... like a calling home." His voice cracked again, softer now, stripped bare. "And I realized I've been afraid all this time. Afraid that what's reaching for us through the mist might take her away too. But maybe—" He stopped, rubbed the back of his neck. "Maybe it was trying to bring her back. To bring all of us back."

Marley's chest tightened. She wanted to tell him yes, exactly, but the truth was messier than affirmation. She didn't know if Annabelle's story would free or ensnare, heal or wound. But she knew silence had already cost too much.

"We'll face it together," she said instead.

He looked at her for a long time, then nodded once.

They left the archive side by side, locking the door behind them. The square was stirring now, townsfolk gathered in clusters, whispering about the impossible sound of the night. Marley saw Evelyn leaning on the café doorway, Mrs. Bennett's apron dusted with flour though her oven was surely cold, Royce perched on the steps of the old hall with his saxophone case at his feet. They were waiting, even if they didn't know what for.

Marley and Damien exchanged a glance. Without words, they knew: the time was approaching. Soon the parcel would open. Soon Annabelle's voice would speak again, not in whispers or visions but in ink and paper, undeniable.

And the town would have to listen.

THE CIRCLE FORMED IN SILENCE, as though each person present understood the weight of what was about to unfold. Evelyn's sharp eyes never leaving the parcel placed in the center of the table. Royce set his saxophone case aside and folded his long fingers together, the knuckles twitching as if yearning to release a note. Mrs. Bennett had dusted the flour from her hands, though streaks of white still clung to her apron. Damien stood behind Marley, broad shoulders squared, as if to shield her from whatever storm might come.

The archive felt smaller now, the old ledgers and shelves pressing in, lantern light casting shadows too long for the narrow room. The air smelled of damp paper, oiled wood, and something faintly metallic, like the tang of anticipation itself.

Marley lifted the parcel from its resting place on the oak table. Her hands were steady outwardly, but beneath the surface a tremor ran through her veins. She set it carefully before her, the wax seal glimmering in the low light. The entwined letters—*C* and *A*—seemed almost to pulse.

"No one has opened this since 1887," she said, her voice low, reverent. "It waited through fire, flood, and silence. The bridge chose to release it now."

A murmur rippled through the circle. Evelyn shook her head, muttering, "Not the bridge. Annabelle."

Marley nodded once. "Annabelle, then."

She slid the letter opener beneath the brittle paper. The wax cracked, the sound impossibly loud. She peeled back the folds with painstaking care, revealing yellowed parchment inside. The paper trembled as she drew it free, the ink faded but legible.

Damien stepped closer, his presence a steadying anchor. "Read it aloud," he said.

Marley's eyes swept the page. The handwriting was bold, hurried, the loops uneven but impassioned. At the bottom, unmistakable: *Callum Marwick, 1887.*

Her throat closed. She drew a breath, then began.

My dearest Annabelle,

If this reaches you, know that I never turned from you by choice. They forbade it—my family, the council, the hands that hold this town in silence. They said our vows would break more than tradition; they said it would unmake the very line they guard. I begged them, Annabelle. God knows I begged. But the seventh night came, and they locked me away as if I were a criminal for loving you.

I heard the bell toll, not for our wedding, but for your disappearance. I tried to run, to cross the river, but by the time I reached the bridge, the mist had swallowed all. They told me you fled, that you abandoned me. Lies, Annabelle—poison to quiet my heart. I know you waited. I felt it in my bones. I feel it still.

I leave this letter in hope, sealed for your eyes. If I cannot free you in life, then let this truth find you in whatever world waits beyond. Our love was not broken by fear, but stolen by those who feared its power. Forevermore, Annabelle. Even in silence, even in shadow. Forevermore.

Callum.

Marley's voice broke on the final word. She pressed the letter against her chest, as though to keep it from slipping away again. Around the circle, silence reigned, but it was not the silence of disbelief. It was the silence of recognition, of wounds named at last.

Mrs. Bennett's lips moved as though in prayer. Royce pressed a fist against his mouth, his eyes wet. Evelyn, unflinching, whispered, "So it was true. The Green Healers weren't just midwives and herbalists. They were keepers of vows. That's why they feared her."

Damien moved forward. His hand hovered over the letter before he finally let his palm rest on the table beside it. His voice was low, gravel-edged. "They tried to erase her. Scratched her name from ledgers, buried her memory under lies. But love... love leaves traces. This—" He tapped the parchment gently. "This is the echo they could never bury."

Marley looked at him. His face was taut, but there was no denial left in his eyes. Only grief, and awe, and something like surrender.

"We have to preserve it," Marley said firmly. "Not just in the archive. In the town's heart. The bell rang to return this truth. We can't silence it again."

Evelyn struck her cane against the floor. "Then let it be known. Annabelle Warren waited, and Callum Marwick was kept from her. Their story belongs to Brookwood, not to whispers in the dark."

The words struck through the room like another toll of the chapel bell.

Marley carefully refolded the letter, though her fingers lingered on the signature. She slid it into a protective sleeve from the archive cabinet, sealing it against time once more. But as she set it in the ledger drawer, she knew it was not being hidden. It was being honored.

Damien's voice was quiet behind her, meant only for her ears. "Forevermore. He meant it. And he left it for her."

Marley turned, her gaze meeting his. "Then we'll carry it too. Until Brookwood no longer forgets."

For the first time since the echoes began, she felt something ease within her—not the absence of grief, but the presence of completion. Annabelle's voice, Callum's vow, the bell's toll: all had converged in this moment.

The circle dissolved slowly, each person carrying the weight of what they had witnessed into the night. Marley and Damien remained last, standing before the darkened shelves. He reached for her hand, and she let him take it. The relics might rest now, but the bond they carried was alive—in the town, in the bridge, in themselves.

The echoes had spoken. The truth had returned. And love, denied for a century, had finally been reunited.

30

A CHOICE MADE IN LOVE

The town had grown quiet in the days since the bell's unexpected toll. The villagers went about their errands with something unspoken in their expressions: relief mixed with unease, gratitude threaded with caution. The bridge, which for so long had loomed over Brookwood as a place of shadow and whisper, now stood bathed in a different kind of reverence. People slowed when they crossed it, touched its railings with a gentleness, as though afraid to disturb its fragile peace.

For Marley, that peace was both a gift and a burden. She had carried Annabelle's story for months, chasing echoes through dreams, journals, relics, and visions. Now, the echoes had grown quiet, yet she found herself still listening for them. Her notebook lay heavy with entries, pages filled with dates, phrases, sketches, fragments of melody and scent. Each morning she flipped it open instinctively, expecting more. Each night she lingered by the window of the inn, waiting for the mist to curl, for Annabelle's presence to rise once more.

But Annabelle was gone. Freed, perhaps. Released.

And that left Marley with herself, with Damien, with Brookwood—and with the silence.

On the evening of the second day after the bell rang, Damien found her on the bridge. The sun was setting low, and the planks beneath her feet glowed like bronze. Marley leaned on the railing, watching the water slip beneath. She didn't hear his boots until he was only a few steps behind her.

"You still half-expect her," Damien said. His voice was quiet, not accusatory, but observant. "Every time you're here."

Marley didn't turn. "Don't you?"

Damien let out a breath, not quite a laugh. He stepped beside her, his forearms braced on the wood. The river shimmered in reflected gold, carrying its secrets out toward the horizon.

"She's gone," he said. "I think we both know that. But it doesn't mean the bridge is empty. Not anymore."

Marley tilted her head, studying his profile. The man who had once clung to denial, who had fought against visions and whispers, now spoke as though the unseen were part of his daily breath. Something in him had shifted the night Annabelle appeared in her fullness, the night Callum's letter was unearthed. Damien carried that change quietly, like a scar healed but not forgotten.

"You've been different since the letter," Marley murmured.

He nodded. "Because it was proof. Not just for you, Marley. For me. For the town. Proof that love was stronger than the stories told to bury it."

They stood in silence. The lanterns along the main road began to flicker on, their glow spilling across the square.

Downriver, a heron lifted from the reeds, its wings gilded by the last light.

Damien turned to her then, his expression bare, stripped of the layers of reserve he so often wore.

"I need to ask you something," he said.

Marley's pulse quickened, though she kept her gaze steady. "Then ask."

He swallowed, his jaw tightening. "Are you going to leave? Now that the echoes have gone quiet?"

The question struck harder than she expected. She pressed her notebook against her chest, as if it might answer for her. "Do you want me to?" she asked softly.

Damien shook his head immediately, almost sharply. "No. That's not what I want." He exhaled, shoulders stiff. "But I need to know if you're here only for them—for Annabelle, for Callum, for the echoes—or if you could ever be here for more. For Brookwood. For..." His words faltered. He looked away, into the current. "For me."

Marley's throat tightened. The weight of the months pressed down on her—their nights of chasing voices, the arguments sharpened by fear, the moments of tenderness stolen beneath the bridge's arches. She remembered the almost-kiss broken by a whisper, the nights Damien had confessed pieces of his grief, the times she had written in the dark by candlelight with his shadow just beyond her shoulder.

He wasn't asking for a promise of permanence, she realized. He was asking if she could stand in the silence and still choose to stay.

"I don't know what forever looks like," Marley said at last, her voice steady but low. "I don't know if the bridge is done speaking. I don't even know if I'm done listening."

Damien's jaw tightened, but he didn't speak.

"But," Marley continued, turning fully to face him, "I know I'm here. Now. And I'm not done. Not with this place. Not with the story. Not with you."

The words hung between them, a thread woven of vulnerability and resolve.

Damien's eyes closed briefly, as though absorbing them. When he opened them again, there was something softer there—relief, tempered with fear. He reached out, hesitant at first, and then placed his hand over hers where it rested on the railing.

Marley didn't pull away.

The bridge hummed beneath their feet, a vibration subtle and warm, as though wood and iron alike were exhaling. It was not the sharp echo of voices past, nor the oppressive mist that once clung to the planks. This was gentler, quieter, like the sigh of a soul finally at rest.

Damien's grip tightened slightly, grounding her in the moment. "Then maybe," he said quietly, "this is where we begin. Not where they ended."

Marley nodded, the sunset painting her face in gold. For the first time, she felt the bridge not as a burden, but as a witness. A keeper of echoes, yes—but also of new beginnings.

The water below carried the last of the light away, and above them, the first stars pricked the sky.

The silence, for once, was enough.

THE DAYS that followed passed like water under the bridge—smooth on the surface, but carrying unseen currents beneath. Brookwood stirred differently now. The chapel bell's haunting toll had faded into memory, and the towns-folk carried themselves as if the air were lighter, as if the bridge itself had eased its long-held weight. Yet Marley felt it constantly, an invisible pulse at the edges of her awareness, waiting for her to test whether the silence was true or only a pause.

Each morning, she rose early and crossed the square, her journal tucked under her arm. She walked the path to the bridge with deliberate steps, pausing often to listen—to the river's churn, to the wind threading through sycamore branches, to the subtle vibration of plank and beam beneath her soles. Damien, ever watchful, often met her there, carrying a thermos of coffee or his lantern though daylight had already claimed the sky. They said little at first, their companionship built on presence rather than explanation.

On the third morning, Marley pressed her palm flat to one of the beams and closed her eyes. She expected the echoes—the faint rush of a woman's sobs, the rustle of a dress, the whisper of a child's voice—but instead there was only the cool grain of aged wood. Her fingers traced initials carved centuries before, weather-softened yet still sharp in places. She drew in a breath, released it, and finally allowed a smile to form.

Damien leaned against the railing, watching her. "You're testing it again," he said, not accusing, not even questioning —merely naming the act as if to ground them both.

"I have to," Marley answered, her eyes still closed. "If I don't listen, I'll always wonder if it's just waiting for me to return."

"And?" His voice was steady, but his hand curled into the railing, betraying tension.

She opened her eyes and looked at him. "It's quiet. For the first time since I came here, it's truly quiet."

Damien's shoulders softened, but his gaze remained

troubled. "Quiet doesn't always mean safe. It could be resting. Gathering."

Marley tilted her head, considering. "Or it could be done. And if it is, what we do now matters more than ever. If we don't fill this silence with something real, the past will find its way back."

He studied her, the furrow in his brow deepening. "You mean us."

"I mean Brookwood," she corrected gently, though her gaze didn't waver from his. "And yes, us too."

THAT EVENING, they tested the stillness together. They returned at dusk, carrying the music box. Damien wound it, letting its melancholy notes drift into the cooling air. Marley braced herself, certain the bridge would answer, that mist would curl, that a voice would rise. But the bridge held its silence, its hum warm but steady, more alive than haunted.

They listened until the last note faded. The air thickened with expectation, as if the town itself paused to hear. But nothing came. No whispers. No shapes. No echoes.

Damien exhaled, tension bleeding from his shoulders. He closed the lid of the box, his hand trembling just slightly. "It's done," he said, voice low. "It has to be."

Marley's throat tightened. Relief mingled with sorrow, the finality of it pressing against her chest. She nodded slowly. "She's gone. But she left us this quiet."

They lingered, the lantern flickering between them. Damien reached for her hand and, for the first time, she let his fingers lace fully with hers without the weight of interruption. No voice split the moment, no unseen presence demanded their attention.

It was only them.

IN THE DAYS THAT FOLLOWED, their companionship deepened into rhythm. Marley joined Damien at the archives, where they cataloged Annabelle's letter beside other town relics. Damien insisted it be displayed with reverence, not buried in boxes as so much of Brookwood's history had been. When Marley placed the letter behind protective glass, her reflection caught in the pane—two women across centuries connected by ink, by courage, by unfinished stories now finally closed.

The townspeople came quietly, reverently, to see the letter and the ring displayed beside it. An old man wept openly, claiming his grandmother had told him of Annabelle's voice calling through storms. A young woman whispered that she'd dreamt of the bridge all her life, but never dared to speak of it until now.

Marley listened, recorded, and offered each voice a place in her journal. Damien stayed close, steady, his skepticism transformed into guardianship. He still flinched at shadows sometimes, still feared that the silence might shatter, but he no longer denied what they had seen.

One evening, as lanterns flickered to life across Brookwood, Marley closed her journal and turned to him. "It's not just Annabelle's story, Damien. It's this whole town's. That's what I came to realize at the circle. The bridge was never only hers—it was everyone's. And maybe that's why it finally let go."

Damien regarded her, the firelight painting his face in bronze. "And you?" he asked quietly. "Will you let go too?"

She shook her head, a small, resolute smile curving her

lips. "No. Letting go isn't the point. Presence is. I don't need to hold on to the echoes—but I'm not leaving the silence empty. I'm here."

The bridge hummed faintly beneath their feet, the same warmth as before—neither warning nor threat, but affirmation.

For the first time, Damien smiled without hesitation. "Then maybe we both are."

NIGHT SETTLED over Brookwood with the patience of an old storyteller, each star pricked into place as if to remind the town that endings and beginnings are only different verses in the same song. The bridge stretched across the darkened river, no longer brooding, no longer shrouded. Its beams caught the lantern light Damien carried, glowing amber instead of shadowed black, and the air itself felt less like a veil and more like a hearth.

Marley and Damien stood at the midpoint, the planks beneath them creaking as if to acknowledge their presence. They didn't speak for several moments. The silence was not heavy but full, as though the bridge itself breathed with them, content at last.

Damien's gaze swept the water below, rippling in the soft pull of the current. "It feels different," he said finally, his voice hushed, as though he feared speaking too loudly might undo the fragile stillness.

"It is different," Marley replied, resting her palm against the railing. The wood was warm beneath her touch—not the chill she had grown accustomed to, not the pulse of echoes, but something almost alive, like the faint heat left in the pages of a well-read book. "It's not watching anymore. It's resting."

He turned to her, lantern glow catching the lines of his face, softening the edges of all the fear he had carried. "So what now?"

The question was heavier than the words themselves. What now—for Annabelle, whose story had been threaded through their days? What now—for the town, which had finally opened its long-sealed chest of memory? And most of all, what now—for the two of them, standing here, hearts caught between past grief and present possibility?

Marley lifted her gaze to the far shore where the sycamore branches leaned over the river. "Now we live. Not for the echoes. Not even for the silence. For this." She tapped her hand against the railing. "For the bridge that finally belongs to the living again."

Damien studied her, lantern swaying faintly at his side. His eyes, weary yet alight, searched hers. "And for us?"

She breathed in, steadying herself. "For us too. But not as a promise." Her voice was clear now, anchored. "Promises bind the future to chains we can't always carry. I can't make promises—not yet. But I can be here. Present. Every day. That's more than a promise, Damien. It's a choice."

He closed his eyes briefly, as if letting her words seep into the cracks of his doubt. When he opened them again, there was no argument left, only a fragile acceptance. "Then presence it is." He reached across the narrow space between them and took her hand, his grip firm but not demanding.

The lantern flame flickered, catching a sudden updraft, and the bridge seemed to hum beneath their joined hands. Marley stiffened at first, half-expecting the mist to roll back in, the echoes to surge like a tide. But instead, warmth spread outward from the beam beneath them, gentle, steady, as if the bridge itself acknowledged their choice.

They both felt it—an unseen blessing, a closing chord.

Marley swallowed against the knot in her throat. "Do you feel it?"

Damien nodded. "It's like the bridge is... grateful." His voice broke slightly, the weight of years of skepticism loosening at last.

Together, they stood as the lantern light gilded the river, as night spread fully overhead. The mist did not return. No voices broke the quiet. Only the steady hum remained, a resonance that did not demand or haunt, but comforted, like a lullaby sung after too many nights of unrest.

Brookwood itself seemed to sigh.

Marley pulled her journal from her coat pocket and set it upon the railing. She flipped to the last empty page and, with Damien watching, wrote: *The echoes have quieted. The bridge hums, and for the first time, it feels alive with the living.*

She closed the book, placed her hand over its cover, and whispered—not to Annabelle, not to Callum, but to the bridge itself—"Thank you."

The hum swelled gently beneath her palm, then faded to stillness.

Damien exhaled, shoulders loosening, as though the years of guarding himself, his daughter, his heart, had at last released their grip. He looked at Marley with something raw, unshielded. "I asked if you'd stay in Brookwood. You didn't give me a promise, but you gave me more than I ever expected. Presence. I can live with that."

Marley smiled softly, eyes damp but unashamed. "Then we'll live in it together."

The river flowed on beneath them, steady and eternal. Above, the stars brightened, their light pooling across the bridge as though even the sky bore witness.

For the first time in over a century, Brookwood's bridge

was no longer a place of sorrow or haunting. It was a place of warmth, of choice, of presence.

The echoes had quieted.

And in the hush that followed, Marley and Damien stepped not into forever, but into the now—hand in hand, grounded at last in love made real by presence.

EPILOGUE: THE BRIDGE BETWEEN

The river had stilled. The bridge, long haunted by whispers and fog, now hummed with a warmth the town had not felt in decades. Marley stood at its midpoint one last time before turning home. Damien was at her side, his lantern lowered, the soft glow brushing against the planks as if the light itself sought permission to linger.

It was quiet in Brookwood—quiet in a way that felt earned.

And yet, beneath the stillness, there was something else. Not an echo this time, but a pull, faint and unrelenting. Marley had thought she would welcome silence when it came. Instead, the absence of voices revealed space for a new sound—an unanswered question that rang as clearly as a bell.

The town had begun to heal. The café was full again, the bakery's ovens warm, the chapel doors left unlocked for the first time in years. Evelyn had even placed the flour tin with its engraved sigil in the front window of the café, declaring Brookwood's history "nothing to be ashamed of." The memory circle had sparked late-night conversations, neighbors leaning across fences and porches, sharing visions once buried.

And Damien—steady, skeptical Damien—had lowered his guard enough to let presence, not promise, anchor him beside her.

But Brookwood was not done. Marley could feel it in her bones.

As they left the bridge that night, she turned to look back. The mist did not rise, nor did the air chill. Yet the old structure seemed to glow faintly, as if lit from within, its planks remembering every name carved into their surface. Marley knew Annabelle had been freed, Callum had been heard. But the story was larger than one couple, larger even than a century of silence.

"Do you hear it?" she asked Damien softly.

He tilted his head, listening. At first there was only the night wind, the murmur of the river. Then, faintly, the sound carried—one she had not expected.

A bell.

Far off, drawn not from the chapel but from another direction. The lighthouse.

Damien stiffened. "It hasn't rung in years."

But Marley knew what she had heard. Not a ring exactly, but a resonance, as though metal had been struck deep within its tower, the sound threading across the water. It was a note both low and clear, and it spoke not of endings, but of beginnings.

THE FOLLOWING MORNING, Brookwood awoke to whispers again—not the kind that haunted, but those of gossip and awe. Several fishermen claimed they had seen a light sweep across the waves near midnight, a beacon long extinguished brought back to life. A child swore she dreamed of a lantern flame housed in glass taller than a house.

Marley listened, notebook open, words racing ahead of her pen. The lighthouse had not functioned in nearly eighty years, abandoned when new shipping routes made its beam irrelevant. But it was more than a structure—it was the first building Callum Marwick's family had helped raise, a symbol woven into the town's foundation.

Damien sat opposite her, the newspaper unopened beside his coffee. He had been quiet all morning, shoulders tense in the way she had learned meant his skepticism wrestled with something deeper.

"It's nothing," he said finally, though his voice lacked conviction. "Metal settling, waves carrying sound. People hear what they want to hear."

Marley leaned forward, lowering her pen. "And what about you, Damien? What did you hear?"

His jaw tightened. He didn't meet her eyes.

"The same thing you did," he admitted at last. "The lighthouse calling."

Marley exhaled. It was not relief, but recognition. Annabelle's story had been about waiting, about love held and denied. But this new thread—it was about legacy, about the town itself.

She reached for his hand. "Brookwood isn't finished with us. The bridge has gone quiet. Now the lighthouse speaks."

Damien's fingers closed around hers, reluctant but steady. "Then God help us both."

Outside the café window, the townsfolk went about their morning, unaware—or unwilling to admit—that another mystery stirred at the edge of the sea.

But Marley knew. And in the quiet, her heart beat with the thrill of it.

The echoes had not ended. They had only shifted.

THE NEXT DAYS passed in a rhythm that should have been comforting, but for Marley it felt like waiting for a note to resolve. The bridge stood serene, the town basked in its newfound quiet, but beneath everything was that undertone—an unanswered hum that tugged her attention toward the coast.

Brookwood's lighthouse had been more than a navigational aid. It had been a sentinel, a witness to generations of arrivals and departures. But after its light went dark in the early 1940s, the structure became a relic, a landmark children dared each other to climb when they wanted to flirt with danger.

Now, though, it was different. People spoke of it in lowered voices, like they had once spoken of the bridge. Marley listened carefully, knowing how gossip was sometimes just history disguised as fear.

One morning, an envelope arrived for her at the café. There was no return address, only a single word scrawled across the front in fading ink: *Illuminate.*

Inside was a brittle sheet of parchment, its edges crumbling. The script was archaic, ink feathered by age.

"When the echoes still and the bridge releases its hold, the light shall rise. Shadows will resist, but truth will not remain buried. The one who bears witness must climb and see clearly, lest Brookwood lose itself to the dark."

Beneath the text was a drawing—a sketch of the lighthouse, its lantern room radiating beams that reached across land and sea. At its base was a circle, a sigil she had seen before in her aunt Clara's journal and again in the ledger with Annabelle's name. The Green Healers' mark.

Marley's pulse quickened. She read the lines aloud to Damien, who stood stiffly beside her, jaw tight.

"It's a prophecy," she whispered.

"It's superstition," Damien countered automatically, but his voice lacked the solid ground it once held. He stared at the parchment longer than he should have, eyes tracing the sigil.

"Then how do you explain this arriving now, just days after the bridge stilled?" she pressed.

He shook his head. "Because people in this town can't leave the past alone. Someone wants you to carry it forward."

Marley folded the parchment carefully, sliding it back into the envelope. "Or someone wants *us* to finish what was started. Annabelle's echoes are quiet, Damien, but this... this feels like the next step."

He raked a hand through his hair, an old habit when his reason felt cornered. "We don't even know if this is authentic. Could've been planted, forged—"

"But you don't believe that," she interrupted softly. "Not really."

His silence admitted more than his words ever could.

LATER THAT AFTERNOON, they walked the narrow path that led toward the cliffs. From there, the lighthouse loomed—its whitewashed walls weathered gray, its lantern room dark against the winter sky. The waves crashed against the rocks below, their spray rising like breath from the sea.

Marley stopped, clutching her notebook to her chest. "Do you feel it?" she asked.

Damien exhaled. "I feel... unease. Like we've pulled too many threads and the whole fabric's about to come apart."

But Marley only saw the symmetry: first the bridge, now the lighthouse. Two structures, two sentinels of Brookwood's memory, each holding its own secret.

"The theme is clear," she murmured, almost to herself. "The bridge taught us about echoes—about listening to the past. But the lighthouse... it's about seeing. About illumination. About clarity."

He turned to her, brow furrowed. "And what if we don't want to see? What if there are things in Brookwood better left in shadow?"

Her gaze held his. "Then why does the light call to us?"

Damien flinched at the phrasing. She had not meant it as an accusation, but it struck as truth.

THAT EVENING, they returned to Damien's study, spreading the parchment across his desk beside Clara's journals, the ledger, and the artifacts from the bridge. The ring glinted faintly in the lamplight, the ribbon folded carefully in its box.

Marley traced the sigil at the base of the sketch with her fingertip. "It's the same mark, Damien. The Green Healers were tied not only to Annabelle, but to the lighthouse too. They weren't just keeping rituals by the river—they were guarding something larger."

He stared at the parchment, finally speaking with a heaviness that seemed to press into his bones. "If that's true, then Brookwood's identity—everything the town believes about itself—could be based on a lie of omission. On shadows, like you said."

"Which means the prophecy is about us," Marley

replied. "Not just me. You too. We've been chosen to climb, to see clearly, because we've already proven we can listen."

He let out a bitter laugh, though his eyes betrayed no humor. "You talk like this is some grand calling. But Marley... every step deeper costs us. Costs this town. Costs my family. Are you ready for that?"

She didn't answer right away. Instead, she opened her notebook and wrote the word *Illuminate* across the top of a fresh page. Beneath it, she copied the prophecy line by line, her handwriting steady despite the tremor in her chest.

Finally, she looked up. "I'm ready if you are."

Damien pressed his palms flat against the desk, staring down at the parchment. For the first time since she had known him, his rational armor cracked—not with denial, but with reluctant acceptance.

"The lighthouse," he said slowly, "isn't done with us."

THE FOLLOWING NIGHT, the town gathered for the winter festival—a tradition that had carried on despite the bridge's hauntings. Lanterns lined the streets, music spilled from the square, and laughter filled the air. Yet Marley's eyes kept straying to the coastline, where the black silhouette of the lighthouse stood against the stars.

As she walked with Damien through the square, Mrs. Bennett caught her arm. The baker's expression was grave, her usual warmth muted.

"You've woken the bridge," she said softly. "Now you'll need to wake the light. But be careful, child. Shadows aren't just absence—they cling."

Marley's breath caught. She wanted to ask what Mrs. Bennett meant, but the older woman had already turned back toward her stall.

Damien noticed the exchange. "What did she say?"

Marley hesitated, then whispered, "That shadows cling."

His face darkened. "Then we're walking into something worse than echoes."

Marley tightened her grip on his hand. "Then we walk together."

For the first time, he didn't pull away.

And above them, faint and fleeting, a beam of light swept across the distant sea.

THE FESTIVAL DWINDLED as the night deepened, lanterns guttering one by one until the town square was scattered with shadows. The last echoes of fiddles and laughter faded, replaced by the steady hush of the sea carrying its endless hymn to the cliffs. Marley and Damien walked side by side along the winding coastal path, the envelope with the prophecy still tucked in her coat pocket like a pulse against her chest.

They had not spoken much since Mrs. Bennett's warning. The silence between them was not cold—it was taut, brimming, the kind that filled with words unspoken because both of them knew what waited at the end of the path.

The lighthouse rose ahead, its dark tower outlined against a sky alive with winter stars. For decades, it had stood hollow, its lantern extinguished, a relic of an age when ships needed its beam to navigate the treacherous coast. But tonight, something about its presence felt less inert, less abandoned.

Marley stopped short, gripping Damien's arm. "Did you see that?"

At first he shook his head, lips parting in automatic

denial. Then it came again—a flicker, faint but unmistakable. A shard of light in the lantern room.

"That's impossible," he muttered. "There's no oil, no wiring. It hasn't been lit in seventy years."

The flicker came again, longer this time, sweeping once across the sea before dying into darkness.

Marley's breath shivered into the night air. "It's starting."

Damien exhaled, long and ragged. "Or we're in over our heads."

She turned to him, eyes steady despite the tremor in her chest. "Both can be true."

WHEN THEY REACHED the base of the lighthouse, the iron door stood ajar. No one in Brookwood had keys—the county had sealed it years ago. Damien ran his hand over the rusted surface, then pushed it open with the gentleness of a man expecting resistance. It groaned but yielded, revealing the spiral staircase curling upward into shadow.

"Do we climb?" Marley asked.

Damien's jaw tightened. "The prophecy said *the one who bears witness must climb and see clearly.* That's you, Marley."

She touched the parchment still in her pocket, then looked up the long coil of stairs. The darkness inside the lighthouse felt different than ordinary dark—thicker, breathing, waiting.

"I won't climb it alone," she said.

Damien studied her a moment, then nodded once. "Then we climb together."

THE IRON STAIRS groaned under their weight as they ascended. Dust floated in the beam of Damien's flashlight, disturbed for the first time in years. Each step rang like a muted bell, hollow echoes spiraling upward.

Halfway, Marley froze. She heard it again—a whisper. Not from Damien, not from the stairwell, but from above.

"Call him home..."

She swallowed hard. "Did you hear that?"

Damien's flashlight wavered. "Don't tell me..."

But then he heard it too. A child's voice, faint and clear, curling down the stairwell like a ribbon of air.

"Say it. Ring it. Call him home."

The same words his daughter had murmured in her sleep.

They climbed faster.

At the lantern room, the glass panes were streaked with salt and age. The great iron lens loomed, fractured and dust-covered, but unmistakably intact. And there—inside the heart of the lens—a flame flickered. Not steady, not fueled by anything earthly, but alive. It pulsed as though in rhythm with the sea, faint at first, then bright enough to paint the room in gold.

Marley pressed her hand to the cold iron railing, her chest tightening with awe.

"The prophecy," she whispered. "It's real."

Damien stepped closer to the lens, his rational mind wrestling, fraying, tearing. "It can't be..." he murmured, but the words fell hollow even to his ears.

The flame brightened, then dimmed, then brightened again—slow, deliberate, like the lighthouse was breathing. Each pulse swept outward, and Marley felt it not only in her eyes but in her chest, her bones, her very blood.

And with each sweep, shadows writhed at the edge of

the glass—figures that seemed to gather, linger, and then scatter, as though resisting the illumination.

"Shadows cling," Marley breathed, recalling Mrs. Bennett's warning.

As if answering, the flame surged once more, throwing long beams across land and sea. The town below stirred. Lights flickered in windows as people woke, pulled from sleep by something ancient, something calling.

Damien gripped the railing, face pale, sweat shining at his temple despite the cold. "This isn't just light. It's memory. It's showing the town what it's been hiding."

Marley clutched her notebook, hastily scribbling: *The light does not guide ships—it guides truth.*

THEY TURNED as a sound rose from below. A bell.

Not the chapel bell. This was lower, deeper, resonating from somewhere beneath the lighthouse itself. It tolled once, twice, the vibration traveling up through the stones, through their bones.

Marley's hand shook as she wrote: *Another bell, another vow.*

Damien caught her wrist, steadying it. His eyes burned with something between fear and reverence. "If this is the next step, Marley, then we've just woken something far larger than the bridge."

She met his gaze. "Then it's not just Annabelle's story anymore. It's Brookwood's."

The flame pulsed again, brighter than before, then steadied. For the first time, it didn't dim. It burned.

Outside, the sea caught its glow, waves gilded in light as though dawn had come hours early. And there, across the water, Marley swore she saw it—an outline. A ship, spectral, moving toward the coast, its sails full against no wind.

She gasped, clutching Damien's arm. "Do you see—"

He saw it too. His grip tightened. "Dear God..."

The ship dissolved into mist, but the flame did not waver.

THEY DESCENDED IN SILENCE, the weight of what they had witnessed clinging heavier than words. At the base of the lighthouse, Marley turned back, looking up at the steady glow above.

The town had gathered at the cliffside now, neighbors whispering, children pointing, elders crossing themselves. The flame had called them.

Damien faced them, his voice carrying across the hush. "Brookwood... has been awakened."

Marley stepped closer to him, whispering only for his ears: "This is where it begins again. The bridge gave us echoes. But the lighthouse—it gives us prophecy."

He didn't argue. He only nodded, his hand brushing hers, not in promise but in presence.

The night deepened, and the lighthouse burned on, its first true sign delivered. Shadows writhed but did not conquer. The flame belonged to Brookwood now.

And somewhere in the unseen depths of history, the Green Healers stirred, their legacy no longer buried.

AFTERWORD

A Reflective Legacy

The Brookwood Mysteries begins, as so many stories do, with silence.

It was the silence of a bookshop whose shelves held more than novels—the silence of Clara's vow, of words written in margins, of echoes that could only be heard when someone dared to listen. Marley stepped into that silence not as an intruder but as an inheritor, though she did not yet know it. *The Bookshop Secret* showed her—and us—that history breathes through the most ordinary doors, waiting for hands brave enough to turn the lock.

From there, the path winds into resonance. *The Bridge of Echoes* carries voices across time, testing whether past promises could be trusted in the present. Each echo reminds Brookwood that memory is never idle—it insists, it demands, it shapes. Marley and Damien began to realize that listening was not passive but covenant: if they carried the echoes, they must also answer them.

The Lighthouse Prophecy shifts the gaze outward, to signals cast against darkness. It asked: what do we guard, and what do we guide? In that season, the town learned that prophecy is less prediction than mirror. The light did not foretell what must be—it illuminated what already was: a community standing on the threshold of its own forgotten story.

The Winter Bell gives voice to stillness. A bell that should have rung but didn't, a vow that had been broken, a bride whose absence echoed for decades. Silence again—but this time charged, asking whether absence could be as loud as sound. Marley and Damien discover that love and loss, entwined, toll not as ending but as call.

And finally, *The Hidden Grove* reveals itself as culmination, not simply continuation. The stones, the spirals, the ledger, the seed—all mysteries unfolded into memory, and memory unfolded into inheritance. What began as secrecy becomes community. What began as whispers becomes vows. What began as one woman's step into a bookshop becomes an entire town's covenant with its own roots.

Brookwood's Legacy

The mysteries are not puzzles to solve, nor riddles to conquer. They are invitations—to listen, to remember, to rise. At every turn, Brookwood asked its people a single question: *Will you keep what was entrusted to you, not as possession, but as promise?*

Marley answered yes. Damien answered yes. The townsfolk, hesitant, divided, afraid—they too answered yes.

And so the series does not close on a solved case or a quiet conclusion. It closes on a circle, still widening. Children's hands pressing seeds into soil. Elders whispering names into bark. A grove alive with bloom and resonance.

The mysteries of Brookwood will always remain, not

locked in secrecy but alive in inheritance. And so, the circle holds:

We remember. We root. We rise.

Brookwood Mysteries
> Book 1 - The Bookshop Secret
> Book 2 - The Bridge of Echoes
> Book 3 - The Lighthouse Prophecy
> Book 4 - The Winter Bell
> Book 5 - The Hidden Grove

ABOUT THE AUTHOR

Jordan Jace is a Pacific Northwest author whose mysteries and heartwarming tales are set against stunning landscapes. With a deep connection to the PNW region's natural beauty, Jace infuses each story with the magic of misty mountains, lush forests, and tranquil coastlines. Jace believes that joy can be found in the smallest moments and the most unexpected places. When not writing, Jace is exploring the world, seeking inspiration in every corner for the next unforgettable story. Discover more at visionsinprint.com

www.ingramcontent.com/pod-product-compliance
Lightning Source LLC
Chambersburg PA
CBHW031202010826

48971CB00013B/1212